ZACK

IN THE COMPANY OF SNIPERS
Book 3

IRISH WINTERS

WINDY DAYS PRESS

COPYRIGHT

ZACK; In the Company of Snipers, 3

Copyright ©2014 by Irish Winters
All rights reserved

Second Edition

This is a work of fiction. Names, characters, dialogues, places, and incidents either are the product of the author's imagination or are used fictitiously. Any resemblance to actual events, locales, or persons, living or dead, is entirely coincidental. The publisher does not have any control over and does not assume responsibility for author or third-party websites or their content.

No part of this book may be reproduced, scanned, or distributed in any printed or electronic form without permission. Please do not participate in or encourage piracy of copyrighted materials in violation of the author's rights. Purchase only authorized editions.

Edited by Cas Peace http://www.caspeace.com

Cover design and author photo by Kelli Ann Morgan,
 http://www.inspirecreativeservices.com

Interior book design by Bob Houston eBook Formatting

ISBN Paperback: 978-1-942895-07-7
ISBN eBook: 978-1-942895-08-4
Library of Congress Control Number: 2014937535

Irish Winter's author website is
http://www.irishwinters.com or irishwinters.blogspot.com

In the Company of Snipers

You can find Irish Winters on Facebook: https://www.facebook.com/author.irishwinters

On Twitter: https://twitter.com/irishwinters1

For news on upcoming releases, sign up for Irish Winters' Newsletter at IrishWinters.com.

For more information about all my books, visit IrishWinters.com.

IN THE COMPANY OF SNIPERS

This series revolves around ex-Marine scout sniper, Alex Stewart, and his covert surveillance company, The TEAM, home-based out of Alexandria, Virginia. An obsessive patriot and workaholic, he created the company to give ex-military snipers like him a chance at returning to civilian life with a decent job.

This is not a serial with each book ending at a cliffhanger. I wouldn't do that to you. *In the Company of Snipers* is a collection of passionate love stories involving women and men who are tough enough to take on the world alone. Each is a stand-alone read, where in the course of an active TEAM operation, one agent comes face to face with his or her demons. The men and women I write about are all patriots and warriors, dealing with what they've lived through or the mistakes they've made

Spoiler alert: Every novel contains adult scenes including sexual situations (some explicit), language, and violence. I don't write sweet romance, so be forewarned.

At the end of each story, it's my hope that you, along with my heroes, will come to realize...

Love changes everything.

One

Schools out already?

Mei Xing glanced at the clock in her kitchen. Time to hurry. Another day of first grade done and no doubt another crayon treasure ready for the refrigerator door. She used to watch for LiLi's school bus from her small balcony. No more. Not since her precocious six-year old had sternly informed her, "Mommy, all the kids can see you."

The bus screeched to its first stop. Mei had just enough time. Out the door and into the open elevator she went, smoothing her hands over her hips just as the bus pulled to the curb. LiLi already held a sheet of bright yellow construction paper to the window, her sweet eyes blazing with excitement.

"Hey, lady."

Mei turned to a man in dark glasses and a dirty denim jacket walking toward her, his steps quick, like he knew where he was going and he was late. He didn't look like a parent, certainly not any of the children's fathers she recognized.

"Yes?" she asked, while she waved another small mommy-kind of wave to her daughter. LiLi waved back, a big grin with her two front teeth missing. She never looked prettier.

"That your little girl?" he asked.

Mei's hackles rose. Protective instincts flashed to the surface. She didn't know this guy. It was none of his business which little girl was hers, not like anyone could miss the distinct American Chinese traits of mother and daughter. The rank combination of sweat, booze, and cigarettes filled her nose. He'd gotten too close for comfort. Too fast.

"What do you want?" She glanced back at LiLi, smiling and bouncing down the steps of the bus, her crayon picture in hand.

"Mommy," she squealed. "Look what I made for you!"

"Excuse me." Mei turned away from the stranger, determined to get LiLi into the safety of the apartment building. "I have to get my dau—"

"Not yet you don't." He grabbed her wrist, jerking her backward and off balance. She nearly fell, forced to rely on the pressure of his hard hand to right herself.

"Mommy!" LiLi screamed.

Mei's heart lurched. Another man had taken hold of her daughter. Same get-up. Dark glasses. Denim jacket. He ran around the front of the bus with LiLi kicking in his arms. The bus driver scrambled after him. "Let her go!"

"LiLi!" Mei launched all of her venom at the man restraining her, fingernails aimed for his eyes.

He grabbed her jaw in his dirty hand, twisting her to view the man who'd taken LiLi. "Take a good look, bitch. You're never gonna see your brat again." With one last twist, he shoved her to the sidewalk and ran around the back of the bus.

Mei scrambled after him, her arms and fingers outstretched to grab his jacket. She reached too late. He jumped into the open passenger door of a mini-truck, slamming the door in her face. She hit the window with frightened, angry fists. "Give me my daughter!"

"Mommy!" LiLi climbed over him, her face blotched with fear, both palms flat to the window and crying, "Mommy!"

"Please!" Mei pleaded for a miracle, pounding the glass with all of her strength. She jerked the door handle, determined to pull the thing off if she had to. "Give her back!"

He grinned, his index finger and thumb turned into a gun. Bang. He shot her with his imaginary bullet.

She wrapped her hand through the door handle. That's exactly what they'd have to do to get away—shoot her. The truck was a piece of junk vehicle. Its handle had to give! As the truck picked up speed, she refused to give up. These guys were not taking LiLi!

The driver applied more speed. Mei stumbled. Her knees hit the roadway. Pain jolted up her legs. *I don't care! Drag me. I'm not letting go!* When the passenger door swung open, she dared to hope. The man jerked it back and forth, slamming it into her.

"Stupid bitch!" he cursed. "Get off!"

"No," she ground out. "Give her back!"

"Mommy!" LiLi's frantic scream spiked another rush of adrenaline. A glimpse of him elbowing the girl off his back caught the corner of Mei's eye just as his boot kicked her full in the face. For one split second, her fingers relaxed. Just barely. Just enough.

Tires engaged once more. The vehicle swerved down the street and away.

Mei dug into the asphalt with her fingernails and pushed to her feet. She ran, but there was no way to catch it. Two blocks down the street and the truck kept going.

God, help me!

When it screeched around the corner and vanished, she crumpled to her bloody knees. *This can't be happening! Who were they? Why LiLi? Why my baby?!*

"I called the police," the bus driver said, one hand to her sweaty shoulder, the picture LiLi had been so proud of in his other hand. "Here. Your little girl dropped this."

Mei hugged the construction paper to her heart, a desperate scream climbing up her throat. Blackest black reached up from the depths of Hell and strangled her. She couldn't even cry. The imaginary bullet had struck true.

LiLi was gone.

Damn. Who's singing in my shower?

Zack Lennox peeled a bleary eye open. Had to be Jake. Only he could get away with singing this early and make it sound good - well, halfway good. The problem was not the pitch or tune, but the depression. The man was good, but he could turn *You Are My Sunshine* into a dirge.

Today was no different. Zack recognized the words to one of the heartrending scores from *Les Mis*. He laid there, his arm over his face to block the early morning light. If only it blocked the song. One hurt his eyes; the other hurt his heart. Yeah. The anguish of every man who'd ever been deployed echoed through those pleading lyrics. *Bring Him Home.*

Singing was the way Jake vented his heartache. He'd come home messed up from his last tour in Iraq, not able to go back to what Americans who'd never been to war called a 'normal life'. Most people didn't realize 'normal' was not an option once a man had been to Hell. Movies and television made 'em look like heroes, but Zack knew better. They were all messed up. Some just hid it better.

The man in the shower roared the last words of the tragic, hopeful song.

Zack growled. *Give me a break.*

"Hmmm." A woman's throaty moan sounded a little too close for comfort. He glanced to his left as a feminine ass plastered itself against his naked thigh. Time to move. He had to get to work, and Jake had to stop singing. Still...that backside was warm and soft. He hesitated. It was early enough. He might have just enough time to—

No. Making love to a sound-asleep woman was not in the cards today. No way. No how. He eased away from...Who was she, anyway? Leaning over her shoulder he brushed the brassy curls aside. *Oh. Carol. Good to know.*

Alcohol might dim a man's senses the night before, but they'd better be sharp when *'good morning, umm, whoever-you-are'* rolled around. She didn't wake up when he leveled his weight off the bed. He stood and looked for his briefs in the dim bedroom light. Not finding them, he opted for a naked stroll to his guest bathroom. After all, it was only Jake in there.

Traipsing down the hall, he stepped over the debris from a damned good time with, by the looks of his place, a lot of friends. Beer and wine bottles littered the living room floor. Cardboard pizza boxes with sauce and cheese wagon-wheel imprints lay discarded on the coffee table where the festivities had begun. He kicked a red and grey hoody he didn't recognize as he shuffled his way to the coffee maker. What he needed now was hot, black, and strong enough to kick-start the week. A maple-glazed donut wouldn't hurt, either.

The first verse of *Ninety-Nine Bottles of Beer on the Wall* pealed forth from the bathroom. Zack dumped in the two scoops of Kona's best, filled the coffee maker with enough water, turned it to brew, and headed for the first and last verse of the too-loud drinking song. Jake had to be stopped. That's all there was to it.

Billowing steam poured from the bathroom door as soon as he cracked it open. The song ceased. He snagged a towel and wrapped it around his waist.

"That you?" a tremulous voice asked.

"You're bellowing loud enough to wake the dead." He swiped a hand over the fogged-up mirror.

"Yeah, well." Jake didn't finish. He always sang when he was depressed, and he was always depressed. All his friends knew that.

"Coffee's on."

"Thanks. You going in today?"

Zack grunted around the toothbrush in his mouth. "It's Monday, isn't it?"

"Thought maybe you could take a day. Maybe we could hang out." The shower stopped.

"Not going to happen. One of us needs to work."

"Yeah, well." Jake's favorite words when faced with reality.

Zack didn't mind. They'd been friends long before the war messed in Jake's head. He wasn't going to turn his back on his buddy now. "Need a favor, though."

"Like?" Jake stepped one foot out of the shower, rubbing a towel over his too-skinny body. He didn't do drugs, Zack was sure of that, but living on the streets was hard on a man. The hot shower had to feel good. He didn't get one often enough.

"Like I need you to make sure my friend, Carol, finds her clothes and makes it to her car some time today. She's still buzzed. Can you do that for me?"

"Sure. Did all the pizza get eaten?"

"Don't know, but there's a box of breakfast biscuits in the freezer. You know how to work the microwave."

Jake wrapped the towel at his waist. "You got a clean shirt around here?"

"Hanging in my closet. Help yourself." Zack smoothed a layer of shaving gel over his head and around his chin. The mirror kept fogging up. He swiped it clean again before taking the blade to his three-day's growth.

"Remember the time you woke up with two chicks in your bed?" Jake made himself comfortable on the closed toilet seat, his knobby knees bouncing with his usual hyperactivity. "That was funny."

"Not my brightest idea." Zack focused on not nicking himself. Stupid things like two hot babes in the same bed caused three times the trouble the next day when he had to tell them he wasn't that kind of interested. He'd made it rule number one to never be that dumb again.

"What's on your docket today?" Zack waited for his buddy to answer. It was a stupid question. A homeless man didn't have a docket.

Jake stilled. "Nuthin'."

"If you've got time, I could use a little help. Remember Lillian?"

"Oh. Her." Yeah. Of course, Jake would remember. She lived two doors down in Zack's singles-only gated community, and she was hot for Jake. Neither of them knew why. Lillian was high-end merchandise; Jake wasn't even in the parking lot of the same mall. It had to be the whole opposites attract thing.

"Relax. She's been in Hawaii. She spends every September there. I'm supposed to pick up Tiki from the vet. They've been boarding her until—"

"Lillian's coming home today, isn't she? You want me to take her dog to her." Jake sounded accusatory. He had a soft spot for the prissy poodle, not the owner.

"Relax. Just get Tiki from the vet and kennel her in Lillian's backyard. It will give you a chance to play with the mutt. You don't have to hang around unless you want to."

"She's not a mutt. When's Lillian getting in?"

"Six p.m." Zack wiped a hot washcloth over his head. Women liked his shaved skull look. Who was he to argue? "Don't worry. You can be out of there before she gets home."

He eyed his friend. A bossy woman like Lillian might actually do Jake some good, but Zack was no matchmaker, another line he did not cross. If a man was going to make a mistake with a woman, well, rule number two came into play. Never stick your nose where it doesn't belong. Folks get to screw up their own lives.

"Sure. I'll get Tiki. She's smart."

"I've got to get moving." Zack glanced at his friend. "You're welcome to stay, but I might be gone awhile. Keep the place halfway clean, will ya? Lock up when you leave."

"How long?"

Zack slung his towel over the shower door before stepping inside. "Don't know. It's a combined effort with a lot of feds–DEA, FBI, ATF, and a few others."

"'Kay," Jake muttered on his way out of the bathroom.

Zack lingered in the shower as long as he dared, which wasn't long. After a quick toweling, he paused to look at himself in the mirror, trying to see what it was women saw. Besides the mocha-colored skin he'd been blessed with from his Jamaican father and his beautiful, green-eyed Irish mother, he didn't see much special.

His nose was crooked from flying over the handlebars of his bike while still in training wheels. It should have taught him to slow down. It didn't. A small curved scar on his chin testified that flying a Humvee over an Iraqi sand dune was not the smartest idea, especially when the top-heavy rig rolled. Speed always enticed him. Life was meant to be lived fast and hard. So far, so good.

He flexed one arm, proud of the rippling effect the taut bicep had over the rest of his upper body. He didn't do steroids, but when he flexed into one of those weightlifter-type power stances, it looked like maybe he used. Truth was, he didn't have to. Genetics supplied the basics; he'd supplemented with a steady bodybuilding program and, voila. There stood the man in the mirror he was today.

Time to roll. By the time he exited the bathroom with the towel once again snug on his hips, Jake had left a cup of coffee on the counter, already doctored with enough creamer and sugar. The debris from the living room was picked up. Two full garbage bags stood at the front door on their way to the dumpster. The quiet words of another opera reverberated tragically from the back bedroom. Poor Jake. Still singing his heart away.

Zack took a long pull on the hot drink. The shower and caffeine energized the day. He sneaked back into his bedroom, grabbed his clean clothes, and tiptoed out like the coward he usually wasn't. The stakeout with Senior Agent David Tao began in less than two hours. Zack didn't have time for female drama.

Back in his living room, he dropped the towel and threw on his uniform for the day, cammie trousers with a black polo where The TEAM's gold logo sat like a small badge high on his chest. He liked his job more than women and speed. That said it all.

Pulling his rifle and handgun out of the gun safe inside his entry closet, he secured them with his gear bag, grabbed the garbage bags, and scrambled out the door with an extra quick step. Just in time. She was up. Jake was going to earn his keep today. His buddy would see the lady back to her car, and Zack would be free to browse the local feminine persuasion whenever he liked.

That's what good friends were for.

TWO

"I already told you. She was wearing a navy blue checkered uniform."

"Okay, ma'am," Detective Frank Bastion said for the umpteenth time. "Take it easy. Let's go over everything again."

"No. I'm tired of going over the same questions and repeating the same answers. You need to be out there looking for my daughter." Mei pushed a hand through her hair, ending with a fistful she wanted to tear out.

The police had arrived quickly after LiLi's abduction, but then these detectives showed up in their fancy business suits and ties. They seemed more interested in every last piece of her personal life than chasing down her missing child.

She sat at her kitchen table, LiLi's favorite soup long forgotten. Back-to-school night, too. Detective Bart Crowder kept walking through her home like he was looking for clues that weren't there. These guys were no help. In fact, they were holding her back. If they wouldn't do it, then she needed to be on the streets looking. Searching. Doing anything but sitting around and answering the same stupid questions.

"Trust me. We're doing everything we can." Detective Bastion placed a consoling hand on her wrist as Crowder came to sit with them. "We're already running an AMBER

Alert, and half the precinct is out there looking for her. Don't you worry. We'll find her."

"How?" She pulled away from his creepy touch. How could he sound so sure? Did he think she was stupid? She'd believe just because he said to? Tears flooded her vision again. She wiped her face and grabbed her sweater off the chair. "Shut the door when you leave."

"You shouldn't go anywhere." Detective Crowder jumped to his feet. "Is there anyone who can stay with you?"

She shook her head. Her parents lived in Sacramento. How could she call them with such awful news? They were ill, her father with cancer and her mother with diabetes. A call like this would only hurt them. She'd distanced herself from anything resembling a social life for so long there was no one else to call. Her world revolved around LiLi. Despair knifed her heart again. In the blink of an eye, her world was gone.

"Why should I stay here?" she asked.

A look passed between the men. She caught a subtle nod from Crowder to Bastion.

"Never mind. We'll be leaving." Bastion reached into his inner jacket pocket and pulled out a business card. "If you do hear from anyone, be sure to contact us."

She stood at the door to her empty apartment and watched them walk toward the elevator, half-wishing they'd stayed and half-glad to see them go. Not once had these two public servants asked about the possibility of a ransom. They made no attempt to hook her house phone up to any of the fancy listening equipment like police do in the movies in case the kidnappers called. All they wanted to know was where she worked. Who was she seeing? How did she spend her time?

Sticking the detective's business card into her sweater pocket, she turned and screamed to her empty apartment. "Then what? If I hear from anyone, then what?"

All the worst what-if scenarios flashed to her mind. The kidnappers hadn't stolen LiLi for ransom. No. That's what the nod must have been about. She wasn't rich or important enough. They'd wasted enough time. Her strength fled at the awful truth. Whoever had kidnapped LiLi wanted her for something besides ransom.

With renewed determination, she snapped her television on and knelt in front of it. At least she had the AMBER Alert. Minutes ticked by. She scrolled through the local channels, despair clutching her throat. Back and forth she went from national news to local, praying for the picture that would announce LiLi's kidnapping. That seemed her only hope. Someone was sure to see. The bus driver had given the police and detectives the license plate number. Wouldn't all the police be on the lookout for a missing little girl? Didn't anyone care?

But normal programming offered no relief. No child-missing alert interrupted any channel. Why was there nothing on LiLi? Mei pulled Detective Bastion's business card from her sweater pocket, rage pounding in her head.

She needed a new phone, damn it! Her old one clicked while it rang, heaping frustration onto despair.

"Detective Bastion," he answered casually.

"Where's the AMBER Alert on LiLi?" she demanded without any introduction. He knew who she was.

"Oh? Isn't it airing yet? Guess I'll have to check for you."

"Do it now," she ordered. The last thing she needed was another liar in her life. Her number one rule was dead right. She didn't need men.

"Yes, ma'am. I will. Is there anything else? Has anyone called?"

"Why would they?" she bit out. He knew better. The nonchalance in his tone confirmed what she already suspected. Bastion and Crowder were useless. Only doing their jobs.

"Just asking, ma'am." He hung up and proved it.

I. Don't. Need. Men!

Mei jumped to her feet, turned out the lights and locked the door behind her.

"Mommy's coming."

Easiest stakeout ever.

Zack watched the blue cargo van pull to the curb from his second story vantage point. David had left to check on their additional array of high-tech video cameras and parabolic listening ears. For the last four weeks, Zack and his senior agent had kept close track of Vincent 'Vinnie' Espinosa, best known as the hitman for Dominic 'Dom' Debargio, a local crime boss. Together, these two arrogant gangsters had gotten national law enforcement's attention through drug trafficking, extortion, and murder. This particular stakeout was huge. All the letters of the alphabet were engaged–ATF, FBI, DHS. Even the IRS wanted a piece of the action.

Espinosa's alleged hideout was headquartered out of the derelict apartment across the street, the target of Zack and David's numerous video cameras and high-tech ears. All they had to do was observe and document. It was boring, tedious work, but after four weeks of court approved wire-tapping and video surveillance, they'd accumulated enough evidence to bring Vinnie down, along with his boss and a few locals. Federal Marshalls were expected within the hour with search and seizure warrants. All Zack had to do was keep an eye on the target. That's all. No problem there. He let the video camera do its thing.

The van was the only thing of interest on the street. It looked like a relic left over from the seventies, a definite five o'clock shadow of rust along its lower edge. The color of the driver's side door did not match the rest of the vehicle. Something about turquoise and navy blue hand-brushed over automotive decay did not make for a sharp looking ride.

Two gangster types scrambled out, grabbed a couple of duffel bags from the back of the van, and headed for the derelict apartment building–mobster Vinnie Espinosa's hideout. They didn't appear suspicious. Who cared what they did? Not Zack. These guys were simply more of the same wannabees–all of 'em losers.

The guns in these young men's baggy pants weren't hidden. Again–who cared? *Not my problem.* Weapons in the duffle bags? Drugs? Bodies? *Not my problem. Keep your eyes on the target, Lennox. Be smart. ATF and FBI are en route. Sleep in your own bed tonight. Mission accomplished. Good job. Well done.*

It was a good plan–until a tiny arm flopped out between the open rear doors of the van.

What the hell?

Zack squinted into his computer screen, then jumped to the window to see for himself. Visions of Iraq flashed instantly to mind. The little arm hung there still as death, a fragile flag of humanity in the unlikeliest of places–a gangbanger's pimpmobile.

What's a kid doing in there?

His gut clenched.

Don't do it, Lennox.

Shoulders squared.

There will be hell to pay.

He unholstered the Ruger on his right thigh.

So what?

Taking the stairs two at a time, he ran straight to the van. When he pulled the creaky tailgate all the way open, memories from another time on the other side of the world assaulted him once more. A tiny Asian girl lay crumpled on her side, her cheek pressed to the metal floor of the wreck. Fragile and pale, she couldn't have been more than six. Dressed in nothing but an orange silk dress, her skimpy clothing was too light for the chill of the late November day.

"What are you doing here?" he asked the unconscious child, knowing full well she couldn't hear him. He didn't care. One thing was sure. These guys had no business with the girl. He lifted her from the floor of the van, cradling her to his knee while he watched his back. Unzipping his jacket, he tucked her inside, feeling her neck for a pulse as he pulled the jacket tighter.

"You poor baby. You're damned near froze to death," he muttered when her chilled body met the warmth of his. A weak pulse fluttered under his fingertips. Reaching for her hands, he lifted both to his mouth, breathing heat onto icy fingers. "Come on, baby. Stay with me. Cry or something. Holler. Get mad. Get mad as hell."

She didn't, but he was.

A door slammed open behind him. Those losers were back. The gangbangers strolled onto the sidewalk, arguing over which of them got to hang onto *the loot*. They hadn't noticed him—yet. The open back doors of their ride concealed him, but Zack had a feeling he was holding their loot. Trouble was headed his way. Big time. He ducked, zipping the girl tight inside his jacket while he hefted his Ruger. There'd be no discussion today. He was keeping this baby.

"David," he whispered into his earpiece. "I'm in the street. Need you here, like right damned now."

"You're what?" David's voice cracked with disbelief.

"Hurry it up. I'm running out of time down here. Out front. Step on it. Now."

"On my way." David must've been close. He charged onto the street as the hoodlums climbed into the van. Too late. Zack had just been made.

"Hey! You!" one of the men roared over the front seat. "What are you doing with my stuff?"

"He's got the girl," the other bellowed. "Get 'em!"

A rain of automatic gunfire blasted through the van. Windows shattered, sending a shower of safety glass over Zack. He sheltered the child. The engine roared to life, coughing noxious fumes from its tailpipe. Rolling to his side, he offered his back to shield the girl while David returned steady fire from the sidewalk.

"There's two of 'em! Get us outta here," one hoodlum screamed. "Move it."

The van peeled away from the curb in a cloud of smoking rubber and squealing wheels.

"Zack." David ran to his side. "What have you done?"

Zack was already on his cell. "Listen Boss, we got a problem. A really big problem."

THREE

"You call this an audit trail?" Putting every ounce of venom she could into her nasty fake-FBI persona, Mei tossed the stack of manila-colored folders across the Washington Metro Police Department technician's desk to emphasize her disgust. "You haven't located half of the information I requested. What kind of department are you running here, anyway?"

The poor woman on the receiving end cringed. Mei almost felt sorry for Kathleen Crawford. One look at her carefully crafted but false FBI ID badge and the Assistant Chief of Police had all but dumped Mei on the hapless technician. He couldn't get out of there fast enough.

"If you'd come back tomorrow, my boss will be able to help better than I can." Kathleen's voice came out high-pitched and raspy, like her vocal cords had all but dried up in the back of her throat. "I must've made a mistake. I've only been here a month. Could you tell me what you're looking for one more time?"

"Maybe you oughta write it down." Mei exuded exasperation. She had to be tough. The day shift supervisor would have never let her in. The thought of all the laws she was breaking rattled her confidence. It couldn't be helped. She didn't care even if it could. After four weeks of single-handedly searching for LiLi, she was willing to do whatever it took. "You're supposed to be able to withstand an audit at any time of day, not just when your boss is on shift."

She poured it on. Subterfuge only worked when her targets were intimidated. Ms. Crawford looked plenty scared. *Good. The more you quiver and shake, the quicker I can get out of here.*

"Agent Xing. Please. I'm sorry. I wasn't aware you had an appointment." Kathleen brushed slight beads of sweat off her forehead with the back of her hand. "But she's really the one you should talk with. She knows a lot more than me. It stands to reason—"

"Fine. My report will show you failed to provide requested information to the FBI. I'm fine with that. Hope your supervisor is. It'll be your name on the line, not mine." Mei opened her laptop with a snap. Sitting at Kathleen's desk, she prepared to record her findings, hoping she looked like the ruthless oriental queen she intended. "Should I enter it as lack of ability? Inadequate training of personnel on shift? Failure to cooperate? How long do you think it will take to fix your problem, Ms. Crawford?"

She drew out the poor woman's name with plenty of sarcasm, intending to elicit the exact panic attack an inexperienced employee might have when faced with the possible loss of her job. Her instincts were dead on. Kathleen looked like she was having a stroke, complete with heart palpitations, hot flashes, and hyperventilation thrown in for good measure. If she licked her lips anymore, they would dry up and blow away.

"Listen. J-j-just l-l-listen. I don't think there's a problem. Like I said, I'm new here. Tell me one more time, and I'll—"

"I don't have time to waste. If you aren't capable, that's all I need to know." Mei waved her hand dismissively. "Now leave me alone. Let me finish my findings. It's unfortunate. It's not a difficult system to query. Even I could do it."

"What if...?" Kathleen huffed a huge sigh, relief showing for the first time at the tantalizing offer Mei had dangled in front of her nose. "What if you showed me how to do it? Umm, if you could run a simple query, I'm sure I could follow your logic, and—"

"What?" Mei peered over her reading glasses. Bait and hook. The poor woman was already caught, and Mei was reeling her in. "You would compromise your password? That's even worse than—"

"No. No. Never." Kathleen's hands shook. "But I could kinda like, maybe open the system for you. Then I wouldn't compromise my password. You'd never see it. You could run one query to show me what you want. Would that be okay?"

"Training you is not in my job description," Mei snapped, straightening to her complete five foot six inches of height. Every inch mattered in her world of deceit, bluff and bluster. She took one step closer, so she could really look down her nose at the trembling techie.

"I just thought...." Kathleen looked up and gulped. The poor woman had hives creeping up her neck, and by now she must need a drink of water in the worst way. "I hoped that would help you, umm, get what you needed."

Mei rubbed her chin and stared. Truth was, she wished she were half as smart as Kathleen. It might be a simple system, but she didn't really have a clue how to get into it. Until tonight, she'd dabbled in amateurish hacking but had only really handled the basic software programs at her old job, the one she gave up when searching for LiLi became a full time occupation. In no way was an automobile inventory system as intimidating as a D.C. Metro Police internal link with the FBI.

If her ruse was going to work, she needed Kathleen to fall all over herself, to be overly helpful in her desire to be rid of the supposed audit and the accompanying mean auditor. "I'm not sure I am allowed to assist. Let me call my superior."

As Mei stepped away with her phone to her ear, she watched her victim's response. Kathleen sat at her desk again, already keying in her password. She fanned her face with a loose sheet of paper. Stepping closer while she pretended a conversation with her supervisor, Mei heard her mutter, "You're okay. She'll be gone in a minute. You can do it. Hold it together."

There was a time Mei would have felt sympathy. Not any more. Ms. Crawford was just another person to step on and over. Mei had a baby to find and the world was in her way.

"My supervisor is not happy, but he did say that I may assist. However, he said to tell you it is not proper protocol for a Federal Agent to query a local system. That is your job. I may show you once and once only. Then it's up to you." Mei kept her expression stern and cold as she nodded in the direction she meant. "I'll send my query findings to the printer over there. Are you in yet or not?"

"Yes." The clerk nodded nervously, her neck and face brightly splotched with the steadily advancing hives and now scratch marks. "I'm in. Thanks, umm, for helping me."

"Whatever." Mei stood directly behind Kathleen, her toes tapping to magnify her annoyance as much as her anxiety. She couldn't get caught. Not here in the main D.C. precinct.

"Let's see how far you can get without my help." She tapped her index finger on her lip, studying the screen over Kathleen's shoulder. "Tell me. Where would an FBI query be stored?"

Kathleen gulped. She moved her mouse to a list of confidential links in a column to the right of the main entry screen. "I've used a couple queries before. I think it's this one right here, but—"

"Just do it," Mei barked. *Stop talking. Do it fast. Get it done. Get me out of here.*

With quick but shaky keystrokes, Kathleen maneuvered through the various menus. "Is this the one?" She glanced timidly up at Mei.

"What do you think?" Mei peered into the screen. Missing children. Endangered children. Known abductions. Child trafficking. There were so many awful selections to choose from.

"I, ah, I—"

"This one." Mei spotted an option for an integrated report. She stabbed the screen with her index finger. "Print it. Now."

Kathleen licked her lips and complied. Her fingers flew over the keyboard. "I'll get it for you."

"Stop," Mei shouted, afraid the very woman she'd just badgered into submission would discover her subterfuge. "I'll get it if you don't mind."

Kathleen froze. Without so much as a thank you, Mei gathered her laptop and strode to the office door, pausing a split second to gather the printed report from the printer tray on her way out. She licked her lips, by now as dry as Kathleen's.

"When, umm, will my boss get the results of the audit?" Kathleen asked.

Mei grunted, "We'll be in touch," and off she went, her heartbeat too loud in her ears and bile creeping up her throat. Never in her life had she contemplated needing so much courage or deceit as she needed now.

It wasn't until she was safely in her car with the bogus badge concealed in her glove compartment that Mei doubled over and vomited the very meager contents of her empty stomach into the street. False bravado took a hard toll. Nothing stayed down anymore. Life without LiLi was killing her in more ways than one.

Straightening, she wiped her mouth and shut the door, hoping no passerby had seen. Why had she worried? She was part of the invisible segment of society, the ones who literally worked their guts out, suffered in silence, and didn't make enough money to garner political clout, much less police support. Her bitterness pushed tears to the surface, but she shoved them back. There would be time to cry later.

Four weeks. LiLi had been missing four weeks, and Mei hated the world of law enforcement with her heart and soul. Maybe everyone else, too. Detectives Bastion and Crowder had only patronized her. When she'd called their supervisor hoping for a show of real concern, she'd been told he'd return her call. She was still waiting.

Her predicament seemed unreal. Was everyone against her? Was everyone in on the abduction of her child? It seemed like it.

After that disappointment, she'd contacted the mayor's office. He was busy campaigning. Her senator talked with her, or at least that's who she thought she had talked to.

Again, he'd said all the right things. He'd get in touch with the detectives. *What were their names? Thanks for calling. I'm glad to help.* Then–nothing.

Now, hoping against hope, she scanned the report she'd stolen. Linked to the FBI's database of missing and exploited children, it listed line after line of endangered children, from runaways to kidnapped, the status of all open investigations, and any known suspects. The difference in this report and the more generic one on the FBI's public website was the accompanying list of known suspects, actual addresses, and phone numbers.

Please be here.

She gritted her teeth, knowing there was no way her scam would've been successsful by going directly into the FBI. She might pretend to be one of them, but to really infiltrate the Bureau? She wasn't that kind of brave. Stupid, maybe. Determined, yes. But truly courageous? Never.

She couldn't read the list fast enough. *Please. Let me find her!*

Line after line declined the name she sought. LiLi Xing. Six years old. Straight black hair in a blunt cut just below her ears. Blue plaid uniform. White blouse. Abducted off the sidewalk in front of her apartment building after school one day. Broad daylight. Missing. No suspects. Prettiest little girl in Saint Charles Borromeo's first grade. Prettiest little girl anywhere.

The sob Mei didn't want to own crept up her throat, along with the bitter taste of bile. Once again, she had put everything at risk, and once again, she'd come up with– nothing!

Striking the steering wheel with her fist, she cried, "Why isn't your name here? Why won't anyone help me?"

The awful truth stared back at her. It was as if her daughter had never existed, like no missing person's report had ever been filed, and no one was looking for her.

Because they weren't.

What do I do now?

Mei glanced at her police scanner, the wisest investment she'd ever made. She now knew police jargon for too many frightening things like actual bodily harm, dead body, sex offender, and dead on scene. And then there were police codes for child neglect, assault with intent to murder, deceased person, and a hundred other realities she'd never needed to know. Until now.

Fortunately, it had proved its worth the very first night she owned it when she'd followed a police call to the Pennsylvania Avenue Bridge over the Anacostia River. Watching through her high-powered binoculars, another smart purchase, she'd watched an officer use a long pole with a barbed hook to pull a body to shore, a very small body. Her hysteria nearly got the better of her, but the corpse was too small. It was someone else's poor baby. A toddler. Limp. Lifeless. So small.

She'd cried watching, but then she got the idea of impersonating an FBI agent. They could get into places she could not–the county morgue, the emergency room, hospitals, and even the D. C. main police precinct. She'd gotten creative then and fashioned badges and official-looking ID cards for other federal agencies. Too soon another call came. Anacostia. An old man claimed he'd found a child in a garbage receptacle. A little girl. Drugged. Nearly dead.

Mei became an Immigrations and Customs Enforcement Officer then. No one at the emergency room questioned when she flashed her phony ICE badge. The nurse led her straight to Claire Langley, the Family Services child advocate assigned to these desperate cases. A plump woman with silver hair, Claire liked to talk, so Mei learned of the comprehensive FBI database for missing children.

"That's two babies in one week," Claire lamented to the young police officer who'd accompanied the little girl into the ER. Mei feigned an important cell phone call and stepped into the hall, not willing to face the scrutiny of law enforcement.

"Yes, and they're both Chinese." He pulled up a chair to sit with Claire in the waiting room, barely glancing in Mei's direction.

"The two-year-old too?" Claire had asked. "The one you found in the river? She was Chinese?"

He'd nodded somberly. "Some of us down at the precinct are thinking there's a child trafficking ring in the area. Looks like it might be straight out of China."

Hope raised its paralyzed head for the first time in days at the startling news. Mei had not known the ethnicity of the first tiny corpse. Suddenly, everything made sense. That's who had kidnapped LiLi. It had to be. LiLi was American Chinese. Mei listened intently.

He sounded so sincere when he said, "It makes me sick."

Yes, but not sick enough to help me find my daughter.

The dark night let loose the first of a late autumn rain, jolting Mei out of her depressing reverie and chilling her soul. She turned her car on and cranked the heater to high. The last time she'd seen her daughter was a sunny day, too warm for even a light jacket. Mei shivered. Wherever she was, LiLi might be cold. Or worse.

FOUR

"I asked if you heard me."

The bellowing voice had to be Kevin Carducci's, as in ATF Director Carducci, the man who'd organized the operation Zack had just bungled. He slipped by the barely open Situation Room door, hoping no one noticed. The last place he wanted to be was where his boss now waged war. Zack had to be in Alex's office by the end of the nasty meeting, where he fully expected he'd get his ass reamed before he got fired. It wouldn't be a pleasant meeting, but this one was much worse.

Everyone knew by now. The whole team. He was a screw up. It wouldn't be so bad, but he really loved his job. Working for Alex Stewart could be a tough row to hoe, but he'd never felt more alive and fulfilled. Heck, most times he didn't even have to use his weapon. Zack bit his lip and clenched his gut. *Way to go, Lennox.*

"I stand by my agent." Judging by the level of volume from the Sit Room, Alex was giving as good as he got, his voice hard as steel.

"I'm not asking if you stand by your agent. I don't care if you think they all walk on water. I'm asking if we have an understanding." Carducci again. Loud. Rude. Arrogant.

Zack grimaced. At least Alex defended him–for now.

"No, sir, we do not."

"Be careful, Stewart. Small time players have no business in a high stakes game. I can make your life very miserable."

Zack cringed. Big mistake, Carducci. No one bullies Alex. A chair scraped. Had to be the boss. If he was on his feet, that meant—

"For the last time. I stand by my agents," Alex snarled.

You tell 'em, Boss.

"Then we're done here," Director Carducci snapped.

"No, sir, *you're* done here. You'll get no apology from me." Alex had the nastiest tone when he was pushed too far. Apparently, Carducci didn't know.

"That's not mitigation, you arrogant fool."

"Exactly." Alex's tone dropped back to a conversational level. "Now we have an understanding."

Zack had to give it to him. The man knew when to charge, all guns blazing, and when to calm. Strategies like that tended to pull the rug out from under pretentious men like Carducci; men who thought paid contractors should grovel at their feet. No one on earth was a better boss or a tougher opponent than Alex. That skill was going to work against Zack today. His turn in the barrel was next.

More chairs scraped, and Zack hurried down the hall. He was in enough trouble. No need to be caught eavesdropping. He barely made it into Alex's office and closed the door, just enough to peek through the crack, when Carducci burst through the Sit. Room doors and stalked to the elevator.

"It's about time."

Zack whirled, startled he hadn't noticed David Tao sitting at the small conference table, his hands folded serenely in front of him. "Damn. Didn't see you sitting there."

"I take it the Director is finished with Alex?"

"More like he's finished with the Director." Zack dropped onto the chair to David's right. It was a small, four-man table. No doubt old man Murphy would be joining Alex. He would complete the murder board. Despite the fact that Zack had been in serious military-like situations with these men in the past, situations where shots were fired and men were killed, his gut poured solid acid. This time was different. The career he loved as an undercover operative would die today. It would hurt.

David murmured, "He is coming."

"And he's not happy, either."

David shot him a 'no kidding' kind of look, but the door didn't crash open like Zack expected with Alex madder than hell and ready to hang someone–like him. That could be good. That could be bad. It gave Zack more time to consider the decision that was going to cost him the job he loved. Even now, he couldn't believe that his saving a girl's life compromised the ATF Op like it had. The TEAM seemed such a small cog in the wheel.

Suddenly, Vinnie had turned invisible. Dom, too. Word was they'd fled the country when Zack exposed the operation like he did. ATF Director Carducci wasn't the only one who wanted his head. Oh, no. There were others standing in line, including the FBI and a few local police chiefs. Heck, even the Navy wanted a piece of him.

Zack scrubbed a hand over his head and stiffened his spine. He and David had spent a lot of time together lately. They'd grown close. Then there were Mark and Harley, both overseas on some operation in Afghanistan. He sighed. *I'm going to miss these guys.*

The door opened. In walked Alex, powerful CEO and boss, with his sidekick, Murphy Finnegan, ex-Army and damned proud of it. Zack's heart started a pounding beat. At least his boss hadn't kicked the door open. He licked his lips and hunkered down, prepared for the bad cop, good cop beat down. He deserved it. *Let it rain.*

Alex took the position directly across from him. Not so good. Zack maintained eye contact, or at least tried to. Alex hadn't looked at him–yet. It didn't make any difference. All those finely honed "I own this damned business" skills were now directed straight at Zack. He waited. *Might as well get it over with. Let me have it. Then I'll leave.*

Minutes passed while Alex opened his leather planner to yesterday's two-page spread. Zack noticed the big black X over a good portion of the pages. That's the kind of guy Alex was. He might keep meticulous notes, but then mark them up in a fit of temper. He might dress the part of a savvy businessman in the expensive gray suit he was wearing, but there was an ex-Marine beneath the burgundy shirt and black tie who could still take a man's head off at a thousand yards– or less.

The man came out of the 22nd Marine Expeditionary Unit at Camp Lejeune, South Carolina, like Zack had. They'd worked together when Alex was getting his covert op business off the ground. Zack was one of his first agents. That had to count for something, didn't it?

At last, Alex lifted his eyes. Icy blues speared Zack clean through. A full on body-slam could not have hurt worse. He wilted. He'd disappointed the one man left in the world he truly respected.

"How is she?" Alex got right to the point.

"Dehydrated, malnourished, and frightened." Zack spoke right up, ready to give his boss every last bit of information in his head. "She's at Children's National Medical Center in D.C. Boss, I didn't have a choice. I–I—"

Alex waved the explanation off with a look of total irritation before turning to David. "What do we know about her?"

Zack clamped his mouth shut. Good. Talking about the girl was a positive sign. Alex had a daughter once. He cared about kids. Good.

"Child Protective Services has taken custody until Immigration and Customs can locate her parents. She's Chinese, so I was able to talk with her a little, but she's only around five years old, maybe younger. It's hard to know for sure." David pushed several photos across the table as he calmly explained. "She's very afraid. I couldn't get much out of her. Different dialects, you understand. I'd be glad to spend more time with her when we're through here."

Alex studied the photos David had taken at the hospital. Zack had been there when the poor little gal came to. By then, she was wrapped in heated blankets, had an IV line in her skinny little arm, and Child Services had been called. The pictures showed everything. They also portrayed a lost child with dark, scared eyes.

"Boss, I—"

"Knock it off," Alex hissed. If looks could kill.

Zack took a deep breath, shut up, and waited.

"So, we've got an endangered child on our hands who doesn't speak English, two gangbangers in a blue cargo van full of bullet holes, and—"

"I've got the van on the surveillance video, Boss, and—"

Another scorching look and Zack's throat squeezed shut. There was no sense in speaking. He was dead. His stupid brain just didn't understand it yet.

"And we've got the duffle bags they carried into the apartment," Alex snapped at him even as he turned to face David again. "Do we know what's in those bags?"

"Fur coats. I ran some preliminary numbers. Street value is close to half a million."

"Furs?" Alex's nose wrinkled. "That's an odd commodity for gangbangers."

"Mother and Ember are working to identify the gang members from the video surveillance Zack mentioned. Metro PD thinks they're 4th Street Tigers. I've got an all-points bulletin out for the van. We're also checking the local precinct's theft divisions to see if they've got anything on stolen furs or vans." David's gaze was as steady as Alex's.

Zack took another deep breath. He hadn't expected to still be here, so all the talk about the little girl and the van had to be a good sign. He rolled the knot out of one shoulder. Maybe he wasn't going to get fired after all.

Alex turned to him. Icy blue had changed to gunmetal gray. Sharp. Cold. Deadly.

"Size it up for me, Lennox."

Zack swallowed hard. *Size it up for me? What does he mean? What's he really asking?*

"Ah," he stalled, his mind racing over all possible answers. David had just summed up the whole debacle. What did Alex want, the damned mess tied up with a blood red bow?

"I guess what we've got here is a little girl who needed help." Zack calmed the moment he opened his mouth to speak. This was that rubber to the road moment when a man stood up and took the blame, right or wrong. "If you want someone's head, it would be mine. I made the call. It's on me. Yeah, David was senior agent, and he backed me up, but I'm the one who screwed the op. If you're here to fire someone, I'm your man."

He blew out a deep breath. These past couple of years would definitely go down as some of his best, but he wasn't kidding himself. Good reason or not, he'd cost the federal government and Alex a lot of money. Someone had to go down. If Carducci wanted blood on a rock, it might as well be his.

"Carducci wants you fired." Alex pushed back from the table, his eyes boring through Zack's head and out the other side.

Zack nodded. He had nothing to say. He didn't work for the ATF, and he cared less what the pretentious man in the thousand-dollar suit wanted. It only mattered what Alex thought, and right now, it obviously wasn't much.

Alex turned to Murphy. Both men looked as bleak as the other. "What do you think, Murph?"

Murphy was the definite good cop to Alex's lethal bad cop. Until now, he'd been quiet. The old guy was in his sixties, thinning gray hair, and the first to admit he wasn't as smart as the new generation when it came to gizmos and computers and such, but he was a good man. Zack waited on him now.

"I don't know." Murphy sighed. "Seems to me we still have an active operation on our hands. I'd hate to lose what corporate knowledge we've got just because Carducci's pissed."

"I don't give a damn about Carducci," Alex grunted.

Murphy's blue eyes twinkled. Zack held his breath. Were these two toying with him? If so, it wasn't funny.

"Just so you two geniuses know," Alex paused long enough to stare him down and keep him wondering. "I got my butt reamed good. You're off the Espinosa case."

He liked the sound of those words. Off. Not fired.

"But you owe me. Big time." Again with the evil eyes. Man, the guy didn't quit. "You're both on this little girl's case. You'd better not screw the pooch, Lennox."

"Yes, Boss." Zack took the hit and let another breath of relief whoosh between his teeth. *Hell, yeah.*

Alex leaned across the table, his fingers laced together and all those pointed, killer skills aimed right at his trouble-making junior agent. "I'm flying out to the Seattle office for a couple days. By the time I get back, I want everything settled. You locate her parents. You find out why a couple of punks had her in the back of their van, and you find a way to make that little girl happy. I want your written reports on my desk, ready for my signature by Monday."

Zack glanced at David. Yes, they were both still employed, but damn, it was going to be a busy week.

"Email me a copy of your final reports no later than Friday night. I'll be home. I'll be waiting." Alex glared. He wasn't finished.

Zack stilled. Here it comes. He braced himself.

"Screw Carducci. I'd have done the same thing."

FIVE

What have I gotten myself into?

Zack groaned. He was an ex-Marine sniper. By definition, a man of action. A dedicated covert consultant on The TEAM, he enjoyed the people he worked with. Most of the time he could handle any assignment his boss gave him, but this one was driving him crazy. He was used to tracking down twenty-one-year-old babes who wanted a good time. Little girls? Never.

He'd been at it since his boss left for Seattle the day before. So far, every search on a missing Asian girl around five or six years old had proved a dead end. There was no AMBER Alert, no reports of missing children, nothing. He'd barely broadened his search to the international arena when David tapped on his desk.

Zack looked up. "You finding anything yet?"

"No, but I have another idea. Let's go visit her." David's leaning over his desk with an expectant look on his face told Zack plenty. No matter what he said next, he was already on his way to the hospital.

"Why?" Zack pushed back in his chair.

David, another Marine, hailed from the west coast and had served in *The Fighting 13th* out of Pendleton, California. The irony of a sniper being a devoted family man and father of four boys never ceased to amaze Zack. Yet that's exactly who David was, as well as a devout Buddhist. He was as big a puzzle to Zack as were most married men in the office, Alex included.

"There might not be much she can tell us," David said, "but we need to see how she's dealing with her strange surroundings."

"She still stable?"

David nodded. "I'll drive."

"Nope." Zack snagged his jacket off the back of his chair. "Sorry, old man. I'll drive. I'd like to get there today."

The playful barb missed David completely.

"So how's it work?" Zack asked once they were en route. Traffic was light as he maneuvered steadily through the busy D.C. traffic.

"How does what work?"

"You know, the whole Buddhist thing and being a sniper." Zack had never asked before, but his curiosity got the best of him. Of all the agents on staff, David was the least prone to stress, anger, or emotion. The ability to control one's emotions was a good skill set for a sniper. It just wasn't one Zack employed twenty-four-seven. No. His peace of mind came from the sleek, black pearl Porsche he and David were cruising in. Pure pleasure, with four hundred and seventy-five horses under the hood, zero-to-sixty in three seconds if he put his foot in it, and a state of the art CDR audio system.

David owned a Toyota, zero-to-sixty in — what? Five minutes? Even the clothes they wore defined them. David was all business, suited up and professional. Zack wore his usual. Jeans. Golf shirt. Leather jacket. He shot a sideways glance at his senior agent. David was married with a wife, four boys, and a home in the 'burbs. How on earth was that living? Boring with a capital D-U-L-L.

Besides, could Zack help it if chicks liked that he was ex-military and built? He worked out. It showed. He liked that they liked. Plain and simple, he indulged the fairer gender, but he wasn't stupid. Pleasure in all forms had its place. He just made sure it had enough room when it showed up and it knew when to leave. The biggest lesson he'd brought home from his many deployments around the globe was that life was short. Don't screw it up.

"Why do you ask?"

"Guess I thought Buddhists were always peaceful," Zack answered, "like the monks in the temples, all Zenned out or something."

"Even Buddha in his wisdom understood the need for strong and good soldiers."

There it was again, an unruffled way of listening and answering that Zack did not have and could not understand. "I guess the key word is good, huh?"

David nodded. "You and I are not like most people around us. We truly understand peace because we've chosen to be good soldiers. We know what it means to fight for peace. You're not so different from me."

Zack mulled David's answer over as they pulled into the hospital zone. David made sense, but he was wrong. He and Zack were worlds apart.

After parking at the curb, they entered the hospital, checked with the information desk, and made their way to the third level. An older woman with a touch of gray at her temples opened the door to the girl's room.

"I'm David Tao." David extended a hand. "This is Zack Lennox."

"You must be the gentlemen who found our little girl." She ushered them in. "I'm Claire Langley, the Family Services child advocate assigned to this poor little girl. I'm sorry I wasn't able to meet you at the emergency room when you brought her in. I had a very busy day."

David nodded to Zack. "Zack here is the one who extracted her from the Tigers."

"Good morning, ma'am." Zack accepted her handshake, but she didn't release him. Instead, she clasped his hand in both of hers and pulled him a step closer.

"You're very brave," Claire said, her kind blue eyes brimming with tears. "I'm so proud to know there are still good men like you in the world."

"Yes, ma'am." He accepted her gratitude, but then she leaned in closer and wrapped her motherly arms around his shoulders. It was enough to make a grown man cry. He patted her back and nodded. Thankfully, she didn't draw it out.

"How is she?" he asked, to divert Claire's attention.

The girl looked lost in the big hospital bed. Sad, almond-shaped eyes darted back and forth until David spoke to her with a few words in Chinese. Instantly, she locked onto him like radar, her little lower lip quivering. Zack watched the miracle unfold. The minute David sat on the edge of her bed, the tiny tyke scrambled onto his lap and buried her face inside his suit jacket. Right dialect or not, he must have looked or sounded familiar.

"My goodness. Let me get her back into bed," Claire fussed. "You don't need to—"

"I don't mind," David interrupted. "I have four sons. Is it okay if I hold her?"

"If you're sure you don't mind," Claire replied. "She's a darling little thing, isn't she?" she asked Zack.

"Ahh, yeah. She is." Who was he to disagree? The little gal was a danged cute kid. She deserved a lot more than a dismal life with a couple gangbangers. He hoped Claire found her a good home. Parents would be nice, too.

David rocked while she nestled inside his arms. He pulled the bed cover up over her to keep warm whatever limbs were not already inside his jacket. She'd calmed and turned into a baby ostrich. David obviously had another talent Zack didn't.

"What happens to her now?" Zack asked.

"She'll go into foster care until we can locate her family," Claire explained. "If we can't find them, she'll be available for adoption. She's a sweet little thing considering all she's been through."

"Do we know what she's been through?" Zack asked.

"For one thing, she's been drugged. There weren't signs of sexual assault, but she hasn't been taken care of. She's very small for her age and underweight." Claire had a sappy look on her face watching David. "Mr. Tao, can you get her to talk? I've tried, but she seems to relate to you better than me. I don't think she understands a word I've said."

"Sure. I'll try." He tugged the blanket off the girl's face. She peeked out with eyes that didn't smile in the slightest, her bottom lip stuck in a pout that made her look too serious for her tender age. He spoke softly in Chinese, but she just stared at him.

"What kind of drugs?" Zack asked, but Claire was no longer listening. Her eyes were glued on the drama between

David and the girl. He'd covered her face again with a corner of the blanket. Slowly, he pulled it down over her forehead until just her eyes appeared. Without a word, he repeated the game one more time. Zack smiled. It wasn't every day he saw his senior agent playing peek-a-boo.

David spoke in the soft musical Chinese language. Very quietly, she answered him back in a soft, two-syllable reply. He smiled and patted his chest, as if maybe he was telling her his name. She reached to touch him, her eyes bright with apprehension as four little fingertips touched his pressed white shirt right where he had just touched. A small word escaped her lips, but the poor thing kept her eyes on him the whole time.

He smiled encouragingly and spoke again. Slowly, she flattened her palm to his shirt, her eyes full of concern for the scary thing she was doing. When he nodded and smiled, she pulled her hand back. Slowly, she reached again, her eyes trained on him.

One more, softly uttered phrase slipped from her lips. He tapped her upturned nose with the tip of his index finger and spoke again. She nodded a quick, scared little nod. At last, her hand was flat against his ribs, but the act of courage proved too much. She whined, pulled the blanket over her face, and grunted until she was once again hidden from view.

Playtime was over.

David wrapped his arms around the tiny human ostrich, his head lowered while he took extra time making sure her feet and arms were covered. When at last he looked up, his eyes glistened. He cleared his throat and secured the blanket again, his hands smoothing over the tiny body latched onto his. Two soft syllables that sounded like "Shay shay," rose from beneath the covers.

"I asked where her mother is," he offered hoarsely as he began rocking. "She said, '*No mama*'."

"Oh, the poor little thing." Claire came to sit at the edge of the bed with him. "Did she tell you anything else? Her name, maybe?"

David cleared his throat and whispered, "Chai Yenn."

Zack had to turn away. He'd held the baby girl. She needed a mother, damn it.

"She doesn't know how old she is, but I'd guess maybe five," David offered somberly. "It's hard to tell. She's very thin."

"I'm so glad you came to visit," Claire said as she reached for his shoulder. "Maybe now that I know her name, she won't be quite so frightened of me. You'd be surprised how many little ones like this we've had lately."

"How many?" Zack jumped at the chance to divert the topic. Dealing with lost children was always a heartbreaker.

"Didn't you know?" Claire asked. "She's the third in the last month, and they've all been Chinese girls. We're working with several agencies–the National Center for Missing and Exploited Children, Immigration and Customs Enforcement, as well as the FBI. Chai Yenn is in much better condition, but she's not the first." Claire shook her head. "Ms. Mei Xing is working with me. She's from the Immigration and Customs Enforcement Agency. I'm expecting her this morning if you'd care to hang around a little longer. You just might catch her."

"Do we have time?" Zack asked David.

He should've known better than to ask. All he had to do was look at the sad but contented face of his friend. David had his arms full of a little girl with no mother. They had plenty of time.

SIX

I can do it. One more time. I can!

Mei swallowed hard, straightened her blazer, and tilted her chin up. She paused with her hand to the hospital room door, needing to be convincing. Claire had come to take the girl to the Family Services office. Today was Mei's last chance to pump the friendly child advocate for information about the child trafficking ring. They were Mei's next targets. She fully intended to infiltrate them. Somehow. The only problem was where to start?

She rapped quietly to announce her arrival, pushed the door aside, and cringed. Two men looked up, their sharp eyes running over her, and immediately she panicked. Could she fool them as easily as Claire? Better yet, could she intimidate them like Kathleen? She gulped past her dry throat and entered. Showtime. Again.

"Why, Agent Xing, how nice to see you." Claire waved her into the room. "I was just telling Agents Tao and Lennox you might drop by. You're right on time."

"Good morning." The muscular bald fellow jumped away from the counter he'd been leaning against and politely extended his hand. Deep brown eyes swept over her again, appraising what they liked and didn't like, no doubt. A wide-open kind of a smile brightened his face, making her very aware when his warm hand engulfed hers. "I'm Zack Lennox. It's good to meet you."

"G-good morning." She returned the favor by raking him up one side and down the other, the same way he'd done to her.

He wasn't half-bad looking. Confidence tugged at the corner of his mouth. Laugh lines crinkled across his forehead. The dark glasses perched on top of his head combined with his leather bomber jacket and jeans made him look like some college preppie, carefree but going places. The man looked like he had it all.

She tried not to notice the ripple of corded muscles down his abdomen when he'd reached for her hand, or the way his shirt fit too tight across his chest. A thick, muscular neck supported his bare bobble-head. She made up her mind right then and there she didn't like him. He thought he was good looking. It showed in his smirky eyes. The man was a player, and she wasn't playing. Maybe, never again.

Pulling her fingers free of his gentle and oddly warm grasp, she turned to the other man, Agent Tao. Now there was a real man. He knew how to handle a child. The little girl was snuggled on his lap. By the looks of it, she knew a real man, too.

"You'll be happy to know Agent Tao was able to learn our little girl's name," Claire announced. "Agent Xing, please meet Chai Yenn."

Little Chai had already peeked out from beneath her cover when Mei entered the room, but the minute Mei looked at her, Chai ducked behind Agent Tao's arm. Hiding. That hurt. Mei had never frightened a child before. All she wanted to do was hold Chai, if only for the joy of feeling a little girl in her arms again. Had she changed so much that a child would hide from her?

Agent Lennox still watched, rattling Mei's confidence even more.

"I am pleased to meet you, Ms. Xing." The older man reached for her hand with genuine hospitality. Now that she'd stepped closer, she could see he wasn't older at all. She glanced back at that Zack guy. They were both around the same age. Agent Tao just looked more mature. Or something.

"I understand you're working with Claire?" he asked.

"Yes." She stalled. The sight of these guys had thrown her off balance. She couldn't put her finger on the reason. Anxiety climbed up her throat, but she pushed it back down. Kept it at bay. Her stomach churned. She had to get the upper hand.

Get tough, Mei. You can do it. Be the ICE agent. Be mean if you have to.

"You the ones who found the girl?" She arched an imperious brow, as least, that's what she hoped for. It had worked before.

Agent Lennox took immediate credit as he lounged back against the counter, his feet crossed at the ankles. "Yes. Just happened to be in the right place at the right time. Snagged her away from the Tigers. She looks a lot better this morning. You should've seen her yesterday."

"I did," she bit out, turning to Claire. Talking with another woman was so much easier. "Are you taking her with you today?"

"I plan to if her doctor releases her." Claire's worried eyes drilled through Mei's crumbling façade. "Are you okay? You look a little flushed. You're not coming down with—"

"I'm fine," she cut Claire off. *Great. Can everyone see through me?*

"Claire mentioned you've been involved with two other Chinese girls found recently?" Agent Lennox asked. "What can you tell us about them?"

Mei bit her lip. She took an extra long minute to brush an invisible smudge off the sleeve of her blazer, fighting her nerves. "We pulled one out of the Anacostia River. The other was found in a dumpster. Why do you want to know?"

He shrugged, his eyes soft and gentle. Inviting. "Where was the dumpster?"

"Behind an IGA store. A transient found her."

"I'm sorry." There was a smirky light in his eyes again. Agent Lennox had long thick lashes that accentuated his good looks, rattling Mei even more, making her feel like–a woman. "I should've asked a better question. I meant, where in Anacostia was she found?"

"I knew what you meant," she snapped. She'd lost credibility fast with that stupid answer. Of course he'd meant which city, not which store. "Near the Eleventh Street Bridge."

A bemused smile shifted over his face. He was laughing at her. She could tell. "What can you tell me about the others?"

This arrogant man was grilling her? Mei stiffened. Time to pull out the snarky FBI agent routine before she really fell apart.

"I don't see how it's any of your business, but if you insist." She poured it on. "The one found in the dumpster is the same age and size, malnourished and dirty with two fractured ribs. She's been placed in a foster home. The other was in the water too long. She was maybe two, maybe three years old. Hard to tell."

The memory of the tiny body at the morgue reached out and pierced Mei's heart all over again. Tears sprang to her eyes. She looked to the door. Another mother was out there somewhere looking for her baby girl; only she'd never find her alive.

Agent Lennox's brows furrowed. Either he was used to working with bitchy women, or she hadn't fazed him at all. At any rate, he had the upper hand and she was making a fool of herself. She glanced at the door again. *I have to get out of here.*

"I'm sorry, but are you waiting for someone?" he asked. "You keep watching the door like—"

"No." She all but growled. "Get on with it. What information do you have?"

He ran his tongue deliberately over his bottom lip, like he didn't know if he wanted to continue the conversation. God knew she didn't.

"As I mentioned earlier, a couple of the 4th Street Tigers had this little gal in their possession." He nodded toward Chai. "Thanks to what you've just told us, it seems whoever's behind it is working a pretty tight area in Anacostia. We'll start canvassing and asking questions. I'll tag a few confidential informants. Maybe they've heard something."

"Child trafficking could be involved," she blurted out the only lead she had.

He nodded, a puzzled expression shadowing his face. "Could be. That would explain a lot. Do you have the clothes from the other girls? We might be able to pull evidence from them, and what was the transient's name? I'd like to talk with him, see if he remembers anything."

Mei shivered. He'd reached the extent of her very limited knowledge. Even Claire was watching now. The floor had turned to shifting sand along with her composure. She was going down.

"The answer to both of your questions is no and no," she snapped, to disguise her rising panic. "I have no idea which transient found her. How would I know?"

"Did you ask?"

Her heart pitched at his probing question. *God, yes! I've asked everybody, but no one knows where she is. No one will help. Will you? I doubt it. You're like all the rest.*

"Of course I asked." She tapped her toe against the polished linoleum floor hoping rudeness might set him back in his place. Those brown eyes of his weren't honing in on her anymore. He looked annoyed. Certainly not cowed like she wanted.

"Sounds like we might be able to help each other, Agent Xing." Agent Lennox turned to his friend even though he'd spoken to her. "What do you think, David? I know the boss wanted us to locate Chai's family, but it seems there's a lot more going on. Want to work with Immigration and Customs Enforcement? Maybe we can help more than just your little friend."

What? Mei's breath caught. She shot a sideways glance to Agent Tao. Was it even possible these guys would help?

His eyes rebuked her before he spoke a single word. "Just so you know, Agent Xing. This *one* has a name. Chai Yenn is a lost and frightened little girl. Right now, she doesn't know who to trust. She isn't just *the girl*."

Her hand flew to the back of her neck where muscles wound too tight for too long ached all the way to the soles of her feet. His reprimand was well deserved, but she couldn't let him see her embarrassment. She'd never meant to imply she didn't care. Everything out of her mouth had come out wrong since she'd opened Chai's door. *Why did I think I could do this?*

"Can you tell me the names of the others? Do you know?" Agent Tao continued with the same gentle chastisement.

"The five-year-old is Zhen Ting. The other is a Jane Doe." Mei stifled her tears. *And LiLi is six and it's cold outside. It's going to snow, but I don't know where she is. And she needs her coat!*

"How sad." He stroked the blanket over the tiny child in his arms.

That tender movement stabbed Mei. The hole in her heart roared with all she had lost. Little Chai Yenn was safe and warm. Everything in the room reminded her that her daughter was not. Chai's tiny hand slumped free of the blanket. She'd fallen asleep in the warmth of this kind man's arms, and Mei could not bear to be in the same room one more second.

"The name Zhen means 'precious treasure' in the language of my ancestors," Agent Tao said quietly.

Mei bit her lip. She was versed in the language of her ancestors, too. *Li* meant pretty. That's why she had chosen it twice. LiLi–for the most beautiful, most perfect daughter in the world. *And I miss her.*

"What's her name mean?" Agent Lennox nodded at Chai.

Agent Tao hesitated, his eyes full of bleak emotion. He cupped the girl's limp hand in his, his thumb softly massaging the center of her palm. "Tea."

The empty word met silence, a pebble dropped into a deep dark well with no bottom. Enlightenment darkened Agent Lennox's already dark eyes, and Mei wanted to shake him. She'd been researching the problem of excess baby girls in far off China since she'd heard the possibility of the awful child trafficking ring. Yes, Agent Lennox. Yes! There were no loving parents to bless this child with a sweet, meaningful name. She's one of those unexpected pregnancies, one of those statistics the Chinese government uses to enforce their success in a program so diabolical it forces parents to choose how to kill their daughters. Let them starve? Drop them at an orphanage and never look back? Drown them in the rice paddies? Smother them and never tell a soul your wife was ever pregnant?

This beautiful baby girl's name was most likely assigned in the depths of some Chinese orphanage where it didn't matter what she was called. She could've just as easily been named after a chair. Or worse.

Mei wanted to scream, *'Do you get it now, Agent Lennox? Life isn't easy for the rest of us!'* Instead, she stared at the floor, tired of fighting the world. She'd gained no leverage today. None. If anything, she'd lost ground along with her composure. There was only one choice. Searching alone these past four weeks for LiLi had taught her well. Attack. Always attack.

"I don't have time for this," she snapped. "You're right. They all have names. They're all lost children, but it's a cold hard world. There are a lot more than three kids on the streets.

I've been working these cases for years, and let me tell you, there are hundreds. Do you hear me? Hundreds. I don't have time to get cozy with every missing kid."

Claire stiffened. Mei had crossed a line and she knew it, but Agent Tao turned to Agent Lennox as if she hadn't spoken at all. "You've given me another idea. I'll check the morgue when we're done here, and yes, I see no reason we couldn't work with Immigration and Customs Enforcement. I'm sure Alex will agree. You know how he is. Maybe Mother can coordinate with the FBI on the evidence as well. The more people we have working on behalf of these children, the better."

"We'll need to visit the other five-year-old," Agent Lennox said. "Who knows? Maybe she can tell us something. What's her name? Zhen Ting?"

Agent Tao nodded approvingly. "I'll visit her."

"I was hoping you would," Agent Lennox muttered. "Looks like you've got a knack with the ladies."

For the first time since the nightmare began, hope surfaced in Mei. These guys actually sounded like they cared, like they were going to do something to help. Maybe they could help LiLi, too? She turned to really look at Agent Lennox, but indifference had replaced the earlier gentleness in his eyes. Now his boot tapped the floor. He had some place else to be. Mei didn't blame him. She didn't want to be around herself, either.

"You are welcome to visit our office." Agent Tao offered one of his business cards. The kindness in his eyes still glimmered, but it was the last straw. Mei could endure no more of the mess she'd made. She headed for the door.

"Agent Xing," he called after her. "How do we contact you?"

He sounded hopeful, but the opportunity was gone. Without answering, she flung the door open and fled, tears stinging her eyes. She'd blown her cover and ruined everything. Intimidating Kathleen had been easy, but she'd only angered these guys.

Selecting the ground floor button at the elevator pad, she clutched her upper arms, rubbing them for warmth she hadn't known in weeks. When had she become so cold? So heartless? *What's happening to me? I do care about Chai and Zhen. I do.*

She scrubbed her arms harder. It didn't help. The cold went clean, clear through. At the sound of voices, she turned. Agent Lennox and Agent Tao had just entered the hall. They stood talking to Claire at the open door.

Mei gulped. In a second, they'd see her. Ducking into the nearest room, she waited for them to pass. They'd never know what a coward she was. The sound of their voices grew closer, Agent Lennox's laced with sarcasm.

"Young lady? You're being mighty generous with that title, aren't you? That chick's got a heart of stone. I've never seen an Immigration Agent act like such a—"

"Do you know what Mei Xing means in Chinese, Zack?" Agent Tao interrupted quietly.

"Heck, I don't know." Agent Lennox stabbed a button on the elevator pad. "Cruella de Vil? Hagatha? Maybe the Wicked Witch from the West?"

Mei squeezed her eyes tight, but the tears came anyway. Yes. She'd become a witch all right. Four weeks of living hell had changed her. She peeked out the door, hoping Agent Tao wouldn't condemn her, too.

"It means 'beautiful star'." He stood waiting at the elevator, shaking his head at Agent Lennox in gentle reproach. "Someone loved her enough to give her a very special name when she was born. I don't believe she's always been the person we saw today."

Mei stifled a sob at his kindness. *My mother gave me my name. I miss my mom. My dad. My baby.*

"Whatever," Agent Lennox grumbled. "It's not like we'll be seeing her again. She couldn't get away fast enough."

How could I stay? I lied to you. She struggled, all of her common sense screaming at her to confess, to run into the hall and tell these guys what was really going on. That she needed their help. That she needed somebody. She didn't make a move.

"I think you may yet be surprised," Agent Tao said as they entered the elevator.

The doors swooshed closed. Mei sank against the wall in the empty room and stifled her tears.

SEVEN

"You know what that little gal needs?"

Mei stopped short when the elevator door opened at ground level. Agent Lennox's question seemed directed at her. Or about her. She'd planned to run straight out the front doors, but now? Was he waiting for her? Her breath hitched at the very real possibility she'd have to face him again so soon. Girding her loins, she leaned forward through the elevator doors, just enough to catch sight of the two men at the coffee kiosk.

Her heart started beating again. He and Agent Tao had stopped for coffee. That's all. They weren't waiting to ambush her, but what was it about broad shoulders beneath black leather that grabbed her attention? Other than the preferred view allowed for a quick getaway? She had to admit, Agent Lennox was built, a veritable V-shape that made Agent Tao look ordinary in comparison.

She angled away from them, still having to pass behind them on her way out.

"A big old teddy bear," Agent Lennox answered himself as he tossed a handful of creamer cups into the trash bin beside the kiosk counter. He still hadn't seen her, but she could hear him. "I'm coming back with some toys. That poor baby doesn't even have her own blanket. She needs one."

"What she needs is a mother and a father." Agent Tao stirred his coffee, his back to Mei.

Her ears perked up at the unexpected conversation. These guys cared. Her feet faltered on her fast track to cowardice.

Tell them.

No, she argued with herself, picking up the pace. Talk is cheap. He won't buy Chai Yenn a single thing. You'll see. He's like all the rest. They promise a girl everything right before they dump her and run away. Men don't care.

He might.

She shook the notion out of her head and hurried out the door and across the street to her car. Kindness among men was rare. That much she knew from experience. Her one supreme rule was her safest course of action. *I. Don't. Need. Men.*

Sliding into her seat, she fastened her seat belt and waited. Following them might be smarter than running away. She might salvage something from her disastrous encounter, at least find out where they worked.

They strolled out of the hospital with paper coffee cups in hand and crossed the street to their car. She sunk lower behind her dash when Agent Lennox pointed his remote at–a black Porsche? That's their company car? Unbelievable. No way was he going to follow through and get anything for Chai. The man was all talk.

They didn't see her when they pulled away from the curb with her following a couple car lengths behind. Traffic was thick which helped her remain hidden, but she nearly lost them on the George Washington Highway. At last, the Porsche pulled curbside in front of a five story, modern-looking building in Alexandria.

Agent Tao climbed out. He stood talking through the open passenger window before a gust of cold wind blew up the sidewalk, scattering leaves and dust in its wake. With a pat on the door and another word to Agent Lennox, he turned and walked into the building.

The way he'd held poor little Chai Yenn told Mei something about him. He must be married and have kids of his own. He looked like the dependable type, and he was kind in the way he'd put Mei in her place, asking about those other little girls the way he had. He cared.

The poor baby in the morgue came back to haunt her. Even good news for Mei was awful for someone else. She chewed her bottom lip. *I can't afford to be soft. Not now.*

The blinker on the Porsche flashed while Agent Lennox waited to pull into traffic.

She glanced inside the building where Agent Tao stood at waiting at an elevator door. These guys must have some pretty good resources if they assumed they could waltz into the ME's office and ask to see the report on a dead child. Confidential informants also meant they had an established network on both sides of the law. Her stomach growled, reminding Mei of her limited budget, resources, and nerves.

Her heart pounded as she contemplated the questions of the day. Should she waltz into an unknown office and act like she knew where she was going when she didn't have a clue? Or should she follow the sports car and see where Agent Lennox went? He might go shopping for a teddy bear. *Yeah, right.*

When Agent Lennox pulled into traffic, she shot one last glance at Agent Tao, steeled her resolve, and followed the Porsche. Keeping a low profile in busy traffic was easy.

Shadowing a showy vehicle easier still. There was no way he could see she was four cars behind him, not with the tiny windows in his vehicle. A dose of humility slapped her full in the face when he pulled his fast little hotrod into a strip mall with a national toy distributor as the main anchor store. She pulled her car into a parking stall, slunk low in her seat, and watched. It took him fifteen minutes, but when he came out, he had a big white teddy bear and a bag in his arms.

He looked happy. She felt sick.

I was wrong. What's happening to me? Why am I so hateful? He didn't steal LiLi. He cares about Chai. Why can't I cut him any slack?

The feeling got worse when he pulled into a seedy part of Anacostia. She hesitated to follow. These were hard streets, places where a person could get killed in broad daylight. A delivery van pulled in front of her, blocking her view.

"I'm not losing this guy," she muttered as she made her decision and swung. Big mistake. He'd parked alongside the curb barely ahead of the delivery van. There he was, right in front of her, flirting with some sleazy-looking woman from his open window.

Mei drove past and hoped he hadn't seen. She pulled a U-turn down the block, intending to park on the opposite side of the street to catch the jerk in the act. No such luck. All parking stalls were taken. She headed in the opposite direction, scrunched low in her seat again. She should've known.

Buying a toy for a kid was easy, but this was the real Agent Lennox, too busy chatting up a hooker to notice anyone else. At least that's what the woman hanging on his passenger window looked like. Her painted on, skintight mini-skirt, itty-bitty turquoise top, and six-inch heels cinched the deal. It didn't take her long to climb inside and shut the door.

Flustered, Mei spotted a place to pull over and park. It was a driveway, so she couldn't stay long, but it allowed a few minutes to watch from her side mirror. That woman was a confidential informant? Yeah, right. He might fool Agent Tao with that line, but Mei knew better. Agent Lennox was only after one thing. *The jerk.*

Something clenched inside her nervous stomach as she watched the rear of the fast car. She pushed it aside, but it nagged like a little green monster, sticking its long pointed green fingernail at her. *What are those two doing in there?*

She reached for her binoculars.

Is he kissing that tramp? It sure looks like it.

Mei adjusted the focus on her binoculars, and—

"Hey, lady!" An angry man in gray coveralls smacked the hood of her car once with his open palm. "You're blocking my business. Customers can't get past ya. Move it!"

"Sorry. I'm moving." Dropping the binoculars to her lap, Mei replied even though the man couldn't hear her. She was so rattled she forgot to look for oncoming traffic. Horns blared. Brakes screeched. She kept going, hoping for one last glimpse of the black car in her rearview mirror as she pulled away.

The jerk was gone.

"I was kinda hoping you already saw something you liked," sweet Mabel Magee drawled in that cute, sexy way she had.

"I might take you up on your offer one of these days," Zack rumbled through a convincing lie. Hooking up with a lady of the street was never going to happen. Still, Mabel was always offering, always helpful, and judging by the way she batted those green contact lens-colored eyeballs, forever hopeful.

"I do like your ride, baby." She trailed a bright turquoise fingernail across the leather seat. Yeah. Most girls liked his car, especially girls in her profession. It was nearly as fast, hot, and pricey as they thought they were. "Black is my favorite color, you know."

He allowed a smirk. Usually, he tagged his CIs on the sidewalk in case he couldn't get them out of said *favorite color ride* once they got in. Zack was no dummy. He was familiar with the lingo of babes on the street, where tricks were cheap and talk was cheaper. The line of hers was only true unless the gentleman she was working happened to drive something red, yellow, or green. The only reason she was sitting inside now was the chilly November weather blowing up her skirt outside.

"You'll let me know if you hear anything, won't you?"

"Oh, absolutely." She had the fullest lips he'd ever seen. How do women do that, make their lips swell like they've used a vacuum nozzle or something on them? Mabel's seemed more pronounced than most. Or maybe it was her odd choice of dark tan lipstick outlined with red. What was she going for, a chocolate cherry mouth?

"Here's a little something for your trouble." He stifled his opinion and offered a couple folded twenties, catnip to the prowling feline. She leaned toward him, her full cleavage on display and begging to be ogled.

"Why don't you stick those bills where no one else can find 'em, sugar?" She licked those full lips again, letting her tongue move extra slow like they weren't already glossed and dripping. Her chest jiggled beneath the tight knit, revealing the embossed impression of two distinct nipples and the lacy view of purple lingerie that wasn't concealing as much as revealing. As cold as it was, she should have been wearing a coat, but Zack knew why she didn't. Mabel used her feminine persuasion in all the best ways. The more that showed–well, the more that showed.

Of course he looked. He wasn't dead. Besides, guys called 'em headlights. Hers were on high beam. How could he miss them? Zack leaned in nearly close enough to touch the merchandise and paused right there. Flirting was one thing. She was another. "You keep talking like that and—"

The oriental gong alert sounded on his cell phone.

"Hey, David, what's up?" he answered hoarsely, the bills between his two fingers, and Mabel still offering a show. He cast one last hungry look down the valley between her breasts and pantomimed a kiss.

She took the money and slowly extricated her long legs from his car, blowing a return kiss over her shoulder.

"I'm at the county morgue. Can you meet me?" Leave it to David to spoil a semi-good time.

"Sure." Zack's gaze lowered to the round backside still planted in the passenger bucket seat. She did fill it extremely well and the hem of her skirt was as high as her cleavage was low. Some kind of tattooed artwork kept peeking out between the top of her skirt and the bottom of her sweater, right above some kind of lacy strap that might have been a thong. The view offered too much enticement. Tattoo or underwear? How did a man not look?

"You need to get down here. I've found something."

"On my way." The tremor of concern in David's voice caught Zack's attention even as he kept an eyeball on the shell game going on with Mabel's derriere. The girl knew how to tease. "What'd you find?" he asked, his attention still wandering.

"You've got see this to believe it. Please hurry."

"Be right there," he said, but he thought, *'And you've got to see this'.*

"Before you take off and leave me." Mabel waited, half-in and half-out of his car like the working girl she was — working it. "There is an old guy now I think about it. He hangs out around the rescue mission. Might be the one you're looking for. Name's Marty."

"He been talking about a little girl, has he?" Zack lifted his gaze to Mabel's face.

"Actually, he's always talking about a little girl. I thought it was his daughter, but I could be wrong. He might be worth checking into."

"Thanks, Mabel."

"Why don't you come back later and thank me in person, Zack baby?" She batted those luxurious lashes. "I'd give you a discount. Might put a smile on your handsome face."

"If you can find out something about those little Chinese girls, I just might." He revved the engine, listening to it purr for a few seconds before he engaged the clutch.

She pouted. "And if I don't? Will I ever see you again?"

Zack smiled. "You never know."

A blustery wind tossed her bright red hair as she got out of the car, looking forlorn. He pulled away from the curb, glancing in his rearview mirror. She got over her loneliness the minute another car pulled to the curb.

Too soon, he was looking down at a stainless steel tray with the remains of a very small body tagged, 'Jane Doe'. "Hell. She's just a baby."

"Two years old," David explained.

"Is anyone looking for her?"

"Not that the police are aware of. They're running a nationwide search."

Zack turned his face from David to gather his composure. The operation was becoming tougher than he'd expected. The morgue always gave him the creeps, but standing over a deceased child as young as the little girl in the tray created another feeling entirely. He wasn't so much disgusted as he was angry. How could anyone hurt an innocent baby? What made some people so evil? So twisted and so damned cruel? He didn't understand. Half of him wanted to punch something, the other half to throw up.

"I've been reading the ME's report," David continued quietly. "It listed an identifying mark on her arm, so I asked to see the body."

Zack peered through the magnifying glass, following the tip of David's ballpoint pen to what looked like a black splotch on the arm of the remains.

"What am I looking at?" As much as he respected his senior agent, David's method of always making a man come up with his own conclusions was aggravating, especially at times like this.

"What does it look like to you?" David persisted.

"I don't know." *Just spit it out. I need to get out of here.*

The longer Zack looked, the edgier he got. Fish had nibbled these tiny hands. The fingernails were gone. No toes remained on her feet. He couldn't even begin to look at her face. The cold smell of death in the morgue had thoroughly squashed any good feeling left from his visit with Chai. She could have ended up on another tray in the same morgue.

Tears blurred his vision. He gritted his teeth and willed them away.

Focus, Lennox. You're a Marine. You've seen worse.

"Look again." David pulled the magnifying glass closer. "Tell me what you think you see."

Damn it, David. Spit it out. Tell me what I'm looking at, so I can get—

Zack looked closer. "What the hell?"

"You see it now, don't you?"

"On a child this small? Why? How?" Zack looked again, disbelieving his eyes. This baby had been marked all right with what looked like a black dragon tattoo.

"Chai is very lucky you found her when you did." David nodded sadly.

"Does the ME have a COD?"

"Not exactly. This little one has been in the water too long. Agent Xing was right. There's no way to know cause of death for sure," David said. "I'm headed back to the hospital and then to the foster family who has Zhen Ting. I want to know if she and Chai have been marked, too. What about you?"

"I think I've tracked the gentleman down who pulled Zhen Ting out of the garbage. He hangs out at the men's rescue mission over in Anacostia. Thought I'd buy him dinner and see what he can tell me. Madam Mim didn't seem to think that was important, but I do. Who knows?"

David rolled his eyes at Zack's description of Agent Xing. "I'm surprised you know who Mad Madam Mim is."

"I've got a kid sister," Zack explained. "She's fifteen years younger. I watched a lot of Disney before I joined the Corps. Xing and Mim have a lot in common, only I think Mim might be nicer."

"We have another problem." David lowered his voice as the ME covered the small corpse and removed the tray. "Alex is on his way back from Seattle."

"Already?" Zack groaned. "Wasn't he supposed to be gone all week?"

"Apparently ATF Director Carducci has some clout in Congress after all," David said. "The boss has been targeted for a Senate investigation. He's scheduled to appear before a committee in the Russell Senate Building later this week."

"Damn." Zack didn't know what else to say. Alex was probably cursing him at this very minute. "He only left yesterday. When's he due in?"

"Seven-thirty tonight."

"Damn," Zack repeated. Could things get any worse?

"Be careful, Zack," David warned. "I have a very bad feeling."

EIGHT

"Who wants to know?"

Marty was smelly, whiskered, tipsy, and suspicious. It seemed his entire face squinted, his lips pursed together like he was thinking real hard when Zack caught up with him. "Do I know you, young fella?"

"No, sir. You don't. Name's Zack Lennox." When the man didn't accept his handshake, Zack sat on the fold-up cot with him. "I was hoping I could buy you dinner in exchange for your story of how you found the little girl the other night."

"What little girl?" His shaggy brows crinkled in suspicion. "Do I know you?" he asked again. "You look kinda familiar."

Zack sighed. Maybe this was a waste of time. Hagatha might be right. "The little Chinese girl you found in the dumpster behind the IGA store. Remember her?"

Another swipe over his face, and Marty blinked a few times. "Oh. Her. I get kinda confused. I used to have my own little girl, ya know. Leastways, I think I did. Sometimes, I ain't too sure 'bout nuthin' no more."

"Come on." Zack offered a hand up. "A good hot meal will help you remember. What do you say?"

Marty pulled his hand away like Zack had just bit it. "I ain't going nowhere. They'll give my bed to someone else. Where will I sleep then?"

"Nah." Zack pulled Marty to his feet. "I'll put in a good word for you. They'll hold it."

"You sure?" He looked across the huge room where a hundred or so cots were set up in rows for another night of shelter from the cold. "Boy, I sure hope you're right. It's awful cold to be sleeping on a park bench. A fella could get his fingers froze off, if'n he don't wake up dead."

"Don't worry." Zack helped Marty into the threadbare green and black plaid jacket laying on his cot. "They'll hold it or they'll have to answer to me."

"Eh, eh, eh." Marty's eyes twinkled. "You must be darned important if you think they's going to listen to you."

They were at the entrance door where a swarthy man stood checking the transients and less fortunate as they came in for a night of warm food and sleep.

"You'll hold my friend's bed until he gets back, won't you?" With those words, Zack pressed a couple bills into the man's hand. He nodded once, and Zack led Marty out into the frosty November night. An early winter storm was blowing in off the Atlantic, kicking the last of the autumn leaves out of the gutter. Marty was right. A man could freeze out here.

"Br-r-r." Marty pulled his jacket tighter. "Gonna be a cold one. Folks are gonna die tonight if'n they ain't careful."

Together they walked across the street to the Fishmonger's Diner where Zack knew he could get a decent meal and hopefully, a private conversation. It was one of Jake's hangouts, a train car-sized Mom and Pop joint right next to Fat Larry's Tavern.

"Howdy, Stan." Marty flashed a high-five to the man exiting the diner.

Stan grumbled and kept on going, flashing nothing back but a whiskered sneer.

Zack steered Marty to the corner table farthest from the door. Setting diagonal to the corner, it avoided the draft while offering the best view of everyone eating, serving, coming and going. He took the corner chair and positioned Marty in the chair to his left, not that the old guy was concerned with covering his back. Zack lived by the simple rule of every sniper. Watch everyone.

The waitress was quick with their glasses of water, and quicker when Zack ordered a round of beers, two large bowls of Fishmonger's specialty, their homemade oyster chowder, and triple-decker sandwiches stacked high with cheese and turkey.

"Will that be all?" she asked politely after she'd delivered the spread.

"How about the biggest slice of pumpkin pie in the house?" Zack clapped a hand on Marty's shoulder. "My friend's a little hungry."

"Coming right up, Hon."

Marty chuckled, rubbing a quick hand over his thinning hair. "You keep being so nice ta me, and folks are gonna think you're my kid or something."

"You got kids?" Zack doffed his leather jacket, letting it slump to the back of his chair.

The old man nodded, working his jaw like he needed to keep his dentures in place. "Yeah. Two. Leastways, I think I only had the two." He scratched the end of his red chapped nose. "'Course, I been on the road awhile now. Ain't seen 'em much lately."

"Well, dig in." Zack sliced his sandwich in half, keeping an eye on Marty. The old man was hungry, licking his lips when he already had a mouthful. After the first bowl of chowder was nearly gone, Zack signaled the waitress for another.

It was at the end of Marty's first sandwich that he turned with his mouth half-full. "I wasn't always like this, ya know."

Zack didn't respond. Tonight was Marty's night to fill his stomach and talk.

"No, sir," he rambled as he tore off another chunk of bread and turkey with his teeth. "I was gonna be an engineer, was gonna be rich and work for NASA."

Empathy swelled Zack's heart. He knew this kind of man well. Marty was one of so many lost souls along the waterfront. His eyes might be rheumy from too many years on the bottle, but his heart was solid gold. Maybe around sixty or sixty-five, gray-haired and missing a couple teeth, he was no more than a scarecrow in a two-bit pair of worn out jeans that someone at the local rescue mission had probably given him. His thin jacket was worthless in the bitter North Virginia weather. Winter wouldn't be any kinder.

"That little gal weren't like you and me," he muttered between spoonfuls of chowder and sandwich. "She had real pretty eyes, kinda slanted like them boat-people back in the seventies. She only peeked 'em open once, but they was real purdy brown." Another couple spoonfuls and he continued, "And she had short black hair. Her lips were kinda blue, ya know, cuz she was so cold. When I first seen her, I just figured she was a doll someone throwed away. She was dirty and she weren't moving at all."

The baby at the morgue flashed into Zack's mind, another cold little body. At least he'd found Chai Yenn in time. Somehow, it didn't ease the fact that the other child had suffered. But why were they all Chinese girls? The Wicked Witch of the West might be right. The operation smelled more and more like a child trafficking ring at work.

"'Course, then she kinda cried." Marty stared across the counter, his mind a million miles away. "She reminded me of...another little girl who...I mighta known...." A drip of cream-colored soup spilled over his bottom lip. The moment stretched.

At last Marty shook his head. "There's just something about a little girl crying that gets to me right here, ya know?" He pumped a weathered fist against his chest, his voice tight and hoarse. "That little baby doll needed me, and I was dang glad I was there. There she was with coffee grounds smeared all over her, and what was I gonna do, huh?"

Defiance glistened in the old man's eyes, as if he needed to justify who he was and what he'd done. Zack nodded, his heart full of compassion. Yeah. Marty had seen better days a long, long time ago. It was hard not to like the old guy. He could've walked away that night, and Zhen Ting would've never been found, but he didn't. That made him a hero. A drunk maybe, but in Zack's book a hero just the same.

"So what happened next?" Zack prodded gently.

Marty lifted the bowl to his mouth and slurped the last of the soup down before wiping his lips with the back of his hand. "Well, umm, let me think."

Zack waved the waitress over for another bowl. "You're still hungry, aren't you, Marty?"

The old fellow's eyes lit up. He dunked half of his sandwich in the next bowl of chowder and ate most of it before he continued his tale. "Well, ya see, I had a hold of her real careful like, cuz I weren't sure if she was hurt, you know what I mean? I grabs up a dirty blanket and I wraps it around her, and I was standing there wondering what the heck was I gonna do next. I mean, what's folks gonna say when they sees me with a tiny little thing like her? I'm just an old drunk–a nobody. Ain't no one gonna ever believe a guy like me."

Zack nodded encouragingly, but that seemed to pique Marty's indignation.

"Well, I'll tell ya what folks are gonna do. Them punks at the IGA don't like guys like me rummaging around the dumpsters. They likes to use us for slingshot practice when they catches us. Heck." Marty peeled his coat and shirtsleeve down, exposing two round black welts on his upper arm. "Look it here, will ya? One of them boys shot me. I don't figure it was a slingshot that time. Sounded more like some kinda gun, it did. They coulda kilt me. It coulda been me laying in that stinking dumpster."

Zack listened and waited. Marty needed to eat. He'd get to the rest of his story as soon as he remembered.

"So I says to myself, I says, Marty, ya gots to do what's right this time. Ya can't worry about yerself when there's a little girl what needs your help." He nodded in self-satisfaction. "Yep. That's what I said. I was standing there, and it was getting colder and colder, but I knew what I had to do. Yessirree. So I clumb outta the dumpster, holding the baby real careful over my shoulder so's I wouldn't bump her poor little noggin, and I walks right in through the front door of the IGA store, and you know what I said?"

Zack shook his head slightly. Marty had a determined glint in his eye.

"Well, let me tell you what I said." He tore off another mouthful of sandwich. "I walks up to the first checkstand and I says real loud, 'I needs help, and I needs it right now'." He thumped his fist to the table. "I did. Yes, I did. That's exactly what I said, and I'll tell you what. You coulda heard a pin drop in the place. Everyone was lookin' at me like I was crazy, only then my poor little baby doll starts moving and fussing, and everyone runs up to see what I found."

"And they helped you?"

Marty nodded. "You better believe they did. The next thing I know, the police are there and an ambulance too, and them doctor guys are taking real good care of my baby, and they got warm blankets, and—" His eyes misted. "And the poor little gal didn't even cry one peep when they stuck that needle thing in her arm."

A tear slipped over his whiskered face and fell onto his empty plate. "My poor baby girl," he sobbed, wiping his face. "She was too sick to cry even when them nice guys was hurting her."

"It's okay." Zack said. "You saved her life."

"Yeah." Marty ran a gnarled hand over his eyes before he stuffed the last of his sandwich into his mouth and started on his pumpkin pie. "That's what everyone was saying. The police came, and they was asking me where I found her, and they gave me a drive to the station, and they was all real nice to me that night. One of them officers even gave me his jacket, you know. Them really warm winter jackets with fur collars?"

"That's the least they could do." Zack noticed the old guy wasn't wearing the warm jacket anymore. The thin waffle weave plaid covering his shirt was definitely not police issue.

"The next night I went back to the store. You know what them mean boys did?" Marty wrangled one of his feet up far enough so Zack could see it. "They all pitched in and they bought me these here boots. Look it. Ain't they nice?"

"Yes, sir. They look real warm."

"They is. They really is. And they gave me a big bag of warm socks and something called protein bars. And they said I was their hero. I ain't never been called a hero before."

"Is there anything else you can think of? Did you understand anything the little girl said?" Zack asked patiently. He'd flagged the waitress for another slice of pie.

"Nah, that's all there was to it, know what I mean?" Marty stared off in a daze. "She was almost dead, poor little thing. Poor baby."

"You're a real good man. You did a great thing saving her like you did."

"I did, huh?"

Zack peered into the old man's humble eyes. "She's in a good foster home right now. Her name is Zhen Ting. It means 'precious treasure'. You found a precious treasure in the trash that night."

"Well, I'll be darned. Precious treasure, huh? Zhen Ting, did you say? That's a real pretty name for a pretty little tyke." Marty was lost again as he stared past the fork in his hand. "I really helped this one. Didn't I?"

"You sure did." Zack thumped his back gently. The old man didn't get much encouragement on the streets. A kind touch from a friend meant a lot.

"I remember something else, now you mention it. She had something in her little mitt." He dug down deep into his dirty shirt pocket and handed a small item to Zack.

Zack held it up to the light. It was an ordinary, black, four-holed button. "She had this in her hand when you pulled her out of the trash?" He turned the button over before he stuck it safe inside his own shirt pocket.

"Yeah. She looked like a little prizefighter with her hand all clenched up in a fist, kinda like she was ready ta punch me in the nose when I found her. Poor little squirt. Darn near forgot about it. Guess I shoulda gave it to the cops, I reckon, huh?" Marty looked expectantly into Zack's face. The soup was gone, along with the sandwiches and pie.

"You ready to get back to the shelter, my friend?" Zack asked.

"Not yet." Marty stared at Zack, waiting and hopeful. "I might meet up with some guys. They might need some help. You know how it is."

Marty sounded a lot like Jake, always working an angle if it meant there was the smallest possibility of a drink in his immediate future.

"Like I said, you're a good man. You ever need anything, and I mean anything, you give me a call, okay?" With that, Zack tucked a couple of bills into the old man's shirt pocket along with his business card. "Where's that nice warm coat the police gave you?"

"Ahh." Marty's eyes roamed around the diner while he patted his pocket. "I'm thinking it's around here somewhere. You know how it goes in my line of work."

Marty's line of work, as he put it, was a hard way to live. Who knew where the coat was by now? Hopefully, he'd spent at least one warm night in it. "You hang onto my card, and call me, okay?"

Marty nodded. "You bet I will."

Zack motioned for the waitress one last time, sliding a couple large bills across the counter to her. "Will you get my friend here another piece of pumpkin pie, ma'am? I'd be much obliged."

"Sure, mister. Pumpkin pie, coming right up." She beamed at the generous tip.

"Well, shucks now." Marty smiled a crooked grin, for the moment just a mischievous old man, up to no good and proud of it. "Ya didn't have to do all this."

Zack stood to leave. "It was my privilege, Marty. You're my friend and friends take care of each other. I'll be waiting to hear from you. You be sure and call."

Marty was already licking his lower lip like a kid at the Thanksgiving table as he pulled the fresh plate of pie toward him. Zack left him with a fork full of pumpkin and whipped cream in his mouth and a gleam of contentment in his eye. As the diner door clanged shut, he glanced back at the man who'd saved little Zhen Ting's life. Marty would be chasing after a bottle before the day was done, but for one night and to one little girl, he would always be a hero.

Zack shivered as he hit the remote to unlock his pricey ride. The sleek black horses reminded him once again that he had it all, while right behind him sat a man who had nothing. Hopefully, Marty would notice the almost brand new leather bomber jacket now hanging on the back of his chair. It might be a little large for the old fart, but Zack hoped he'd at least get one night's warmth out of it. A hero deserved a helluva lot more.

NINE

Mei searched online for The TEAM, looking for a way inside. Surely it listed job openings and maybe an online job application, at least something to get her inside the fancy building in Alexandria long enough to steal an ID badge, or whatever they used. The well-designed homepage flashed onto her screen in brilliant red, white, and blue.

The TEAM
Covert Surveillance
Owner and CEO
Alexander B. Stewart
Ex-Marine Corps Scout Sniper

Symbols of every branch of the military lined the banner at the bottom of the screen. There was no 'about me' page, no links for further information, no tabs for FAQs, and no Facebook, Twitter, or other social network icons. Only two phone numbers, one east coast, the other on the west coast, graced the site. She groaned at what the lack of information undoubtedly meant. Alexander B. Stewart didn't need to advertise. His clients knew him. And he wasn't hiring.

Try as she might, she could not get past The TEAM's firewall either. Her hacking skills were weak at best, but one failed attempt after another made two things crystal clear. The business could afford an excellent computer programmer, and maybe it wasn't such a fly-by-night outfit after all. It had to be involved with counter-intelligence somehow. The design of their home page said as much. They were too good. Too secure.

"What am I going to do?" She pushed away from her kitchen table, angry at that Zack Lennox guy all over again. What did he have to worry about anyway, with his leather bomber jacket and Ray-Bans perched on top of his shaved head like some preppie college boy? He was another privileged kid whose parents probably paid his way; a guy who didn't have a clue when it came to what really mattered in life. *The jerk.*

But...he had rescued the third little girl. He'd risked his life to steal her away from those gangsters. As much as she wanted to dislike Agent Lennox, she couldn't. Not completely. Her feelings confused her. *Why do I hate him? I was so rude. Why couldn't I at least have been polite?*

The succinct information on the website tantalized. "You guys know something," Mei muttered to herself. "I know you do. You can get into the ME's office. You're rich. You're— men."

Hopelessness dragged its long black fingernails across her weary shoulder blades. Time was running out. She had to get into their office. It was just a matter of how.

Coffee brewing already? The familiar aroma energized as much as it concerned Zack. If Mr. Coffee was already on and brewing, that meant—

"You got anything yet?"

That meant Alex had worked all night after a long cross-country flight. Barely at his desk, Zack turned to face his over-the-top, flaming type-A, and very hyper boss. Not a good way to start what already promised to be a busy day.

"Morning. Went back to the hospital yesterday to see how she's doing, and—"

"How is she?"

"She might be released today if—"

"You found her parents yet?"

Zack shook his head. "Not yet, but—"

"Where's David?"

Zack sighed. There was no sense talking. Alex had too much caffeine in his system to shut up long enough to listen.

"Here, Boss." Thank goodness David had come in early. "Mind if we meet in the Sit Room?"

Alex didn't answer, just turned on his heel and marched straight to the Situation Room.

"Watch out," Zack muttered out the side of his mouth. "He's already wired."

David nodded in agreement. "I called his house. Kelsey said he hasn't been home yet."

"Figures."

His hard-charging boss could be a pain in the ass. How did his sweet wife put up with him? As quick as the conference door shut, Alex hit the floor running. As usual, he positioned himself across from them.

"Let's get something straight. My first concern is our little girl. She's our primary mission here. How is she?"

David took the lead, so Zack let him. Alex and he were the concept of yin and yang personified; one's calm balancing the other's lack of it. "Physically, she's okay. Her name is Chai Yenn. She's eating, and she's safe. The hospital released her late yesterday. She's at Child Services until they can place her with a foster family, which could be as early as today."

"But?" Alex leaned forward, his fingers drumming the tabletop.

"I know it's out of our control, Alex, it's just that—"

"She's not happy, huh?" Alex asked, his intensity more and more annoying. "You're right. It's out of our influence. What else?"

David took a measured breath and began again. "There have been two other Chinese girls found in the same area. One was pulled from a dumpster, the other drowned in the river."

"Where?"

"Near the Eleventh Street Bridge along the Anacostia Riverwalk Trail."

"Let me get this straight." Alex stilled. "Three, and they're all Chinese girls? How old?"

"We have two five- or six-year-olds in protective custody–Chai Yenn and Zhen Ting. The child in the county morgue was maybe two."

Zack straightened his back. He recognized the look. The caffeine buzz was gone. The predator in Alex had just shown up for work.

"Those are babies," he hissed.

"Yes," David agreed. "Another thing. I checked with the Medical Examiner's office. All of these girls have been marked with a tattoo."

"A black dragon tattoo," Zack added.

"Where?"

David pointed to the backside of his bicep. "I researched that specific design. The tattoo signifies a child trafficking ring in Mainland China. Have you ever heard of Lenny Huang?"

Alex clenched his jaw. "I've heard of him. He runs the Black Dragon Syndicate. You're sure the tattoo is his mark?"

"Yes, but that's not all." David slid a CD across the table to Alex. "In my internet searches for Mr. Huang and his syndicate, I came across an online video game called Black Dragon Conquest. The object of the game is to smuggle children from various Chinese ports and then sell them to international locations around the world, including Washington D.C. and New York City. The younger the child, the greater the risk, and the higher the player's score."

Zack shook his head in disbelief. David had been busy.

"I walked through the game as far as I could," he said. "In fact, I've spent most of the night on it. The challenges include imaginary beasts, law enforcement demons, mazes, caves, and natural disasters." David swallowed hard. "The worst challenge is called the Monsters of all Monsters. The *MOM*. She's depicted as a terrible beast with five heads that eats the children alive if they escape. It's a graphic, bloody game."

"The bastard's set up a child trafficking ring right here in D.C.," Alex muttered, his voice hard. "Right here in my neighborhood."

"I still don't know what the color-coding means, but I found green and red dragons, too. If we've got three children with the black dragon tattoos, there are a lot more little girls in trouble."

"What do you think the colors mean?" Zack asked.

"I honestly don't know," David admitted grimly. "They might designate the country these girls came from, or where they're going. It might mean rating or pricing. I'm just guessing."

"The game may not be connected to Lenny Huang at all," Alex said.

Zack's gut clenched. No. Alex didn't believe it either. The game was no coincidence, not since they'd found the girls at the same time. His gut told him true. Alex was right the first time. A syndicate boss from a world away had opened a despicable business on the east coast.

"I need to decipher the game," David said. "Perhaps there are clues I'm not seeing. Can you spare Mother or Ember?"

"You bet," Alex said quickly. "Todd can help, too. He's sharp with computers."

Zack turned to Alex. "How do you know Lenny Huang? I don't recall any ops involving him before."

"Interpol sent a report on him just yesterday," Alex said. "He's ruthless and extremely powerful. They've been watching him for years. What do you have, Zack?"

Zack cringed. It was hard for an over-achiever like him to have hit so many dead ends, especially when David had found so much. He pulled the puny evidence bag from his pocket. "Not much. The old guy who found Zhen Ting gave this to me. Not sure it's worth anything. He said she had it in her fist when he pulled her out of the dumpster. Could be a piece of trash for all I know."

Alex grimaced at the single, black button. "This is all? A button? Nothing from your CIs?"

"Not yet. None of my informants have heard a thing."

"Which only means this kind of business hasn't touched them yet," David said. "Most people wouldn't recognize human trafficking if they saw it."

Alex called over the intercom for Mother to join them. She joined them at the table with her cup of coffee, taking the chair at the head of the table at Alex's right.

"Morning, Boss. Whatcha need?"

He handed her the CD. "I want you and Ember to dig into this game. Find out everything you can, highest scoring users, who created this piece of crap, everything. Zack has something, too." Alex held out the evidence bag. "What can you do with this?"

She took it, her nose wrinkled like she could barely see the tiny button. "What is it? Oh. Sure. I'll take care of it. I know a guy. Get back to you as soon as I know where it's been. Umm, Boss?"

"What?"

The atmosphere in the room shifted. Zack swore he could feel Alex's hackles rise. Mother always walked a fine line with the boss. As good as she was, she seemed to push his buttons without even trying. She was by nature a collector of other people's personal information, a huge off-limits zone for him she never seemed to appreciate. Or respect.

She kept on going. "I've been in your office."

"So?"

"Well, so." She glanced at Zack and David for emotional support–or something. Zack leaned into his chair, offering nothing but observation to what might be an entertaining morning after all. "You have reports all over your desk. They're all from old operations. I coordinated them with you. What are you doing in there?"

Alex pushed away from the table, staring at his nosy techie. "What do you think I'm doing?" he asked icily.

"I don't know. At first, I kinda thought you were using those paper copies to prepare for the Senate investigation. You're all holed up in here with your door closed. Looks like you're studying for a bar exam. The place is a mess."

"Is everyone worried, or just you?"

"Well, that's what I'd be worrying about but, umm, am I worrying for nothing?" Her voice changed from smug to downright nosy. "Then whatcha doing in there, Boss? You been working all night again, haven't you?"

Zack pushed back from the table. *Here it comes. Watch out.*

"Do you recall our first black op into China a couple years ago?" Alex asked quietly.

"Sure do. You sent Murphy, Roy, and Mark. Roy got dysentery so bad he had to come home early. I never thought a black man could look so white."

"That's the one," Alex replied. "I need the name of the kid they ran into in Beijing. He wasn't part of the operation, but the discovery of Chai Yenn got me thinking, especially with the Interpol alert on Lenny Huang. Didn't that kid have something to do with an adoption agency in Mainland China?"

Mother stared for a few seconds. She paused, blinked a few times, and continued. "Tony Brown. His name was Tony Brown. He was a tall, skinny kid. Looked like he should've played for the NBA. Mark got a bunch of pictures of him."

Alex sighed. "I knew you'd come up with it."

"Oh yeah." Mother had her smug on now. "He went over there with his parents on some kind of a mission. Let me think. It was either UNICEF or Save the Children." She stirred her coffee. "No. Now that I think about it, he was there as an envoy for Charity Adoption Services. He and his parents went from orphanage to orphanage to set up arrangements between the United States and China so Americans could more easily adopt Chinese orphans. The only problem was they couldn't get enough little boys to make it work. Plus, they ran into a few diplomatic snags. You know how it is working with China."

Zack's mind instantly caught what Mother had not said. If they couldn't get enough boys, did that mean there were too many girls in China, the only country on earth known for its one child law, where parents were known to favor sons? His gut was talking to him again, pouring acid into the dilemma of all those unwanted baby girls. Was that how Chai Yenn fit into the picture? Was she part of some bizarre adoption scheme gone wrong? Was she one of those throwaway babies?

"Are you thinking Tony Brown and Lenny Huang are connected?" Zack asked.

"I don't know." Alex shifted in his seat to face Zack. "But Tony Brown was in the meeting yesterday. He works for Kevin Carducci."

"The ATF Director?" Zack hadn't seen that one coming. There was no such thing as coincidence. Stars only lined up when they were meant to. What was going on?

Alex turned back to Mother. "Find Mr. Brown's itinerary. I want to know who he talked to, their current location, and a good contact number for them. I don't want the people he said he talked to, though. He probably doctored the information he reported to the State Department when he got home. Whatever you do, do not contact Mr. Brown. Understood?"

"Got it, Boss. When do you need it?"

"As soon as you get back to your desk. Why? Are you too busy?"

Zack caught the sarcastic dig under Alex's question.

"Oh, no. Ember and I are updating the project manager system, that's all. We'll work your request first like we always do." She handed Alex a four-by-six picture. "But take a look at something else while I'm here."

"What am I looking at?" he asked, annoyed as he peered at the photo.

"Just my latest hacker," Mother replied smugly. "She's got her camera link up while she's trying to hack our system. Doesn't even know she's broadcasting."

"But we're still secure?"

"You bet. Would I let a hacker in?" She rolled her eyes. "Am I not the Mother around here? See, I've created a little program to sends me an alert whenever—"

"Just asking," Alex interrupted, placing the photo face down in front of him. "Thanks. That will be all."

She cringed. "I've got one more question."

"Of course you do." Alex turned to her. "What?"

Zack allowed a smile to tug at his lips. His boss was fast approaching the need for more caffeine. Now would be a good time for Mother to take the hint and leave.

"You've got a lot of boxes behind your office door."

"Yes. They need to go to the Senate committee today."

"All of them?" Her eyes widened in exaggerated surprise.

"That's the intel from the ATF Op. Get Todd Chandler to run them over to the Russell Building." Alex's tone ratcheted tighter with every busybody question.

"Why Todd? I mean, he's new here. Did you notice he's got a crush on Ember?"

Zack tried real hard not to smirk.

"I think I hired Todd to work," Alex snapped. "That okay with you?"

"Sure." Mother stood, not noticing his less than gentle reprimand to mind her business. "He's a cute kid. Ember likes him. Me too."

Zack bit his lip to keep from laughing out loud.

"I'll get the information you need." She sashayed out of the Sit Room like the queen bee of the hive. "You want anything else, you know where I'll be."

Alex glared at Zack.

It was going to be one of those days.

TEN

I can do this.

Mei snapped the bogus ID badge onto her belt for another long day of disappointment. Dressed in her usual attire for undercover work–navy blue skirt, white blouse, and black heels–she hoped she looked like the scary federal agent on the badge. If she could only stop shaking.

It was another cold day. She was colder. Her daughter needed her cute, pink winter coat, the one with the fur-lined hood. Mei clenched her knuckles to her mouth, willing the sob back into her chest. *Stop it. You have work to do. LiLi depends on you. Stop it, right now.*

Glancing one last time into the mirror, she hissed to her reflection, "You don't have time to be soft. Who will find her if you don't?"

The stark, cold face of an angry American Chinese woman stared back. She used to be pretty, but now her dark hair was pulled into a tight knot that brooked no soft tendrils or femininity. The day for pretty make-up and smiles was past. All Mei needed was to keep her head down and blend in.

Despite the bitter chill in the weather, she opted for no coat. Not until LiLi was home would she be warm again. Resolute steps took her to the elevator and out to her assigned parking stall. Everything weighed against her, even the frost on her windshield. While the engine warmed the inside of the car, she scraped the windows clean. Shivering in the arctic breeze, Mei shook the melting cold from her fingers and climbed back in. At least the heater worked.

Today, I will find her.

Shifting the car into reverse, she pressed the accelerator, slowly backing up. The driveway had been salted. Snow was in the forecast, but had yet to arrive. The steering wheel shuddered. What now? It didn't take long to find out the rear tire was flat. That solved one problem. There was no longer any reason to worry about fuel, at least not today.

Parking the car again, Mei grabbed her computer bag, squared her shoulders into the wind, and gritted her teeth.

Today, I will take the bus.

Zack's fingers tapped a steady beat on the table. Sitting around the Sit Room doing nothing but talking drove him crazy. The minute the op ended, he planned to ask for an assignment overseas. Exciting or not, he needed something a whole lot more physical to do than meeting with Alex or Mother

"Here's the contact information you asked for on Tony Brown."

Alex scanned what Mother handed him. "Put it up on the screen."

"Thought you'd never ask." She flashed the info to the overhead.

It showed the individuals Brown had contacted. She'd organized the info by orphanages visited, persons contacted, dates, times, and length of each conversation. All of the names were Chinese except one: Mr. Reginald Richards, attorney, Washington D.C.

"That's our man. David, you and Zack—"

Mother flashed another list overhead, interrupting Alex. The profile of Mr. Richards, an adoption lawyer who specialized in overseas adoptions, replaced the previous list. The room was silent as Alex, David, and Zack absorbed the attorney's list of clients and his fees. Mr. Richards catered exclusively to the rich and famous. There were a few well-known celebrity types on the list, as well as diplomats from all over the world. His adoption fees ranged into the millions and all the children he'd dealt with were between the ages of newborn to eight-year-olds. All girls. Hundreds of girls.

"See this?" Mother used the laser pointer to indicate the far right column titled *EXOTIC*. "These are bi-racial children with one Chinese parent. Apparently there's a market for girls who have different and unique looks."

"I want this dirt bag," Zack muttered under his breath. "All he's doing is selling babies."

"Do we know why Brown contacted Richards all the way from China?" David asked.

Mother shrugged. "Ember and I were talking about that. If the right people got their hands on the right baby girl, they could turn her into a model, maybe even a movie star. It's all about marketing and appearance. A blue or green-eyed Oriental woman would make a breathtaking model. She'd be a real money-maker for some of these cosmetic companies."

Alex growled and pushed away from the table. "Only if they were halfway decent people to begin with, and I doubt it. We're not tackling an operation this big without federal backup, the FBI for sure. Contact them, and Immigration and Customs. Let them run with it."

Zack glanced at David, and immediately wished he hadn't.

Alex noticed. "What's going on? You two have something else to say?"

"Ah, Boss, sorry," David stuttered. "I should have mentioned sooner. ICE is already involved. We ran into Agent Mei Xing when we checked on Chai Yenn yesterday. She's assigned to the case."

"Good. Work with her. Let me know what you find out. Anything else?"

"Not right now," David replied.

"One last thing." Alex stood. "I'm putting Todd Chandler full-time on the case with you. Put him to work. In the meantime, I'll contact Interpol and see what they know about Huang." With that final command given, he was out the door with Mother on his heels.

David didn't move an inch. Neither did Zack. Working with Todd was a good thing. The kid had skills, some of them computer related. He was a good fit for the rapidly expanding operation. It was the other assignment that stuck in Zack's throat. Work with Cruella de Vil? Just thinking of another confrontation with the snarky woman gave him a chill.

"You want to call her?" He turned to David. "I mean you are senior agent and all."

Before he had a chance to answer, Mother peered back into the room. "Excuse me, David, but you have a visitor."

And there she was, the ICE queen herself.

Zack jumped to his feet, a product of all the politeness trained into him from childhood and the Corps more than anything else. Agent Xing actually smiled when she entered the room. Okay, so it wasn't a very happy smile, but it did crack her face a little bit. She politely shook hands although she still kept the contact brief, limp, and insincere.

He scanned her once from head to toe. She wore no wedding band, and why he noticed bugged him. He didn't care about the uppity woman. Hell. She wasn't even what he considered attractive. Her cheeks were gaunt, and her hair was pulled back tight enough to pull even the hint of a smile off her face. *This chick's wearing the same clothes as yesterday. What? Did she work all night?*

"How's the investigation going?" She placed her laptop on the table while she accepted the chair he'd offered.

"What investigation would that be?" Zack asked as he and David resumed their seats.

"Why, Agent Lennox, the investigation on Chai Yenn, of course." She smiled again, which irked him more than when she was rude.

She wants something.

"Like I said, what investigation? The last time we met, you said you worked alone. Isn't that what you heard, Agent Tao?"

David nodded, his index finger tapping his chin like he was thinking.

"You gentlemen must think I have a lot of nerve." She didn't appear fazed in the least.

"You think?" Zack pushed away from the table.

"I'm sorry. I acted badly at the hospital, but I'm here to offer the assistance and total cooperation of the entire Immigration and Customs Enforcement Agency."

He caught the first tell. Federal agents used acronyms. They assumed everyone spoke their language. This woman was not who she pretended to be. He leaned back and looked closer. She'd also spoken her apology too quickly, as if they tasted bad on her tongue and she had to spit them out before she changed her mind. At least she had the good grace to lower her eyes. Long eyelashes fluttered against creamy cheeks. David might be right. She might be someone's daughter after all. She'd almost bordered on feminine for a second there and, damn it anyway. Why'd he notice?

"I apologize." She lifted her chin to look directly at him. Intelligent dark eyes caught him off balance, like she'd reached across the short distance between them and landed a good, hard sucker punch. She blinked once, and he had to think why he was angry with her. *Oh yeah. This woman's heartless. She's trouble. Besides, the hag's not good looking. Much.*

Zack stood to leave. He had CIs to chat with. David could deal with her.

"I think it's important we focus on who we're really working for." David spoke very quietly. "Both of our agencies owe Chai Yenn and Zhen Ting the best work we can do. They are the important ones. Not us. We must put our differences aside and work together like the professionals we are."

Damn it, Tao. Zack stopped at the door. That was another annoying thing about David. He was a sniper. The man knew precisely how to hit his target and what ammo to use. The gentle reminder he'd just shot struck home like a live round of guilt. Mei nodded her total agreement, as if that helped. A ripple of unease poked at Zack. Everything was not as it seemed with this chick, but he sat again.

What am I not seeing?

"Ma'am, we'd be pleased to share all the information we've gathered over the past twenty-four hours, but we would also appreciate the same professional courtesy from you." David was the quintessential diplomat. "Is there anything you'd like to tell us?"

"That's why I'm here." She folded her hands in front of her and wiggled her hips, seemingly eager to please and still throwing off vibes of deceit. "My office has narrowed the search to two attorneys in the D.C. area who deal in overseas adoptions. I have a proposal to—"

Zack cut her off. "We already know about Reginald Richards."

"You do?" Her eyes registered surprise. "What, umm, else do you know?"

"He's facilitated the adoptions of hundreds of Chinese girls in the last few years," David offered.

"And he's made a boatload of cash," Zack added. "'Course, I bet you already knew that."

"Well, yes. Of course, I know that." She shifted in her chair. "Let's see what else you've got."

Zack caught the second tell. Agent Xing blinked rapidly, and those once calm hands were squeezed tight. No, make that wringing, as in twisting her fingers like they were rags. The game changed. She might've known about Richards, but she hadn't known about all those adoptions or the money he was bringing down. Zack pulled his chair up to the table, watching for other tells. She had his undivided attention now.

He set the trap. "He specializes in exotic children."

Bingo. Her brows raised. She didn't have a clue what he was talking about.

"Exotic? As in..." She let her words trail away, doubtless thinking she was baiting him.

He leaned forward and shrugged like he could care less. "You know. Unusual physical characteristics. Hair color. The shape of their face. Anything to make their looks unique. Physical attributes that fall outside their ethnicity."

She sucked in a quiet gasp. He had her now. Hook, line, and sinker.

"Like a Chinese American with blue eyes?" she asked quietly.

"Well, yeah," he admitted. Awareness trickled into his perfectly set trap. The earth shifted. Why had she come up with that specific example? None of the girls they'd located were Chinese Americans, at least as far as he knew. What wasn't she telling them? What did she know?

She licked her lower lip and glanced down, but her eyelashes fluttered. She was biting her lip–hard. Suddenly, she flattened both of her palms to the table.

"Let me show you what else we have on Richards." David interrupted the fishing expedition. Just as he flashed the attorney's profile on the overhead, Alex stormed back into the Sit Room with Mother on his heels.

"Shut it down!" he demanded as he slapped a picture in front of their guest. "Who the hell are you?"

Mother reached around David to turn the overhead off, then scurried out the door.

Zack stared dumbfounded. What had Alex so spun up?

"No, I...I—" Agent Xing caught her breath. She stood to leave but Alex grabbed her wrist, forcing her back to her seat.

"You're not going anywhere, Agent whoever you are. We're checking Immigration and Customs. Answer me. Who are you?" He crowded her personal space with pure hostility.

"Mei Xing. I am Mei Xing. That much is true." She crumbled. "I'm not an agent for Immigration though. I'm just...I'm—"

"You'd better come up with a better story," Alex bellowed into her face. "You've been trying to hack my server. What the hell are you looking for?"

A single tear trickled down her cheek.

"And you can knock that crap off. Fake tears won't work. If you think for one minute—"

"I'm a mother!" she screamed back at him. "That's all. A mother. Do what you want. I don't care. I'll do whatever it takes to find her. Do you hear me?" She wiped the tears off her defiant face, meeting him head-on every inch of the way.

Now Zack was hooked. *A what? A mother? Find who?*

Alex lowered his voice and pulled his chair against hers. "Who are you trying to find?"

"What do you care?" She was the angry one now, their roles reversed. "Turn me in. Call the police. I should've known you guys wouldn't help, either."

"Now wait a minute—"

"Why should I? You're all the same." She shoved her chair back, preparing to stand, although he still held her wrist. "Well, let me tell you something. I don't need men!"

Once again, Alex refused to let her rise out of her chair.

Zack was impressed. This woman had actually barked back at his boss, a feat few had tried. The stare down continued, but he'd caught desperation in her voice loud and clear. The men in her life had failed her.

"I'll ask one more time," Alex said calmly. "Who are you looking for?"

She hesitated, glancing at the door.

"I haven't called anyone, Mei–if that's your real name. No police are coming to get you."

She melted, her lower lip quivering as her demeanor softened. One more minute of the stare down continued before she burst into tears. "LiLi." She hiccupped. "I'm looking for my daughter."

Say what? Zack looked closer. Mei Xing was scared. That's why the tough girl act. She'd been scared at the hospital, too.

David grabbed the box of tissues from the nearby credenza and pushed it into her hand. She took several, wiped her face, and tried to compose herself.

"Come on now, don't cry," Alex soothed. "Tell me what's going on. Tell me about LiLi."

Mei hiccupped again, the tissues against her mouth and nose. He still gripped her wrist, but she didn't seem to mind. Dark eyes flicked over his face, searching. At last she dabbed her eyes and spoke. "My little girl. She was coming home from school. She's only six. One minute, she's getting off the bus. She's smiling at me. The next minute, some guy attacks me and...They stole my baby," she whispered. "In broad daylight. Right in front of me. They took LiLi."

Tears poured down her cheeks, and that didn't help. Zack's defenses went right out the window. Her story stabbed his heart. What the hell was going on in Anacostia?

She pushed the picture of herself peering into her laptop computer screen back toward Alex. "I met your agents at the hospital, so I followed them. You guys can get into places I can't, and I...so I...." She fingered her very official looking ICE badge, and just that fast Hagatha was back. "What else could I do? I couldn't get past your stupid firewall!"

"Yeah, well, that's not going to happen." Alex chuckled softly as his hand moved from her wrist to her shoulder.

"But you don't understand. I've been looking for so long, and she's just six."

Zack glanced at David and Alex. Alex was patting her shoulder like he did this kind of thing every day. David looked genuinely concerned, but neither of them seemed as affected as Zack felt. "Boss, umm, I'll go check for any missing person reports." He had to get away. "And I'll find out about any AMBER Alerts that might have—"

"I already know." Mei glared at him through teary eyes. "They never issued one. I'm not important enough."

"Who the hell told you that?" he asked in amazement at the bold-faced lie.

"No one. It's just that the detectives asked me a lot of questions. They said they'd issue one, but they never did. Then another man called. He wouldn't give me his name, but he said he worked with the police. He told me I had to file a missing persons report first, and—"

"Wait a minute." Alex stopped her. "A missing person report? Are you serious? They didn't treat this as an abduction?"

She buried her face in her arms and sobbed. "I've been everywhere–the police, my congressman, the governor. No one will help me."

Zack turned away. Something about the woman was sucking him in, and it had to stop. She sounded desperate and sad. So much in love with her missing child.

"Someone's been telling you a helluva lot of lies," Alex said gently.

"I know," she squeaked. "I can't trust anyone. Everyone's against me."

Zack never thought he'd live to see the day. His boss had pulled Mei into his arm. The sight of her crying against Alex's shoulder shook Zack. The haughty ICE agent had been reduced to a little girl. He turned away.

"Everyone isn't against you," Alex said quietly, "but someone's done a good job of hosing you. How about if we find out about the AMBER Alert business? That shouldn't take long. Then we'll find your little girl, okay?"

"Really?" Mei lifted her head. "You'd really help me? After all I've done?"

"Yes, ma'am, we will." Alex nodded to Zack and David. "You work with my two agents here, and we'll find your little girl. We'll find LiLi."

"But why?" She hiccupped through another stifled sob. "You don't know me."

Alex was quiet for a minute. "It's what we do, Mei. We do what others can't. Or won't."

"Thank you," she said timidly. "Thank you very much."

Alex turned to Zack and David. "David. Come with me. Zack, stay with Ms. Xing. See what else she knows."

ELEVEN

"You must hate me," Mei said, her voice hushed and tired.

"No, ma'am. I don't." Zack would've agreed with the statement earlier, but after spending hours with her, he didn't know how he felt. Some of her story made sense. Some didn't. The detectives she described and named did not work for the police. He'd checked. And the mysterious man on the phone who'd told her there'd be no AMBER Alert? Another dead end. Zack had worked plenty with the police officers. There was no way they'd blatantly disregard a mother's plea for help. Heck, most of them had children. If anything, they were over-the-top rabid dogs when it came to crimes against kids.

Too many other things didn't add up. Someone was one step ahead of her all the way. Or she was lying. He would've agreed with that conclusion the day before too.

"So tell me again. Why do you think your daughter is caught up in the child trafficking ring?"

She sighed another long drawn-out sigh, like she'd done with every repeat question. "Because it's the only thing that makes sense."

"Where'd you hear about it?"

"At the Emergency Room. A police officer told Claire the whole thing smelled bad."

That surprised Zack. "You were at the ER? When?"

She blanched white, her dark lashes bleak against the pale of her skin. "After they found the second little girl in the garbage."

"You saw her?"

"Yes," she whispered. "I went to the morgue too."

"You what? How could you do that?"

"I had to make sure."

"How did you know we'd found Chai?" he asked gently. This woman was one surprise after another. He couldn't get the baby at the morgue's partially decomposed body out of his mind. How could she?

"I bought a police scanner when LiLi first went missing. I had to." She looked away. "Then I used my, umm, influence to get into wherever I needed to go."

He didn't know what to say. No wonder she was gaunt. The woman was running on empty. "How many fake IDs do you have?"

"As many as I need."

Inexplicably, his hand reached across the table. Her hand was ice. "You won't need them again. I'll help you."

She didn't answer, but there was definite fire in her eyes when she eased her hand out from under his.

Mother tapped at the door and peeked in. "Hey, Zack. Got a minute?"

"Sure. Be right there." He turned to Mei. "I'll take you home as soon as I'm finished."

She nodded tiredly. "I'm not going anywhere."

"So, how's your new girlfriend?" Mother said the second he stepped up to her desk.

"Whatcha got?" Zack ignored the catty question. She never changed. Leave it to her to pick up on the vibes he wanted to ignore. The woman had radar. Yeah. Mei's story touched him. So what?

"I asked a friend of mine to run your little button through his new generation RXD spectra-analysis machine." She handed him the evidence bag. "He works for a private lab that handles some of the country's toughest forensic evidence. The new analyzer they've got can scan a sample in microseconds. It breaks it down to 20 millimeters of—"

"Just tell me if it's worth anything." Zack waved her technical explanation off.

"It's worth seven dollars, just for one button. It's got three diamonds in it. They were covered with grime, but that's not what's important. Look at this." With a flourish, Mother set a colorful bar chart with a conglomeration of vertical lines on her counter. "The spectra-analysis report lists everything that came into contact with the button." She pointed to one particular green line. "See this right here?"

He followed her manicured fingernail. One word leapt off the page. "Cocaine? That little girl's been around cocaine?"

"At least the button was. Look at this." Mother traced a thin yellow line, but too many other words vied for his attention. Coffee. Watermelon rinds. Lard. Vodka. Dog feces. That beautiful baby was buried beneath sludge. She'd suffered. Someone hurt her, tossed her out like garbage. If not for Marty....

"Zack." Mother's voice softened. "Zhen Ting had the button in her hand. I can prove it. See this yellow line? Those are her skin cells."

He could barely speak.

"And these two lines here." She highlighted bright orange and brown lines. "I eliminated yours, but two other people touched it, only I don't know who they are. I've got nothing to compare."

"Could be Marty." Zack scrubbed a hand over his face. "He handled it."

"Or whoever dropped her in the dumpster," Alex said. He had come up behind them, his hand to Zack's shoulder as he peered over the counter at the report.

Mother kept going. "I've got more. This button is made from a shell found in New Guinea. The only place in the world that uses buttons like this is a high-end men's suit shop in *Le Marais,* Paris, France. They've got some kind of an exclusive contract."

"Bet it's expensive," Zack muttered.

"Let's just say you'd be spending a month's salary to buy a suit there, unless you're making a whole heck of a lot more than I think you're making." Mother usually crowed when she was successful, but this time she was subdued.

"More pieces of the puzzle." Alex cut to the chase. "Who bought it?"

"Here's the list." She produced another sheet of computer paper. "Recognize anyone?"

One name leapt off the page. Mr. Tony Brown.

"How is this guy involved?" Zack asked. "He's everywhere."

"That's what you and David are going to find out," Alex said easily as he and Zack stepped away.

"Thanks, Mother." Zack rapped his knuckles on her countertop before he left. "Good work."

He wasn't prepared for her tender smile.

"Get 'em, Zack." She dabbed her eyes with a tissue. "Don't let them hurt any more little girls like the pretty baby you found. She and Zhen Ting deserve justice. Someone needs to pay."

His thoughts exactly. All he could do was nod. It seemed the op was hard on everyone, not just him. He turned an abrupt about face and joined his boss.

"Speaking of David, did he already leave?" Alex asked, looking around the deserted office.

"I think he was stopping by CPS on his way home."

"Child Protective Services? Again?"

"He's checking another lead."

Alex rolled his eyes. "Sure he is. More like he's checking on Chai Yenn. How about you? Still working with our little mother?"

"I was about to take her home when Mother called. Poor woman took the bus here. Guess she had a flat tire."

"And?"

"I don't know, Boss. Someone's trying damned hard to keep this kidnapping from going public."

"You believe her?"

Zack nodded. "Yeah. It doesn't make a lot of sense, but I do."

"David checked the AMBER Alert. No report of a missing child was ever filed."

"The detectives were fakes. Maybe everyone she thinks she talked with, too. She's sure hard set that her daughter's abduction is mixed up with the child trafficking ring though."

"I don't know how," Alex breathed quietly. "More likely she latched onto the first thing that made sense. She's desperate. See what you can find out about the father. As long as you're taking her home, sweep the place for bugs.

Someone's intercepted every move she's made. Whoever's behind it, they've got to have her place wired somehow."

"But why? She's just a single mom working a dead end job. She's right. She's a nobody."

Alex shrugged. "It doesn't make sense, but have you felt her back?"

That came out of the blue. "Ah, no. Sure haven't."

"I noticed when she fell apart. Mei Xing is thin as a rail, Zack. That woman is killing herself looking for her daughter." Alex aimed his index finger at the Sit Room. "If what she told us is the truth, we need to find her little girl, and we need to do it fast."

Now it was Zack's turn to blow out one of those long suffering sighs like Mei had been doing. "I'm on it."

Just take me home.

Once inside the sleek sports car, Mei fastened her seat belt, pushed back into the leather seat, and tried to ignore her luxurious surroundings. There was a time a car like this one would have impressed her. No more. Agent Lennox guy had it all. The parking garage he parked in was protected from the weather. He didn't even have to scrape windows on his Porsche. And here she was, sitting in the same seat where only yesterday some working girl had wriggled her disgusting butt. Ewww. The irony did not escape Mei. Just the fact that she was here proved she was inconsequential in the grand scheme of things, almost as low as that hooker.

The soft yellow glow of the overhead lights faded as Agent Lennox pulled the vehicle up the ramp, punched in his secure access code, and pulled silently into traffic. This was the last place she wanted to be, beholden to another rich man. The night traffic slipped by.

"Can I get you something to eat?" he offered. At least he was polite.

"No, thanks. I want to go home."

"I still have one question."

"And what would that be?"

He'd already downloaded everything from her laptop, and grilled her for hours. What could possibly be left unanswered? The only reason she'd allowed the miserable day to unfold the way it had was because Alex Stewart made her believe. Almost.

"There are still a few things we didn't get to. All I want to know is why the attitude?" Agent Lennox didn't rise to the challenge of her nasty remark like she expected. "Why were you so hostile with David and me at the hospital yesterday? You didn't even know who we were before you ripped our heads off. What was that all about?"

He'd never understand. How could he?

"How far would I have gotten if you knew who I really was?" She flipped the stolen badge snapped to her belt. How dense could he be? "I've done so many illegal things. If I'm going to find my daughter, I can't be weak. If that comes across as mean and nasty, I'm sorry. I really don't care what you think of me, Agent Lennox. I have to find her."

There. Now leave me alone.

She turned back to the window. People flew by in their nice clean cars, oblivious to the mess that was her life. The night was dark and her mood darker. Another day without LiLi was another day wasted. Mei bit her thumbnail and pushed the fear down one more time.

"Where is her father?" he asked gently.

That was another thing. Why was Agent Lennox being so nice and civil? Why did he act like he cared?

"He was a friend in college," she snapped.

"So you two didn't marry?"

"No, Agent Lennox, we didn't marry." Resorting to sarcasm, Mei riveted her eyes to the outside scenery one more time. "He was a medical student with a different plan for our future than mine. When he found out I was pregnant, he packed up and left. I haven't seen him since."

This agent was persistent, but dragging up the sperm donor mistake from her past didn't help. *Sheesh. Kick me while I'm down, why don't you?* She hadn't thought of Christopher in years, and she didn't want to think of him now. He'd left her high and dry and run home to Mommy and Daddy like the privileged spoiled brat he was. In doing so, he'd avoided the responsibility and inconvenience of a baby born out of wedlock. Other people might not have a problem with that scenario, but the only heir to the most prestigious cardiovascular surgeon in New York City had to be above reproach. He had a reputation to protect.

"What's his name?"

"Christopher Elias Jones the Second." The name fell from her lips like ice.

"The heart doctor's son?"

"You know him?" Great. Agent Lennox and the biggest mistake in her life were probably best friends. Wouldn't it just figure?

"No. Only what I've read in the paper. He did the heart surgery on the Vice President last year."

She preferred the gloomy scene outside her window to the gathering disquiet inside the car. Who cared what Dr. Christopher Elias Jones the First did? After he'd offered to buy Mei's silence for a million dollars, she'd never seen him again. He didn't care about her or his only grandchild. No. The important thing was to ensure neither Mei nor LiLi interfered with his son's career. A baby with someone *like her* might not look good on a résumé. That she told him in no uncertain terms to go to hell hadn't set well with the self-absorbed physician. His son, either.

"There's no chance he or his parents might have abducted your daughter?" Agent Lennox parked at the curb in front of her low rent apartment in Anacostia.

"I don't see how. They've never seen her." A quiet sob sneaked up on her. For too long, Mei had blamed herself. Something was wrong with her. She wasn't good enough for Christopher. Mei knew better the moment she first held her newborn daughter. It was never about her or LiLi. Neither was it the fact that she was Chinese American. No. Christopher and his parents were the problem. It was best they were out of her life. They'd never be good enough for LiLi, not if they lived to be a thousand.

Mei stared at her bleak world, the cold rain drizzling like she wasn't already cold enough. His hand settling over hers startled her, but when she turned with all her angry words ready to fly, she caught the light in his eyes. The tenderness was unmistakable. For that single moment in time, it seemed he saw her. She wasn't invisible.

"I can't begin to imagine what you've been going through," he said kindly.

His genuine concern took the venom out of her. It would be nice to hold the hand he'd offered, to believe he meant what he said.

"Tell me the truth, Agent Lennox. Don't lie. Do you think we can find her?"

He didn't blink or look away. "You heard my boss. If he said we're going to find your daughter, then we will."

"But you don't believe she's part of the trafficking ring, do you?" she asked accusingly, daring him to contradict her. Yes, those manly eyes were kind, but she'd been lied to before.

"There's no way to know for sure, at least, not until we do some more digging. I think it's unlikely a human trafficking ring from Mainland China would grab an American child off the street, even one of Chinese heritage. Still, it's possible. They might have grabbed her to replace another child."

"You mean, like a child who died? A little girl they might have...killed?" Her voice cracked. It was time to go before she fell apart.

"I'm sorry. I didn't mean th—"

"Forget it." Mei stiffened her chin and raised her head. "Thanks for the ride."

"It was my pleasure."

I seriously doubt that. No man appreciates a bitchy woman.

She unfastened her seat belt and pulled the door handle. Somehow, during the time it took her to get to her feet, he'd raced around the car and was offering a hand up. She waved it away.

"I'm fine. Goodnight." Mei turned away, wanting nothing more than to put the disastrous day far behind her.

Agent Lennox followed. "I'm coming in with you."

"You don't need to." *I don't want you to. This isn't a date.*

He didn't argue, but neither did he leave. With one flick of his wrist, the Porsche winked back when he remote locked it.

"You don't need to walk me to my door, Agent Lennox. Really." *Surely, he had better things to do? Like leave.*

"Give it up, Agent Xing." Without asking, he slid out of his jacket and placed it over her shoulders.

She noticed. God, how she noticed. Warmth flooded the cold pit in her heart, the stone dungeon she carried everywhere. The man she wanted so much to hate had just been kind, and he'd done it automatically, like it was no big deal.

"I'll escort you to your apartment. After I make sure you're safe, I'm going to sweep for listening devices. It's very possible someone's bugged your place."

She pulled the warm leather around her, shivering as heat replaced the chill. It was hard not to notice the masculine smell mingled with the leather, wrapped up in his jacket like she was. "You really think someone's eavesdropping on me?"

"It's the only thing that makes sense. Someone has to be intercepting all your calls."

She wasn't going to argue, but why would anyone bug her? She didn't know anything.

He waited at her side while she keyed in the secure access code to her apartment building. Once again he held the door, his hand at the small of her back while he ushered her inside, and once again warmth surged up from her toes. His touch felt so good that it hurt. She shrugged away from him, but he didn't seem to notice she meant to avoid him.

"Think about it," he said as they walked to the elevator. "Those weren't real detectives you talked with. Someone set the whole thing up in order to abduct LiLi, and then to prevent you from getting the help you needed."

Her mind went blank. Intrigue of that scale belonged in movies, not her pathetic excuse of a life.

"Which floor?" he asked.

"Second." She fingered the supple feel of his expensive jacket, the men's cologne imbued in its lining rising up into her nose like incense. This guy had it all. He could afford to be nice.

The elevator ride was quiet. They didn't speak again until they were at her door. The dismal feel of her apartment met her full force when she opened the door and flipped the light switch, a big contrast to the interior of his car.

"Don't mind me. I'll only take a minute," he said as he stepped inside with her. For the first time, she saw the holster across his broad back, two pistols tucked under his arms. They'd been hidden beneath the leather jacket now draped over her shoulders.

Her eyes drifted over his profile as he proceeded into the room. For a big dumb jock, he wasn't bad looking, bald but attractive in a primitive way. He was the kind of guy who decorated himself with tattoos and chewed tobacco. Thick biceps flexed when he unsnapped what looked like a walkie-talkie on his belt. Huh. No tats. Only clear rippling skin rich with the color of a mixed heritage. Well, okay. So he didn't have a tattoo that she could see. It didn't mean anything. She'd already seen his choice of women. She knew his type.

"Would you like coffee or tea?" she asked, just to be nice. He was, after all, helping her again. It's not like she'd asked him to.

His eyes lit up at her less than enthusiastic offer. "It's late. You sure you don't mind?"

"I could fix..." She turned to her sparse kitchen where a half box of granola, three apples, and a couple more spoonfuls of instant coffee awaited their demise. "I'll make coffee."

While he walked through her neglected home, she set her teakettle to boil and placed two mugs, two spoons, and what was left of the sugar and creamer on the table. He might as well know he was not going to get his usual cup of caffe-mocha-latte-whatever he was probably used to drinking every morning. All she had to offer was plain old Folgers freeze-dried. If it was good enough for her, it was good enough for him. He could take it or leave it.

The simple sight of the sugar bowl in the middle of her table brought LiLi's pouting face to mind. Like all kids, she loved sweets. Mei had to watch her or she'd spoon sugar on her waffles. Over the syrup. Maybe with chocolate chips. Mei's resolve buckled.

God, I can't do this alone anymore!

"Copy that." Agent Lennox 's voice rose strong and confident from her bedroom where he was checking for listening devices. She stared when he entered the kitchen, dumbfounded at the odd coincidence. It was as if he'd just answered her.

"I'm sorry," she murmured. "Did you say something to me?"

Did you hear me? Are you the answer to my prayers?

"Sorry. Didn't mean to be loud. Just chatting with the boss." The darkest chocolate eyes smiled back at her, warm and melted. Inviting. Comforting.

"I only have instant coffee," she said to break the connection. What was she thinking? He didn't care. Not really.

Agent Lennox pulled out a chair and sat, watching. She glanced sideways at him. He was the first man to sit at her cheap dinette set. He made it look small and fragile, sitting there with his hands on his knees like he was. Somehow, he also made it look good.

When the water heated enough, she poured two cups and sat opposite him, ignoring all those masculine traits her eyes kept pointing out, his big work boots for one. The man had huge feet, so of course his thighs were large, too. But his lashes were long and thick. Men didn't usually have eyes as deep and dark as his. Those lashes made them deeper. Sexier. She shook the foolishness out of her mind. *I don't care if he has three eyes as long as he finds LiLi.*

"Did you find what you were looking for?"

"Only the best coffee I've had in a long time." He uncurled his fingers. There in his left hand rested two square little things, each with a wire hanging off it.

Her jaw dropped. "You're kidding me—"

"I never kid about good coffee, ma'am." He cautioned her with a finger to his lips.

Someone's been listening to me.

She couldn't breathe. All this time, someone out there knew. They'd heard her cry, swear, and scream. They'd heard her call the police and the detectives. The hospitals. Her senator. They'd heard everything. Worse, they'd physically been inside her home. She wrapped Agent Lennox's jacket tighter, glancing at what had once been her sanctuary.

His eyes searched hers. "You wouldn't happen to have any rice, would you?"

Rice? Now? He's hungry? This late at night?

She went to her empty cupboards and returned with the granola and one bowl. "This is all I have. If you want milk with your cereal—"

He took hold of her hands and the box of cereal between them. "It will do. Thank you."

She caught the tender look in his eye. He'd seen her bare cupboards. Now he knew.

Yes, I'm living on the edge of poverty. Deal with it. I certainly have.

Instead of taking the box, he shook his head. "Another time. I'd better get going."

He downed his coffee in a gulp. At the door, he turned to her and tapped the deadbolt. "Make sure you use this."

She gulped. He'd found listening devices inside her home, and now he was leaving? Her anxiety must've shown through. Suddenly, he was back at her side. The air he brought with him was filled with the distinct odor of leather, and — power? Safety? Her heart stuttered. She looked up into fierce brown eyes that seemed to see through her carefully constructed wall. His arm curled protectively around her. For one split second, her lips parted.

"Don't leave your apartment until I pick you up in the morning. Understood?" An emotion flickered across his face. One lightning quick glance at her mouth, and he took a step back, releasing her. "I'm an early riser. Will six a.m. be too early for you?"

"I'll be ready, Agent Lennox," she whispered, her angst gone with the strength in her legs.

He nodded, opened the door without looking back and was gone.

Mei turned the deadbolt like he'd instructed. A chill shivered across her shoulders when she glanced at her empty apartment. Someone had been in here, and that person had left listening devices to track her every word and move. There might be a bug in her car, too. That meant they knew she had a police scanner. They knew she'd been to the hospital. They knew everything.

She sank to the floor, for the first time afraid to be in her own home. Agent Lennox's jacket sank with her. She pulled it closer, burrowing into the warmth and the odor of a man who might care. The empty rooms stared back at her. No longer friendly. No longer safe.

"I can't stay here."

TWELVE

Where the hell is she?

After pounding on Mei's door until he was afraid he'd wake her neighbors, Zack did the only thing he could do. He picked her lock, easy enough since the deadbolt was not engaged like he'd told her to do. *Damned ornery woman.*

It didn't take long to search the two-bedroom dive. By then, he was livid. He had no idea where she'd gone or if someone had abducted her, too. He doubted that scenario, but the obvious fact remained. Whoever'd planted those bugs was no longer receiving any intel from Mei's apartment. They might've gone looking for her. Anything was possible.

Like an idiot, he'd changed her flat tire before leaving last night. In an attempt to breach the stone cold wall she'd built around her, he'd done something to help her, but it had only provided the means for her to run around town and get into more trouble. Not his brightest idea. Zack thumped his steering wheel with the heel of his palm, cussing her as he drove past her parking stall. The wreck was still there. She must have taken the bus. How could he help if she refused to listen?

The drive to the office was faster than usual because his emotions ran straight down his leg and into the accelerator. Somehow, the purr of those four-hundred and seventy-five horses worked their magic, soothing the ragged edges off the already troublesome day. Now, if only he knew where Mei was.

The seemingly simple chore of locating Chai Yenn's parents had quickly morphed into a human trafficking operation. On top of an apparent child abduction, it seemed to include someone spying on a woman too poor to afford food, but too pig-headed to do as she was told. He parked his pride and joy in its assigned stall and opted for a run up the two flights to his office to burn off what was left of his irritation.

Alex would already be there and demanding. *Great. What am I supposed to say? I lost her? I screwed another op? Damned woman.*

He pushed the fire-door open and entered ground zero. The aroma of an early pot of coffee welcomed him. Did the man never go home? Annoyed, he rounded Mother's empty desk on his way to his workspace. At least the office busybody would miss the round of fireworks.

Two very elegant, long legs that ended in bare feet stretched into view. Mei?

"Where have you been?" he muttered quietly. What was she doing in his chair, all sprawled nice and comfy, his leather jacket wrapped around her like a blanket? Still dressed in the same clothes as yesterday, she yawned like he'd disturbed her from a sound sleep. "I was picking you up this morning. Remember? You were supposed to stay put."

She blinked wide-open eyes, still waking up. Yeah. The deer in the headlights look was a new touch, somehow soft and feminine. So was the length of silky black hair hanging off the slightly disheveled knot at the back of her very hard head.

"Take it easy. I found her downstairs," Alex said from behind him.

And then he was really mad. "You slept in the lobby?"

"No, I—" She pushed her hair off her face, straightening in his chair. "Umm, yes. I had a flat, so I took the bus."

Despite himself, it was hard not to miss how cute she looked when she pushed her butt back and folded her legs beneath her.

"I fixed your flat," he growled, not ready to ease up on her.

"Relax. I let her in when the front door alarm sounded. She's been camped out here waiting for you," Alex intervened.

Zack shot his boss a look. It would've been nice if someone had told him.

"I couldn't stay there," she said softly.

He didn't know who to be angrier with. "So you trot down here in the middle of the night?"

"Lay off," Alex said. "No harm, no foul. You got the bugs?"

Zack reached inside the pocket to his team jacket and pulled out the two nasty listening devices, by now deep inside a noisy paper bag of noisier dried rice to prevent anyone from listening.

Alex took the bag, inserted two fingers to shuffle the rice aside, and viewed the contents. "Radio Shack specials, huh?"

"Already dusted them for prints. They're clean," Zack muttered, not sure why he was angry. Obviously, Mei was capable of taking care of herself. Why should he worry? Wait. He wasn't worried, was he? The notion didn't sit well. He glanced her way. Slumber still clouded those dreamy browns.

A woman waking up was just plain sexy. Why did it have to be her?

"Since you're both here." Alex nodded toward his office. "Let's decide on our next step."

"Okay." Mei pushed to her feet, sliding both arms into the too-big leather jacket. She looked like some high school cheerleader in her boyfriend's letterman jacket the way the thing dwarfed her. Zack calmed, thinking about how cold she'd been last night. Black leather looked good on her now that he had time to actually look. Long legs. Leather. Yeah. She could be damned good looking, in an uptight sort of way.

"I was going to take you to breakfast," he said to soften his outburst. "You should've waited for me. You've got to be hungry."

Just that fast, the jacket was off her shoulders and tossed to his chair. Mei reached to the back of her head and wound the loose strand of hair nice and tight. Hagatha was back. Good looking was gone.

"I don't need your pity," she snapped. "We have work to do."

He followed behind her and Alex, watching her smart ass twitch from side to side as she seemed to lead the way. Exactly who was in charge here? It sure looked like she was. Despite her brief thaw of the night before, she was back to ice queen status. As soon as they were seated at the small conference table in Alex's office, the inquisition began.

"Your boss took my badge." She glared at Zack like he'd done it.

He shrugged it off. "Good."

"I can't work without it." Very delicate eyebrows dropped into a severe V. Cruella di Vil? Yeah. That's who she looked like when she glared like that.

"What are you telling me for? Tell him." Zack nodded toward Alex. "You could do serious time if you got caught. Next time I'm at your apartment, I want the rest of them. Should've taken 'em last night."

She tapped her toes like she'd done in the hospital, glaring the same way, too.

Well, two can play that game, sister. He glared right back. Damn. She had pretty eyes. Pretty mean eyes.

"You been having phone trouble for awhile now, have you?" He shot a volley her way.

"Yes. Why?" she hissed.

"Because that's what cheap listening devices do to phones. You ever think of that?" *Bam. Full in the face. Take that, Miss High and Mighty.*

She blinked. He gulped. How did she do that to him! One minute capable, downright tough, vicious and cruel, but the next frightened and scared, which only meant she never was tough in the fist place. *Argh!* He couldn't keep up. Vulnerable and mean did not go hand in hand. The frightened woman ducked back behind the cover of the Wicked Witch of the West, and he let her. A witch he could deal with.

"Your boss interrupted me yesterday, Agent Lennox. I have a proposal that might break the case open. Remember?"

"And that would be?" Zack slouched back in his seat. He was done trying to help. He shot a look at Alex, who still hadn't said anything. Zack's sense of foreboding snapped to attention. His boss looked way too comfortable.

Damn. These two have been talking. Something's going on.

"I want to go undercover as a married couple."

Oh, hell no. Zack nearly laughed out loud. Would have if Alex hadn't finally engaged, his fingers steepled together and tapping to beat the band. Caffeine and Mei were a bad combination.

"She's got a good idea, Zack. You two could infiltrate Richards' office as a married couple. Find out if he's involved with the Black Dragon Syndicate like we think he is. Might lead you straight to the children." Alex sounded like he was asking, but he wasn't.

"But we have no evidence those guys took her daughter." Zack was not going down without a fight.

"We have no evidence they didn't."

"If they've got a lawyer like Richards on their payroll, they've got money. They'd have no trouble bugging my home. Who else could it be?" Mei tossed her two cents worth into the ring.

Zack tossed it right back out. "Money does not equate to motive." He focused on his boss. "Motive. Means. Opportunity. Why would a child trafficking ring steal her daughter and bug her home?"

Alex shrugged. "Why not?"

"Sounds like a lot of trouble." Zack gritted his teeth. "That means they've got fake detectives, telephone operators who intercepted every one of Mei's calls, and someone ballsy enough to break and enter."

Alex leaned forward. "Think about it. Whoever's behind the abduction killed the forty-eight hour window essential to finding a missing child. They covered their tracks and diverted attention. It smacks of organized crime. She could be right."

Mei followed the conversation like a tennis match.

Zack bit his lip rather than say, 'She could be wrong'. The woman he'd finally glimpsed behind Hagatha was hanging on by a thread. Wrong or right, the fact remained. A child trafficking ring did exist. Little girls were endangered. And LiLi was somewhere out there without her mother.

"Wouldn't David be better for this operation?" Zack pushed back from the table, definitely drawing the short end of the stick again. "He is Chinese. Mei's Chinese." *And I don't want to do this.*

"You and Mei are closer in age." Alex cut him off at the pass. "And you'll make a more believable couple."

"Why's that?" *Because she's bitchy, and we already fight like we're married?*

"Look at the two of you." Alex smirked.

He was right. Who'd doubt when a latte-colored man and a Chinese American woman showed up to adopt an exotic child?

"Yeah, but Boss...."

The last thing Zack wanted was to spend another day with Mei. Feeling sorry for her did not equate to a twenty-four-seven partnership, much less an undercover sting that might take who knew how long. It could last days, weeks, and heaven forbid, months. They'd have to pretend to live together. No way.

Alex stared back at him.

Zack stifled his next good excuse. The decision had obviously already been made, maybe before he'd even rolled out of bed this morning. "Never mind. Will do."

"Good. Mother will put your undercover identities together. You'll be wired. David and Todd will be in a nearby listening post if needed. All you have to do is keep me informed. Besides..."

"Besides what?" Zack looked at his boss's smirky face. The man could irritate the horns off Satan.

Alex extricated a small photo from the inside of his suit jacket and handed it to Zack. A little girl of Chinese descent smiled back at him. Aside from the big toothless grin and happy face, she was a miniature version of Mei. There was only one difference.

"Is this your daughter?" Zack asked Mei, stunned into submission.

She nodded, her lips pressed tight.

Zack couldn't win. He was going undercover with Mei, to play husband to her wife. There was no sense arguing.

LiLi had blue eyes.

"You two love birds ready?"

"Shut it, Todd," Zack hissed. "Don't think because you're in the van I can't get to you."

"Copy that," Todd replied cheerfully. "Just checking on the honeymooners."

Zack's fist clenched. His earpiece might be small enough to fool Attorney Richards, but having a smart ass like Todd Chandler in a man's head only made him cranky. And Zack was plenty cranky. At least Alex hadn't given Mei an earpiece. Yet.

"We're moving," Zack muttered as he climbed out of his car and walked around it to open the door for his 'wife'.

Today he was Quentin Burns and she was Amelia, the millionaire co-owners of an up and coming software firm. He'd driven his Porsche to add to their undercover backstory, but Alex had taken care of them in every other way. They looked quite the wealthy couple. Mei wore a simple black dress, a color that only made her features more severe, like that was possible. The fur-lined winter coat helped disguise her narrow frame. Ember had taken her to a high-end salon for hair, make-up, and nails. It didn't help. She looked the epitome of pampered wealth, but beauty could not disguise the starving look in her eyes.

For the first time in a long time, Zack was in a business suit–white shirt, black tie, the whole clown get-up. He ran a finger under his collar, loosening the tie so it didn't feel like he was choking. This was funeral attire. He couldn't wait to get out of it.

Mei stood next to him on the sidewalk. The earth shifted. He should be getting used to the off balance feeling by now. It seemed to happen every time she got too close. He purposefully avoided resting his hand at the small of her back. They were supposed to be married. That gesture might make someone think they liked each other. He didn't want to blow the whole op right off the bat.

"Can I help you?" The elderly woman behind the receptionist desk peered over her wire-rimmed reading glasses. The brass nameplate on her desk declared her to be Ms. Marjorie Bradford. She wore her hair in the same fashion as Mei's, all knotted into a tight little bun at the back of her head, only Ms. Bradford's hair was white. Pure white. Who was she anyway, Richards' mother?

"Mr. and Mrs. Quentin Burns to see Attorney Richards." Mei stepped right up and took charge, like that was a surprise.

"You'll need to fill out the paperwork and agree to a background check." The secretary handed Mei a clipboard with several forms. "When can you return for your follow-up appointment?"

"Why do we need another appointment?" Zack asked.

"Young man." Ms. Bradford scowled sternly, not a hint of a smile in her voice. "Child adoption is a serious undertaking. It will take several appointments to work through all the legalities. Besides, we can't approve you and your wife until we know for certain that you can afford the retainer fee now, can we?"

Zack cocked an eyebrow. "Fee?"

"Oh, yes." She nodded as if to confirm her words. "There's a one million dollar fee, upfront and non-refundable. When you make your selection, there will be an additional charge depending on the age of the girl. Didn't you know?"

"Tomorrow," Mei interrupted before Zack could phrase a proper rebuttal to that kind of robbery. "We can be back tomorrow. First thing in the morning, if it's okay."

Ms. Bradford checked her schedule. "We have an opening at 9 a.m. tomorrow. Will that work for you?"

"We'll take it."

"Whew." Todd blew out a long drawn out sigh in Zack's ear. "A million bucks? Boss ain't gonna like that."

Zack grunted. He didn't have much sympathy for Alex right now. Let him pay. It might teach him for being such a smart ass.

"Honey." Mei stabbed him with those stiletto eyeballs of hers. "Can you help me?" She nodded him over to one of the chairs in the waiting area, the clipboard and pen in her hand.

No endearments came to his mind, at least none he could say out loud. They sat together and began filling out the paperwork with their fake address and personal information while Agent Chandler snickered. Zack gave his earpiece five hard taps with his index finger.

"Ouch!" Todd cussed. "Knock it off. You're hurting my eardrums."

"Good," Zack muttered quietly. "Now shut the hell up."

"Copy that," Todd replied in a much softer voice.

"I don't know what to put here," Mei whispered, pointing to the line where she was supposed to indicate the age and gender of the child they wanted to adopt. The frightened mother was back, and darn it anyway, Zack's heart dropped right on cue. How did she do that? One minute he didn't want to be anywhere near her, and the next he was ready to kill anyone who intended to hurt her. She had him so twisted, his brain hurt trying to keep up.

"Female. Six years old," he said brusquely. "That's who you want, isn't it?"

It must have been the hard reality of having to write LiLi's age and gender down on paper that shook Mei. She lowered her head and–damn it anyway, he felt like an ass again. He'd made her cry.

"Do you want me to do it?" he asked, more gently.

She shook her head and dashed the weakness away. The rest of their phony financial information took no time at all. Zack cleared eight figures yearly–on paper.

"There." Mei handed the completed forms to Mrs. Bradford. "We're ready to see Mr. Richards now."

"Oh, you won't see him today. My goodness, no." She shook her head, her face wrinkled like a dried prune. "What do you think tomorrow's appointment is for? Be sure to bring the money. Small denominations. No cashier checks."

"But I thought," Mei choked. "I thought...."

"Let me get this right." Zack secured Mei inside the crook of his arm before she fell apart and blew the op. "You want us to bring the money before we get to meet Richards?"

"I need to see it. Yes." Ms. Bradford sniffed like that was obvious.

"But we're here now," Mei argued.

"But he isn't," Ms. Bradford retorted.

"But you said—"

"It's okay," Zack intervened. "Tomorrow's fine."

"But I thought—" Mei couldn't finish.

"Come on, Amelia." He turned his anxious wife toward the door. The last thing they needed was for Hagatha to make an appearance and destroy what little good they'd accomplished. "We have plenty to do today. Tomorrow is fine."

She finally spit it out once they were on the sidewalk. "I thought we'd be able to see some of the children."

"Would've been nice." He opened the car door and waved her in.

"All he's doing is selling babies," she whispered as she folded her long legs into the passenger seat. He tried hard not to notice how elegant those black silk stockings looked in his car. The high heels Ember had selected for Mei didn't look so bad either. What is it about high heels on long slender and very attractive legs? They made Hagatha look good again. Of course the rest of his body noticed.

"What'd you expect?" He needed to keep some emotional distance between them. "The man's as crooked as they come. He's not exactly running a family friendly business."

"But...." She fastened her seatbelt as Zack shut her door. She was crushed. He got that. He just hadn't expected to feel the same way.

"Todd." Zack called his surveillance crew. "Today's a no-go. Tell Alex to put a million together. You heard the lady. Small bills. We'll be back in the morning."

"Already advised the Boss. Said no problem. Swing by the office in the morning—"

"We're swinging by now."

"Copy that." The seriousness of the op must have gotten through Todd's hard head. He'd stopped teasing.

THIRTEEN

"I've been thinking about what you asked about LiLi's father and his parents." Mei swiveled in her seat to face him. "Do you think Christopher's father might be behind it?"

"Alex is checking that lead." Zack studied the traffic in his side mirror before he pulled away from the curb. The pleasure of driving his car instantly soothed him. There's nothing like four on the floor to make a man forget he's on a blind date with a woman who doesn't even have a nice personality going for her. "Did you know your boyfriend moved to England to pursue a graduate course in oncology?"

"No, I didn't, but...Excuse me? Alex is checking what lead? Are you checking on me, too?" Mei's voice went from mildly pleased to openly hostile as the questions poured out of her mouth. "You guys didn't believe a word I said, did you?"

Zack grunted. "You really want me to answer that, Miss ICE agent? Or are you Miss Metro PD right now? Or maybe you work for the local paper? The FBI? Hell, I don't know. Tell me which one of you I should believe."

Mei did something he hadn't expected. She chuckled, a very little coughing, choking kind of a chuckle. It wasn't a laugh by any means, but it was different. "I guess I'd have double-checked my story too, huh?"

"You think?" He forced his eyes to the road. Mei was quicksand, and he was tired of not being able to catch solid footing around her.

"So. What have you found out about him and his parents? Are they involved? Did they do it?" She leaned onto the console, bullying him for answers. Mei was ten kinds of impatient, pushy, demanding, and, oh yeah, impatient all over again.

"Man, you never quit do you?"

"Would you?" She bristled.

"We're checking, okay? For hell's sake, give us time to do our job. You might not believe it, but everyone in my office is on your side, and some of us are working exclusively on your case. Hell, I got married, and I don't even recall popping the damned question."

"I really do appreciate everything you are doing to help me," she muttered.

"Don't worry about it." He blustered as if angry. "It's all I dreamed it could be."

"But it's not enough."

Zack bit his lip to keep his big mouth shut. Nothing would ever be enough for this woman. He got that. He understood. Really, he did. She wanted her daughter back, and until then everyone around her was going to be miserable. He just didn't want to be her very own personal whipping boy.

"I'll never get married," she said quietly.

That came out of the blue. He ended the conversation before it started. "Me either."

"Why not?"

"Because I'm smarter than that," he shot back.

Two blocks down the road he spotted the tail, a black Lincoln sedan following at a respectable distance, but following nonetheless. He made a quick right turn and parked curbside. Oddly, a baby boutique happened to be in the right place at the right time.

"Since we're adopting, let's go shopping for some baby stuff." Before she got a word out of her mouth, Zack was out of the car. While he ran around it to open her door, he rang the boys in the surveillance van. "Hey, Todd. You still there?"

"Whatcha need?"

"I'm two blocks north of our last location. Think I've got company. Got a black Lincoln on my six. Check it out?"

"You bet."

Mei's eyes were wide with questions when he opened her door, but he cut her off. "Humor me. We've got someone watching. Let's make it look good."

He pulled her up and out of the car. Unexpectedly, her high heels did not handle the curb very well. She fell into his arms, a nice surprise.

"You're going to have to do better than that," he whispered as he swung her onto the sidewalk, enjoying the feel and weight of her delicate body.

Mei hugged him with a trifle more affection, her hand on his arm while glancing down the street.

"No," he ordered, his index finger to her chin as he redirected her gaze toward him. "Don't look at them. Just me."

So she did, surprising him yet again. She really could be obedient.

Zing. He looked down into those mysterious dark eyes, suddenly holding Mei the way a husband would hold a wife.

Tenderly. Gently. For a fraction of a second she looked up, her eyes two dark pools of secrets he didn't know yet. Her breath caught. So much worry and pain shone in those dark pools, and something else. Trust. She'd finally found someone she could trust. Him.

Zack gulped at the revelation. All at once, it was important to untangle the hard knot at the back of her head, to feel the silk of her raven hair falling through his fingers. More than anything else, he wanted to see her smile again, to hear her really laugh. Standing there on the sidewalk of Rosslyn, Virginia, Zack just wanted Mei to be happy.

Heat radiated from the delicate fingertips on his chest. The scent of cherry blossoms washed over him like an invitation. The tiniest glimmer of hope materialized.

As she leaned in slowly, her chin tilted upward. The distance vanished between them. Her breasts pressed against his chest. Her right thigh warmed his left thigh and he was very aware of her hip. The busy street noise faded. His lips brushed hers, just asking, just wishing. So soft and willing. She relaxed against him with a sigh, her hands circling his neck. Tenderness for this woman exploded in his heart.

Zack pulled her off the ground, his lips pressed harder to hers. He hadn't planned to kiss her, but she needed to be kissed—to be loved. It felt right. Mei kissed him back, her arms tight around his neck and her feet no longer touching the sidewalk. A soft, sad sound escaped deep from within her throat. This woman needed so much more than one kiss.

Her tongue skimmed his lips, and he let her enter, another pleasant surprise that just possibly she might want him the way he was beginning to want her. The busy city fell away. One minute they were kissing, the next she was hammering his mouth, demanding more, her tongue pushing against his with rampant hunger. Their teeth collided. She laced her fingers around his ears, pulling him into her and biting his lower lip. It seemed she poured all her loneliness and pain into her kiss, like if she gave it away she could be strong again.

A ragged moan lifted out of her. He let her win, let her take what she needed. The ferocious fire of her hunger roared through him. The memories of all those other chicks in his life vanished in the heat and passion of this one real woman. At last she pulled back, panting into his still open mouth, breathless with the daring thing she'd done, her fingers clutching his collar.

Dark eyes sought his. Regret flickered. Anger, too. He prepared for a slap. It didn't come. Instead, she burrowed under his chin, breathing hard, and he let her. This fierce, mean woman was in his arms, trembling, her heart pounding against him like it belonged to a scared little girl. Her slender body hugged into him. His fingers traced the sharp edges of her spine and shoulder blades. Alex was right. Mei was starving, and not just for food.

"I like this," he whispered, his own heart pounding a noisy beat. She wasn't the only one who was scared. He'd overstepped the invisible line between agent and client, and he'd done it with the Wicked Witch of the West.

She didn't speak, and he was glad. There were no words for the tender moment. Like a happily married couple, they stood there in each other's arms. He absorbed the feeling that had sprung up between them, stroking her cheek when he pushed a stray wisp of hair behind her ear. She had delicate ears, a soft curl of skin that looked more like fine bone china beneath his rugged fingertip.

When she lifted her face, Mei searched his with wondering eyes, and he couldn't look away. Heck. He could barely breathe until she took a step back.

"There. Was that good enough, Agent Lennox? Do you think we fooled them?" She nodded sideways in the direction of the Lincoln.

She couldn't have hit harder if she'd punched him square in the solar plexus. He actually felt dizzy. He'd kissed–Hagatha.

"Let's get it over with. I have work to do." With one hand still in the center of his chest, she pushed away.

"Wow," Todd breathed in his ear. "Were you and Ms. Xing—?"

"Shut up," Zack growled.

"No, I was going to say, good plan. You sure fooled—"

"Drop it!" Zack snapped his earpiece off. He followed his *wife* in a daze, trying to catch his breath and his equilibrium, only now he had to deal with the fact that Todd and David had heard and probably seen them. The operation just kept getting better and better. He began to seriously consider a divorce in his immediate future.

Mei didn't speak as she passed through the aisles of the store, and she didn't smile. Neither did he. He couldn't, not with his heart stuck in his throat like it was. The kiss had singed a heated spike straight through to his soul. It still burned.

He watched her, though. Pretending to be happy while walking through a baby boutique was hard work for a mother with a missing child. Her fingers skimmed the rail of a pink baby bed occupied by a fluffy teddy bear. For a second, she faltered. Her lips tightened, and he wanted her back in his arms. Mean as she was, she was hurting, bleeding from a hole so deep she truly had nothing to offer the world but pain and anger.

Wordlessly, he went to her side and secured her trembling body under his arm. She could hate him; she could hurt him. He wouldn't let her fall apart. "Let's go."

"Yes," she said quietly, all her bravado drained and her energy with it.

They left the store the same way they entered, together, but very much alone. He opened the car door for her. Pretending to tie his shoelace, he scanned the street for the Lincoln. It had moved and was parked half a block ahead of them on the other side of the street.

He discreetly activated his earpiece again. "Anything?"

"The car is registered to a Mr. Robert Smith. He reported it stolen two nights ago."

"You call the police?"

"Waiting on your say so."

"Do it. Let's give this joker something to think about."

"Will do," Todd replied.

"Thanks, Todd."

"No problem. See you back at the office."

Zack rounded his car, glancing at the Lincoln. Darkly tinted windows made it impossible to see how many people were in there. Who were they watching, him or her?

"How about we grab something for lunch before we head back?" Zack asked as he pulled away from the curb and drove past the Lincoln. "I know a sushi bar if you'd like."

"Okay." Her voice was very soft in the quiet car.

He sucked in a big breath to apologize. "Hey, listen. I'm sorry, Mei. I was out of line. I got caught up in the moment, and—"

"Forget it."

"No, really. I'm sorry." He rested his hand on her arm.

She brushed him off. "Drop it."

"Where is he?"

Mother looked up from her computer screen. "Who? Alex?"

"Yes, of course I mean Mr. Stewart," Mei hissed. Agent Tao wasn't anywhere in sight. Who else would she want around this place? She glanced into the work bay with its black granite counters, polished steel trim, and leather office chairs. Even at work, these people lived better than she did.

"He had a meeting with the Interpol Director." Mother glanced at Agent Lennox. "What do you need? Can I help?"

"I need a quiet place to work," she snapped. "Is anyone in the Sit Room?"

Mother shook her head. "It's all yours."

"Do you need anything?" Agent Lennox offered.

Why was he still here? Didn't he get the hint? She'd certainly given him enough.

"I need my laptop. I left it with your boss."

"He figured you might need it." Mother lifted the laptop up to her counter. "Here it is."

"Thanks." Mei slid it over the edge and turned toward the Sit Room. She had work to do, and she needed time to think.

Time was running out. LiLi was still missing, and darn it, Agent Lennox was standing there, his eyes boring through her every defense. How did he look right through her like that? The man was annoying.

"What?" She bit his head off again. "What do you want now?"

His eyes flashed, but he stepped back just like she knew he would. Men didn't stand up to an alpha female. As kind as he'd tried to be, that's all he was, another weak, spineless—

No. She couldn't finish the rant. Nothing spinning around in her head was true, not when it came to Agent Lennox. He might not engage in verbal abuse when she taunted him, but he wasn't like Christopher at all.

She stormed off to the Sit Room and shut the door behind her. Taking the first empty chair at the table, she fired up last year's Christmas present from her boss at the car dealership. His banner year in sales had translated to a bonus for her–a MacBook Pro, and about the only friend she had left.

Her stomach hurt from eating too much, but all the western-style sushi filled with raw Alaskan salmon, cucumber, onion, and avocado tasted delicious, and having actual food in her stomach felt good for a change. Agent Lennox must have known she was hungry. He'd played her like a fool, somehow figuring out that sushi was her one culinary weakness. Unfair!

It didn't help when he ordered tempura shrimp and salmon sashimi that melted in her mouth. She was so hungry, she couldn't stop stuffing her face, but now she was ashamed. Had LiLi eaten at all today? Was she even warm?

Mei brought up the website on Attorney Richards again, but instead saw the tender look in Agent Lennox's eye when he'd kissed her. He might have initiated it, but she ended up being the one who'd all but assaulted him. She couldn't help that either. The gentleness he'd offered filled the aching hole she'd carried since Christopher had deserted her at the first hint of morning sickness. Not until Agent Lennox lifted her into his arms did her starving self take over, and like the sushi, she couldn't stop. The hungry beast within had come roaring out to devour everything in its path. Him.

Poor Agent Lennox. Poor LiLi. Poor me.

She slapped the laptop cover closed and buried her face in her arms on top of it. Agent Lennox wasn't in the room, and yet he was. Why now? Why him? It made no sense. She was on the most desperate hunt of her life. The last thing she needed was a distraction so strong, an attraction this fierce.

The door cracked open and a red-haired man peeked inside. Mei straightened and brushed her emotions off her face. "What do you want?"

"Ah, ma'am," he said politely. "I didn't mean to disturb you, but I made some fresh coffee. Would you like a cup? I can bring it to you."

"No, thanks." She shook her head, but changed her mind. "On second thought, yes. I could use some coffee."

"We've also got tea, juice, or milk." He took a step into the room. "I'd be glad to run out and get you something to eat if you're hungry."

"Coffee will be fine," she insisted.

He returned in two seconds flat with a tray filled with a big mug of coffee, creamer, sweetener, a plastic spoon and a small plate of pumpkin cookies. "Here you go," he said. "Thought you might like a snack about now."

"You didn't have to do this," she said, surprised he was thoughtful.

"This?" He raised his brows. "It's is just me being friendly. Don't think twice. I'm Todd Chandler by the way." He placed a napkin beside her cup and the cookies alongside her laptop. "I was with David in the surveillance van. 'Sides, I get hungry when I'm undercover. That was a tough thing you did today. I imagine you're starved."

"Not really. We stopped for lunch on the way back."

"You did?" Todd did have a charming smile. Mischievous green eyes smiled too. "It's good to know old man Zack remembered how to treat a lady."

She didn't respond, just sipped her black coffee and let the warmth of it soothe her rattled nerves. Agent Lennox did know how to treat a lady. That was the problem.

"He's worried about you." Todd lingered at the door. "Thought you might want to know."

Mei heard what Todd really meant to say. He'd overhead her snap at Agent Lennox, and thought he needed to run interference. That's all. That's what men did. They covered for each other.

"He'd die before he let anything happen to you. Hope you know that, too." Todd shut the door and left her alone with the very unsettling thought.

She didn't see that one coming. *Agent Lennox would die for me?*

FOURTEEN

"What are you gals up to?" Zack had to ask. Mother looked like she was in a trance after her less than friendly encounter with Mei. Ms. Xing remained hidden away in her self-imposed dungeon, the Sit Room. Just as well. He leaned back in one of Mother's many extra chairs, folded his hands behind his head, and relaxed for the first time all day.

"We're playing the game David found. Black Dragon Conquest," Mother answered without looking up. "It's sick, and I don't mean sick in a cool way. Whoever wrote the file format for the game has one disgusting, twisted mind."

Ember glanced at him. "You know how in most games you get to kill monsters and minions of the evil overlord? Well, in this game you're not the hero; you're are the minions of the beast. You hunt children. I'm at the twenty-second level. I'm rich. I've got over eight million yuan," she shrugged, "but I feel really creepy."

"No," Mother murmured. "This game's not about fun. I'm leaning toward a different approach. I'm thinking we need to stop playing and take a look behind the scenes of the game."

Ember arched a mischievous brow at Zack. "Oh, oh. That means compilers and debuggers. You might not want to hang around for this part."

Mother turned to him, a determined glint in her blue eyes. "There isn't a game on the planet I can't break."

"Hold up. Before you start disassembling and decoding, can I join you for a minute?" Todd asked. "Hi, Ember. She's got you playing, too?"

Zack caught the shy look Ember shot Todd, and the way she made room for him to pull a chair alongside hers. Hmm. Mother might be right. Something was up between these two kids.

"Boss treating you any better?" Mother asked.

Todd scowled his answer.

"That'll pass. Don't let him get to you." Zack chuckled. "He's hard on new recruits."

"Why? I'm not some FNG. I was Army, like old man Murphy. I've done my time."

Zack grunted. "Might be good if you don't keep reminding him you're a pansy-assed Ranger for one thing."

"What? You telling me to embrace the suck?" Todd grumbled. "That's all I do around this place. He looks right through me."

"Don't matter. Either way, you've got to prove yourself first. That's the way the Boss is. Until he sees you in action, you're just a wannabe on his payroll. Might as well be a fobbit."

"What are you guys talking about?" Mother demanded. "Is it more of the military speak no one else gets?"

"Just guy talk." Zack smirked. "A fobbit's a Ranger who plays it safe and never leaves his forward operating base. You know, like a rabbit too scared to come out of his hole in the ground."

Todd shook his head instead of answering.

"And FNG is, umm, just the latest new guy in the squad. It's not a compliment," Ember grinned. "You know how it is. They might all be soldiers, but each service thinks it's better than the rest."

"Cuz we are." Zack snorted. "Ask the boss. He'll tell you."

Ember thumped his bicep with the clenched point of her knuckles. Hard. "You Marines. All the same."

"And your point would be?" Zack glowered. His intimidation factor would've worked if he and Ember hadn't known each other for years. The day he worried her was long gone. True, Alex tended to hire more Marines than snipers from other services, but again, that's just the way the guy was. When it really came down to it, he was looking for certain kinds of men, their choice of military branch aside. Murphy, Harley, and Todd were Army. Ember, Navy. The only one not associated with a branch of service was Mother. And of course, Zack was a Marine through and through. A big 'Oorah' echoed in his head. Once a Marine, always a Marine. Oorah!

"Right now I just want to keep my job," Todd muttered.

"Then break this darn game," Mother said. "That'll make him take notice."

"Think I just did. Look at this." Todd pointed to the maze of tunnels Mother's video character had just entered. "Make your scary dude bump into this wall. Right here. See?"

"Why?"

"Easter eggs, Mother. I found Easter eggs hidden in the game."

Her eyes lit up. "Way cool."

"Wait. What the heck are Easter eggs?" Zack pulled a stool into Mother's workspace and joined them. He'd played a few video games in his time, but no way was he as sharp as these addicted gamers.

"You Marines wouldn't understand," Ember teased, leaning away from Zack's hefty fist aimed at her bicep. "Ouch. Don't hit me," she giggled, rubbing her arm despite the fact he'd never made contact. "Okay. I give. Easter eggs are hidden rewards. They might allow a player to jump ahead in the game, rack up points, or find clues. Stuff like that."

"But they also expose data and coding," Mother said. "Every game's got vulnerabilities. The key is knowing how to compromise and use those weaknesses so no one knows you've been inside their event decisions." She winked at Zack. "It's kinda like politics."

He had to smile. Mother was the consummate gamer, online and off.

"Yeah," Todd said. "It's fun when you're playing a fun game, but this one is just plain scary, and it's in Chinese. I can't figure some of it out."

"David can translate." Mother reached for her phone and dialed the senior agent.

Zack made room for David at the terminal. Before long, more and more agents stopped by to watch.

Mother turned to explain. "The hero in this game is named Jiāng-shī."

"Which is Chinese for zombie," David said quietly, "and zombies deal in death. The creature sucks the life force out of anyone he encounters."

"What's the matter with you?" Mother glanced over her shoulder at him "You sick or something? You're awfully quiet."

He scrubbed his face with one hand. "It's this game. It's evil."

"Maybe I can help." Todd took over Mother's joystick. "Watch this."

Zack and David leaned into the screen while Todd moved the zombie hero through one cavern after another with its basket of eleven little gingerbread-type cookies.

"What are those supposed to be?" Zack pointed at the basket.

"Children," David said tiredly. "Jiāng-shī's mission is to deliver these eleven children, more if he can acquire them while he is inside the cavern."

"Where's he taking them?"

"I still don't know," David sighed.

"Right. We haven't gotten far enough in the game. All we're doing is raking up points and winnings," Ember said.

Zack rested his chin on his fist as he watched Todd move the zombie along a stone path in a dark cave. Sometimes gold glittered along the floor or in the walls. Each time the zombie touched the gold, a display at the bottom of the screen changed.

"You guys ready?" Todd turned to his audience, his eyebrows lifted in mischief. Without waiting for an answer, he clicked on a stone wall blocking the hero's way. As it disintegrated, it revealed Chinese lettering in two very distinct columns.

"Wow," Ember exclaimed, her long slender fingers on Todd's knee. "Good job. Look what you found."

David scanned the script. "Stop. Don't move a thing. Let me read it."

Everyone paused until he pointed to the first set of letters. "These are eleven names."

"The names of the children?" Todd asked.

"Possibly. But," David straightened in his seat, "that last name is not a child's name. It says R. Richards."

"What's the other list?" Zack asked.

David peered closer. "Numeric."

"Now watch." Todd moved the zombie hero again, pushing him farther into the cavern. As Jiāng-shī advanced, he pulled a root hanging down from the ceiling. A panel creaked open and a ghost materialized, wavering in and out of focus.

"It's one of those Easter eggs I found. What's this spooky guy saying, David?" Todd turned the volume up. "It's talking in Chinese. I don't understand."

David cocked his ear toward the computer as everyone quieted to hear the ghostly incantation. "The creature is Yōu Líng, the dark soul. It sounds like he's relaying delivery instructions, but it's in code. *Four must travel to the city of stone workers. Four go to the city of the lady. Three are destined for the city of light.*

Mother gasped. "Is he talking about Paris? It's the only city of light I know."

"Then where's the city of the lady?" Todd asked.

"New York? Maybe the lady's the Statue of Liberty," Ember interjected.

Mother turned to Zack and David. "You guys ever heard of the city of stone workers?"

Zack shrugged. "Might be Egypt. Stone workers built the pyramids."

"Never mind. Watch this." Todd moved Jiāng-shī to the tunnel exit, where Todd clicked his mouse over the second square stone to the right of the arched opening.

Immediately, two gray wraiths swirled around the basket of children, chanting and buzzing. The wands in their long bony fingers emitted fiery sparks that sizzled into the heads of the gingerbread children. Childlike cries screeched above the buzzing noise of the wraiths until the sparks faded. Tendrils of orange smoke drifted over the basket. Jiāng-shī's zombie face split into a toothy grin as he bowed to the wraiths.

David pushed back from the game. "I can't watch it anymore."

His reaction sparked Zack's interest. The game just got more and more bizarre. "What are they doing to those kids?"

Todd zoomed in to enlarge the head of one of the gingerbread children. Zack cursed. A dragon tattoo had been burned into the face of each cookie child.

"And look at this." Todd was excited now. He enlarged another head. A green dragon was burned into that child's face. Another showed a red dragon. "Sick, huh?"

"Wait," Zack growled. "Go back to the list you found."

Todd did as he was told.

"Which of these names got the green dragon tat?" Zack asked.

"Heck, I don't know. Wait a second." Todd flashed back to the screen where the branding had taken place. Enlarging the screen even more, he was able to decipher Chinese characters on one of the children. Everyone turned to David.

"Li Ming," he interpreted. "It's a little girl. Her name is...Li Ming."

"Now go back to the list," Zack ordered.

"Already doing that," Todd muttered, working the joystick as fast as only a gamer knows how. Everyone leaned into the screen. Sure enough, Li Ming's name was there as well.

"Poor Li Ming is going to...where, Todd?" Mother asked.

"Wait for it." Todd worked the keyboard, adeptly matching the names on the list to the gingerbread children in the basket. By the time he was done, they knew exactly which child was going to Paris, New York, or Egypt. They also knew each child was a female.

"Wait. Something's not right," Zack muttered. "We've got three little girls with the black dragon tattoo right here in Anacostia."

"The city of stone workers doesn't mean Egypt," David murmured.

"I know! The Masons were stone workers," Mother declared with gusto. "George Washington designed D.C., remember? He was a Freemason and pretty high up in the ranks, too. He incorporated their symbols throughout the city's design when he put L'Enfant in charge."

"That's a conspiracy theory," Todd muttered. "No one believes that. It isn't true."

"Oh, yes it is," she declared.

"It's got to be D.C.," Zack said. "That means these children are coming to Richards or he's already got them. We're looking at a freaking purchase order. That's how these guys are communicating with each other. This isn't a game. It's e-Commerce. It's how they're selling children."

"Why's his name on the whole order if he's only getting four of the eleven?" Todd interrupted.

"Damn it," Zack hissed. Expletives he couldn't say in mixed company sprang to mind. The evidence was clear. "Because his business is international. We need to decipher those tattoos. I'll bet a month's pay they're like barcodes."

"You might be right," David said.

"Ah, guys." Todd had continued to work through the game. "I still need to know what the witch with the wand was chanting."

"I forgot. Play it again," David said tiredly. "Sorry."

Todd clicked the second square stone to the arched exit again. The wraiths repeated the chant.

David paled. "I don't know what it means, but she said, *'Even if you live, you'll die'*."

"Them poor little babies are all cursed," Mother whispered.

"Like hell." Zack stood so quickly he knocked his chair over. He stabbed the computer screen with a condemning finger. "These girls aren't cursed. He is. It's Richards who's cursed, and every person who's working for him."

And I'm the one who's going to put him down.

FIFTEEN

The following morning, Mr. Quentin Burns and his wife, Amelia, were back at the attorney's office with the prerequisite fee.

"Is that the money?" Mrs. Bradford asked when she spied the hefty aluminum briefcase.

"Yes, ma'am." Zack lifted it to hand it over but she declined, shaking her head with her lips pursed in that dried prune way she had.

"I don't want to touch it, but I do need to see it. Please set it on my desk."

That was an odd request, but Zack did as he was told. She peered down her nose at the stacks of one hundred dollar bills when he opened the case. "You call those small bills?"

"They are to me," he replied with his best fake-millionaire nonchalance. After the revelations of the video game, he was in it to win it. Cold hard cash didn't get turned down too often. He was willing to bet it wouldn't today, either. "What'd you expect? Twenties?"

Ms. Bradford sniffed like she was offended by the filthy lucre. "Fine. Keep it. Mr. Richards will see you now."

She ushered them into the attorney's office. Reginald Richards motioned them to sit in the chairs in front of his desk while he finished a telephone conversation. When he hung up, he leaned his elbows onto his desk, his lip curled as he ran his gaze over them both.

"Mr. and Mrs. Burns, or whatever your names are, you say you're looking to buy a little girl. That right?" Attorney Richards was used to dealing in human commodities. He didn't bother with the euphemism of adoption. A dark haired, olive skinned man, Zack pegged him about five ten, maybe two-hundred-fifty pounds. His hands were rough and calloused, not the hands of a pencil-pushing lawyer at all, and his face was just as rough. A scar on his forehead gave the appearance of a perpetually raised eyebrow. The man had jowls. He looked more like a nineteen-fifties era gangster than a lawyer.

"It's Quentin Burns, Mr. Richards. And this is my wife of eleven years, Amelia—"

"I don't care what your names are." Richards waved the explanation away. "Let's get straight to the point. Your background checks came back clean. Marge says you got the dough. That's all I care about. Most people lie about their names anyway, so it don't matter one way or the other. What matters is you two understand what I'm going to tell you next."

Mei reached for Zack's hand and he squeezed it, surprised she wanted any contact with him. The woman drove him crazy, cold one moment, hot the next.

"You wrote down here that you want a little girl around six years old." He glanced at the form they'd filled out the day before. "A Chink. That right?"

You sonofabitch. Zack bristled at the derogatory slur. "I'd appreciate if—"

"Yeah, whatever." Richards tossed a card across the desk. "Take this. It's a couple foster homes you can check out. Take your pick of the litter, but I want you to know what you're doing's illegal. Buying babies and children is against the law. Make damned sure you don't go blabbing where you got her."

"Yes." Zack answered simultaneously with Mei. She was wound so tight, her nervousness vibrated straight up his arm.

"I gotta be honest with ya. I really do this kinda stuff to save them little girls' lives, ya know." Richards waxed noble. "They got no chance of a decent life over there. You ever seen one of them orphanages in China? All they want is sons, so the baby girls gotta go somewhere. I'm here to tell ya, them places are a stinking mess. Everyone knows these kids are better off over here, no matter how they end up."

"What about the adoption papers?" Zack asked. His fist curled. He needed to get Mei out of here before he decked the lying buffoon. The image of eleven gingerbread children remained stuck in the back of his mind. Richards needed to be branded, and Zack was the man for the job.

"You get the papers when you picks the kid. You'll come back here, and we'll finish the deal. You got a problem with that?"

Zack shook his head. "No, sir, but I want to make sure—"

"I don't care what you want. Get out of here. I've got bigger problems than a couple rich snobs who can't even make a kid." With that snicker, he waved them to get out of his office.

As if on cue, Ms. Bradford re-entered the room and escorted them back to her desk. Just in time, too. One more minute of listening to the evil man, and Zack would've wreaked some vengeance for Chai all over Richards' ugly face. He wanted to.

Mei held tightly to his hand, and this time he didn't just press his other hand to the small of her back. He pulled her close, she was trembling so hard. They'd just come face to face with one of the most despicable men he'd ever met.

"Please take a seat." Ms. Bradford motioned toward the chairs next to her desk. "Did he give you the addresses?"

Zack slanted the card at her. "Got 'em."

"Just checking. He starts rambling about those poor little girls and he forgets sometimes. Reggie really is a good man."

"And pigs fly, too," Todd muttered in Zack's ear.

Not now, Todd. I'm already mad enough for the two of us.

"If you don't find what you're looking for at either of those homes tomorrow, let me know. We don't keep all the available children in one place. Security, you know."

"Tomorrow?" Mei's voice creaked. "We can't go until tomorrow?"

Zack tightened his grip on her.

"Certainly not," the annoying secretary replied.

"Why not?" he asked. "We've done everything you've asked, and you expect us to wait another day?"

"Tsk, tsk, tsk." Ms. Bradford peered down her nose through her glasses at her computer screen, her fingers flying over her keyboard. "These things take time. I can hook you up with other options if you don't want to wait, but if you give us a day, we can make sure you have more of a selection. Your choice. What shall it be?" She paused, her quick fingers suspended over her keyboard.

The trap was set. Zack had no choice. Of course he and Mei needed to view as many children as possible.

"I guess we'll wait until tomorrow then, won't we?" He could not restrain his sarcasm.

"I'll give you the address for a third home since you're so eager." She leveled a volley of sarcasm right back at him. Her fingers hit the keyboard. She acted like she was hooking them up with a used car instead of a child. Someone needed to knock her on her ass, too.

Zack offered the briefcase again.

"Not today." Her expression could not have been sweeter. "I only needed to see it. You'll pay when you take possession. That way, you're as guilty as we are."

"You're cold."

Mei shivered at Agent Lennox's words, but it wasn't from the chilly weather. The gray clouds scudding across the sky were nothing compared to the desolation in her soul. Another day without LiLi was more than she could handle.

The drive back to the safe house had been quiet, the shock of being in the presence of a truly evil man more than she'd anticipated. Attorney Richards hadn't even tried to hide what he was doing. The man dealt in human flesh, as if children were nothing. Her skin crawled thinking about him, yet he'd only done it because he assumed he was talking with someone as low as he was. Her skin crawled even more. She'd sunk to his level.

"I'll turn on the gas log," Agent Lennox offered, already on his way across the room to the fireplace.

Standing frozen inside the two story foyer, she couldn't handle the safe house either. The plush lifestyle it represented irked her to her core. The vaulted ceilings, fine moldings, and huge brick fireplace reminded her she was living the life of a queen. LiLi was not.

Everything had been different last night. Agent Lennox avoided her, and she didn't blame him. After their unexpected kiss on the street, he'd become an easy target, always too close and kind for his own good. She knew she was hard on him. The kiss had been a mistake. She never should have let him get inside her defenses. He was trouble, a womanizer, a pretty boy, but so gentle in the way he'd held her. One minute she intended the kiss as nothing but subterfuge, the next, it seemed she could not stop. His touch had ignited a ravenous hunger and a wildfire. All her defenses melted. The only way back was to push and shove. So she did.

Poor Agent Lennox. After one particularly nasty barb about him being nothing but a spoiled rich kid, he'd retreated to the couch and television while she locked herself in one of the four bedrooms. It seemed a good arrangement–then.

Mei stood frozen in the doorway, unable to enter and unable to leave. The longer she stood, the more she wanted to run. There seemed no way to hurry the drawn-out process of the undercover operation along.

Agent Lennox turned to her, waiting for what, she didn't know. He had a fire blazing. The man had the patience of a saint, but then, he should. He had to be getting paid enough to watch over her. The oriental gong of his cell phone jolted her out of her very depressing dilemma of whether to leave or stay.

"What's up?" he answered after checking his caller ID. He stilled, listening as he watched her. His brows furrowed, and Mei's heart stopped. It had to be bad news. She could tell.

"Who's that?" His piercing look drew her into the room. "You're kidding? Under the same bridge?"

She walked to the fireplace, her heart on the verge of panic. Which same bridge? The Eleventh Street Bridge? The Pennsylvania Avenue Bridge?

"How?" His dark eyes registered no emotion, but something cold glittered there. Whoever he had on the other line, they were talking about death. Someone had died. Who? LiLi?

"Guess that takes care of that." He paused. "Okay."

When he stiffened, Mei clutched his wrist. "What's going on?"

He held up his index finger for her to be quiet.

"Tell me," she demanded.

His features softened. Her blood pressure spiked. *It's LiLi. They found her.*

"Where?" he said quietly. "Okay. Got it. Right. We're on our way."

She whirled around, intending to go right back out the door. They'd found her daughter. That's what Agent Lennox was talking about. She had to leave, but he grabbed her wrist before she got too far away, his expression hard as granite while he continued the conversation.

"That isn't going to be easy," he muttered, his eyes sharp and focused on her. He was quiet another moment, before he said, "Got it. Thanks, David."

"Tell me," she ordered the moment the call ended. "What did Agent Tao tell you? Who died?"

Agent Lennox stowed his cell phone in his pants pocket before he spoke. "They found another little girl, Mei. David will call with the details as soon as he gets to the hospital."

"How old?" All her worst fears.

"Around six."

"Where is she now?"

"Children's National Medical Center."

"I'm going." She pulled away, her heart in her throat.

"No." Somehow, Agent Lennox was in front of her, blocking the door. "We're going to stay on task and—"

"No, we're not. I don't care if you go with me or not. I'm going." She pulled out all of her nastiest skills. "I have to know. Get out of my way."

"No. We stay." He didn't move, just stood there with his hands palm forward like he was trying to capture a frightened animal. "By the time we get across town, David will be at the hospital. He'll call. Then we'll know for sure. Besides, if we screw the mission, we'll never get back inside Richards' office. We need to stay the course."

"I can't. I...I...can't. Get out of my way." The man was stupid to think he could stop her. Nothing could. Weeks of fury propelled her into him, punching, scratching, and kicking. He had to get out of her way. Now!

She never got a lick in. He had her wrists neatly trapped at the first strike.

"We stay." He never raised his voice, just pulled her against his chest until she had no choice but to look up at him. "You've got to trust me. David will call. Trust him. For hell's sake, trust someone."

"No!" she spat. "I don't need men. I don't need—"

"You need me!" he bellowed. "God, Mei, stop fighting me."

"But I can't. What if...?" She bit the words off before they saw the light of day. *What if it is LiLi? What if...?*

Fear suffocated her. Time had run out. It was bound to happen. The odds were always against her. This time it was her daughter. She'd have to go to the morgue again. Mei twisted away, trying with all her pitiful strength to best the man who held her fast.

"I don't need anyone!" she shrieked, so close she could've bit him. "Let me go!"

Men hated screaming, bullying women. Agent Lennox needed to hate her enough to let go. He flinched, but instead of releasing her, he wrapped her up in his arms, burying her head beneath his chin, his hot breath on the back of her neck.

"No, Mei. No. Hear me for once. Just listen."

In one split second her resolve melted. Wrenching sobs broke out of her in painful, ripping spasms that felt like they were tearing her apart. "I can't. I've worked too hard, and she's so little."

"It's not her," he whispered. "Trust me, Mei. It's not LiLi."

"You don't know that," she groaned. "Let me go. Let me see if—"

"No. I'm not letting you go." His arms wrapped her tightly, her head still against his chest. "We stay. We wait for David. That way our cover's still intact. He'll call. You'll see. Then we'll bring Richards down along with every other bastard who's in this with him."

In one fell swoop, he lifted her feet off the floor and carried her to the couch in front of the fireplace. Agent

Lennox settled her onto his lap, encircling her inside the steel bands of his arms from which there was no escape. She'd landed facing away from him, his head pressed tight to the back of hers. Orange flames licked the fake fire log, but all she saw was LiLi's blue eyes staring back. The tears she'd held back burst forth, drenching her face and the sleeve of his dress shirt.

"I want my baby," she sobbed.

"You're not alone," he whispered hoarsely, smoothing one of those big hands over her head and shoulder like he needed to calm her. With an irritated yank, he pulled the tie from his neck and tossed it away, nestling her deeper into the crook of his arm. "I wish I could get that through your hard head."

She cried. All she had was her hard head, as he'd just put it, along with a police scanner, a laptop, and an all city bus pass. That's all that had gotten her this far, and now she'd failed. It would be Agent Tao verifying her baby's body. It would be....

"Is she dead?" she asked, unable to look Agent Lennox in the eye. "Is the little girl—" She choked. Saying it once was awful enough.

"No." He smoothed a gentling hand down her spine and up again to rest between her shoulder blades. "She's alive. The Coast Guard put extra patrols on the river in that section of Anacostia. They got to her in time. Believe it or not, they're on your side. Hell. Everyone is."

"Who's doing this?" she whined. "How could anyone hurt babies?"

The pain eked out in sobs she could no longer restrain. Only his arms kept her from falling apart and she needed him now, needed the smell of leather and sandalwood in her nose to keep the other smell at bay, the odor of the antiseptic morgue and that other mother's dead child. The memory twisted her insides. There'd been no joy in her life for too many days. Even the breaks in the case were tragic. The hope that LiLi still lived seemed to rely on other children dying. The awful paradox suffocated her.

"I just want her back." She pressed her face into his bicep, pulling more of his smell into her soul, trying with all her heart to wrap herself so deep she could finally feel again. *Save me, Agent Lennox. Please, please save me, too.*

"We're going to find her." The chords of her only lifeline rumbled deep in his chest and against her ear. She clung to him for all she was worth. "I promise. When we do, we'll save all those other little girls, too."

Another reality crept onto the couch with them. Mei heard it beneath her ear. She felt it in the puffs of heated breath against her neck. It trickled wet and warm where he rested his chin. He was crying, too. The mantra she'd clung to for so long seemed weak and foolish. Maybe she did need this man. Just this one.

SIXTEEN

Zack held Mei gently at first, and then as tight as he dared. As harsh as she came across, there was a fragile strength to this woman that spoke to the warrior in him. For the second time in as many days, she'd stirred the deepest chambers of his heart. He'd had serious girlfriends before, but none like Mei. Her mother's anguish resonated with him, awakening feelings he'd not felt before.

He wiped his face. She didn't need to know what a sap he was. The lovely scent of cherry blossom filled his nose, oddly comforting in the middle of the bleak ending to another fruitless day.

These were the toughest times in war, when imminent battle was delayed and the wrecking ball of testosterone-driven rage was asked to hold and wait. Stand down. Maybe tomorrow. Maybe not. Soldiers grew antsy. Tempers flared. All the pent-up dread and fearful expectations had to go somewhere. He used to pump his highest numbers during down times like that, if only to vent the energy he could not expend against the enemy. It seemed to help. Too bad this wasn't then.

All he could do was hold her and hope it was enough. The visit to Richards' office had to have been excruciatingly difficult for Mei. Picking her up and trapping her on his lap was the only thing he could think of to break through the hard wall she seemed intent on maintaining. Oddly, she'd leaned into his arm, content to let him hold her but not willing to face him. Her cheek rested against his bicep instead of his chest. He understood.

"I heard you and Agent Tao," she said tiredly. "Something else is going on, isn't it?"

"Yes. The police found another body. A man was killed tonight under the Eleventh Street Bridge."

"Is he part of this?"

She didn't jump up and run like he'd half expected. "We think so. His name was Tony Brown. He worked for ATF Director, Kevin Carducci."

"Who killed him?" Her body softened against him.

"We don't know yet, but given the location, it might be the same people who dumped these little girls."

"What's ATF?"

"Alcohol, Tobacco, and Firearms." Her question surprised him. She had fake ID badges for every other federal agency. Why not the one Carducci directed? It struck him as an odd piece of coincidence or sheer, damned luck. Suddenly, he was glad she'd missed that particular one. She might not be here in his arms now. She might be laying under some bridge like Tony Brown.

"Oh." She sighed again, her body tucked into his arm like she belonged there. The fire was warm. Zack stretched his legs and relaxed his grip. She wasn't going anywhere. They might as well be comfortable. Tomorrow was shaping up to be a heck of a day.

The feel of her slender figure tucked against his stirred feelings he'd struggled with for days. She was an exotic beauty when she let her guard down. With her dark eyes against creamy golden skin, everything about her was elegant and rich. Not rich in the ways of the world, but in qualities of devotion, perseverance, and fortitude. She had an inner strength that defied the world. Her fierce love for her daughter touched him to his core. For the first time in his life, he could relate. Because of Chai Yenn, he understood.

She shifted in his arms, a quiet murmur on her upturned lips. Tender, soft lips. Close and warm, her cherry blossom fragrance tantalized and teased. With the pleasant pain of her body against his, Zack wanted her in every sense of the word: in his arms, in his bed, and in his life. But not this way. He quelled the impulse to cover her sleeping mouth with his. Now was not the time. Surprised at the depth of his feelings, he tucked a strand of loose hair behind her ear and placed a soft kiss on her forehead instead of her lips.

Reality stole his breath. *I think I'm falling in love.*

Denial came fast and hard. *Oh, hell no.*

Just as quickly, another emotion surfaced, an intense protective instinct to hold on tighter. This woman was different, his feelings for her uncharacteristically passionate, so why had his heart suddenly pounded? Why was his mouth dry? Best question of all, why had he ever kissed her in the first place? The pleasant taste of her lingered. It created a craving that never left his mouth. He pressed his lips to her forehead again and closed his eyes. *God, maybe it is love.*

A familiar oriental gong vibrated in his pocket, jerking him out of the enlightening reverie.

"Talk to me," he whispered into his cell.

"It's not Mei's daughter," David answered promptly.

Zack let out the deep breath he hadn't known he was holding. "Good to know. I'll tell her."

"Claire was at the hospital. She's having a hard time."

"Aren't we all?" he asked as Mei stirred in his arms, her breathing slow and steady. "How bad is this little girl?"

"She's in intensive care. Someone spotted her from a tour boat. They're the ones who pulled her out of the river. A nurse happened to be on board, so she started CPR. By the time the police got there, the girl was breathing on her own. How's Mei?"

The thought of another baby girl hurt and abused like sweet little Chai and Zhen sickened Zack. He looked into the sleeping face of his charge. Even asleep, she looked angry. Her forehead crinkled into a small V between her brows, and her lips were thin and tight. He smoothed his palm over her arm, wishing he could do more.

"She's sleeping," he said. "It's been a tough morning."

If they were lucky, they'd find LiLi today. If not—

He pushed the thought from his head. All Zack had to do was infiltrate the foster home and let the Tattle Tales he intended to plant do the rest of the job. The whole façade seemed futile, but they had no other leads. With the trail a month old by the time Mei's plight was made known to the local authorities, there wasn't much else to go on.

An AMBER Alert now broadcast regularly. Authentic police detectives had interviewed Mei, and The TEAM's mission had become twofold–find LiLi, and bring the perverse business down at all cost.

Mei seemed to take it well when he told her David's heartbreaking news, but then she'd broken down again. The rest of their evening turned into a roller coaster with Mei calm one minute, tearful the next. There was no joy to be had when another child lay fighting for her life in the hospital, only gratitude it wasn't LiLi.

"Are you sure you can do this?" Mei eyed him as he shifted his car into park. "I mean, you're not a father. You've never had a child."

"No problem," he replied. It was just a house full of kids. How tough could it be? "You ready?" He hurried to help her out of the car, cocking his elbow for her to take.

"Yes." She linked her hand at the crook of his elbow. She was different today. Maybe it was because they were going to meet some of the girls, or maybe because she'd gotten a good night's sleep. He didn't know why. It just felt good not being a target for a change.

"Comm check." David's calm voice sounded in his earpiece.

"Loud and clear," Zack responded as he closed her door and locked his car. This was an easy day. He glanced at the stern yet pretty woman at his side, planning where to take her to lunch afterward. If nothing else, Mei needed food to sustain her temper. "We're going in."

"Copy that."

Apprehension first entered his mind when he spotted security bars on the windows and painted basement window glass. He relayed the observation to his buddies in the van and rolled his shoulders to feel the weight of the holstered firearms at his sides. For now, those pistols were hidden beneath his jacket. It never hurt to be prepared.

"No alarm system in view. Hold on a second. Let me activate the Interceptor." He reached into his pants pocket and hit the switch on another of Mother's inventions; a device no bigger than his key fob which could detect any type of detection system on the premises that might pick up on or interfere with his earpiece and comm link. It was a spy versus spy contraption, no more amazing to Zack than the woman who'd come up with it. Why Mother didn't go into business for herself and make a billion off her techie inventions was a puzzle he could not solve. Maybe she thrived on the abuse from Alex, or maybe it was the abuse she gave him. Who knew?

"Take it slow," David advised.

There wasn't a blade of grass outside the house. An eight-foot high wooden fence concealed the backyard, allowing no visibility. Any other time, the scenario would have felt like a trap. The hair stood up on the back of his neck. It was a trap– for all those children.

"No indication children live here," Zack relayed to David. "No toys in the yard. No trikes. No swing sets. Nothing."

"They don't let them outside to play."

"They don't want the girls to run away." Mei hugged into his bicep.

He scanned the bleak industrial neighborhood where the lone house stood. It didn't offer much in the way of the big friendly places he'd grown up in, where kids called everyone's parents Mom and Pop. It didn't offer much at all.

They climbed the five concrete steps to the porch and knocked on the door. The planks on the porch were weathered and split. Chipped gray paint covered everything.

"First Tattle Tale in place," Zack said as he pressed the device above the hole where a doorbell had been. Tattle Tales were another of Mother's genius inventions. Wireless and nearly invisible to the human eye, they resembled common everyday household items: the head of a tack, a vinyl bumper pad one might use to muffle a cabinet door, even a speck of plaster. But the video and audio feed they provided was clear as a bell. Crystal clear.

"Receiving," David confirmed.

An older Chinese woman jerked the door open, startling Mei. Zack pulled her under his arm.

"You Burns?" the woman snapped, a lighted cigarette dangling off her lip.

"Yes, ma'am. Quentin and Amelia Burns. We're here to—"

"I know why you here. Me Jun."

"Her name means, 'to be truthful'." David supplied a useless piece of trivia that Zack instantly filed away for a later laugh. This woman had nothing to do with the truth.

Jun opened the door and waved them into the dark interior of the home, a hallway that opened into a room to the right and another hallway straight ahead. Before he moved, Zack pressed another Tattle Tale to the wall beside the front doorjamb, giving David his first view of the interior. The devices were simple to install, no tougher than touching the door with his fingertip.

"Receiving second feed," he acknowledged the transmission.

An older man waited at the junction of the halls, his arms thick and his clothes baggy. Zack angled Mei so she walked on his other side, away from the stranger. Narrow halls made for perfect ambushes. Not today. Another Tattle Tale went active.

"Third," David said, as calmly as ever.

Jun directed Zack and Mei into an empty room with a sliding glass door on the opposite wall. "Sit. You wait here," she barked as she left, shutting the door behind her.

Zack went to the glass, wishing he could shield Mei from whatever was on the other side. He couldn't. He wasn't prepared himself.

"Looking at maybe fifty Chinese females, all under the age of ten, maybe younger," he relayed to his buddies in the surveillance van as he secured the fourth video/listening device to the window frame. Dozens of girls crowded the expansive room; some playing quietly, and others chatting. The child sitting alone beneath the window caught his eye. She sat with her legs curled beneath her, rocking back and forth, her arms wrapped tightly around herself.

The room was Chai multiplied. The lack of smiles, the sea of orange dresses, and the bareness of the gym-like room took his breath. No adults supervised the playtime, if that's what it was. There seemed to be no need. The girls were oddly calm and orderly, not like any kids he'd grown up with.

"Any signs of abuse?" David asked.

"Other than the fact they're here?" Zack asked, searching for signs of sickness and physical assault. "Nothing obvious," he rasped. "God, David. You should see this."

"I do," he answered somberly.

"She doesn't look well, does she?" Mei watched the girl beneath the window. "They're all so thin. I don't see LiLi."

"Don't get your hopes up," he reminded her, his arm around her again. "She might not be here."

The door behind them opened. Jun barked at several girls as they scurried inside. Their faces were expressionless and almost resolute, too mature for their tender ages. Like little orange soldiers, they lined up against the wall and turned to face Zack and Mei without a word. He activated Tale number five to document what was happening inside the room. Stark reality dawned on him. He might not have brought enough Tattle Tales.

"These girls four year to seven year. They good. Strong." Jun lit up another cigarette. "You like?"

"Hey there." Zack offered his hand to the first little girl. "How—"

"You no touch! You no talk!" Jun screeched, the cigarette bobbing on her lip. "These girls no talk, so you no talk."

Zack shrugged. Fine. Whatever. He wasn't here to make trouble, but what a stupid rule. "How are we supposed to get to know them if we can't talk to them?" he asked.

"You buy first." Her crabby face wrinkled like she was trying to intimidate Zack.

Give me a break. He stared her down. This was a cold-hearted madam, pure and simple, a pig of an older woman who sold little girl flesh to the highest bidder. A troll by any other name.

"You want?" She jerked her head toward the girls, her palm held open. "You pay?"

He shook his head. "No, ma'am. I—"

"Then you want see babies now?" she screeched again, impatient and rude.

"Yes," Mei spoke up, preventing Zack from saying what had sprung to the tip of his tongue.

The older woman snapped at the girls. They left as quickly and as quietly as they'd entered.

He leaned into Mei's ear. "What'd she say?"

"She told them to go away." Mei's voice sounded firm, but he saw the tremble. "No one wants ugly dogs."

"Are you two okay?" David asked kindly. It had to be hard for him, too.

Zack couldn't speak with Jun nearby. He tapped his earpiece to signal affirmative.

"You come. Now. You come." Jun screeched from the hall, her hand on her hip and a glare in her eye.

Zack tucked Mei under his arm, stepping between her and their obnoxious guide while his mind worked the gaping flaw in the logistics of this illegal trade. How had all those uber-elitist couples been introduced to the children they'd adopted? There had to have been an agent involved, someone who'd circumvented the very distasteful selection process. Like a lawyer? Yeah. That had to be how they facilitated the transfer of ownership, one shark to another.

SEVENTEEN

The nightmare continued.

Jun waved Zack and Mei to another set of doors. The moment she opened them, a wave of uncleanliness assaulted his nose, the odor of too many unchanged diapers and vomit. Oddly, no children cried from within. No coos or giggles either.

Mei grimaced and covered her nose with the back of her hand as she followed Jun into a long narrow room. Five baby beds lined one wall; four playpens lined the opposite wall. There were no windows. The aisle in the middle of the room accommodated one changing table, a metal shelf of diapers, clothing and other baby supplies. Each bed held two infants, separated by a wooden board placed widthwise. The playpens contained two or three toddler-sized little girls, sitting or standing. Dozens of eyes turned to the sound of adults at the door.

Zack froze at the doorway, taking in the sight. He meant to position another Tattle Tale, but his heart failed. The room looked more like a kennel, a pound, where children were penned like animals. All those little girls' eyes were pairs of almond shaped lasers to his soul. Yes, the cages were baby beds and playpens, but the sheer magnitude stole his breath. This was the nursery?

"Send me a feed," David reminded him.

Mei stood waiting, her face ashen. "Come," she said softly, her hand reaching for him.

Zack pressed the Tattle Tale to the doorframe before he stepped into the room. David's soft gasp in his ear was the only confirmation he heard that the video device was sending. His lungs seemed incapable of pulling in air. Too many babies watched him. He clutched Mei's fingers, pulling her arm into his as together they moved from playpen to playpen and bed to bed, looking into the face of every girl.

These little ones were as serious and unsmiling as the older girls. Each had the same short haircut and the same mirthless eyes staring back. One little girl stood at the side of her playpen, her thumb in her mouth and drool on her chin. The second he looked at her, she lifted her arms to be picked up. He couldn't resist. Innocently, Zack reached out to tousle her hair.

"You no touch." Jun wagged her bony finger at him from where she stood at the door. "No touch. No talk."

And he'd had enough. A man can only be bullied for so long, and he'd had a gut full.

"What if I want this one?" He picked up the little gal with the upstretched arms, the one reaching for him, and seated her tiny butt on his forearm. She was a delicate little thing, maybe one and a half years old, with the saddest eyes. He only wanted to put a smile on her all too serious baby face. That's how he was made, to give women what they wanted no matter how old they were.

Jun sputtered.

The fragile little lady on his arm looked up at him. Instinctively, he cupped her head. She fit so easily in the palm of his hand. Two pouty lips puckered into the saddest smile as she laid her head against his chest. The flutter of her heartbeat against his melted him. The baby looked up at him, and he fell into her eyes. The universe shifted. A tiny baby sigh escaped her lips, and his big tough, ex-Marine heart fell a thousand feet.

David was saying something in his ear, but all he could see was Mei looking at him with sudden tenderness and mouthing the word, *'No'*.

It was too late. He'd been smitten by the power of love at first sight and smitten hard. Somehow, when he'd chosen her, the baby had also picked him.

Jun's beady eyes lit up. "You like? You take? Good. Good."

Here he was, a highly trained soldier–a sniper. He'd been through combat. He'd seen orphans and motherless children before. Hell, the world was full of them, but until this moment they'd all moved around him like a human sea he wasn't really part of. They were nameless. Not his problem. Medics treated them. He might toss handfuls of candy, but for the most part, a sniper's life was lonely. He'd lived a remote life that facilitated his mission.

But standing there in a stench-filled room with a fragile life in the same hands that had squeezed off death-dealing rounds all over the world, Zack couldn't breathe, much less think. A warm feeling for which he had no resistance flooded his body from head to toe, taking his common sense with it. Something rare and wonderful had just happened. He couldn't pretend it hadn't.

Mei came right away to him and tried to pull the little girl out of his arms.

"Don't." He turned away from her, maintaining careful hold on his baby. "This is the one...I want."

"No." Mei elbowed him, her determination in high gear. "We must see them all."

"But you don't understand." He heard his mouth working. For some reason his brain was no longer attached to it.

"Remember why we are here?" she hissed, her eyes as hard and cold as Jun's.

Zack stared. Oh, hell. He was an idiot. Plain and simple. He'd let his emotion get the best of him–again. They were not here to rescue or select. Not yet. Not today. His brain had slipped a gear, popped a clutch.

Reality hit him hard when she eased the child from his grasp and replaced her in the filthy playpen. Mei knew how to hold a baby. He blinked hard, looking down on the little girl again. She'd scrambled back to the side of the playpen and pulled herself up, her fingers clutching the netting until she stood again, her eyes glistening with *'Please take me home. Don't leave me'.*

He gulped, reaching for the baby girl again.

"No." Mei was not so gentle this time. She dug her nails into the back of his arm, pulling him away.

"Not yet," he growled, twisting out of her grasp. "I can't leave her."

"Yes, Agent Lennox, you can." Mei jerked him again, forcing him to look down at her.

Zack looked down at the wolverine on his arm. Man, she had mean eyes, she was right. They were on a mission to find her daughter. That's all. Just LiLi.

"We are through here." Mei hissed a rapid string of scolding Chinese at Jun.

The older woman waved her hand, pointing to the front door. "Go then. No baby for you. Who care? Go." She blew a puff of cigarette smoke at them. "You two very stupid."

Mei's fingers pinched all the way through his leather coat as she pushed him away.

"No," he groaned.

"Yes," she countered quickly.

"I can't just—"

"You will." Mei's whispered command cut through the daze.

Zack steeled himself. *She's right. What's wrong with me? I'm on a mission. I can't screw this op, too.*

His feet moved. Something annoying kept buzzing in his ear. He walked out the door, his heart pounding painfully hard as he dutifully resumed the husbandly role of a childless rich couple. Jun slammed the door behind them, muttering about stupid Americans. He walked down the five concrete steps in a daze and held the car door for Mei like a good husband should. He turned the ignition and started the ride he loved, but something was wrong. It didn't shine like it used to. He got behind the steering wheel and drove down the road. The engine didn't purr anymore either. No joy eased up from the throttle to his palm. The gearshift felt cold. The whole damned car felt hollow. Empty.

After two blocks, the buzzing in his ear was the last straw. He jerked the elegantly designed vehicle to the curb while he pummeled the steering wheel, dash, and anything within reach. When that wasn't enough, he threw himself out of the car. The sight of his sleek machine poured more fuel on his already roaring fire of disgust. Zack hauled back and hit the pearl black beauty. Pacing back and forth, his frustration escalated. He kicked the side panel because he knew kicking the tire would only break his foot. Nothing helped. He raked his fingernails over his head, full of self-loathing that knew no bounds. The gentle weight of that child still rested against him, her fragile head against his heart. A mighty groan rose within, one he could not allow to spill out. All he had was this stinking car!

At last, Mei's voice broke through the rage. "Agent Lennox. No. Please stop."

He stilled, taut in the chilly November morning, heaving great breaths that didn't give any relief. The muscles in his arms twitched. It was hard not to strike her, too.

What have I done? Why didn't I take that baby out of there? I could have.

The bitter word dug at him. *Coward.*

"I have to go back."

"No. It's not why we went there. We're on a mission." She threw the word at him like it meant something, clutching his elbow like he might fall. "Can you drive?" she asked.

He glared down at her, nothing but anger ready to spew. Instead, he growled, "Yeah. I can drive."

She held his door while he took the wheel. That was odd, her holding his door. The world had turned upside down. Nothing felt right. He turned the ignition, his head full of unvented anger. The starter growled back at him. The damned car was still running. Mei hurried around to her side, and once again, they were ready to go. Too late the thunder in his head stilled and he knew what the buzzing sound was.

"Zack, listen to me." David's panicked voice registered deep inside his ear canal. "Can you hear me?"

"Not now." He peeled the earpiece out of his ear and tossed it to the floor, fogging the window in front of him with his heavy breath. Shit. David and Todd had heard everything. Not only heard, but seen. He screwed the op. Soon Alex would know. It didn't matter. Everywhere he looked, sad dark baby eyes stared back at him. The memory of that orphaned feminine soul still fluttered against his strong male heart, a heart that could have saved her.

He punched the steering wheel again.

"Agent Lennox is very angry."

"I heard," Agent Tao answered quietly. "What can I do?"

"He wants to be alone." Mei peered out the back window of the safe house. She'd called Agent Tao the moment Agent Lennox tossed his leather jacket to the floor and headed to the backyard. The two pistols holstered beneath his arms made her very nervous, given the explosive rage she'd witnessed. He sat on the picnic table, his feet on the bench and his hands on his knees. His back was to the house and his face to the six-foot high fence surrounding the yard.

"His car is full of dents," she murmured.

"He punched it? I was afraid of that."

"You heard everything?"

"Yes."

"He won't like it."

Agent Tao sighed. "He picked up one of the babies."

"Yes," she whispered. Agent Lennox couldn't hear her, but she felt deceitful talking about him behind his back. "The home is a very terrible place. We must find all of these foster homes are, and the police need to raid them."

"We're working on it. Alex is already in touch with the FBI, Interpol, and local authorities."

Agent Lennox stood, his hands to his hips, staring over the fence. He slipped the holster off his shoulders. After he folded the belt and set the weapons on the table, he dropped to his hands and knees, pushed his feet behind him and began doing push-ups. Mei counted ten. Still he pumped, his palms pressed to the concrete patio. Up. Down. Faster and faster.

"I need to fix something to eat," she said. "He will be very hungry."

"He won't be hungry," Agent Tao said. "If he comes up swinging, call me. But if he assumes the hero pose, I think he will be okay."

"The what?" Mei asked. "The hero pose? What is that?"

"A yoga position," he explained. "Zack will look like he is kneeling, sitting back on his thighs. If his palms are open and facing up, it means he's relinquishing his bad energy to the universe. He is seeking balance to cope with the anger he feels."

Mei glanced at Agent Lennox. She'd lost count of how many push-ups he'd done. He'd slowed. The push-ups took longer. Sweat dampened his back and glistened off his head and neck. It looked more like he was seeking to kill himself than to find balance.

"Let me know if I should come over," Agent Tao said.

"I will. Thank you."

She hung up, her eyes glued to the angry man outside the window. At last, Agent Lennox stopped at the highest point of a push-up, his arms outstretched, his full weight supported on fisted bleeding hands. Beads of sweat dripped off his brow, nose, and chin to the concrete beneath his face.

Mei winced. The position had to be extremely painful on the hands he'd just used to batter his car. Blood stained the concrete patio beneath his fists. Still he held. She couldn't take her eyes off him.

At last he sank to a prone position, his nose pressed to the ground, his elbows cocked at his sides to pump again. He didn't. Very slowly, he lifted to his hands and knees. Sitting back on his haunches, he faced the fence. Just as Agent Tao had predicted, Agent Lennox assumed the hero position.

Mei ran to the refrigerator. Those hands needed ice. The man needed food. She had to find a way to help. When she returned to the window, her tears fell. There sat the big proud man who had tried so hard to help her, his face buried against rock-solid forearms. Despite his skill and training, his wealth, or his prized possessions, he couldn't do a thing to help a little girl stuck in a pit of an excuse for a foster home.

Her heart melted. She turned away. He would come in when he was ready.

The last thing any man needed was for a woman to see him cry.

EIGHTEEN

Zack and Mei were on their way to the second foster home, and of all things, they were driving a rental car. He'd called his repair shop to tow the Porsche. When the cocky tow truck driver asked what had happened, Zack rudely told him to mind his business. The car reminded him of the tiny soul he'd deserted. He wanted to pound it all over again.

This morning, he hid behind dark glasses and bandages. Mei had taken care of the wounds on his hands the night before while he tried to recover some semblance of pride. She wanted him to see a doctor. Not going to happen. Mei insisted there were broken bones that needed x-rays. He told her to leave him alone. She finally stopped nagging.

Mei needed to stay out of his way. As long as his little girl remained in that wretched place, he wouldn't allow himself the comfort of medical attention. It didn't make sense, and yet it did. How else could he maintain the link with her if not through pain?

Determination steeled his mind. Somehow he was going to save every last child caught up in this stinking business. Every last one.

"How do you do it?" Zack growled as he maneuvered through the tangle of early D.C. traffic. The safe house was across town from Anacostia. Too far. Alex should've planned the mission a lot better.

Mei answered just as he knew she would. "There is no choice. What else would you have me do, Agent Lennox?"

That set him off.

"For one thing, stop calling me Agent Lennox. Zack. My name is Zack. Would you please just call me Zack?" He slapped the steering wheel, sending a stabbing tremor up the side of his hand and into his arm. Out of sheer aggravation, he hit it again. Pain. More pain.

"I'd rather call you dear."

"What?" He snapped her head off again, not understanding.

Unfastening her seat belt, she leaned across the console, her fingers gentle on the sides of his face. "I would rather call you brave and kind and darling."

"God," he groaned, pulling the rental to the curb at those unexpected endearments. Easing her body across the console, Zack buried his face in her neck with great heaving sighs. The fragrance of cherry blossom soothed, but he was letting her in too deep, the last thing he needed.

She stroked the back of his neck, her fingers trailing comfort over the edge of his ear while he tried to resist. "We're the same in so many ways. You're a Marine, and I'm a mom, but we do what we have to do. We don't ever give up."

Zack cringed at her inaccurate assessment of his glaring fault. He'd defied his very nature by walking away from that baby yesterday, giving in to the mission instead of doing the right thing. The memory was eating him alive.

"I can't get her out of my head," he muttered.

"Shush now, Zack. It's hard. I know." She patted the center of his chest, one arm around his shoulder like they were friends, but he caught the difference. Mei had just used his name. Where was the cold and condescending ICE agent? Hagatha? Cruella? It would be easier to deal with someone hard and calculating, but not someone who cared, who understood.

"Please don't hurt yourself any more." Mei rested her head on his shoulder. "I can't bear it."

He stilled. What was it about this woman? One minute mean, the next pouring kindness all over him.

"I don't even know her name." The anguish clawed its way out of him. "I'm sorry. I'm such an ass, I didn't realize the pain you've been in."

"No. You are a very good man."

"Then why do I feel like crap? Why do I feel like a stinking traitor, like a damned Judas?"

She took his face in her hands and pushed his dark glasses up from his eyes to rest on the top of his head. "Because you have a good heart. You care for a little baby, but you don't even know her name. We will find her the same as we'll find LiLi. I promise."

Mei kissed his lips as sweetly as he'd ever been kissed, but Zack didn't feel the pleasure of it. His breath caught in his throat. Did she just tell him the same lie he'd been telling her?

The second foster home was different than the first. Cleaner. Quieter. The girls seemed healthier. Not really what he'd call happy, but better.

Zack and Mei walked through the child-filled rooms behind dark sunglasses and a shield of indifference. They didn't hold hands. They didn't pretend they were a loving couple. No one screamed at him. Most importantly, he didn't touch a single little girl.

The only good thing that came out of it happened when Mei asked if there might be any other foster homes to visit. She came away with another address, while he left six Tattle Tales behind. The tour ended quickly. Zack ushered Mei to the passenger seat of the rental and closed the door as soon as she was inside. They were headed to another foster home. He wanted them done and behind him as quickly as possible.

"Did you get that?" He pressed a finger against his ear to reduce the background noise interfering with his comm link. David had the location of the other foster home and Zack needed his senior agent out of his head.

"Yes. Got it. Good job. Now that we've seen the inside of Richards' foster homes, we cannot wait. I mentioned it to Mei yesterday. Alex is working on a plan with the local authorities, the FBI, and Interpol this morning to bring all these homes down."

"Today?" Zack climbed behind the steering wheel and closed the car door.

"As quickly as they can gather sufficient forces. You've just given us another address to follow up on, which makes the operation that much larger. It's critical we sweep in on all of these places at the same time. We cannot risk endangering the children any longer or allowing the people running the homes to escape. Alex's plan includes Richards' office, too."

Zack glanced at Mei sitting beside him. Their time together was coming to a close, and if the upcoming takedown worked correctly, all those girls would be out of danger. She might find LiLi, although he doubted it. But if the plan of Alex's didn't go smooth, there was no telling what would happen. All kinds of bad scenarios filled Zack's mind, running the gamut between people like Jun running away to save themselves, or blowing the homes sky high to obliterate the evidence. How far would Richards go to save his hide?

Zack already knew the answer. These children weren't human beings in Richards' eyes. They were inventory, and the foster homes were nothing but warehouses to store his inventory. Hell, the man would probably burn them down just for the insurance if he could get away with it.

"Ah, Zack, how are you feeling today?" There was a definite note of unsolicited concern in David's calm voice.

"Fine," Zack snapped, pulling the earpiece out and tossing it onto the back seat. The last thing he wanted was to talk about his feelings. There was no joy in listening to the cheap economy vehicle's engine turn over either. He missed his car. He couldn't kick a rental.

"I have an idea." Mei's hand was warm on his arm.

"Yeah, what?" Somehow, since the day before, they'd switched polarities. She was strong; he was falling apart. He was rude; she was patient. "I don't want breakfast if that's what you're going to say. I don't want anything."

"I've been thinking about the girls lined up in the hall yesterday. It didn't make sense. It's not like that man was taking them outside to play. And didn't Ms. Bradford say they don't keep all the available children in one place?"

"You need to know the police are going to take down all of these foster homes as soon as they can. Maybe today." Zack let her have the bad news bluntly.

"But what if there are more?" Mei gasped. "How will I ever find my daughter?"

He gripped the steering wheel and stared straight ahead. She'd just voiced his own dilemma; how to save one at the expense of so many others.

Mei's breathing was now audible, short, fast breaths because her heart was pounding as she dealt with the sudden change in her expectations. He tried to soften the blow. "We can't let any of the girls suffer, not now that we know how bad it is."

"You're right," she agreed quickly, and he had to look at her. She didn't sound as upset as he expected. "Then we need to go back to the first foster home right now. Let's get your little girl out of there before they have a chance to move her, or before the police swarm in and overrun the place. You want to get her, don't you?"

"Say what?" He looked twice. She might as well have told him the sky was green.

"I think they were already moving some of the girls yesterday. Remember the girls in the hallway that I mentioned before? They looked like they going somewhere. Maybe there are other foster homes we don't know about. This is our only chance."

Mei's choice of words did not elude him. *Your little girl. You want to get her. This is our only chance.*

What the hell was she thinking? It didn't matter. His mind kicked into high gear. They still had the money. It could work. He'd have to keep David and Todd in the dark, though. Hell, he'd have to go against every correct protocol for The TEAM. It might put the whole operation in jeopardy, but it's not like he hadn't done that before. Alex would be one mad bastard, but wasn't he the one who'd said he'd have done the same thing by rescuing Chai Yenn? Zack would be fired for sure. He weighed the odds. Other than that, it just might work.

He looked into Mei's eyes and saw the love shining there. She was a different woman since his meltdown yesterday, but he'd been such an ass all morning. He looked away.

"Zack." She leaned across the console again, turning his face to hers, not blinking even once. "Let's rescue one baby at a time. We know where your little girl is. I know you will do everything to help me find LiLi. I trust you."

Great. What a way to kick a man when he's down. He shook his head, trying to catch his equilibrium. It was impossible around this woman. Either she was crazy, or he was. Right now, he didn't dare guess.

"Who are you?" he asked, cupping her cheek in his hand. "Just when I get you figured out, you change."

Closing her eyes, she tipped her cheek into his palm. "Someone who knows what it's like to lose your child. I can't let that same thing happen to you."

"That's the problem. She isn't mine."

Wise brown eyes peered back at him. "She is if you love her."

NINETEEN

Mei gulped.

They were back at the first foster home. Agent Lennox had parked in the same place they'd parked the day before, and for now, the money was safe in the trunk of the rental. He'd turned off his earpiece and stowed it in the glove compartment. All she had to do was be brave one more time.

"I'll go in alone," she said, trying to sound confident.

"I should go in with you."

"No. They'd see your hands and wonder what happened. Besides, you don't speak Mandarin. I do."

He hadn't taken his eyes off the dismal home. "What if you run into trouble?"

"I won't." She hoped. It seemed a more dangerous operation now that they were back and she was really preparing to go inside all by herself.

"Here." He unholstered one of his pistols from under his arm, checked the magazine and handed it to her grip first. "Take this."

"I don't need a gun."

"Take it," he insisted. "I'll feel better if you can protect yourself while you're inside."

"I have no place to hide it." She didn't want the weapon near her, much less when she fully planned to be carrying a child with her. "Besides, I don't know how to use it."

He frowned, the gun still in his outstretched hand. "Do you ever do what you're told?"

"I did. Once. A long time ago. Maybe." She would have smiled if she weren't so scared.

"I doubt it." He secured his weapon and faced the house again.

Taking a big breath, she opened the door and stepped outside. The chill wind of the dismal day reminded her to pull her jacket tight. Her knees shook as she made her way back to the front door. As quick as she rang the doorbell, Jun answered, only this time she barely opened the door a crack.

"Why you here? What you want?"

"I'd like to talk to you about one of the babies my husband and I saw yesterday."

Jun peered past her to the car where Agent Lennox waited. "Where other car? Why he not come with you? He scared?"

"No, he stayed in the car because he has your money." Mei played her ace in the hole. "We're willing to pay you for the child if you will let us take her with us."

Jun's eyebrows shot up, but she recovered quickly. "How much money you got?"

"May I come in?" Mei resorted to her alter ego. "Or are you going to keep me standing out here in the cold while you ask stupid questions?"

That did the trick. Jun opened the door and stepped aside for Mei to enter. "You want same baby he like yesterday?"

"Yes. Do you still have her?"

"Maybe." Jun glanced down the hall where a group of older girls stood in a line. All dressed in their orange dresses, they looked like they were waiting for a fire drill.

"What's going on?" Mei asked.

"We moving," Jun admitted. "Again."

"What do you mean, you're moving?" Mei's heart skipped a beat. Was the baby already gone?

Jun shrugged and walked toward the hall where the girls waited. "Come. We talk money. Then we talk baby."

"No." Mei stood her ground. "I want to see the baby first. Once I have her, we'll talk money."

Jun glanced over her shoulder. "I think you come now. We see baby you want." She lit a cigarette as she walked, so Mei followed. The money was secure for now. She intended to signal Agent Lennox once she had the little girl safely in her arms. There was no way their plan could fail.

Once in the hall, she spotted the man she'd seen the day before. He stood at the back door, his arms folded over his chest. A look passed between Jun and him that Mei couldn't interpret. He nodded, but Jun kept leading, so Mei continued to follow. Her fingers clenched with worry. Saving this child meant everything right now. Then it was LiLi's turn.

The smell of the place hadn't improved. Mei took a deep breath before Jun opened the nursery doors. Once again, every child's head turned to her. All those eyes. The bleakness of their situation encircled Mei, an invisible snake that constricted the joy out of saving just the one. All of these children needed rescue.

Jun marched over to the playpen where the baby girl lay sleeping on her stomach. With the cigarette bobbing on her lip, Jun reached into the pen and jerked the baby up by her arm. The poor little tyke blinked, her lips puckered up for a cry that never came. Jun shook her once like she needed to shake the sleep out of the baby.

"You want this one?" she snapped. "You like? Yes? No?"

"Yes." Mei couldn't take the baby from Jun fast enough. She smothered her to her chest. "She is the right one."

"How much money?" Jun glared. "You say we talk money when you have baby. How much?"

"What do you want for her?" Mei asked. There were so many others. If Jun asked for less, maybe she could rescue one or two more.

"I think not." Jun's face crinkled into an ugly sneer as she glanced over Mei's shoulder.

Too late Mei saw the young black man sneaking up behind her.

Too late she felt his fist in the side of her head.

Too fast the reeking floor reached up and swallowed her alive, along with the child in her arms.

Where the hell is she?

Zack drummed the steering wheel through bandaged fingers. Every tap hurt. He didn't care. Mei had been in there too long. Something was wrong. The old dude he'd seen inside with Jun yesterday was out and about today. He'd already made two trips to the dumpster at the end of the driveway, even waved once when he spotted Zack in his car. Still no Mei. Still no signal.

How long can it take to grab one baby and run?

Low gray clouds raced overhead on their way westward. If she didn't come out soon and at least give him the signal to bring the cash, he'd have to turn the engine and the heater on. His gut screamed. The cold was the least of his worries.

"Come on, give me a sign, damn it." He grabbed the door handle, rolled the stress out of his shoulders, and watched the front door. "Wave to me, Mei. Do something."

The door of the house opened, but it was Jun. She waved all right, a fast come-quick kind of a wave, and Zack bolted out the door.

"Come now," she called to him. "Baby girl sick. You must come now."

He ran. One step hit the porch before he heard the vehicle screeching toward him. A blue van? That blue van. He froze. Which way to go? Forward or retreat?

"Must come," Jun screeched. "Hurry. Hurry."

The vehicle swerved over the yard. There was no time to think. He reached for his cell phone and stabbed the preset number for Alex. Mother answered.

"They're moving the girls," he bellowed.

"They what?" she asked. "Zack? Is this—?"

"Hey, you!" Two thugs scrambled out of the still-moving van.

"Mei's inside," Zack yelled at Mother. "Get someone here now. Send help."

4th Street Tigers ran at him, guns drawn, murder in their eyes.

"Where are you?" Mother demanded. "Hold on. I'm sending—"

"We're at—"

A blinding light exploded in his head. Pain crashed against his skull.

"Mother!"

"Aw. He's calling his mommy," someone taunted from very far away.

He dropped to his knees, the phone on the ground beside him. Darkness descended.

Jun lunged.

He grabbed her bony ankle.

She hit him again.

TWENTY

Something smelled bad. Real bad.

Zack squinted through murky vision. He would've opened both eyes, but one was stuck shut. Swollen shut. A man shouldn't feel so damned bad. His whole head seemed swollen shut. Nose. Ears. Mouth. Darkness parted only to reveal more rolling darkness that made him dizzy. Like he wasn't dizzy enough.

She hit me. Oh hell, did she hit me.

It was hard to make out anything in the cold dark place where he lay. A thin layer of slimy mud cushioned his cheek, offering relief. Breathing would've felt better without the burning stone in his chest.

The fog in his head lifted. Both arms were pulled tightly behind his back, making breathing constrained and difficult, but he was alive. Maybe alive was a good thing? Stiff and cold, his bandaged fingertips slid along the plastic zip ties strapped around both wrists. His feet were bound together the same way. Tight.

Details surfaced slowly through the haze in his brain. Jun. That damned mean Jun. The 4th Street Tigers. Even the blue van showed up for roll call. Mei was in there somewhere, lost in his head. Alex, too. Nothing made sense. The cold felt good on his cheek. Sleep beckoned. If only he could breathe.

He lay there gasping like a fish out of water. The ground moved and swelled. Breathing became all-important. Thinking, too. That's what Alex always railed on. He expected his agents to think. *Once in a while, just think.* But Zack's brain pounded inside his skull and thinking hurt. If that wasn't bad enough, just trying to breathe felt like it was killing him, too.

His needs became more primal the longer he lay there.

Air. I need air.

Someone groaned nearby.

"Mei?" Zack grimaced. He'd have thought of her eventually. And then he knew his mouth was full of blood, maybe a couple broken teeth, too. He spat the clot out and called again, but his voice carried no impact or volume. He croaked anyway, "Mei."

There was no answer, and the feeble attempt had taken all his strength. He lay listening and shivering. Something at the back of his mind recalled that shivering was a good thing. It was only when a man stopped shivering he had something to worry about. Of course, he probably didn't care much by then.

Think! Alex's voice screeched at him from out of nowhere.

"Damn it, Boss," Zack rasped. "Leave me...alone."

Think, Zack. Think.

"You're bugging me. 'Sides...I'm trying...to die here."

Think.

"Think I'm...losing my mind."

He stilled. Alex wasn't really here. Good. A man deserved peace and quiet when he's trying to draw his last breath.

"Mei?" he asked the darkness. She was here a minute ago, wasn't she?

He rolled to his back and pushed his hands into the mud. Every muscle screamed to lie back down. Somehow, he managed a sitting position, but that only made him dizzier, like it was possible. The ground moved in a circular wave, up and then down, around and around.

The darkness whispered a word he dreaded. *Concussion.*

"Yeah. Yeah. Maybe...if I live." His hoarse voice echoed. Echoed...Echoed....

"Ah, hell."

Pain slammed his ribcage. Inhaling fire, the blackness took what little breath he'd drawn. Barely able to squeeze a breath in, he tried to think and think fast. Mei had to be here. Maybe between the two of them, they could figure something out.

"Mei." He groaned like an old man and then he rested and listened. There was no answer. All he heard was wheezing and coughing, choking and spitting. His. Breathing shouldn't be so noisy.

Another sinister thought joined the last. *Punctured lungs. A man could die from that.*

He pushed the warning out of his head.

"Mei?" he croaked again.

She whimpered. Finally.

"Can you...hear me?" Nausea and vertigo buffeted his meager hold on gravity. His mangled gauze-covered fingers pressed into the mud behind him. They still hurt from when he'd pounded his car. A little more pain hardly mattered.

Why was it so important to sit up in the first place?

"Agent Lennox?" She sounded as bad as he did.

"It's...me," he hissed. For awhile, neither said anything. It was all he could do to maintain the tripod thing he had going between his butt and his hands behind his back. He listened to mud squishing as Mei moved toward him.

"I'm tied up."

"You...hurt?"

"I feel funny, like I've been drugged." Again more squishing, scraping noises until she bumped into his legs. "Are you hurt?"

He laughed, a strangled coughing sound that didn't sound like a laugh at all. "Hell...no. I'm...fine."

Her body pressed against his thigh. Another good thing. Now he knew her exact position. And she was warm. He had to make the best use of the time he had left. She had to live.

"Lis...ten." Breathing was harder now, his lungs thick and sluggish like they breathed soup instead of air. "Boot. Knife."

"Are you telling me you have a knife in your boot? Left or right?"

"R-right."

She fumbled, but eventually pulled the knife from his inside boot sheath. He winced, gagging back bile at the nauseating sawing motion when she cut the tie at his ankles. Every little movement created swells he could not control. He willed himself not to throw up.

She scooted along his thigh, grunting funny little sounds until they were sitting back to back. Her fingers searched his wrist for enough space to slide the knife. He gulped. Shaking more than helping, he stretched his arms as far apart as his strength would allow. Fire filled his lungs at the simple movement. Mei needed room to work, but the knife she was working with was razor sharp. Maybe those bandages would protect him if she slipped. Maybe not.

"C-cold?" he asked between bone rattling shivers.

"Same as you," she muttered. "I need to get you out of here."

"'Kay," he rasped. "That...be nice."

A flush of something warm trickled over his cold skin. Instantly, it chilled. Damn. She'd sliced him. It wouldn't take long now. Maybe it was just as well. Now he'd die quickly. He sagged onto his side.

"Hey," she muttered. "Your turn. Cut me free."

Oh, yeah. That was the least he could do before he died.

"Gimme...knife." He reached for her in the dark, feeling down her arms until he came to where her hands were tied together. She held the blade down, a real good safety precaution considering how little control he had over his shaking fingers, and the fact he couldn't see. Dark walls closed in. Lack of blood will do that.

"Be careful. It's sharp," she cautioned, like he didn't already know how much he honed his own knife.

"Uh huh," he grunted, taking the slippery tool carefully out of her grasp. And then he felt it on his wrist. It wasn't him. It was her. "You're...bleeding?"

"No," she lied. "I'm not."

"Are too," he muttered. "You're cut. So...sorry."

He fumbled the knife, nearly losing it. Multitasking was impossible with clumsy, fat fingers. Talking, cutting, breathing, and trying not to die all at the same time was hard. He focused. One thing at a time. His fingers searched between her slender wrists for the width of a razor sharp knife. She was a smart woman, stretching her arms apart to help the blade maneuver.

After one sharp slice and one painful grunt, she was free. He leaned into her solid back, both hands to the ground for support.

"Give me the knife. I can cut my feet apart now."

He complied, handing the knife in a wide arc around her, handle first so he didn't hurt her by mistake. As soon as she was free, she turned and cradled him, tipping him backward onto the muddy ground, his head in the crook of her arm. At last. He could breathe again.

"Lis...ten," he rasped.

"I'm listening, Agent Lennox. What do you want me to do?"

"Get...help."

Mei looked at Agent Lennox's battered face through the dim, dark light where they'd been dumped. It looked like some kind of a warehouse. The floor was definitely cold concrete with a layer of mud that had no doubt been frozen before their bodies thawed the upper crust. A square opening high overhead allowed the only light, a scant beam of the late afternoon sun. But it was enough to scare her. The big strapping agent who'd helped her so much now lay struggling to breathe, and there was nothing she could do to help. His jacket was gone. Hers too. The left side of his head was swollen and blackened with blood. Plus, he was going into shock. He wheezed, every word a struggle. She had no way to keep him warm.

"Mei..." He choked and spit. "Must...go."

She hugged him one last time. "I don't want to leave you."

"Got to."

With her forehead to his cheek, she felt him shiver. Agent Lennox was twice her size, maybe more. As usual, he was right. She had to go. Easing her body from beneath his, Mei lowered him onto the damp, dirty ground. "You have to hang on. I don't have LiLi yet, and you promised you'd help me find her. You hear me?"

One side of his mouth lifted in a sad attempt at a smile. "Yeah...promised."

"You don't have your baby girl, either." She smoothed both hands over his chest, scared this might be her last moment with him. "I'll be right back."

"Hey," he groaned, his hands searching in the dark for her. She clasped them both to her lips. "Should've told you...sooner. You're...really...something."

She kissed his fingers. "Please, don't die. I should have told you. I love you, Agent Lennox."

He groaned again.

"I'm sorry I've been so rude to you." All her sins spilled out of her mouth. "You've only tried to help. Don't die, Agent Lennox. Please. I love you so much."

"Mei." He gasped for air.

"Yes?" She guided his hand to her mouth for one last kiss.

"Zack. Call me...Zack."

Alone never felt so cold.

Zack listened to Mei's tentative footsteps squish through the mud as she walked into darkness, and then he was alone. It was okay. Time she left anyway. The cold was colder now, but he'd stopped shivering. It didn't matter. Slumber beckoned, and he was tired. The pain in his chest commanded what little concentration he had left, and sent him writhing for any position that offered a chance to breathe easier. There was none.

Can't breathe. I'm drowning in my own blood.

At last, it got the best of him. With gritted teeth, he let it have its way, and collapsed into the slimy mud. Darkness swarmed his thin hold on reality. The war came back to him. So much injustice in the world. Damned Taliban. Damned child murderers. Poor, poor children everywhere. He drifted. Poor Mei. He'd failed. Still didn't find LiLi like he'd promised. Poor, poor Mei.

Alex?

Zack opened his one good eye. His damned boss was peering down at him through a long foggy tunnel. *How'd he get into the war?*

The man had a blinding bright light that, well, blinded. Zack squinted, shifting his head to avoid the sharp poke in the eye the light offered. *My hell. Can't a man die in peace?*

"I've got you, son."

Two strong hands eased him out of the mud, cradled him, searched his neck and chest. Being handled hurt. He couldn't breathe again. Neither could he talk.

"I've got you, son."

Yeah, well, let me go. You're killing me.

Alex covered Zack with a blanket that felt like heaven it was so warm, but he still couldn't breathe. Hands lifted him onto a board, but Jun was back. She stabbed him in the side this time–with a knife. Damned, mean Jun. The knife felt long and sharp, but oddly, he could breathe better. Maybe she was good for something, after all. Or maybe she'd turned into a medic with a scalpel? He groaned the illusion away.

Doom whirled on the cold November breeze. Fractured skull. Punctured lungs. Hypothermia. *Yeah, yeah, yeah. I'm dying here. Let me be.*

"You've got him now?"

Alex just would not shut up.

"Yes, sir. We're taking him to Washington Central."

"Boss?" Zack gasped. If the nightmare really was real, if that one guy really was Alex, he needed to ask him something.

"Yes?" Alex leaned over him.

Zack blinked. Alex looked bad. Really bad. Kinda sad. Kinda mad. Awful dirty. He didn't usually look so bad. Maybe it wasn't him.

"Umm." Zack blinked. Thinking hurt. He'd wanted to ask something. Didn't he?

"You're going to be okay." Alex rested his hand on Zack's forehead, like he was checking him for a fever or something.

"Mei?"

"She's okay," Alex said, but Alex was lying. Zack could tell.

"My Mei?" he asked again. "She's good? You sure?"

"She's fine, but you're sick, son. Lie down and shut up."

Okay. Zack closed his eyes. That sounded more like Alex. He believed now.

Mei was okay.

TWENTY-ONE

"How you doing?"

Zack saw Alex's face close above him. Too close. By then he'd been cleaned up, stitched up, and warmed up. The hands he'd abused his car with the day before were properly treated and encased in thicker bandages. They felt numb. And numb was a good feeling. He could breathe, something a man appreciated a lot more after he'd nearly suffocated on his own body fluids. The only problem was he'd woken up in a hospital, not his favorite place.

"Better," he wheezed. "So...I'm gonna live...to fight another day?"

Alex patted the top of Zack's head. Their manly relationship was always different than most. Alex was a hard man to get close to. Zack never knew how he'd done it. Just one of those things that happens when you fight side by side with a guy, save his ass once in awhile, and cover it the rest of the time. "No fighting for you for awhile. Looks like someone took a brick to that hard head of yours."

"Didn't see the bastard who...threw the first punch." It was still hard to breathe, much less talk.

"What did you see?"

Zack looked up into his boss's blue eyes. Alex always looked so serious.

"Stars, Boss. I saw...stars." *Sheeesh. What a stupid question.*

Those blue eyes smiled for a second, but his boss was going to ask him again. Alex did. "What was different at the foster home this time? Think."

Alex's favorite word–think. It made Zack smile. The word had saved his life.

"Yeah. Know what you meant. The blue van for one thing. Chinese driver...heavy set, five ten, dark clothes." Zack stopped to catch his breath. "Same blue van...at the ATF stakeout."

"Same driver?"

"No, those guys were black. This guy...definitely Chinese. Kinda chubby."

"Where was Mei while you were getting the crap beat out of you?" Alex wasted no time going straight for the jugular.

"Inside, Boss. She...ah, went inside."

Blue eyes bored straight into Zack's lying eyes. *Man up, Lennox. He knows.*

"It's my fault. We were going to...buy the little baby girl. Had all the money. Had to help her. Couldn't leave her. Not again."

Whether he was too beat up to control himself or because his heart hurt thinking about the little girl he'd lost, but tears filled Zack's eyes. He'd just confessed to stealing a million dollars to buy a child. Alex already knew he'd turned off his phone and earpiece. Lennox had screwed the mission. Again. He'd be fired for sure, but worst of all, he'd lost his one chance to save that baby. He'd failed the most important operation of his life.

"Did you...did you see that place? And she's so small." Reconciliation morphed into anger. "I couldn't leave her," he declared.

A glimmer of something drifted through those icy blues. Alex looked–pleased?

"I've got news for you. You saved every single one of those little girls."

"What?"

Alex nodded. "It was your call to Mother that brought the whole world of law enforcement down on those foster houses. And yes, I've seen the place. We even got the girls they'd tried to move before we got there. Caught the blue van and the men driving it, too."

Zack didn't know what to say. He was delirious. That's it. Alex was a by-product of the pain meds. He closed his eyes, hoping the next time he opened them his boss would be gone. He wasn't.

"Do you need a drink?" Alex held the glass while Zack sucked down a huge swallow through the straw.

Okay. That did it. I'm hallucinating for sure. Alex is helping me get a drink? No way.

"We got Richards and his secretary, Ms. Bradford, too. Remember her?" Alex kept talking. "She turned state's evidence and gave the FBI all of her documentation. Mother and Ember are helping sort through it. Oh yeah, and speaking of the one million dollars? It was in the blue van. Still marked. Still in the same bag. You didn't steal anything."

"And the babies? I mean, Boss, that little girl in the first foster home. I mean, where are all those little girls?"

"Some are in the hospital. Some are going home to their real parents." Alex paused.

"Their real parents?"

"They're not all orphans. Some of those little girls were abducted from China. They need to go home. They have families who love them."

Okay. That was news. He hadn't thought of that possibility. He'd been focused on saving one baby girl. That's all. He'd developed a plan where she'd be part of his life, where he'd take care of her, feed her, keep her safe and clean, and make her smile every single day. A good nanny could take care of her while he worked, but he'd be home every night. The boutique where he and Mei had stopped had a cute pink bed, perfect for his little girl. He had a plan. It would work. It just didn't include parents.

Another little girl came to mind. "LiLi wasn't there, was she?"

"No, but I didn't think we'd find her in this mess, did you?"

"No, of course not." Zack groaned. "How's Mei? We need to find her daughter, Boss. You know that—"

"You let me worry about that, okay?"

"Yeah, but she's been through so much, and—"

"Knock it off. My job is to locate LiLi. Your job is to listen to your doctors and take care of yourself. Can you do that without screwing it up?"

Zack shrugged. "Does she know yet?"

"I told her. Mei's a tough little gal, Zack. Don't underestimate her. Do you feel like sitting up for awhile?" Alex raised the hospital bed without waiting for an answer.

"Thanks, Boss." Sitting up didn't hurt this time, but it didn't help either. The baby girl had slipped through his hands. LiLi was still missing. Mei would be crushed.

"Don't look so glum. You're alive. Mei's alive, and you're a hero."

He didn't feel like a hero.

"You need anything before I leave? A drink? Pain meds? Anything at all?"

"No thanks." Zack fingered the call button with his clumsy, gauze-covered mitts. The joy of living through attempted murder faded with the knowledge of failing Mei. Maybe he'd ask for a pain med after all.

"How about a little company?"

"No." Zack shook his head to protest when Alex opened the door.

There stood Mei with her arms full of a pink-checkered baby blanket. She came to Zack's bedside and set the bundle on his lap. "I have someone who wants to meet you," she said.

The sweetest little girl with dark almond-shaped eyes blinked up at him. She didn't smile. She didn't coo. Her hair glistened clean and black around a pink baby face, and she smelled refreshingly of baby powder. All his pent-up worry turned to relief when he grabbed that little gal and pressed her to his face. She resisted for a moment, but let herself be hugged.

"I'd like you to meet your little girl, Song Chang. Baby Song, this is the big strong man who rescued you and all your little friends. This is Agent...This is Zack." Mei's voice sounded soft and motherly, until she burst into tears. "I thought I'd lost you."

He gathered her into his bed alongside Baby Song, overcome and damned happy. Zack couldn't speak, just held those special ladies while Mei tried to compose herself, and Baby Song watched with serious eyes.

"You could have told me," he muttered to Alex.

"Nah. This is better." Alex had taken up residence on the only available chair. "You deserved a little scare after scaring the hell out of me."

"Yeah, well." Zack choked. They were here. His girls.

"The Tigers dropped you through a hole in the floor of an abandoned warehouse over in Anacostia. They roughed you up pretty good first. Dropped Mei on top of you. Landing on you protected her fall, but it didn't help you much."

"How'd you find us?"

Mei raised her hand shyly. "You told me to get help, remember?"

Zack shook his head. He couldn't be certain of anything. "Hell of an op, Boss."

"You're telling me? I was in a meeting with the FBI, Interpol and the State Department when you got through to Mother."

"I do remember that." Zack rubbed the bruised side of his face with the back of one hand. "Someone clocked me. I think it was Jun."

"She won't be running any more orphanages where she's going."

"You got Richards, didn't you?"

Alex could not have looked more pleased. "The police caught up with him at his place in Georgetown. He thought he could work a deal. Even made a statement to the press about how it was all a big misunderstanding, how he was innocent."

"Innocent, my ass," Zack growled, pulling Mei closer. She looked so pretty there in his arms. Who'd a thought?

Alex chuckled. "Funny thing. Ms. Bradford is Reginald Richards' aunt. She took very meticulous care of her nephew's business. FBI's got names, addresses, even pictures of a few couples involved in the scandal. She kept track of the children who got sick or died, and how they disposed of bodies. Made our job a lot easier, but it sure surprised the hell out of Richards."

Mei shivered, and Zack automatically kissed her forehead. Her hand on his chest felt warm and good. Baby Song watched with big wide eyes. She hadn't made a peep yet.

"Do you remember me, little girl?" Zack asked. Of course she didn't, but he had to ask. "What happens now, Boss?"

Alex had a funny light in his eye as his gaze shifted from Mei to Song and back to Zack again. "The Office of Family Reunification is all over it. They've already made contact with several Chinese families and are bringing them Stateside to be reunited with their daughters. It's national news. I'm proud of you."

"How many girls were recovered?"

"Over three hundred at the last count."

Zack leaned back into his pillow. Praise from Alex meant a lot, but the thought of all those little girls caught up in the ugly business was more than he could stomach. Baby Song chose that moment to reach her fingers to his nose, watching him closely while she cranked it one way and then the other. Mei made an unusual noise that sounded a lot like a giggle.

"Hey, you," Zack murmured as Song continued her exploration of his face. She patted his cheek with the softest angel touch that melted some of his heartache away. "It's very nice to meet you, Baby Song."

"Ah, for hell sakes." Alex stood, scrubbed a hand over his head, shaking his emotions off his face. "I'm going back to work." He turned to Mei. "I hope you know nothing's changed. We're still looking for your daughter."

"Thank you," she said quietly.

"No, Mei. Thank you. You saved our guy's life." He paused, one foot out the door and one foot in. "Almost forgot. You had company at your apartment last night, Zack. The Tigers tore it apart."

"They what? Was Jake there?" Zack startled.

"No one was there, but it's a crime scene right now. You can't go home until the police release it. Then it needs to be repaired."

"What'd they do to it? How'd they—?" Zack automatically thumped his hip for his wallet, keys, and cell phone, which of course were not there. "They took my wallet. They've got my ID—"

"Relax. We recovered it. Mother's holding it for you."

"Why'd they do that?"

"According to all their BS graffiti, they want you to stop messing with their boss."

"I'm not messing with their boss."

Alex cocked a quizzical eyebrow. "Yeah, you are. Richards, Debargio, Espinosa, the Tigers–they're all in this together."

Things were starting to line up in Zack's head. "We can link Tony Brown to Carducci. We can link the Tigers back to Debargio and Espinoza. Want to bet Carducci knows Debargio?"

"I'll do you one better." Alex was back inside the room. "I just finished the Senate Investigation. Remember that?"

Zack gulped. Oh, yeah. That. It's a wonder he still had a job.

"Of all the senators on the committee, who do you think voted to sanction me and my business?"

The way Alex's eyebrow spiked told Zack this was a tasty bit of inside info. "You tell me."

"Does the name Stephen Lord ring any bells?"

"Whoa. The big mouth from New York?" Zack knew Senator Lord by default, and not in a good way. He was a well-educated Yale man from a family of old money. He'd grown up in privileged Hyannis Port, Massachusetts, but moved to New York after he lost the bid for governor in his home state. Known for his hard stance against the military, he'd been trounced in the election.

Alex nodded. "One guess who he plays poker with every Tuesday night."

"Carducci?" Zack tried that on for size. "Man, we've sure got a lot of players in the game."

"We do. Which means you and Miss Xing will be under lock and key until it's finished. Todd and Ember are outside. Right now they're contending with a pesky reporter, but they'll escort Mei and the baby back to the safe house. You'll stay there when you're released. Sound good?"

"Sure." What else could Zack say? Recuperating with Mei and Song nearby sounded like a damned good idea. He looked at her to judge her acceptance of the new plan. "You okay with that?"

She wouldn't meet his eyes when she answered. "Of course."

Mei was blowing his socks off, as if he'd had any on. The whole experience they'd just lived through had changed everything. Here she lay, contentedly in his arms discussing his moving in with her. Sure, they were in a hospital bed, and he was feeling fairly harmless, but still. Two days ago, she'd have lanced him with one sharp barb and tossed him out with the trash.

"I've got work to do," Alex muttered. "Do what your doctor tells you for a change, Zack. Can you handle that?"

He caught the sarcasm. "I'll try."

"Try hard." Alex shut the door and left.

The silence in the room stretched. Something crazy was happening. Zack couldn't lose it, but he didn't want to move too fast, either. Still...he needed help with Song and a woman's help would be better. Hers would be best.

"Tell me about Song Chang." He changed the subject. "Does she have parents? Do we, ah, I mean do I get to keep her?" If Mei noticed his poor choice of words, she didn't let on.

"No. Song Chang doesn't have any parents. She's out of an orphanage like Chai Yenn. Claire was thrilled that we, umm, you are able to take her." Mei was having as hard a time as he was keeping them separate in her mind. Good to know.

"Claire knows about all this?"

"Oh yes. She's in the middle of placing hundreds of little girls in legal foster homes right now. I think she wants to adopt you herself. She's so proud of everything you did."

"We, Mei. Everything *we* did. Going back to get Song was your idea."

With all their talking, she'd moved into the very personal zone under his chin. His weary heart stuttered for a better reason than death this time. The crazy day on the sidewalk flashed back to his mind, the first time he'd kissed her. She'd surprised him. Hell, she'd almost knocked him over with the intensity of her kiss, not something he was likely to forget. Here she was again. Fragile and strong. Mean and gentle. So close, and yet so far.

He tilted his head down, just in case she needed reassurance, or whatever it was she'd needed that day. He still wasn't sure. "Would it be okay if I—?"

"Yes." She covered his mouth with hers, her fingers on the side of his jaw, pulling him close and ending his question. Ah, the kiss hurt like crazy, but he wanted more. The sweetest tongue traced over his stitched lips, blessing him, tasting him, and he returned the favor.

She eased back, her hands cupping his cheeks. "I'm sorry. I shouldn't have—"

His turn. Using his arm for leverage behind her head, he forced her face back to his and squashed her doubt away between their lips. Now was not the time for much physical interaction, but he wanted more of this luscious woman. Hunger for her roared over him, exhausting the very limited reserve of strength he had left. As he ended the contact, she snuggled against him and he was sure. There would be another time. But for now, Baby Song waited in the crook of his other arm like she didn't know how to be a real baby, and another little girl was still missing.

"I'm sorry we didn't find LiLi," he whispered.

Mei placed a finger on his swollen lips. "Yet."

TWENTY-TWO

Zack eased onto his feet. He'd only been in the hospital four days, but enough was enough. Time to check out and get back to normal again. His punctured lung caused a little more trouble than his concussion, but he was tough. A Marine didn't admit to pain, and he sure as hell didn't waste time lying around in hospitals. He wasn't going to start now. By the time he'd dressed, which was a joke with bandaged fingers, Mei arrived, and just in time.

"Good. You're here. Could I ask you a favor?" he said, knowing the next question would push the limits of their relationship.

"Sure." She came straight to him, her eyes soft with concern.

"Could I ask you to button my shirt?" That ought to give her a hint of what else he needed.

"Of course." She reached for his collar, her fingers gently bumping his chin and neck while she fastened the first button. By then her eyes had drifted down to his jeans and the next dilemma. He could go without tucking his shirt into his pants, but they needed to be zipped.

He watched her, breathing the fragrance of cherry blossom and the very feminine essence that was Mei. All of her clothes were shabby, except for what Alex had procured for Amelia Burns. This woman needed a new wardrobe and a smile. Her fingers trembled and she had a cute way of biting her top lip, pulling the left side into her teeth only to pull it out and do it all over again. For some crazy reason, their close proximity unnerved her.

"I never thought I'd be asking you to button my shirt," he whispered, reaching both arms around her to rest his bulky hands at her back. "Unbutton, maybe."

Her breath hitched at his gentle innuendo. She glanced at his zipper. "I suppose you need help for...that, too."

He had to pull her in close so she couldn't see his smile. He couldn't risk hurting her feelings, not as fragile as he knew she was. Any other day, he'd have ventured a salacious grin and an all out 'hell yeah', but not today and not with Mei. Not yet.

"I hated to ask." He stifled the urge to take his feelings for her to the next level. "I won't watch."

The soft grunt from her throat told him she didn't believe him, but he kept his word. Of course, he didn't have to look to know what was happening when her fingertips grasped the zipper pull, her other hand on the snap, and his body on high alert. The zipper stuck. She tugged harder, pulling the fabric between zipper start to zipper finish taut and stiff. He clenched his sore fingers inside the gauze. Maybe it wasn't such a great idea.

"It's stuck," she muttered, leaning down to–see?

He rested his hands on her shoulders, his stupid heart working on a drum roll at her innocent position. Any other time...

She gave the zipper a mighty tug and up it came, along with everything else down yonder.

"There," she said as she met his eyes, her fingers still working on the troublesome button. "Got it."

"Thanks." He changed the subject as the button fastened. "Where's Song?"

"She's with her very first babysitter."

"Let me guess." He blew out a slow deep breath to clear what was left of his brain. "Bet that's Kelsey."

"Your boss is very persuasive. He and his wife have stopped a couple times to visit while you've been in the hospital. Todd and Ember set up LiLi's old baby bed in my room at the safe house. Kelsey has a way with babies. Song almost smiled."

"If anyone can get that little girl to smile, it will be Kelsey. She loves children." Zack focused on Kelsey to keep his mind off Mei.

A hearty knock at the door interrupted them. "I hear there's a grumpy-assed Marine in here. The nurses want him the hell out of their hospital," Todd groused as he and Ember came into the room. "Oh hey, Zack. Are they talking about you?"

"Shut up, Ranger Rick," Zack muttered, glad to see Mei had bodyguards with her, but thankful they hadn't been immediately on her six.

That Todd and Ember showed up to help him was cool. That it looked like they were getting serious was an added bonus. Ember was the creative, free spirit in the office. A man never knew what color hair she'd show up in, what crazy getup, or what new tat or piercing might grace her voluptuous movie star persona.

Today she was blonde, her hair soft and natural for a change. Her body was definitely her canvas, and judging by the way Todd never took his eyes off her, he was into art. The crazy woman should've gone to Hollywood she was that gorgeous. It made Zack smile. Ember had always seemed a little lonely. She deserved a good man in her life. And Todd? For an ex-Army Ranger, he wasn't so bad.

"Want me to grab a wheelchair for you, old guy?"

"No. I've got this." Zack stood for a moment, testing the truth of his words. There is nothing like the threat of a wheelchair ride to motivate a man. "And what's this 'old guy' crap? You're what, five years younger than me?"

"In dog years," Todd teased.

"Let's move." Zack put an end to the banter. He was tired already. After the latent sexual tension with Mei, the bed in the safe house was calling his name.

"Yes, let's get you home," she said.

Zack glanced down at the little lady's hand resting on his forearm. Did she just say 'home'? Judging by the shy smile on her mouth, she'd heard the slip, too. If it was one.

He made it all the way into the hall before the head nurse intercepted his plans.

"Where do you think you're going?" she asked sternly.

"I'm outta here," he answered, straightening to his full height, minus those few inches he needed to stoop just to keep breathing.

"Not like that you're not." She glowered.

"Yes, ma'am. I am," he argued, knowing full well what she was getting at. Just then an orderly barreled down the hall with the damned contraption known as a wheelchair. Todd snickered.

"Sit," the nurse commanded, her index finger pointed at the seat of the wheelchair. What was it that made her think she could take on a Marine?

"No, ma'am—"

"The wheelchair is not negotiable, Mr. Lennox." Her pointy finger stabbed the plastic seat. Damn, she had the whole alpha dog thing down to a science. "Either I escort you to the curb, or you will not leave the hospital. Am I understood?"

There was no way around her. When her toe started tapping, he knew he'd met his match.

"Yes, ma'am," he muttered, relinquishing his pride much to Todd's delight.

"Shut it, Chandler," Zack warned as the nurse adjusted the footrests and took her position behind the wheel.

Everything got worse. Todd had his cell phone out. "Smile!"

Not long ago she'd been buying formula for LiLi.

Now Mei was filling her cart with something a toddler would eat. Claire said Song would need formula to supplement her diet. They'd given her a thorough physical and found her underweight and malnourished. The child's condition worried Mei, so she bought anything that would boost the baby's weight. Claire had provided food stamps, special vitamins, and diapers. All Song needed now was love.

Ember and Todd were on the other side of the market, shopping for necessities like meat, potatoes, bread, and butter.

Zack rested comfortably at the safe house with two other bodyguards until they returned. Alex certainly meant business when he said she'd be safe.

She paused at the wine aisle, looked at the blushing shades of zinfandels, merlots, sauvignons, and rosés. Once upon a time she might have lingered, but not today.

"Look." Ember held up a bag of tangerines from the checkout line where she and Todd waited. "Do you think Song will eat these?"

"She might," Mei said, scanning their full cart. These two knew how to shop. Packages covered with white butcher paper told her they'd bought plenty of meat, but she also noticed a bag of potatoes and lots of fresh vegetables, not to mention a box of glazed donuts, several bags of snacks, and a tub of red licorice. Her stomach growled at the sight of all the food. It had been a long time since she'd had junk food in her house, but it looked more like these two were ready for a party.

Ember and Todd chattered like a couple kids. These two were very touchy feely with each other. Ember's hand was comfortable on Todd's waist like they knew each other well. Mei looked away, her feelings a slippery slope of past promises broken, the pain of her missing daughter, and one handsome man who'd stood by her. The question was—would Zack stay?

She'd seen his choice of women. Everything about the man oozed ego and sex appeal; from his muscular body, the confident way he walked, and even the car he drove. She couldn't wrap her mind around the abuse he'd taken—for her and from her. His passionate response to holding a motherless child seemed to have awakened the dead part of her soul. She hadn't seen that coming. The sight of the innocent baby in his big hands had jolted her universe. And yet....

LiLi is still missing. What on earth have I done?

She paid for her groceries while the bag boy filled two grocery bags with what she'd bought for Song.

"You ready?" Todd scooped her bags out of her arms and into his cart. "Come on, ladies. Time's a-wasting."

Ember circled her arm through his while they walked out the automatic doors together, her head on his shoulder and a definite glow in her eyes. With her blonde hair and his red, they made a charming couple. Their appeal was further enhanced by the fact they both had green eyes, hers more vivid, his calmer. Mei walked behind them, feeling like an old woman compared to their youthful enthusiasm. She caught the way his hand smoothed over Ember's butt when he unlocked the tailgate of his Tundra. They had it bad for each other.

Todd made short work of stowing the groceries in his vehicle. Ember ran the shopping cart three parking stalls down to the cart return rack. In no time they were back at the safe house. He delivered the groceries to the kitchen while she and Ember put everything away.

"You want to see something cute?" Ember nodded toward the living room. There lay Todd on the floor with Song sitting square in the middle of his chest and a pink sock monkey in his hands. Each time he snuggled the monkey into her, making silly animal noises, she turned away.

"She never smiles," Mei said quietly. "It's like she doesn't know how."

"Poor little munchkin," Ember said. "She hasn't had anything to smile about until now."

Mei and Ember stood at the kitchen doorway, watching Todd play with the baby.

"Are you two done putting stuff away?" Zack asked from his prone position on the couch. The minute he spoke, Song twisted around to see him.

"Wow. She sure knows you," Ember commented, "and yes, the food's put away."

"Hi, Baby Girl," Zack said tiredly to Song. "Who's the funny guy you're sitting on? Smack him once for me while you got him pinned down."

Instantly, Song lifted her arms for Zack to come get her. He rolled to his side, but Todd beat him to it.

"Stay put. No need for you to move." He settled Song alongside Zack. "Here you go."

"Thanks." Zack pulled Song into the crook of his arm.

"Looks like you've got white boxing gloves on."

Zack lifted one hand. "It does, doesn't it?"

"That's what happens when you beat the hell out of your car."

"Can it, Todd," Zack muttered.

"Okay. We've got work to do." Todd held his arm out to Ember.

She ducked into him, giggling. "We're installing a few more Tattle Tales around the place. Want to be sure you kids are safe and sound."

Todd paused at the front door. "Just so you know, Song's baby bed is in Mei's room. Ember's room is next to hers. Yours is the other side of Mei's, and mine's across the hall. I put your gear bag in your closet. Any questions?"

"Thanks, guys," Zack said.

Mei followed behind them and locked the door. When she turned to Zack, her breath stalled. He looked so right sprawled on the living room couch, especially holding his baby. Mei let her eyes scroll over his chest, stomach, and down his long legs to his stocking feet. The man was built of muscle and iron. A sudden heat flamed to life inside her when her eyes met his. Instantly, her practical side took over. *Stop this foolishness. Get a grip.*

"How are we doing?" She tried to sound stern, but the contentment in the room enveloped her. Being with this man and this particular baby brought another feeling into the safe house; the happy sensation she used to have with LiLi. It seemed so long ago.

"You said 'we'." His deep, soft voice rumbled, and her practical grip evaporated. The man who'd risked life and limb for the baby in his arms looked exhausted and irresistible at the same time.

"Song looks happy, doesn't she?" Mei changed the subject as she knelt beside the couch. A new world of possibilities pounded in her heart at every word from his mouth. The instant her hand brushed the hair on his arm, desire ignited. The poor man was bruised and battered, but his eyes were dark and hazy. She knew a man in love when she saw one. Whether he'd said the L word yet or not, the practical, determined side of her was losing ground. Fast.

"I like that word." He stroked her cheek with the back of his bandaged fingers, barely making contact. "*We.* It has a nice ring to it, don't you think?"

Thinking was not her strong suit right now. Even through tape and gauze, his gentle touch had coaxed the flickering ember inside of her into a raging inferno. His deep, sexy, baritone voice was doing some very fine stroking, too. Every ragged nerve-ending in her body calmed at his velvet touch.

She brushed his flirtation aside. "I think you're on pain medication. That's what I think."

He would not be put off. "After we find LiLi, would you let me take you out for dinner, say, in Hawaii? I know a little place—"

"We'll have this conversation when you're not on drugs," she said with firm conviction, but her cheeks heated under his attentiveness. Her fingers trembled. Whatever was going on between them, it had to stop. "I'm putting Song to bed. Then I'm going to bake some—"

"But we're finally alone and I want you." He pulled her against him, his hand encircling her waist. She stiffened. All of her very dead erogenous zones sprang to life. If his mittens strayed too far south, she'd combust. Too far north, she'd ignite.

His eyes zeroed in on her mouth. *This can't happen.* Her fingers rose to his lips to intercept, those poor stitched lips that looked like they needed a kiss to make them feel better.

"You're supposed to be resting," she whispered, every stern admonition gone from her very sensible head and her voice nearly too hoarse to be heard.

His ragged lips claimed hers hesitantly. The heat of the moment exploded inside her. He pulled her against him even as he breathed his need into her, like that was in anyway possible. Her whole body responded to the feel of his hip against her stomach, the length of his hand along her ribcage. Practicality flew out the window, while all those delicious feelings surfaced with a heated rush.

When he trailed moist, hot kisses into the crook of her neck, her plans for dinner faded away. Her heart pounded wild, wanting, and so tempted. He was the masculine soul her feminine soul craved, the rugged complement to her softest places, and the steel to her weakness. Every fiber in her body ached for his touch. Desire coursed from his lips to hers and all the way to her toes until...a soft little hand patted her cheek.

Mei leaned back to see Baby Song yawning from her comfy corner of Zack's other arm. Embarrassed she had gotten lost in his arms, Mei caught her breath and a thin shred of common sense. Their amorous moment had been pre-empted. Just in time.

Zack released Mei long enough to kiss the top of Song's head. Then he kissed Mei again as passionately as his tender lips allowed. "I want a rain check," he breathed, his voice husky and low.

Her own desire burned on her cheeks. She looked up into hooded eyes that regarded her with so much raw emotion it took her breath. She trembled, suddenly saved and more frightened than ever.

"I don't know how it happened. One minute we're strangers, and the next...." What could she say? We're living together? We're in love? We're–what? Nothing felt right. Her words to him in the abandoned warehouse came to mind. Did he remember she'd blurted her feelings, that she'd told him she loved him? Had she spoken too soon? Could she really trust him? Her heart said yes, emphatically yes, but it had played her wrong before.

"And the next thing you know, I'm living with you," he said, his face filled with tenderness, his brown eyes pulling her in like a magnet she could not resist. "You're going to regret saving my life because I'm not leaving, Mei. You know that, don't you?"

She shook her head, wanting so much to believe. "No," she whispered. "I don't know anything of the sort."

"It's true," he declared. "Get used to it. I'm here to stay if you'll let me."

Mei nestled into his arm. Okay. He might not have said he loved her, but what he said helped.

"I have to ask you something," she said, still struggling to stifle the hope blossoming inside. "That day in Anacostia. You were talking with, umm, a woman."

He tipped back from her, grinning. "You followed me?"

She should've been embarrassed, but before she risked any more of her heart, she needed to know. "Who was she?"

His grin deepened. "Are you jealous?"

"No. I just...want to know."

"Mabel Magee," he answered, not a note of hesitation in his voice. "She's a CI, a confidential informant of mine. I've got a few in the area, a couple more in downtown D.C. Why?"

"She looked like, umm—"

"A hooker." He said the hard word for her. "She is."

"How do you know her?"

"She's a friend of my buddy, Jake." Zack tipped farther back, his arm still around her but the smirk on his face full of warmth. "She's been around. Jake, too. I can always trust them to tell me the truth if anything's going on I should know about."

"Who's Jake?"

"A Marine, only not as lucky as me." His arm tightened around her. "That okay with you?"

She couldn't meet his eyes. Of course she was jealous. It just surprised her she'd been jealous then. She'd hardly knew him.

"I've had a few girlfriends," he admitted. "I'm no saint, but Mabel's not one of them. No way I'd bring someone like her into my home. She's trouble."

"It's okay, you don't need to tell me anything else."

"Not unless I want to." He pulled her into his face again, planting a kiss on her cheek. "And I want to."

Baby Song chose that moment to latch onto his nose, twisting it like it belonged to her sock monkey. Mei smiled as this darling baby girl studied the big people in her very different life. How strange everything must seem to her. And then it happened. Song wiggled one big wiggle from the top of her head to the tips of her ten little toes. A tiny smile split her all too serious face. She made her first baby sound, a soft little coo. One syllable of angel-speak, but it was enough.

"She's happy," Mei said as she leaned into Zack. The joy of the simple milestone in Song's life meant so much more sharing it with him.

"Of course. All my girls smile."

"All your girls?"

"Yes," he said. "You. Song, and very soon, LiLi."

TWENTY-THREE

"We've got trouble," Todd muttered. "Ember. Get the door. No one gets inside."

Zack raised himself up on one elbow to see what was going on. It was the second day he'd been at the safe house and up until now, things had been quiet and restful. He and Song were relaxed and snuggled on the front room couch, napping and enjoying the smells wafting from the kitchen. Mei had decided to bake banana bread, a nice touch on a cold autumn afternoon. Todd kept a low fire in the fireplace. The place almost felt like home.

Ember hit the door just as someone rang the doorbell and pounded on it at the same time. She cracked it, leaving the safety chain in place. "Can I help you?" she asked before the uninvited visitor could say a word.

"We're here to interview Zack Lennox. Is he here?" a woman's abrasive voice asked in no uncertain terms.

"There's no one here by that name," Ember said evenly. "You must have the wrong information."

"You're lying," the pushy woman declared. "See my station's helicopter overhead? I couldn't get past you at the hospital, but you can't hide from Channel 16's Eye in the Sky. Now let me in. I don't have all day to play hide and seek."

"I'm sorry," Ember continued sweetly. "Like I said, there's no one here by that name. I live with my boyfriend. Todd, honey? Can you come to the door for a sec?"

Todd jumped up from the computer where he'd been monitoring the Tattle Tale feeds. Ruffling a hand through his red hair to muss it up, he stepped to Ember's side, his hand going immediately around her waist. Placing a noisy kiss on her cheek, he faced the reporter.

"Sure, hon. What's up? Someone selling vacuum cleaners?"

He unlatched the security chain to get a good look. Between the two of them, the view was still blocked, but Zack angled his arm out from beneath sleeping Song's sweaty little head. The baby snored softly. He'd draped a blanket over her to shelter her from view and to keep off the chill from the open door. Sitting with his hands on his knees, he waited, prepared to move.

"I wasn't born yesterday," the reporter snapped. "Zack Lennox is here and I know it. I'm not leaving without an interview. The FBI has taken credit for everything, but I know better. The public has a right to know what really happened. I want a minute of his time."

"Listen, lady." Todd yawned and kissed Ember again. "Like my girl said, you got the wrong place. Sorry about that."

"You and your boss think you're pretty clever, don't you?" She tried a different attack. "You're the same two who were at the hospital. Well, I've got news for you. You can't hide him forever and two can play that game."

"Whatever." Todd shut the door slowly but deliberately. "See you around."

"What the hell?" Zack growled when Todd and Ember shut the door and turned around.

"Do you believe the nerve of her?" Ember growled.

"Damned nosy reporter," Todd muttered. "Name's Victoria Levitt, ace reporter at the Independent Virginia Chronicle. She wants a story, and guess what? You're it."

Zack shrugged. One newspaper was the same as the next to him. "She blew our cover," he muttered tiredly. "We've got to move."

"You up to it?" Ember asked.

"Sure as hell not up to meeting the Tigers," he declared. "Let's pack. Alex has another safe house across the river in Pennsylvania. We can be there in an hour."

"What's going on?" Mei stood at the kitchen doorway, her cheeks flushed. Zack's heart thudded to an abrupt halt at the sight of her. How did she do that to him, fill his senses from all the way across the room with just three words?

"We need to leave. The press knows we're here. The minute this gets out—"

"It's already out," Ember muttered from the window where she kept an eye on the reporter. "Ms. Levitt is standing on our front porch holding an interview without you. Her cameraman's filming. We're screwed. Oops. Damn. She saw me."

Zack stood, rolling the ache out of his back and assessing their exit strategy. "Then we go now. Mei, grab some things for the baby. Todd. Get the car running. Grab your gear, kids. We gotta roll."

"That won't work," Ember advised. "Another Channel 16 news van just pulled into the driveway. They've got you blocked in."

"I'm calling Alex," Todd said, his cell phone already to his ear. "He needs to know."

The conversation was short and not so sweet. Zack could hear Alex bellowing from where he stood. Poor Todd grimaced and held the phone away from his ear.

"We're on our way," Alex's disembodied voice declared loudly and angrily. "Be ready to move when we get there."

"Ah, Boss. We're not going anywhere. She's got the driveway blocked."

"Who said you were taking your vehicle?"

"Right. What's your ETA?"

"Should be there in twenty." The phone went dead

"Man," Todd muttered. "I hate when he's spun up. Can't get a word in edgewise. Wonder how he knew."

"Probably because Mother monitors all the news channels," Ember said. "Channel 16 runs an Eye in the Sky breaking news bite. That's their claim to fame. They're first on the scene all the time."

"It also means anyone with a television is standing on our front porch right along with her," Zack said.

"Or anyone with an instant news update on their cell phone," Todd said.

"If that...woman," Zack bit his tongue at the word he wanted to say, "if she broadcast our address, the Tigers know where we are. Shit. We don't have time to wait for the boss to show his ugly face. I need more ammo. Now!"

"On it." Ember doffed her casual sweater, revealing her double holster and the two weapons she carried, while opening the front closet. "Ruger 9mm. Double stack?"

"No. Single."

She tossed him a box of 9mm ammo, plus two loaded magazines. "Have at it."

Zack caught Mei's frightened gaze when he caught the ammo. Setting it on the end table, he scooped still-sleeping Baby Song into his arms. "Grab some things for Song to eat and drink and come with me."

Mei's eyes opened wider.

He waited at the kitchen doorway while she grabbed a box of crackers, a can of baby formula and two baby bottles. There hadn't been a need before, but he needed to explain how the safe home really operated. When she came to his side, he proceeded down the hallway to what looked like another closet door. It wasn't. Opening it revealed a metal door, with a keypad where a doorknob would normally be.

"This is the safe room. There's food, water, a restroom, a bed, and a telephone inside. Once I lock the door, the only way out is when you open it from your side. Enter one-eight-one into the keypad."

Mei entered the code, her fingers shaking. "You should stay with us. Your hands are still healing. How can you use a gun?"

The door eased open automatically, releasing a whoosh of cooled air into the hall. He ushered her into the room, his hand to the small of her back. Handing the baby to her, he peeled the bandages off his fingers. Little Song fidgeted as she opened her sleepy eyes.

"I'm taking care of that right now. Turn the heat up in here. You've got a phone, television, and a computer. I'll call you when it's clear."

"Zack." Mei's voice cracked. She took a step toward him. "Don't. You're not ready."

Damn it, he wanted more time with her. He brushed a quick kiss into her forehead. Duty called. "Marines don't run, Mei. Stay in here. Whatever happens, do not open the door. I'll be back as soon as I can. Understood?"

"Zack!" Todd's bark from the other room gave her no time to answer. "Git your ass out here."

He closed the door, listening for the soft sound of compression hydraulics sinking the master lock into place before he turned to answer. With Mei and Song safe, he grabbed his pistol out of his gear bag and hurried back to the center of the house. "How many?"

"Two cars just arrived. Twelve Tigers." Todd crouched at the bulletproof window beneath the couch where Zack had just lain. "Looks like Ms. Levitt might be caught in a crossfire. Should I let her in?"

"Yes," Zack hissed as he crouched at the opposite side of the room, facing the backyard. A civilian was a civilian whether he liked her or not. "Make it quick."

Todd opened the front door. "Get your dumb asses in here," he growled, motioning Ms. Levitt and her cameraman to speed it up.

No sooner said than done. Ms. Levitt ducked in as quick as a sacred rabbit, her cameraman on her heels. "Oh thank you," she said, her damned microphone in her hand and her cameraman still recording. "Looks like I'm going to get my interview after all."

"Shut up!" Ember roared from where she crouched in the kitchen. "This is all your fault, you dumb bitch!"

Zack slammed the loaded 9mm magazine into his weapon with a grin. *Yeah, Ember. You go, girl.*

"Another SUV just rolled up," Todd reported. "Seven more bad guys hitching their pants up. Dumb asses."

"You call the police?" Zack asked, stretching his sore fingers to limber them up for what lay ahead.

"Soon as Todd got off the phone," Ember answered, her pistol aimed out the kitchen window, also bulletproof glass. "They're in transit."

"So you're the famous Zack Lennox," Ms. Levitt purred.

Zack shot her a cold glance, surprised at the heated look in her pale blue eyes and her low cleavage. She was turned on? Now? He turned away, mad enough to push her back outside.

"What they packing?" he asked Todd or Ember.

"Sawed offs. Uzis. Typical gangbanger shit," Todd answered.

"I got five creeps sneaking around back here," Ember muttered. "They've got ARs."

"We've got bulletproof glass and steel reinforcements. Let 'em try shooting through that," Zack reminded his team.

"I got a world of hurt in front," Todd answered. "Damn. Someone brought a LAW to the party."

"You're shitting me?" Zack growled. "An M72? Are you freaking serious?"

Any other day, the stark fear staring back at him from the once cocky reporter might have been enough to make him offer her an explanation. Not today. Let her figure out that the Tigers she'd summoned with her brash reporting had a light anti-tank weapon in their arsenal. Bulletproof glass didn't stand a chance.

A spray of lead hit the outside of the home. Zack debated opening the safe room to these two geniuses from the press.

His decision was made for him when a battering ram impacted the front door. There simply was no time for any more hospitality.

"These guys are serious," Ember muttered.

"You ready?" Zack asked. Protocol was simple. Sit tight. Alex and the police were on the way. Until the safe house was breached, they would not return fire. But the minute that happened, Zack was ready. He'd already planned which Tiger to hit first, second, third, and how high or how low. Another SUV rolled across the lawn, dropping Tigers out of open doors before it came to a stop.

"Looks like an even fight," Todd quipped. "Five more. That's what? An even two dozen? Great! Eight for each of us." He turned to the folks from the press. "You folks wouldn't happen to know how to shoot, would you?

Ms. Levitt shook her head quickly. Her cameraman, too. "No. That's your job," she squeaked.

"Figures." Todd turned back to the army facing him from the street. "Might have made an interesting story seeing how you're so brave and all."

"Not bad odds," Zack rasped. "I've been in tougher fights."

"Oh yeah? When?" Ember's eyes were intent on whatever was taking place behind the house.

Zack would have obliged with the details of his escapades high in the Hindu Kush, but time had run out. The noise from the battering ram ceased because the idiot with the LAW loaded it, and unfortunately, he knew which way to aim.

"We got incoming," Zack yelled. "Front door!"

BLAM!

The house shook on its foundation when the 66.mm shell blasted through the door and exploded into the interior wall. Ms. Levitt screamed like a loud-mouthed siren with no shut off switch. Ember turned to face the smoke from her location behind the kitchen table, now on its side and scant protection from any type of ammunition. She was the farthest away, but Zack and Todd had their hands full. No sooner was the door breached than another spray of bullets peppered the entryway, throwing plaster and woodchips into the home. The Tigers at the other side of the house let loose with a barrage of their own, automatic fire etching across the bulletproof glass until visibility was no longer possible. Ms. Levitt kept the siren turned on high and loud.

"Ember!" Zack yelled through the smoke and debris.

"I'm good," she answered. "You?"

"Good," Todd shouted. "Stay safe!"

Zack ran to the front door before any of the gangbangers could enter, dropped to his side on the floor, and fired death into the yard. Shrieks and angry voices punctuated the two seconds of silence when he discarded the empty magazines and reloaded in one swift, smooth movement.

Todd took his turn returning fire, still crouched at the now-broken picture window. Angry shouts and screamed curses were the only indicator of his success. Too much smoke still filled the house to know for sure what was going on outside.

The moment Todd reloaded, Zack took over, meeting the barrage from outside with steady shots from side to side. These Tigers were cocky and arrogant, not trained snipers by any means. As a result, they'd come in too close, thinking they could enter quickly once they blew the door. Guess again. Zack couldn't see clearly through the smoke, but what he could see, he hit.

"Stop!" Todd yelled out.

Zack shot a quick look his way. Todd had his finger to his ear. Zack reloaded, but it seemed the war ended as quickly as it started. Eerie silence reigned, but Zack had had enough. He didn't know who was alive out there, but he was ready to send them to their maker.

"Who's next?" he called through the open door.

No one answered. Sirens shrieked the local PD's approach. Good. Help was on its way, but it wasn't there yet. Adrenaline magnified every noise and sight, pumping up Zack's senses, pushing the sixth sniper sense out into the yard, feeling for the enemy. The universe seemed to be holding its breath and Mei was waiting for him. This needed to end because he did not trust her to be obedient and stay put.

"Step it up, kittens. I can't wait all day," he ordered impatiently. "You've got to the count of three before I come out and finish the rest of you. One!"

He cocked his head to listen, but still no answer. "Sitrep," he snapped to Ember and Todd.

"Backyard is clear," Ember answered.

"Too much smoke in the front yard," Todd reported. "Looks like someone popped a smoke grenade. Too murky to see. Alex called. ETA in sixty seconds."

Zack held his breath, still on his side and still trained on the deadly silence outside. There was no way he'd killed all the Tigers. Someone grunted. Another cried about someone hurting him, and Zack dared to hope. The police weren't there yet. Was Alex?

"All clear," David Tao's friendly voice finally sounded.

"All clear," Zack echoed. "You coming in?"

A ramrod straight shadow evolved out of the smoke into Alex Stewart.

"You sure shoot your mouth off when you're seriously outnumbered, don't you, Lennox?" he scolded his agent.

"It's a little trick I picked up from a sniper friend of mine." Zack clasped Alex's proffered arm and pushed off the floor. "An old guy once told me what your enemy doesn't know–your enemy doesn't know. Sometimes all you've got left is ego. Praying like hell doesn't hurt, either."

"An old guy?" Alex offered an arched brow.

"Damned glad to see you, Boss." Zack let Alex pull him into a man hug, more of a shoulder and chest bump than a hug. The police had arrived. Some of the smoke outside had cleared. It looked like David Tao had the scene under control.

Ember emerged from the smoky kitchen, stepping over the debris from the grenade, her pistols holstered. "Hey, Alex. Took you long enough getting here."

"Where's Todd?"

"Here." Todd raised one hand from the bullet-pocked picture window. "Mei and Song are in the safe room. We're all good."

"Where are *they*?" Alex growled, his nostrils flared as he took in the scene of his now-destroyed safe house. "Where's that sonofabitchin' reporter?"

Zack turned to the ridiculous scene of a smart-assed reporter on her hands and knees, hiding behind her cameraman who himself cringed behind his camera, like that was any kind of tactical gear. "Alex Stewart, meet Ms.

Victoria Levitt, ace reporter of some piece of shit rag in town."

She actually scrambled to her feet and smoothed her hand over her disheveled hairdo, like Alex cared what the hell she looked like. Stepping forward with her chin tilted up, she offered a dazzling smile and her hand, which promptly crumpled against the hard wall of Alex's chest when he stepped into her comfort zone.

"You risked the lives of my team, an innocent woman and a child to get your damned story," he bit out, towering over her enough that she had to take a step back.

"The press has the right to report on any—"

"Your press privileges ended when you set foot on private property, Ms. Levitt," he hissed. "You recklessly endangered civilians. You could've gotten killed yourself, not that I give a shit about that. There will be consequences."

Again with the chin tilt. Ms. Levitt ran her gaze up and down the angry man in her face. "Freedom of the press," she said. "I know my rights. You can't threaten me."

"Get the hell out of my house," he spat. "I'm not threatening the likes of you. I'm promising."

"I...I—" She straightened her hair again, looking for her microphone. "I was just leaving." It took her all of one second to grab her mike off the floor and catch up with her cameraman, who was already out the door and in police custody.

"Maybe we shouldn't have saved her life after all," Todd muttered as he nodded toward the reporter, herself now in cuffs and screeching up a storm of protest.

Zack headed down the hall to retrieve Mei, but before he did, he needed to make sure. "We all clear?" he asked one last time. If nothing else, he wanted to assure Mei the battle was over and the good guys won. She might have to hang back until the debris was cleared, but the good news would help her calm down.

Todd stepped to the front door, now blackened and hanging off its hinges. He waved to David. "Hey. How's it going out there? You need a hand?"

Zack glanced back. Leave it to Todd to always ask if he could help. The damned kid would be senior agent in no time. Zack never heard David's answer. All he saw was the hit. Todd jerked backward, his hand to his chest and his mouth opened in surprise like he was horsing around. Like he couldn't believe what was happening. Like he wasn't shot.

Alex grabbed him before he hit the floor.

Ember screamed. "Todd! Oh, my God! Todd!" She was suddenly across the room and on her knees beside him, her hands covered in dark red blood, the kind of blood that pours out of a man's pulmonary veins. Alex cradled him, checking for pulse and hope. Zack caught the bleak stab of pain that flashed in his boss's eyes.

"No!" Ember had her hands frantically all over Todd, her cheek to his cheek, her breasts to his chest, her mouth on his mouth, trying to pour life back into him. She cupped his chin. "No, no, no! Don't leave me, baby. Don't go!"

Zack moved away from the safe room in slow motion, his body turned to lead and heartache. Mei didn't need to see this. *God, no.*

Todd lifted a bloody finger to Ember, tracing her lower lip. His mouth moved. Zack wasn't close enough to hear what he said. The pain on Ember's face was bad enough. Todd's hand dropped. The sound that ripped from Ember stopped

Zack cold. He'd heard it before, an angry, pain-filled keening hurled heavenward from the shattered heart of a buddy or a loved one left behind.

Alex pulled her against him, his eyes dark and hard.

"He's leaving me, Alex," she sobbed. "He's...already gone." She collapsed on top of Todd, and suddenly Zack heard the sound of triumph from the front yard.

"I got him! I got Lennox!" a man's voice crowed.

Zack stepped around Alex and Ember with murder in his heart. When he cleared the door he saw the braggart; a Tiger with his face to the ground while two policemen muscled him into submission. Still he yelled. "I got him! I got him!"

"Who are you talking about?" one of the officers asked.

"Five K for Lennox." The braggart's sweaty face glistened with pride. "That's the deal. Sweet. It's all mine."

"Oh, yeah? Who's paying a bounty for Lennox, tough guy?" The officers handcuffed the killer and pulled him to his feet.

"Who do you think?" the gangster sneered.

Zack barreled into the gangster, taking him back to the ground with his fists in the man's ugly face. "That man you just murdered ain't Lennox, you freaking dumb ass! You killed the wrong man!"

The police pulled him off and pushed him away, but Zack launched himself again, this time his hands at the man's neck, choking him with all the strength his mangled fingers had left.

"You're Lennox?" the fool gasped. "You?"

"He was my friend," Zack growled when David Tao pulled him away, his hand in the middle of Zack's chest. "He was a kid! You killed the wrong man!"

"Settle down," David said, his own dark eyes glistening. "Ember needs you. Mei needs you. We all need you. Settle down."

"No!" Zack choked, raking his fingernails over his head, full of anger he was not yet ready to release. But David was right. Ember's sad lament echoed from the inside of the house.

"He's dead," Zack told David. "Todd is...dead."

David nodded. No more words were necessary. Zack swallowed his anger and turned to the awful scene where Alex still cradled his newest agent and the woman who'd loved him. Todd never felt the bullet that pierced his heart, that left him gasping for life already gone. Sirens wailed in the distance, bringing medics for whom there was no longer a patient to save.

"God." Zack rammed his back into the wall behind him, still ready to fight the world. He couldn't breathe. He couldn't swallow. Worst of all, he couldn't face Ember.

Paramedics scrambled around the crime scene. Alex relinquished his hold on the young man, crushing Ember into his arms until she had no choice but to let Todd go. There was no miracle cure this day. No way to change the awful thing that had happened.

Junior Agent Todd Chandler had fallen in the line of duty.

TWENTY-FOUR

The only one missing was Ember.

Zack stood with Mei at the grave, the rest of his somber teammates all within arm's reach. Together they watched the honor guard present arms and take the twenty-one shots with such perfect accuracy that the sound of their report evolved into three single volleys.

Job well done, reservists.

Thirteen folds to the flag of glory, and twenty-one shells tucked within the heart of the red, white, and blue.

Good job, Marines.

A short but precisely measured walk to the grieving parents, and the flag that had covered Todd's heart was now pressed against the bosom of the mother he loved. And who loved him. Her son. Her boy. Her darling baby. Silent tears fell into the folds of color. His father held his mother tight.

God bless you, Agent Todd Chandler. Fellow soldier. Hero. Friend.

Mei sniffed. Zack steeled his heart. He'd stood here too many times in the past. It always hurt. He saw her step out from a small black sedan then, her slender shape shrouded in billowing black. Ember. She didn't join the rest of The TEAM. His heart ached so much worse with her all the way over there, alone.

At last, the leaden December sky relinquished its hold on all the sorrow of the day. The ice cold rain fell on restless and resting alike. Ember pivoted on her heel and walked in the opposite direction. Uphill. Toward the Arlington Amphitheater. And solitude.

Zack stood with Mei, watching her go.

"Poor Ember. I must talk to her," Mei offered.

"No. Let her go. You know how it is. She wants to be alone."

He turned with Mei and walked away.

Arlington was quiet once again.

Two new agents were assigned to guard Mei and Song. Junior agents Rory Dennison and Connor Maher were a couple of the best. Alex had moved everyone to a secure hotel suite in Alexandria, not far from The TEAM's office, so Zack went back to work. He was the early bird, like Alex. It was just the way some folks were made, hard-wired to greet the morning sun and start the day. No more lying on the couch. No more downtime. Injured or not, Zack was a man at war.

The office was silent when he arrived. Mother sat staring at the blank screens in front of her. She was the privileged one. She had to know it. Alex pretty much gave her whatever equipment she asked for without question or hesitation. He trusted her implicitly and because of that trust, her workspace became the heart of The TEAM, the place where everyone eventually came for technical expertise, support, and sometimes gossip. She excelled at it all. Not today. Zack avoided her. She might want to chat. He didn't.

Want to or not, he watched her. For the first time in a long time, some of her screens were dark, while others transmitted static and snow. Only a couple relayed images, and even they were muted. Nosy, I-know-something-you-don't-know Mother didn't seem to see them. She shrugged out of her black suit jacket, letting it fall to the floor.

Only a week ago, he'd watched Todd sitting with Mother and Ember as they unraveled the mystery of the Black Dragon Conquest. Zack could still see the unmasked delight in his friend's green eyes when he'd discovered the Easter eggs. And now he was gone.

After the hours they'd worked, after all the good they'd accomplished, karma should have been a hell of a lot kinder. Absentmindedly, Zack rubbed tender fingers over his ragged lips. Everything hurt. His hands. His mouth. His heart most of all.

Mother sniffed. Great. The last thing he needed was to hear someone releasing their grief while he bottled his inside.

"I'm sorry," she said sadly. "I didn't know you were already here."

Zack looked at her to see who she was speaking to. He should have known. Alex was already here. He must've spoken to Mother. She answered, "I've usually got more energy. In no time at all I'll be able to leap tall buildings again, and run faster than a speeding bullet and...and..."

Zack cringed. Mother's overabundance of words had just sabotaged her.

"I'm sorry, Boss," she cried. "I can't do this today."

I should've stayed home–if I had one.

"Why don't you come into my office?" Alex offered gently, nodding toward his open office door. "Zack? You too. Come on."

No. Not yet. Not now.

He saw the glint in his boss's eye. Alex wasn't asking.

"Coming," he growled.

"I'll be okay." Mother blew her nose into a couple tissues. "I just need a minute."

"Come on, Sasha."

Great. Mother grabbed her box of tissues and followed Alex like a whipped puppy. It was a rare day when anyone called her by her real name. Alex was being kind today, the last thing Zack needed. Kindness offered was the toehold that would crack the door to everyone's grief, and he did not want to go down that road. Work was a better remedy.

Work your guts out. Try to forget. Never let 'em see you cry.

Zack followed anyway. He'd barely sat down at the smaller conference table when Murphy entered, quiet and somber. Then David. Within minutes, Alex had everyone in his office except poor Ember. Who would have ever guessed her sweet love affair would end this way?

Kelsey must have baked because there were homemade cinnamon rolls on Alex's table, and he'd made a pot of coffee. It smelled good, but no one made a move. The frosted rolls sat waiting for Todd to show up and snag the first one. Like he always did. Before....

"I'm proud as hell of you guys," Alex said.

Good way to start, Boss. Kick us when we're down.

Zack clenched his fists in front of him at the table. Stitched and broken fingers complained at the pressure. He did it again. Everyone's morale was low. He'd lost enough people and friends in his life to understand where their heads were right now. They'd done their best. Damn it. They should be doing a victory dance instead of mourning. But life can change on a dime. That's just the way it was. He stared at his hands, clenched them again, and planned revenge.

"How's Chai Yenn, David?" Alex turned to the senior agent at his side.

The question must've surprised David as much as it did Zack. He looked sheepish, like he'd been caught. Zack watched the cat and mouse game begin that Alex was so good at.

"She's...she's living with my family," David said, gulping as he faced Alex. "Once Nancy heard—"

"You're her foster parents then, right?" Alex asked calmly.

"Yes." David looked guilty. "She never went into a foster home. I couldn't let her."

Mother reached over to squeeze his hand.

"Congratulations." Alex didn't miss a beat. "Chai Yenn is a lucky little girl. I'm glad you and Nancy have her."

Me, too. Zack nodded toward David, a man's unspoken approval. David understood. That's why he was senior agent.

Alex turned to Mother. "Tell me about Tony Brown."

Here we go.

Mother didn't need prompting to continue. A good manager knows how his people think, and Alex knew talking was her therapy. Who didn't know that?

A light flickered in Mother's blue eyes. "Remember the button Zack found?"

"I do."

"Okay, so I checked the list of customers at the shop in Paris, and Tony Brown was on the list all right. Only the suit he ordered was a forty-eight regular, and Mr. Brown wears, umm, sorry, wore a thirty-six long."

Zack turned away. Too soon those knowing blue eyes of his boss would catch him in their beam. He wasn't ready.

"So then I checked a couple other things," Mother rattled on. "Do you know why he was in Paris in the first place?" She didn't give Alex time to answer. "Well, I'll tell you why. Tony Brown was on ATF business with his boss, Director Carducci. You want to know who wears a forty-eight regular?"

"Carducci." Again Alex's voice was incredibly calm.

"Right. So I got to thinking. If the little girl from the dumpster had a button from Carducci's suit in her hand, he must've had a hold of her right before she was dumped, don't you think?"

"Whose skin cells besides Zhen Ting's were on the button?" Alex asked patiently.

"Still don't know, but the spectra-analysis proved that person is diabetic. And do you want to know who's diabetic?"

"Carducci?"

"Right again." Mother didn't crow like she usually did when she impressed her boss, but Zack could tell she was pleased. She had a way of radiating when she was right. An annoying way....

"Good job."

"But there's more."

"Okay, what else?" Alex was infinitely kind today.

Zack understood. Really, he did. He'd been in this exact situation too many times in the past. The most important thing everyone needed was to acknowledge their grief and their strength. It made sense. The only way forward was through. Zack just wasn't ready to go through. Not yet. He had work to do.

"I've been checking on Tony Brown. You're right. He was on the mission to China with his parents, but I got to thinking." Mother was on a roll now. "He didn't seem like the kind of kid to get involved in child trafficking. I mean, one minute he was trying to help the orphans in China, and the next minute he smuggled babies? It didn't feel right, so I ran his cell phone records again. He only called Richards one time while he was in China. You want to know who called Richards a couple times a week during the same time frame?"

Alex raised an eyebrow. "Carducci again?"

Mother nodded.

"Did I tell you I don't pay you enough?"

Now you're just sucking up, Boss. Zack drummed his fingers together. Much more of the mutual admiration society BS, and he'd have to ask to be excused.

Alex put a hand on Murphy's shoulder. "How's the van coming, Murph?"

The older man looked tired as he spread a diagram in front of Alex. That piqued Zack's interest. "Found this inside the backdoor. I had a hunch before, but now I know how the little gizmo works. Look at this little arm right here. It's an aperture that springs the latch. It's remote operated. It proves someone wanted our guys to see the door pop open at that exact moment. Zack and David were set up. Chai Yenn was bait."

"Do we know who triggered it?" Alex asked.

"Well now, that's tricky. It's triggered by a cell phone signal, so I asked Mother to track all the cell towers within the area of Espinosa's hangout. Looks like David and Zack had company that day."

Zack straightened in his seat. *What sonofabitch did that?*

Murphy slid an eight-by-ten photo across the table. Zack craned his neck to see. It showed the plate glass window of a storefront a couple doors down from the Espinosa hangout. A black Lincoln sedan reflected in the window. Zack leaned closer. This windshield he could see into. There was a man at the wheel of the vehicle holding a cell phone up to his face.

"Looks like Carducci needs reading glasses," Alex commented drily. "Anything else?"

Carducci? The bastard who wanted me fired? Zack's blood began to boil. Now he knew where he was going after this meeting.

Murphy continued. "The FBI wants to talk with you about Shawn Washington, you know, the gangbanger who killed Todd. Washington claims he's got a big fish on the hook. He wants immunity first. The FBI wants you there when he talks."

"Immunity for the punk who killed one of my agents?" Alex shook his head. "I don't think so. Tell them no deal. We've got enough evidence to put Carducci away with Washington and Richards as it is."

Murphy pushed back from the table. "One last thing. Remember all those furs that came out of the van?"

"Yeah. What about them?"

"Metro PD tracked them to an estate sale in Vermont. An elderly gentleman left an estate of antiques, furs, even a vintage Morgan—"

"He got a name, Murph?" Alex gently interrupted Murphy's rambling.

"Valentine. As in Sophia Valentine, Carducci's wife. Her father passed last spring. Those furs were from his estate."

"It doesn't make sense." Alex straightened in his chair. "Why would Carducci dump furs on Espinosa?"

"Hell, I don't know, Alex. Could be a payoff. Furs are easy enough to move." Murphy's voice betrayed his weariness of the whole affair. Zack agreed. There were so many angles to the operation it was hard to know who was doing what to whom.

"Thanks, Murph. You've always got my back." Alex was saying all the right words. Zack had to give him credit. The man knew his team.

The door cracked open and an ashen-faced Ember walked in. Instead of sitting at the table with everyone else, she took a seat by the door. Zack bit his lip. Dressed in an all black and very tight fitting pants suit, she'd chosen to hide her eyes behind dark glasses. He should've thought of that. A pair of Oakleys would provide the wall he needed.

Alex swiveled his chair to face her, his hands on his knees. "Ember. You didn't have to come in today. Why are you here?"

She didn't speak, just faced him behind the shades.

"Say your piece, but then I want you to go home," he said gently.

Ember had dyed her pretty blonde hair black, a harsh contrast against her pale skin. She raised her chin and handed Alex a sheet of paper. "I've got the Cayman Islands for you, Alex."

Zack detected a definite note of coup de grâce in her soft, sad voice.

"ATF Director Kevin Carducci has seventy-two million dollars in various bank accounts in the Caymans. They all track back to a single point of origin." Her voice quavered, breaking Zack's heart all over again.

"Whose?" Alex asked.

"Interpol's most wanted man on the planet. Mr. Lenny Huang. He's behind the Black Dragon syndicate."

"I know who he is." Alex watched Ember. "Are you okay, kiddo?"

She looked away and Zack wanted to go to her, muss her hair, hold her and let her cry. It just wasn't his place. It was Todd's.

Alex laid the report on the table in front of him and looked around at his team, slowly making eye contact with those who could. When he'd made the complete circle, he looked down at his hands, still splayed on the paper Ember had given him.

"I know how much this particular operation meant to all of us, but we're not going to pursue the China connection any longer. D.C. Interpol Director, Mr. Daniel Peters called yesterday. Told me to butt out."

David opened his mouth to protest, but Alex held his hand for silence. "It's all good. We'll butt out. It's their op. Let them bring the bastard, Lenny Huang, down. Guess they'll call if they need us. In the meantime, we'll take care of Carducci. And when we're done with him, maybe we'll go after Debargio, Espinoza, and the 4th Street gang, too."

Zack's hands were instantly on his armrests, ready to push off. As difficult as it was to get on with the business of living, that's exactly what everyone would do, simply because that's all there was to do. That was life.

Alex caught Zack's eagerness to leave. "You're another one who shouldn't be here."

Zack steeled his face and offered nothing back.

"Why are you?"

"I have to do something," Zack ground out, his heart clenched as tight as his fists.

"You can't bring him back."

But I can make someone pay.

"What about Mei's daughter?" Zack barked. It was either bark or fall apart.

"Go home, son." Alex's words were soft and sad. "Trust me. I haven't forgotten LiLi, but I can't lose you, too."

Steel doesn't cry, but it does choke up when someone hits below the belt. Mother sniffed into her tissues. Ember coughed a tight little cough, her hand to her mouth, and Zack wished like hell he were the one lying six feet under at Arlington. It should have been him who'd gotten shot. Not Todd.

"We do an ugly and a damned tough job in the world," Alex said. "Sometimes we take a beating while we're doing it. We're branded assassins and mercenaries. We get investigated, and most times we get hung out to dry by a federal government that wants to look good without really being good. It's been a helluva week. We've lost a brother and a friend."

He seemed to struggle for his next words. "It's not easy. It sucks. And it hurts. You all know the Marine Corps motto is *Semper Fi–Always Faithful.* I'd like to think that's how we'll finish this op. We'll be ever faithful to our country, always to each other, but especially to our own fallen friend and brother. Todd Chandler was a damned good man."

Zack felt the mood in the room shift, just the tiniest fraction. Damned if Alex hadn't done it again, made a course correction so small as to be almost imperceptible. The man looked sad, but proud. *How does he do it?* Zack straightened his shoulders ready to follow his boss into whatever hell he aimed to go.

"Let's finish what we started," Alex spat out his last words. "Get this sonofabitch."

TWENTY-FIVE

"Come here, little one."

Mei gathered Song out of Zack's arms and settled the sleeping baby back into the crib. Again. The little girl ended up with him in his bed at least once or twice every night. All Song had to do was make the smallest peep and he was at her beck and call. It was sweet in a way. He tried to be quiet, tiptoeing into Mei's room so he didn't disturb her. She'd lie there and listen while he got the baby a drink, talking quiet baby talk to a child who had yet to make more than a quiet coo once in awhile. He'd snuggle with Song until they both fell back to sleep. Mei would give them enough time before she'd reverse the scene; tiptoe into Zack's room and return Song to her own bed.

Mei stood at her bedroom window, thinking. When Alex had first sent Zack home from work, he'd been angry. As beat up as he was, Zack wanted to be with his team. Mei understood. Not being able to change the tragedies in life was a bitter reality, but spending time with her and Song mellowed him out. He'd chatted with Rory and Connor. That helped, too.

The hard day came back to her. She'd been in awe knowing that Zack, Todd, and Ember stood in harm's way, protecting her and Baby Song without hesitation. Ironically, Todd had been right when he'd said Zack was ready to die protecting her. Zack was, only it was Todd who'd ended up fulfilling the prophecy. The look in Zack's eyes when he'd retrieved her from the safe room was shattering. She knew without a word something terrible had happened.

The fierce bond of warriors knotted Zack to Alex to David and then to their fallen comrade that morning. Like a chain forged in fire, no words were needed as they'd knelt around Todd and watched the medics do their work. The bond was so real Mei could almost reach out and touch it. They called it brotherhood, and those brothers loved their brokenhearted sister like no one else could. Ember's grief still sliced to the core of Mei's heart. As awful as it was not knowing where LiLi was, she still had hope to cling to. Poor Ember had nothing.

The wind whipped against her window. December had come with a great blizzard that brought the nation's capital to a swift and icy standstill. There was no wind with the storm, just snow piled quickly into a thick, icy blanket covering everything. The landscape had changed into white lumps that used to be cars, narrow paths that once were sidewalks, and streets meandering between mounds of plowed and shoveled polar precipitation.

This was the season when people stayed inside their heated homes and made merry, but Mei's heart was cast out into the world, wandering the snowy streets and worrying after her stolen daughter. There were no colored lights in the strange new hotel room. She had no time for merriment.

It was during quiet times that despair crept into her heart. Her arms missed the feel of LiLi's warm little girl body hugged up against her in quiet slumber. Her lips longed to speak nursery rhymes, to sing songs, and taste chocolate milk and maple syrup kisses. Her nostrils yearned for the smell of her child's minty toothpaste breath and lavender scented baby shampoo. Mei ached for each touch, sound, and sight of her stolen child.

As thankful as she was to bring Baby Song into her life, the knowledge that this child was safe and sound only emphasized the fact that her child was not. Where was LiLi now the days were cold and winter so deep? Was she safe and warm somewhere? Did she have enough to eat? Was she sick? Was she clean? Were the people who had her kind and decent, or did she cry herself to sleep at night because she was afraid? Please God, was LiLi even alive? Mei blocked the pain and tears before they took over. Despair came too easily. She refused it yet again. She'd cry after she had LiLi back in her arms.

Turning at the sound of Zack's bedroom door quietly closing, she watched him enter her room. His eyes instantly strayed to Song's bed.

"You took my baby," he whispered.

"She needs to be in her own bed."

"I know." He came to her side. "I just like to snuggle with my girls."

The transformation in him touched her. From the moment he'd picked Song up out of the dirty playpen, he had revealed an amazing heart. Zack seemed to live to make Song smile, the way Mei had once lived to make LiLi smile. He'd be an excellent father if his plan to adopt his little girl succeeded. Baby Song loved him. Mei did, too, but things had happened so fast between them. She needed to slow the momentum. Nothing must get in the way of her finding LiLi, not even a handsome man with a beautiful baby.

"I know you." He wrapped his hands around her waist, pulling her back into his chest. "You're thinking about LiLi."

Mei leaned against him. "What are we doing? Are we fooling ourselves?"

"Fooling ourselves? About what, Mei? About Song? LiLi? About us?"

"About everything, Zack. What have we done? We aren't even married, yet we have a child? What's that about? What have we done to Song?"

Zack gazed at the sleeping baby. "I think we've done a great thing for Song."

Mei could read the love on his face the moment she mentioned the baby's name. The anguish for her child reared its ugly head again. Mei didn't begrudge the love he had for Song. She just wanted LiLi, too.

He tilted her chin up with two fingers, his eyes searching her face. "You think I've forgotten, don't you?"

Mei turned away. "No. It's just that—"

"We haven't found LiLi yet," he finished for her. "We've been looking in all the wrong places. She's still out there."

Mei tried not to cry, but Zack's strong arms made her weak. All her work had been for nothing. She was not only off course, but now she was dead in the water, taking care of another woman's child instead of her searching for her own. Pointing to the frigid wonderland beyond the window, her fear hiccupped out of her. "I want my baby...in here...with me."

"I know Mei." Zack smothered her against him, his voice soft and low in her hair. "We're catching our balance, that's all. This has been hell week. As far as Alex is concerned, finding LiLi is my next assignment. He doesn't know how to give up. Neither do I."

"I'm afraid I'll never see her again." Mei wiped her face with the sleeve of her robe as she regained her composure. Her moment of weakness embarrassed her. Zack had just lost a good friend. She should be comforting him.

"Come here." He scooped her into his arms and carried her into his bedroom, settling her neatly beside him in his bed, robe and all. "I bring all my best girls here."

She sighed as he covered them both with his blanket. Dressed in pajama bottoms and a T-shirt, Zack's body was rock solid, the same as his self-confidence. She pressed against him to listen to the steady rhythm of that good heart beneath his chest muscles. It sounded strong and sure, just like him.

Mei relaxed. He was always gentle with her even when she'd been a beast. The comfort of his strength warmed her as Zack shared the weight of her awful world. He reached to the nightstand to turn off the light, pulling her into the crook of his arm. Listening to his steady breathing, she closed her eyes. No wonder Song fell asleep in his arms.

His hands smoothed down her arm and back up again as he settled onto his pillow.

"I've been so mean to you," she admitted, her fingers roaming up his neck to secure themselves around his ear. His scalp prickled with the day's growth.

"Nah. You've been fine. Don't worry about it."

"Why do you shave your head?" she asked, her hands smoothing over his scalp. She used to think it bare and vulgar, but somewhere during their time together his bare head had become a badge. Zack Lennox was who he was, exposed for all the world to see, like him or not. Hair wouldn't change the man.

"I started shaving it when I joined the Corps. Guess I thought it made me look tougher, meaner. Why? Don't you like it? You want me to grow it out?"

"No." She brushed her forehead against his scratchy chin, breathing in the just-showered smell of the man she loved as her fingers roamed over his head again. "I like you just the way you are."

They lay quietly together, her heart pumping with pleasure at her position tight against him. He always smelled so good; a hint of leather and–him. She drank in a deep breath, willing the comfort of it into her soul.

"Do you ever untie that knot thingee in your hair?" he asked mischievously, his fingers plucking the tight bun at the back of her head.

"No." Her heart pitched, not sure if he was talking about her hair or something else. Suddenly, she didn't want to be closed off and fighting the world by herself. "But I could."

His hand cupped the side of her head, his fingers smoothing over her tightly pulled hair, the pad of his thumb on her cheek. "I'd sure like to see the real you," he coaxed, peering into her face. "I know you're in there."

Mei forgot how to breathe when he leaned in to place a feather-soft kiss on her forehead. It wasn't enough. She shifted to a sitting position at his side, releasing her hair from the army of bobby pins that had restrained it for so long. Her heart pounded at what the simple action really meant. This was a huge step, an undressing that would bare her soul again. Questions flooded her mind. Did she truly have anything left to give this man who'd only and always chosen to stand with her? Did he really want her? More than anything else–how could he?

"Yes," he growled, his fingers combing through her tangled tresses. His breath hitched when he shifted his weight to his elbow to bury his hands in her hair, turning it into a cape for her shoulders. "My hell, Mei. You're a whole different woman."

"Zack," she whispered timidly, scared at what might happen next, but finally willing. "I don't want to be alone anymore."

"Are you sure?" he asked tenderly. "I'm not pushing you, Mei. Don't think you have to do anything you're not ready for. Honest. I'm happy just being here with you."

"Please kiss me. Like you did the first time. Like you...." She left the words unsaid. *Like you love me.*

"Are you sure?"

"Yes," she whispered, quieter still. *Kiss me. Love me. Help me feel something besides the awful hole in my heart.*

He groaned, reaching his arm around her, his hand gentle at the base of her skull as he pulled her into his face. "There is something you must know before we do this, Mei. I meant it when I said I was here to stay. I can't explain it, but I..." He paused and she turned her head. Rejection was always better when you didn't have to take it face first.

Zack smoothed his hands over both her cheeks, cupping her so gently as he forced her gaze back to him. The room was barely lighted from the outside. His eyes glowed with so much tenderness and she was afraid. There was so much more at risk. Her child. Her soul.

"Mei," he whispered, again closing the distance between them. "All I have to give you is everything I am. I love you with every piece of my heart, every breath, and every minute of every day. I don't want to ever leave you. Are you good with that?"

There were no words. Her heart swelled and broke at the same moment his lips captured hers, no longer asking as much as telling her of the strength in this good man's heart. Their groans meshed as their tongues entwined, and she came undone. The starving woman emerged again, famished for love she didn't have to earn or deserve. He moaned when she pushed him back to his pillow, tearing his clothes off to bare his body to her. Her robe and gown flew to the floor.

"I love you, Mei," he reaffirmed over and over, her desire stoked higher and hotter with each endearment.

The softest light exposed his body to her; the flat, square panes of his chest punctuated with small, dark nipples, which hardened beneath her scrubbing palms. Heaving abs barely strained beneath the weight of her body. His hands cupped tight at her backside, gently separating the cheeks of her ass when she lowered herself onto him. Her body opened itself to him, welcoming all he had to give.

"You are beautiful." His deep voice rumbled through her, encouraging her daring act of life. "So beautiful." His fingers flexed again, pulling her closer. "Come to me, Mei."

She cried at his sensual command, sinking him into the deepest, softest, most broken parts of her body and soul. There was no struggle to her taking of him, no resistance to her assault as she ravaged and insisted, pulled and pushed until she straddled above him, her shame tossed aside along with all her fears. He simply never let go. Not once. He just let her ride and rock until there was nothing left of her, until she was no more alone or separate. Until she and he occupied one and the same space and time.

The gentlest hands in the world reached up to cup her face, his thumbs wiping the tears she hadn't realized were spilling over. "Hey," he muttered. "Why so sad?"

"I'm not. I'm...I'm...." There were no words to describe the incredible conflict within her heart. How could one woman feel so saved and still so broken at the same time? So found and still so damned lost? There was no happily ever after to her life. There was only sustenance along the way, and she needed all this man had to offer just to survive another day. "I'm so happy you love me."

"Ah, Mei," he muttered as he rolled her onto her back without breaking contact. "My turn."

He grazed her lips, his hands reverently caressing her body, skimming lightly over her cheek, down her neck, and coming to rest at her breast. Heat coursed through him, but he wanted to do this right. Mei was no ordinary woman. She was all he'd ever wanted but never knew he needed until now. The pain and loss of the past days were somehow easier to carry with her at his side.

The depth of his feelings for this woman evoked every nerve-ending in his body. Strumming his thumb across her hardening nipple, he captured her mouth, breathing in the delicate essence of her feminine body. Making love had never felt like this before. He couldn't taste enough or touch enough. Mei had become fire and breath–and life. His all.

The delicious fragrance of cherry blossom tantalized, singeing his nose with a scent that would never leave. The brush of her hair on his arms teased in the most pleasant way. Her lips and tongue were honey, more needful than food or drink.

He moved against her fragile strength, lowering himself carefully onto and into. Eagerly, she wrapped herself around every inch of him, her body arching into his, ready and wanting. Everywhere he touched, softness, warmth, and womanly desire accepted, and in the way that only Mei could–demanded all he had to give.

He gave. For a sensation-filled, exhilarating moment, he wanted nothing more than the physical pleasure he'd anticipated since their first kiss on the sidewalk in Rosslyn. He'd wanted her then, and now that he had his hands all over her, he wanted her all the more. In the heat of a ferocious hunger, he filled her in another exertion of total surrender. The release of body and soul ripped out of him. Now. Now. Now!

She offered all, grinding her lovely body against his as they melted together, her fingernails clenched to the back of his shoulders and the sweetest murmurs floating up to his ears. He'd found heaven in the arms of this beautiful, mean, desperate woman. There was no turning back. Only more.

"I'm going to make love with you...every day...for the rest of my life," he vowed.

"I...love...you," she answered, each word a prayer he so did not deserve. The tremble in her voice resonated to the deepest cords of his heart. This was what he'd been searching for all his life, the genuine surrender of a real woman's heart.

Mei sighed, breathing him into her soul. The scent of him mingled perfectly with hers. The feel of his rough, naked body empowered her femininity in every sensuous way possible. Beneath the midnight curtain of her silken hair, his hands explored, pinched, and smoothed. Like softest rain on a summer day, she poured herself all over him again, kissing every part she could reach.

Within a very few minutes, they were once again enfolded in the exquisite flames of intimacy, striving with and against each other, pulling and pushing, angling for deeper, better–more. Her body remembered the mechanics of sex, only it had never known this depth of pleasure. He coaxed and teased. Her body responded easily and happily, drawn out of its shell by this most tender warrior.

Zack sounded tired, drawing in huge breaths when they finished their third go round, but her libido seemed to be revving up. Now it was her turn to coax and tease, his to respond. At last, he rolled her to her back again. The darkened room lit with shuddering fireworks that exploded her skyward. Up. Higher. Into forever....

She closed her eyes and succumbed to the fall back to earth and into love. He cradled her tenderly, the heat of his mouth in her neck as he fell with her. Starlight. He'd turned her into pure starlight.

"I love you," she whispered, snuggling into the delicious warmth of his world.

"You are mine," he whispered in return, his voice as ragged as hers. "All. Mine."

TWENTY-SIX

Alex really ought to know better by now.

Zack always had a problem with the word *obedience*. He took one day off like his boss requested before he walked to work the following morning. Early downtown Alexandria was void of most tourists but busy with delivery trucks, shop owners opening their stores, and the sounds of another workday. Despite the chilly wind blowing with it, the smell of the Potomac wafted uphill, energizing everyone in its wake, him included. The love of a good woman had worked wonders for him. Despite the ache in his heart at losing Todd, he felt more balanced today.

Safety was another of those words. It was something he provided, but rarely accepted. He didn't need to be kept safe from the wolves of the world. The wolves of the world had it backward. They needed protection from him, and he intended to begin the hunt for them today. Stitched and healing hands or not, he was done being obedient and safe.

A shiny red fire engine roared by, its siren screaming. Zack kept walking. All the truck did was remind him how much he missed his car. For now, the pearl black beauty was parked in The TEAM's parking garage to keep it safe. He did not trust hotel valets or parking.

The damned fire engine blasted its horn up ahead, making a sharp right turn that startled Zack out of his reverie. The engine had turned onto the same street as The TEAM's office building. It couldn't be. There were plenty of other businesses on the street. It could be a cat in the tree. It could be....

What the hell?

He ran to intercept the fire engine. Black smoke poured from The TEAM's subterranean parking lot. He dodged fire hoses, as well as the firefighters scrambling around him to the underground nightmare. There was no getting past Battalion Chief Burgess though, who stopped him at the barricade.

"Stay behind the line," the very stern man commanded.

"That's my team in there," Zack insisted

"No, sir, that's *my team* in there," Burgess bit out. "It's a crime scene now. No one crosses my line."

"What the hell happened?"

"Bomb went off in the elevator shaft."

Zack's heart plummeted. Alex was the office early bird. Was that his black truck barely visible through the smoke belching out the garage entrance?

"Anyone hurt?"

Burgess shot him a grim look. "Only if they were in the elevator when it blew."

"My boss..." Zack couldn't finish the thought. *Alex.*

"Was he in there? Are you certain?"

"Maybe." Zack's mind pinged, searching for any reason Alex would not have come in early. He couldn't come up with a thing. All he could do was stand and try to breathe.

"Your boss own a truck? Might have been a big diesel?"

"GMC," Zack ground out. "Parked across from the elevator?"

The fire chief's demeanor softened. He waved Zack around the barrier. "The fire's out. Come with me."

The paramedics had just rolled onto the scene. Burgess called to them. "Don't know if we need you guys. Go see for yourselves."

Zack groaned as he entered the blackened catacomb that had once housed five company vehicles and enough parking stalls for the twenty or so agents on staff. Most of the destruction was contained at ground level. The scene was surreal, everything opposite the elevator shaft blackened or twisted. Not even the elevator call buttons remained on the wall. Worse, Alex's truck had been blown to the other side of the garage where it rested on its side. The chassis and tires still smoked. None of The TEAM's SUVs survived the blast.

He shot a glance into the farthest, darkest corner where he'd parked his pride and joy. At least it had survived unscathed, but his small piece of good fortune paled at what he did not see and could not find. Alex.

It should have been me.

"I can't say officially, but my best guess is someone planted a pressure bomb," Burgess said, pointing to the gaping hole, now filled with water and blackened puddles of ash. "We'll know for sure once we finish our arson investigation, but in a case like this, the bomb usually explodes after a person calls the elevator. They don't even have to set foot inside. Soon as the elevator hits the hydraulic bumper at ground level, it detonates. Looks like someone wanted to make sure they got their point across. They used more than enough explosive. Probably SEMTEX. Maybe dynamite."

Zack listened for any comment from the firefighters about survivors or body parts, but deep down, he knew. His gut clenched at all the evidence. Anyone standing in front of the elevator door would have been incinerated on the spot. Blown away. Turned to ash.

"Any bodies?" he asked, his voice dry and weak.

First Todd. Now Alex. They both died instead of–me.

"Can't get into the blast zone yet to know for sure," Burgess responded, his hand to Zack's shoulder. "It's still too hot. You doing okay, son?"

"I'm good." Zack gave the customary USMC reply, although catastrophic pain engulfed him. "Need to call my guys."

A sizzle of electricity arced from exposed wiring within the blackened shaft. Firefighters hurried around him. They had work to do, while he seemed capable of nothing more than standing like an idiot and gawking, his phone in his hand and dread stuck in his throat. *How do I say the words? Alex is dead.*

He turned from Burgess and shook the paralysis of shock off. Later. He'd deal with his personal feelings later, so he stabbed in the preset numbers and focused. First Murphy, then David, and Roy. By the time he'd finished, his resolve shattered. He had one more call to make. The hardest one of all. Kelsey....

The world spun sideways. He stuck his phone deep into his jacket pocket as grief climbed out of his heart. How much could they stand? It seemed the earth had tilted the wrong way on its axis. Revolved backward. Nothing felt right. A wave of vertigo slanted his vision. His knees wobbled and down he went, unable to take his eyes from the smoking hole where Alex had...died. Unable to make the last call and break his sweet wife's heart.

Not this. Not Alex. God, not Alex.

Burgess yelled for the paramedics, but they couldn't help him. This kind of pain wasn't treatable. A rage unlike any he'd felt before exploded from deep inside. Zack cursed the man he'd served; the man he loved. *Damned stupid type-A, have to be first, have to know everything. Jesus Christ, Alex! What'd you go and do this for?*

Memories deluged him like a home movie he couldn't shut off. The first time he'd met the intense man he'd eventually call Boss was on a flight to Baghdad, where they'd worked a successful black op together. He and Alex had completed their last mission near the northwestern borders of Pakistan. They were equals–almost. Born the same year, but Zack went one step further in his career to become USMC gunnery sergeant. Alex called it good at staff sergeant because of his family tragedy.

But he never lost his heart. Not really. Zack had been honored and privileged to witness the man's marriage to sweet Kelsey in Hawaii. They were made for each other; two kids with messed up lives who had latched onto each other and done good.

Zack scrubbed an ash-covered hand over his face. Alex's death would kill her. Hell. It was killing him. His heart pounded from the cavernous, sucking hole death always left in its wake. Tears rolled down his face, and he didn't care. He stared at the smoking pit that used to be an elevator. Nothing mattered anymore.

"Get that sonofabitchin' thing off me!"

Zack's ears perked up. He turned toward the sound of that angry voice.

"I'm not dead, you freaking moron!"

Alex?

A familiar stream of the most welcome expletives in the whole world resounded from the stairwell where two hapless paramedics were transporting a very angry man to ground level.

"Let me walk, you bastards! I'm not crippled!"

Strapped to the gurney and soaked from the building's mandatory fire suppression system, Alex was bleeding, dirty, and mad as hell. Zack stumbled to his feet, wiping his face and so damned relieved. For once, Alex's wonderfully wide range of cuss words was music to his ears.

"I don't need this damned crap on my face." Alex peeled off the oxygen mask, but just as quickly the medic put it back on.

"Yes, sir. You do."

"Boss," Zack choked, not sure how much emotion Alex would allow in his present condition. Oh, what the hell. He charged the gurney, needing to touch the lucky bastard to make sure he wasn't seeing things. "You're alive," he ground out, his stupid eyes filling with tears. "You dog. You're alive."

"What?" Alex bellowed, blinking through the grime on his face. Both of his eyes were bloodshot. His nose was bleeding and he looked like he'd been in one helluva fight. "Zack! What'd you say?"

Zack grabbed his boss's bloodied hand, wanting to kiss the guy, but smart enough not to. "Never thought I'd be so glad to see your ugly face."

"What?" Alex shouted again, his hand fisted around Zack's. "Speak up. I can't hear you."

"The blast ruptured his eardrums," one of the medics said, pointing to the blood running down Alex's neck.

"What'd you say? For hell's sake, speak up." Alex looked from medic to Zack, those bright blue lasers shining out from beneath the soot and blood.

"Where'd you find him?" Zack asked.

"Stairwell." One medic pointed his index finger upward. "Looks like he might have changed his mind after he called the elevator. He was already headed up when the elevator set off the bomb. Percussion threw him into the first floor fire door. Knocked him down and out."

Zack gripped Alex's hand tighter, but it looked like encouragement was the last thing Alex wanted. He was hell bent on getting on his own two feet.

"And he's got an irregular heartbeat." The same medic grimaced as Alex tried to undo his straps again. "We're taking him to the emergency room. Is there anyone you can call to meet us there, maybe someone he'll listen to?"

"Yeah, cuz it sure isn't us," the other poor medic muttered, wrestling to redo the straps to keep Alex on the gurney.

Zack grinned through his tears. *That's my boss!*

"Sonofabitchin Debargio tried to kill me!" Alex bellowed, tearing the blood pressure cuff off for the third time. The medic put it back on. Patiently and firmly, he began the process of inserting an IV line. Alex brushed it away until both medics strong-armed him.

"I'll call his wife," Zack said. "He listens to her. Where are you taking him?"

"Georgetown," both medics said at once.

Zack almost laughed with relief. The determination on his boss's face proved it once again. When Alex was angry, all was right with the world.

"You're going to the hospital, Boss." Zack tapped his shoulder to get his attention. There was no sense talking to him, but just the fact that he'd caught Alex's attention seemed to do the trick. Alex settled while the medics completed their assessment and inserted the drip line. The adrenaline in his system made it difficult, he was shaking hard enough to rattle the gurney. Here was a side of the man Zack had not seen before–mad as hell but scared, too.

"Get my guys, Zack. Call 'em. All of 'em!" He was in no condition to give orders, but Alex yelled them just the same. "We're going to get that sonofabitch Debargio if it's the last thing I do."

Zack nodded. Yeah, Alex might be a little beat up right now, but he was going to be fine. The man ran on anger and caffeine. They didn't make 'em any tougher.

"David knows what's going on." Alex still bellowed. "Talk to him. Do it today!"

Zack pointed at the ambulance making its way slowly down the driveway toward the medics and their unwilling patient. "You're going to the hospital, Boss. We'll take care of Debargio."

Alex couldn't read lips. Aggravation glittered in his bleary blue eyes but he nodded, resigned that he was no longer in charge. When he caught sight of the smoking carcass of his truck, he reached for Zack, gripping his forearm wrist to elbow.

"Call Kelsey," he growled. "You be the one to tell her. Don't let 'em scare her."

"You know I will." Zack pulled his cell phone out of his pocket to prove he meant to do just that.

"Zack." Alex's voice cracked. "Tell her...tell her I love her."

"Shut the hell up. Tell her yourself," Zack roared, frowning like a bastard at that stupid request. Alex better get that through his damned thick skull. He was not going to die.

While the medics loaded him into the back of the ambulance, Zack fulfilled his word. This call he could make.

"Hey, Kels. Yeah, this is Zack. Hey, listen. It's about Alex."

TWENTY-SEVEN

"He can't hear the phone ring, so call me any time," Kelsey whispered down the line. "They gave him something to help him sleep."

"Is Libby staying with you for awhile?" Zack had to smile. It was so like Kelsey to whisper even though Alex couldn't hear.

"Yes. Mark's on his way home from Afghanistan today, so she's keeping me company. She's pregnant, you know."

"I'll tell the guys. We can use some good news for a change. Listen, Kels, I'm sending two of our new recruits over to keep watch at your place. I doubt you'll have any trouble, so don't worry."

"You sound like Alex."

Zack paused. Was that good or bad?

"He always tells me not to worry, too."

"You shouldn't. You'll like these kids. They're both ex-Marines. Gabe Cartwright's a big goofball, and Taylor Armstrong's real quiet. Like I said, it's only a precaution. Let them keep an eye on things while you take care of Alex. Metro PD offered up an office until we can get back into our building, so if you can't reach me on my cell, call me there."

"Thanks, Zack. Tell everyone we're good."

Zack hung up. Kelsey sounded like one of The TEAM. No matter how much they were hurting, they always answered with the affirmative, "I'm good."

He turned to face Murphy, Roy, and David. "What's the plan?"

Murphy had commandeered office space from Metro PD when Zack ran Kelsey to the hospital. Metro hadn't been overly generous, but the broom closet sized office they'd offered up was better than nothing. At the moment, the men of The TEAM were a ragtag outfit gathered around a four-by-six wooden table and a borrowed murder board. There weren't enough chairs, so no one sat. Mother and Ember were holed up in another part of the station, trying to accomplish their work on borrowed computers. Zack was in jeans and his leather jacket, still covered with soot and mud and smelling of smoke. Murphy, Roy, and David were not as dirty, but their clothes smelled of smoke as well. Emotions ran high.

Murphy nodded toward David. "The plan is we talk with David. Guess he and Alex have been discussing—"

A sharp rap at the door interrupted him. Just as quickly, a tall man in a crisp, black business suit walked in like he owned the place. "So this is where you're hiding."

Zack's hackles rose. Whoever he was, this stranger had just jerked the wrong chain on the wrong day.

"Who the hell are you?" Despite his words, Murphy extended his hand in friendship.

"Interpol. Director Daniel Peters. You must be Finnegan." The intruder returned the handshake. Peters seemed to know everyone, addressing all four men by name as he made the rounds, shaking everyone's hand and making direct eye contact. When he was done, he zeroed in on Murphy again.

"I'm here to enlist your services, unless you'd rather sit around here wasting time instead of going after the man who damned near assassinated your boss."

"Alex mentioned you and he were organizing a three-pronged offensive against Debargio, Espinosa, and the 4th Street Tigers," David said. "How close to implementation are you?"

"Today," Peters shot back. "Now. This very minute."

"Good." Roy rubbed his hands together. "I'm ready for a little payback."

"Me, too," Zack admitted. It was time to not be on the receiving end for a change.

"Wait." Murphy held up his hand to slow the conversation. "Let's hear the plan first. We're not going off half-cocked like—"

"What? You need warrants before you're willing to make an honest effort?" Peters removed several folded documents from his inner suit jacket pocket and slapped them on the table.

Zack caught the sarcasm leveled at Murphy. Peters was a hard charger, and no, The TEAM did not always need warrants to proceed. That was the responsibility of the entity hiring them. Alex knew a thing or two about business law. His contracts stipulated proper procedure. It might not always work out, but that was another story.

"Now you mention it, yes, a warrant is exactly what I want to see, especially if we're throwing in with you Feds." Murphy took a seat at the change in Peters' attitude and pulled his glasses out of his shirt pocket to read the warrants. "These only cover Debargio's residence and Espinosa's hangout. I thought you said this was a three-way?"

"We don't need one for the Tigers," Peters snapped, his brows wrinkled and his fingers arched into the table. "They reek of probable cause. Didn't one of them murder an agent of yours recently? A Todd Chandler?"

Icy fingers slithered up Zack's neck at the way Director Peters tossed out Todd's name like it suited his purpose. *"A Todd Chandler,"* like Todd was just another statistic. Peters seemed intent on inciting instead of enlisting.

Peters' impatience escalated while Murphy took another long minute to finish reading the warrants. The thing about a confrontation with Murphy was he did it passively, but effectively. There was no temper or aggression, although his lack of engagement could be damned aggravating.

Peters drummed his fingers on the table.

Murphy kept on reading.

"What part do you want us to play?" Leave it to David to insert a modicum of diplomacy to take the tension out of the room. Damn him, anyway.

"Is this all you've got? The three of you and him?" Peters nodded toward Zack.

Zack bit his lip. There it was again, the insolent condemnation behind the push.

"I don't need anyone else," Murphy said. "They're the best agents—"

"Fine." Peters cut him off. "You four will go after Espinosa. I trust you can stick to the ground rules this time?" He glared at Zack.

"No problem," Zack answered, ignoring the innuendo and trying real hard to follow David's diplomatic lead and not punch Peters' arrogant face in. "What are they?"

"Simply that this is a synchronized offensive strategy. You will get into position, but you will not proceed until you have my signal to do so." Peters seemed to have a problem and Zack, apparently, was it. He wasn't addressing Murphy, David, or Roy. No, he was speaking directly to Zack like he was the only one in the room. "All three attacks will commence at precisely the same moment to prevent one of these targets from alerting the other two. Am I clear?"

"Do you want us to get these guys, or are we going to keep playing mine's bigger than yours?" Zack rolled his fingers into a fist. He got the point. Despite the fact he'd brought down the child trafficking ring, his rep for bungling the ATF Op remained. Didn't it figure? One screw up had effectively wiped out the good he'd done?

"What three attacks?" Murphy asked.

"Metro PD will apprehend the 4th Street Tigers at their hangout and take them out of the picture," Peters replied. "At the same time, you guys will intercept Espinosa at his place in Anacostia. You know the area. You'll go in hot. Hit him hard. At the same time, my men will apprehend Debargio at his place in Maryland. If we do it right, we'll be home for dinner tonight. Understood?" He glanced around the room, making eye contact with all four of them again. "When can you be ready?"

Murphy scrubbed a hand over his chin. "That might be a problem. At the moment, all of our equipment is part of a crime scene. We can't get to it."

"I can get you everything you need. What else?" Peters retorted.

"Comm links would be good," Roy said.

"I've still got the surveillance van," David said. "There should be enough comm links and ammo in there. We may not need any Interpol assistance."

"Tattle Tales?" Roy asked.

David nodded. "If you've got your weapons and gear bags, we should be good to go right now."

"Guess we won't need your help after all," Murphy said to Peters. "When do you need us in place?"

Peters seemed to relax. He checked his watch. "In two hours. Call when you're at this location." He tossed a business card to Murphy. "If you can't follow my orders, I need to know now."

"We'll be there," Murphy said evenly.

"You are to contact me with any deviation in this plan. Understood?"

Murphy rolled his eyes. "I've done a few covert ops before, in case you didn't know."

"Fine." Peters cast one more disparaging glance at Zack before he strode out the door.

"Whew," Roy chuckled. "Something's sure got his panties in a twist."

Zack watched the door Peters had exited through. His gut was talking to him. He hated when it did that.

Once again, Zack stood waiting at the place where he'd first met little Chai Yenn. Only now the van lay in pieces at the Metro D.C. evidence garage. Chai Yenn was safely ensconced in the stronghold of a loving family. Hundreds of little girls were either on their way to better lives in foster families, or restored to their real families.

He couldn't help feeling a little smug this afternoon. The mistake he'd made had turned out to be a very good decision. Following his gut affected so many little girls for the best, including the two waiting at home for him. He smiled. The word had a nice ring to it. *Home.*

Zack knew the type of man he was after. According to intel, Espinosa saw himself as the godfather of this particular neighborhood. Untouchable. To prove it, he had planned a horrendous crime wave to supposedly make history, starting New Year's Eve. Word on the street was there'd be no place to hide. Zack intended it to be true–for Espinosa.

The plan was straightforward. Zack and Murphy would enter Espinosa's hangout through the front entrance, while David and Roy entered through the rear. As far as The TEAM was concerned, today was the day for good old Vinnie to put his money where his big mouth was.

"You ready?" Murphy asked, as he and Zack flattened themselves to the side of the building. Zack scanned the empty scene. The streets had been plowed and sidewalks were shoveled, but even during the four weeks of undercover work on the ATF Op, he'd not seen the place so deserted.

"We have a go." David relayed the latest word from Director Peters. "Move out."

Murphy went first, edging along the brick building, his rifle tight into his shoulder. Zack had chosen his pistol, a compact Ruger 9mm fitted with a centerfire laser, instead of a rifle. Doorways and corners offered too many blind spots in clearing a building. Close quarters brought risk and death up too close and personal.

He thumped Murphy's shoulder from behind and took over the lead. They moved in sync, alternating the point position while the other covered the rear. They'd no more than cracked the front door when Zack sensed something wrong. The place was deadly quiet. Hollow. By the looks of it, Espinosa's hideout had no heat either. The resulting busted water pipes had created a science fiction kind of landscape of frozen spray throughout the inner halls and stairs. Sheets of ice covered the floors. Vapor clung to the men as they proceeded into the building.

"Murphy? Zack?" David's voice came through loud and clear over their earpieces.

"Yes?" Murphy answered.

"Join us at the back staircase. You're not going to believe what we found."

"Yeah well, you're not going to believe what we've found either," Murphy muttered.

Zack shuffled his feet, sliding along the slippery, frozen carpet to the side entrance where he and Murphy joined back up with Roy and David. The place was macabre. No sound. No lights. No people. The back staircase was worse. There in lifeless color hung the frozen bodies of Espinosa's two lieutenants: Gus and Dick.

"Judging by the holes in their foreheads, they've been executed like Carducci," David said.

"Say what?" Zack growled, surprised he didn't know that development. "When'd that happen?"

"Yesterday," Murphy answered as they headed back to their surveillance van. "Sorry, son. My fault. With all the commotion with Alex, I forgot to mention it. David went to the Carducci home yesterday morning with the Metro Police. Carducci was already dead."

That surprised Zack. First Brown? Then Carducci? This morning Alex, and now Espinosa's two buddies? "Who's behind these murders? The Tigers?"

"Possibly." David intervened, halting on the curb as they headed back to their van. "Wait here. Whoever's it is, they made it look like Carducci hung himself from his second floor banister. The ME was not convinced. There were too many defensive wounds on Carducci's arms and hands. He definitely fought his attackers. There's something else you need to know."

Zack caught the warning in David's words. "What else?"

"Alex has continued to actively investigate Debargio. He's got an account in the Caymans the same as Carducci. Alex showed me dates, transactions, deposits, and money transfers–all originating from the identical account in Mainland China."

"Lenny Huang?"

David shrugged. "It's hard to know for sure. We haven't been able to link any of the transactions directly to Huang, only to Mainland China. Interpol is pursuing that end of the investigation, but it seems obvious."

Zack had to bite his tongue. It made sense. If Lenny Huang was the mastermind behind this crime spree, Zack wanted a piece of him, preferably his head.

"There is one more thing." David glanced around like he was nervous. "Alex also has a dossier on Senator Lord."

"Yeah. I knew he was suspicious of Lord. How's it going?"

David's hesitation only lasted a second. "According to Alex, Daniel Peters suspects Senator Lord is Lenny Huang."

"Say what?" Murphy sputtered.

Zack couldn't have been more shocked, either. A United States Senator? Running the most despicable crime family in the world? From the Senate floor?

"How'd he come to that conclusion?" Roy asked. "What's he got on Lord?"

"Peters didn't say, but after he made the claim, Alex had Ember dig into it. It didn't take her long to track an email correspondence from Huang to Richards. The IP address originated in Georgetown."

"She tracked it to Lord's residence?"

David nodded.

"So that's our next stop," Zack said. "Let's go."

"Before we get into the van again, there is something I need to do." David pressed a finger to his lips. He pulled a bug detector from the back of the van and proceeded to sweep the inside compartments with meticulous care. To Zack's amazement he found two listening devices; one fastened beneath the steering wheel column and the other on the back of a monitor in the rear of the van. He left them where he found them, but switched on the jamming device installed in all The TEAM's business vehicles. Once outside, he swept the exterior of the van. Nothing.

"Alex suspected as much," David whispered. "Someone is very interested in our intelligence gathering."

"Who?" Murphy growled.

"Whoever's tying up all the loose ends," Zack replied quietly. "Looks like Lord if you ask me. Time to pay him a visit."

"No kidding," Roy muttered.

"Now wait a minute." Murphy slowed the conversation down. "I know we're all ready to fight. Seeing Alex like he was this morning's got us all itching for a payback, but are we sure about what we're doing? We can't waltz into Lord's home and accuse a Senator of being the Chinese mastermind behind a string of unsolved murders. No one's been fingered for any of them yet, and Lord's already laying for Alex as it is. Do we want to give him more ammunition?"

"Maybe not, but do we want to wait until he kills the Boss?" Roy asked. "He came close."

"How about we stick to what we do best, Murph?" Zack asked. "If I can get into Lord's place, I'll plant a few Tattle Tales and see what we come up with. If I can't get in, we'll check in with Peters."

Murphy shook his head, clearly undecided.

"Come on," Zack cajoled. "I'll be in and out before you know it. We owe it to Alex."

"But that's breaking and entering, plain and simple. What if you get caught?"

Zack shrugged. "I don't plan to."

TWENTY-EIGHT

Zack hit the ground running, his Ruger tight against his chest and his mission clear. He needed to get inside Senator Lord's palatial, white brick colonial-style mansion in the upper crust neighborhood of historic Georgetown without being detected. The home looked quiet, but challenging. It had a helluva lot of windows.

The west side of the home offered three at ground level and another two at the second story, all facing a charming carriage-house where the upper level housed a possible studio apartment, judging by its one curtained, east-facing window. The ground level boasted a single standard-sized window without the curtain; another chance to be spotted and the mission blown before it started.

Zack's challenge was to avoid notice from all those points of view as he infiltrated the grounds and entered the residence through the side door, also facing the carriage-house. His primary goal was simply to bug the good Senator's establishment from one end to the other. If Alex was right and Lord was Lenny Huang, the world needed to know.

To avoid all those points of view, he entered the snow-covered yard along the west side of the carriage-house, where a walkway had been cleared. The last thing he needed to leave behind was boot prints.

Murphy monitored surveillance from within the now-sanitized van parked at the front of the neighboring home. The listening devices had been disabled. Roy had settled at the rear of the property toward the east, where a dense patch of oak and pine provided thick camouflage. David was set up opposite Roy's location, also in the cover of brush. From these positions, they could easily provide backup if needed.

Zack was bound and determined he'd be the one taking the risk despite his recent injuries. They were yesterday. This was today. Besides, he was going into the residence on Echo Protocol, The TEAM's descriptor for getting the hell out of a tight spot before the sound of your voice could come back to you.

"You seeing this?" Zack whispered over his earpiece as a single individual exited the side door of the mansion and entered the carriage-house. The man's square bulk made identification simple.

"Vinnie Espinosa," David and Roy responded in unison.

"Copy that," Murphy muttered. "Guess that answers our question about an alarm system. You seeing any sign of dogs?"

"Negative," Zack whispered, his body flattened against the carriage-house, listening intently. Now was not the time to be distracted. With his adrenaline pumping on high alert, every nerve in his body became a highly sensitive receiver gathering input from all directions. He waited, analyzing the men's voices as well as the sound of footsteps on wooden stairs coming from inside. A chair scraped against the floor.

"Two individuals inside the carriage-house," he reported.

David's voice spoke calmly through the earpiece. "Assume Debargio is on the property as well."

"Hmm," Zack said. "Two gangsters on the premises. That kind of changes things, don't you guys think?"

Roy chuckled. "Is it breaking and entering to enter a guy's home because you're afraid for his life?"

"I don't know. You afraid for the Senator's life, Zack?" Murphy asked.

"Terrified," Zack muttered as he planted a Tattle Tale to the outside window frame of the carriage-house and stepped back. No sense of urgency came from within, so he turned to the house and entered quickly through the side door, just in case Senator Lord might need his help from the gangsters in his garage.

"Number one is in place. I'm inside," he whispered as he eased the door closed behind him. "Wait. I think I hear Lord. Someone is screaming, 'Help me. Oh please. Help me'."

"Good one," Roy muttered. "Sure glad you're inside where you can help."

"Gentlemen," David's calm warning came through loud and clear. Playtime was done.

"Proceeding into the home," Zack said.

"Copy that." Murphy's canned response became a trail of breadcrumbs. He knew where Zack was at all times. Zack knew he knew. It was tactical risk assessment every step of the way. Nothing more. Nothing less. Nothing better.

Two doors stood closed inside the side entry, one at his left and right. He paused, listening for any sound to indicate a maid or housekeeper might be at work in the residence. Nothing. Very carefully, he eased the door to his right open, revealing a mudroom complete with laundry and shower. Empty. Silently, he tried the opposite door. It opened to a chilled pantry. Also empty. Before taking another step, he pressed the second Tattle Tale to broadcast from the side door.

"Number two is in place. You receiving, Murph?"

"From carriage-house and side door. Clear as a bell."

So far so good. An elaborate gourmet kitchen gleamed ahead. Tiled floors, copper pans hung overhead, and stainless steel appliances, sinks, and countertops created a very utilitarian ambiance. He'd expected something more...snobby. This workspace looked like someone actually used it. The basement door stood ajar in the far corner beside a row of windows facing north.

Zack continued into the residence, searching for Lord's den where he planned to leave another Tattle Tale or two. The silence of the house raised his hackles, making him edgier and more alert. He'd expected to encounter staff, maybe a few maids. That no one was home unsettled him. The sensation grew.

He proceeded past the lavishly decorated dining room and up the ornately carved staircase that most likely led to bedrooms and such. Zack did not require a tour. Only one Tattle Tale was needed. He placed it at the base of the second level open banister newell, where it could pick up whatever might transpire at ground level.

"Coming in fine," Murphy advised. "You found the den yet?"

"On my way." Zack descended quickly, every nerve taut and on overload with anticipated input. The problem was there was no input. The place felt oddly vacant for a man at the center of D.C. politics and a very active socialite wife.

At the bottom of the stairs, he passed into a living room filled with a grand stone fireplace and leather couches.

Everywhere artwork was displayed in fancy framed pieces, or life-sized gilded statues. A heavy wooden door just past the living room revealed the Senator's den. Zack cracked the door and entered, closing it silently behind him.

"Found his *love me* wall," he muttered to Murphy.

Pictures of Senator Lord with past presidents, various Hollywood celebrities, and notables throughout the world adorned every wall of the man's study. Throughout the room, his suave, slicked-back hair and bright eyes watched Zack at his clandestine work while he placed two Tattle Tales, one at the doorway and the other behind Lord's desk.

"See what you mean," Murphy grunted. "He does like to look at himself, doesn't he?"

Zack did a double take when he exited Lord's study and spotted the bronze bust of the senator ensconced in an alcove at the opposite wall. Without thinking twice, Zack pressed a bug to the underside of the bronze chin on the pretentious bust. Lord never looked so good.

"Sorry, Murph. I couldn't resist that last one. First and upper level complete."

"Copy that." Murphy's faithful reply came quickly into his ear. "Basement next?"

"Yes." Zack walked stealthily into the kitchen. With Espinosa and Debargio on the premises, he was antsy to get the job done. Things had gone extremely well so far. Too well. He didn't want to push his luck. "Give me two minutes and I'm out of here."

"Door's open," Murphy replied easily. "Coffee's on."

Zack proceeded past the bank of four ovens set in a travertine-tiled wall, two industrial sized refrigerators, and more culinary instruments than he knew what to do with. His mind went to Mei living in her ratty apartment and making do with next to nothing while these people had so much. All Mei wanted was her daughter. Her needs were so basic. What made Senator Lord happy? Anything?

Zack had no more than entered the heavy door to the basement when he heard it. The side door of the house had opened and closed. Someone else was in the house. At the same moment, he got Murphy's warning. "Espinosa to your left."

"Anyone else?"

"Negative."

With no place else to go, Zack stood watching through the crack in the barely open basement door where he could see into the kitchen and all the way to the side door. Espinosa plodded into the house like the moose he was. He looked quite comfortable opening one of the refrigerators like he already knew where everything was kept.

After loading up a tray of cheese and deli meats, he opened a handsome wine-keeper Zack hadn't noticed. It looked more like a wooden cabinet instead of a temperature-controlled wine cellar. Espinosa selected two bottles, stowed one under his arm and secured the hefty snack tray while carrying the other. He nudged the wine-keeper door closed with his foot and plodded back the way he came, elbowing the side door open.

"Looks like old Vinnie's a glorified gopher," Murphy said quietly as the side door shut behind the mobster.

"Am I clear to go?" Zack asked quietly, the encounter too close for comfort.

"Yes. Espinosa is back in the carriage-house. Go now. Be quick."

Zack intended to be better than quick; he planned to be greased lightning. He placed one Tattle Tale at the top of the steps facing the kitchen. Gliding down the basement steps, his heart beat urgently fast. It was past time to leave.

Still in unpainted sheetrock, the staircase was hung on slats that opened on the right side while the left side was solid wall. It gave the steps an airy feeling instead of the tunnel-like effect most basement staircases evoked. With his gun drawn and ready, Zack placed the final Tattle Tale on the partially framed wall directly opposite the staircase. As far as he was concerned, that was pretty darned good for a place where not much happened other than storage. Feeling a little smug with his success, he pivoted on his heel to retrace his path upstairs, when—

"Sonofabitch!"

"Zack?" Murphy asked in alarm.

"Damn it! Holy shit, Murphy! Sonofabitch!" Zack honestly could not stop his lips from spewing profanity. Adrenaline had just dumped a huge burst of fight-or-flight into his system. His mouth dried up at the same time his stomach pitched. Now he knew where Senator Lord was. Good hell, did he know.

"Zack?" Murphy's loud, urgent voice in his head only made the scene more surreal. "Answer me, damn it!"

"Give me a second." Taking a few steps back, Zack grunted, his hands to his knees and his heart jack-hammering in his head and chest. "Just found...the Senator. Number eight is in place." He stepped to the side of the Tattle Tale, so Murphy could take in the view.

There between the wooden slats of the basement steps, wrapped in asphyxiating but clear plastic sheeting, were the gray, bloated faces of Senator Lord and his wife, Carma Sue. White zombie eyes stared through the wooden planks of the steps in unseeing condemnation of Zack's trespass through their elegant estate.

"Holy shit." Zack scrubbed his face and blinked hard at what he was seeing.

"Looks like they've been dead a while," Murphy commented drily.

"Ya think." Zack hadn't recovered yet from the sucker punch of shock he'd received. He swallowed hard, wanting to spit if he could only gather enough saliva to do so. It wasn't physically possible, not with the shock of the ugly sight still reverberating through his system.

"Guess we know why Debargio and Espinosa are here."

Zack couldn't answer right away. He needed a second to get his balance. This was the ugliest thing he'd seen in years; two corpses in definite decomp leaned together like lovers between the wall and stair joists. "How long you think, Murph? Days? Weeks?"

"Hard to say," Murphy answered. "They look plenty ripe. A couple days maybe. Can you determine COD?"

Zack shook his head grimly, not wanting to get close enough to determine cause of death. He peered between the steps, not really noticing anything that resembled a bullet hole until he walked to the open side of the staircase. Carma Sue had a black mark at her temple.

"Gunshot, by the looks of the missus. Execution style. Right temple. Definite stippling, but I am not moving these bodies to check any further. Let the ME figure it out. That's his job."

"No need. I'll contact him when we're done here."

David's voice calmly joined the conversation. "Movement from the garage. Debargio and Espinosa entering the house. Side entrance. Stay put."

Zack glanced around the basement for cover. He didn't need any more surprises. The place provided multiple choices to hide, with an unfinished closet-sized room across from the bodies and facing the stairs. Stacks of industrial-sized paint buckets offered decent camouflage with a view. He leaned against the wall behind the buckets, thankful for the solid support.

Within seconds, Debargio and Espinosa's voices traversed through the house and toward the front entry. By now, Murphy should be getting an earful as well as plenty of video.

"Zack. They're waiting for someone. Haven't mentioned a name yet."

"Copy that." Zack focused on the heavy footsteps and muted conversation overhead as he calmed his heart rate, trying real hard not to look at the bodies only feet away. But zombies still had eyes, and these were staring right at him. An icy chill slithered up his back and neck. He shook it off and focused on the living, breathing guys upstairs who could kill him.

"Whoever they're waiting for, they don't know why he's late." Murphy relayed another scrap of conversation.

"What are the chances of two bad intels during one op?" Zack asked.

"You mean us being sent to Espinosa's hideout when he's here?" Roy asked.

"Yeah, and Interpol going to Maryland when Debargio's not there." Zack surveyed the scene displayed before him.

The basement was giving him the creeps in a big way. "Why didn't Peters know that?"

"At least now we know Lord is not Huang," Roy said quietly. "Not if he's been dead for a few days."

"He couldn't have ordered the hit on Alex either," David joined in.

"Movement your way, Zack." Murphy's report stopped the chitchat. "Looks like—"

The furnace kicked on, the hum of it blocking the overhead noise, and suddenly, Zack lost all communication.

"Murphy? David?" He tapped his earpiece for a reconnection. "Roy? You guys out there?"

Nothing. He'd lost everyone. The question he'd put to his senior agents worried him now. Why were two task forces sent on wild goose chases when the real action was going down at Lord's mansion? Only Lord was no longer running the show–if he ever was. Two bad intels on the same operation? No way. Something smelled bad, and it wasn't just the zombies in the room.

His sniper sense shuddered up his back. Zack pulled an extra magazine out of the ammo bag on his hip and stuck it in his jacket pocket. Impending trouble had a way of broadcasting its arrival like a tornado. Something evil was coming. He could feel it. Time to be prepared.

The basement door opened. Fluorescent lights flashed to life overhead. Heavy footsteps thumped down the stairs. Two pairs. Zack leaned deeper into the shadows of boxes, crates, and paint cans. Two sets of milky zombie eyeballs seemed to follow him.

"Might as well get the mess outta here while we're waiting." Espinosa's booming voice filled the concrete crypt.

Zack spared a quick look. Even dressed in his expensive three-piece business suit and fine winter trench coat, the burly gangster looked the part of a bouncer from one of Debargio's seedy nightclubs. Nuggets of gold glittered on fingers as thick as pork sausages. His massive hands looked too big to be functional, but Zack knew the reputation of the monster who wielded them. Espinosa liked to use his hands. Nothing satisfied him more than the brutal beatings he'd personally administered on his way up the corporate mobster ladder. His ham-sized hands were always his first weapons of choice. And they were lethal.

Debargio was as big and square as Espinosa, but he didn't like to get dirty like Vinnie did. He considered himself the brains of the business and a gentleman. Smart enough to keep one step ahead of the law, he'd built a kingdom based on drug trafficking, extortion, and murder. Word on the street was Debargio wasn't afraid of anyone, and opposition had better believe him or they disappeared. Zack watched as the two thugs angled Senator Lord's wife out from beneath the stairs. Vinnie kicked a plastic container the size of a small footlocker out from behind the bodies. With a few grunts and groans, they manhandled Carma Sue until she was folded in half and somersaulted head first into the container. It was tight, but with a few snapped bones and well placed punches, Carma Sue was redesigned to fit.

Espinosa pressed the lid into place while Debargio watched. Without a word, they maneuvered a nearby hand truck with its gruesome cargo back up the stairs. Zack needed to spit or throw up. Handling corpses was something he'd never gotten used to. The sight of Carma Sue reduced to a rectangle turned his stomach. Heat flooded his throat, bringing the sensation of claustrophobia with it.

I have got to get the hell out of here.

TWENTY-NINE

Zack listened to the hum of the furnace while it continued warming the home. Now that Debargio and Espinosa had left the side door open, all the warm air was being rapidly expelled into the great outdoors. Contact with Murphy was indefinitely delayed. It spoke volumes to Zack that these two gangsters were doing their own dirty work. Apparently, Debargio and Espinosa had disposed of their buddies a little too soon.

"Murphy? Anyone?" He tapped his earpiece again. Still nothing.

Several long minutes passed before the gangsters returned. Debargio took a seat on the bottom steps and left Espinosa to wrestle Senator Lord's plastic-wrapped corpse all by himself. When Espinosa finally dragged the Senator clear of the steps, he let the body drop. Lord's once arrogant face impacted with a soggy crunch against the concrete floor.

Bile stroked the back of Zack's throat. He squeezed his eyes shut for a second, not wanting to watch but knowing he had no choice. He needed to keep an eye on these two thugs,

"She was a heavy broad," Debargio said. His winter coat must have been a hindrance to heavy lifting. Sweat glistened beneath his salt and pepper hairline as he leaned his elbows against the stairs, still not lifting a hand to assist his buddy.

"You ain't seen nothin' yet." Espinosa dragged a larger plastic container across the floor to Lord's body. "Well, what do ya know? This guy's too tall for the box."

"Told you to get it done before they turned into party balloons," Debargio wheezed, still watching Espinosa do the heavy lifting.

"Don't get why we gotta move 'em at all. Hell. Just burn the joint down. Let the cops find a couple roasted cadavers. What would it hurt?"

"Boss don't want no fire. He wants enough time to get outta town."

"Would've been nice if he'd told us that to begin with. You always listen to him?"

Zack's ears perked up. *Boss? What boss?*

"Long as he keeps paying me I do. You shoulda dropped these two jokers in the river a couple days ago and sunk 'em, like I told ya. Then we wouldn't have to do it now."

"Well, I been a little busy, ya know what I mean?"

By now, Lord's body lay across the container. There was no way a six-foot plus gentleman was going to fit in the box, not without a lot of remodeling. And the smell. Zack hadn't noticed it until these guys started forcing the zombies into tiny spaces.

"Come on. Take a load off 'fore ya give yerself a stroke." Debargio waved Espinosa to sit. "By the time the Feds pull their heads outta their asses, we'll be gone."

Zack cringed, hoping Vinnie had enough sense to refuse Dom's unbelievable offer. Really? Sit and chat in the stink of the place? Zack could barely stand to breathe.

"Okay, but not for long." Espinosa sank onto the nearest crate. Unfortunately, it was right outside the closet where

Zack stood. The crate creaked. Espinosa fanned his heavily jowled face with splayed fingers. "Gotta get this guy outta here. He stinks."

Ya think! Zack pinched his nose shut and breathed through his mouth.

"We're almost done. Then we can blow this town and head for someplace warmer, maybe a tropical island." Debargio pulled a gold case out of his inner suit pocket and removed a single cigar. "Would you like that?"

"Just don't wanna work with Chinks no more." Espinosa scrubbed one of those boxing-glove sized hands over the crew-cut stubble of his head.

"What's a matter?" Debargio's brow spiked. "You don't like money all of a sudden?"

"It ain't the money." Espinosa stretched his hands in front of him and cracked his knuckles. "It's all them little girls. Don't like the way they looks at me."

"What? Scared? Don't everyone look scared when they look at you?" Debargio laughed a wheezing, wet kind of a laugh. "Oh, that's rich. That's real damned rich."

"Come to think of it, they do now ya mention it."

Zack clenched his Ruger to his chest, disgusted beyond belief at the crude way these men discussed the children they'd sold like meat. *Give me a reason, guys. I'll show you scared. Hell. I'll show you dead.*

Debargio turned serious as cigar smoke billowed from between his thick, red lips. "We don't have to worry 'bout no more Chinks, anyway. Stupid Richards sells a kid to a Fed. How dumb can a dumb guy get?"

"He won't last long, Dom. Don't worry 'bout it. I took care of ya. Got a friend inside the joint. 'Fore long you'll be reading about that crooked shyster in the obits."

"Can't happen soon enough." Debargio's cigar smoke filled the cramped basement room adding to the sickening scent of decay. "Selling them girls was a good deal when we started the business, wasn't it?"

"Yeah. Yeah, it was." Espinosa's head bobbed in agreement.

"Shoulda kept the inventory down, though. First rule of good business and that's where we went wrong. Never shoulda listened to old Stevie. Couldn't move them girls fast enough once they started pouring into the country. Standing inventory ain't never good thing. That's when all our problems started."

"Dumb ass." Espinosa kicked the body on the floor. "He's a piece of work, ain't he?"

"He is now." Debargio laughed again. The two men sat chuckling at their sick brand of humor while Debargio finished his smoke. When he blew out the last putrid puff with lingering satisfaction, his voice turned somber. "Guess old Gus and Dick was sure surprised."

"I ain't gonna lose no sleep 'bout them." Espinosa waved off Debargio's comment. "They got what they had coming. I never trusted neither of them guys. They had too many ideas about how to run things. Always thought they knew better than me. Dick was out to get both of us. Shoulda bumped him off sooner."

"Same as that smart ass, Stewart. If it wasn't for him and his guys sticking their noses in our business, we'd a been home free."

"Yeah. That damned guy didn't know when to back off." Espinosa cracked his knuckles again as he stretched and stood. "I tried, Dom. Honest, I did. I sent my boys over to the home to dispose of that Lennox guy and his Chink girlfriend when they first started poking their noses in your business, but did I kill him? No. I coulda, but I told my boys just rough him up. If he dies..." Espinosa shrugged. "Not my problem. And then I sent my boys over again to knock down his apartment. I told 'em to leave a little note, you know? Spell it out nice and clear so Stewart gets the message, but do he listen? No. He keeps coming at me. What was I gonna do? You tell me. Then that Lennox fella killed a bunch of my boys in the gunfight. My boys only got one of Stewart's. Sounds like I'm the one what still owes him a payback if you was to ask me. I'm just saying."

"Yeah, but your boys got the wrong one, Vinnie," Debargio said softly.

"So they ain't the smartest. Who cares? What else was I gonna do?" Espinosa had himself spun up by now. All Zack could do was watch the man's broad back as he paced the floor, gesturing dramatically with both hands.

"You done good," Debargio mumbled. "You took care a business. That's all you coulda done."

"Guess Stewart knows we mean business now. That bomb shoulda splattered him to hell and breakfast. Wonder what the last thing was that went through his mind?" Espinosa waxed almost pensive.

"What ya think?" Debargio burst into a fit of sputtering laughter. It took him a minute to stop wheezing before he could talk. "It was his ass. Damn, that's a good one, Vinnie."

"Real funny. That's about as stale as the smoke you're blowing." Espinosa wrinkled his face as he waved both hands. "Don't know how you can sit there and enjoy a good Cuban with the stink in here."

"Yeah, yeah, so, now what?" Debargio turned serious, his eyes on the tall, lanky problem at hand.

"We improvise. What'd ya think?" Espinosa turned to the offensive work waiting on the floor. With an enormous grunt, he tipped the plastic-covered body head first into the container. Lord's head thumped with a sharp crack of skull against concrete. Zack winced. The container tipped over. Vinnie was getting nowhere. Packing Lord was a two-man job.

Espinosa wrangled the body into a standing position, his arms wrapped around Lord's arms and chest. Zack looked away, his eyeballs scarred for life. More of the nasty putrid odor emanated from the plastic wrap. How could Espinosa stand to touch the corpse like he was? If these guys didn't hurry and get it out of the basement soon, Zack was in trouble. He never could vomit quietly.

Kicking the container against the basement wall to the far right of the stairs, Espinosa got the leverage he needed to complete his task. Zack flattened against the wall of his closet, hoping his cover held despite the fact he was almost entirely in Espinosa's view. While Debargio sat and watched, Espinosa folded Lord in half the way he'd done with Carma Sue, and pitched him into the now stationary container.

Zack gritted his teeth and choked back the impulse to hurl, the scene too disgusting to watch. He would've liked a pair of noise-cancelling earplugs so he didn't have to hear the squishing, crackling sounds of Lord's corpse being reconfigured to fit plastic corners and walls. At last, the disjointed Senator was unceremoniously crammed into his final resting place. Espinosa stretched several lengths of duct tape around the container, since the lid did not come close to fitting. Lord's feet extended beyond the plastic cover, but the tape held. For now.

My hell. Get him out of here.

Espinosa situated the container onto the hand truck. The body was packed and ready to go, Lord's head and feet both aimed toward the ceiling. Espinosa turned to Debargio, his hands on his hips like he'd accomplished a great feat. "You pushing or pulling?" he asked point blank.

Vinnie's direct approach surprised Zack. Neither of these guys seemed to be the boss, so exactly who was? They'd mentioned a boss earlier. The damned child trafficking ring just kept getting bigger. Who else was there?

Debargio stared at Espinosa for a full minute before getting to his feet. Apparently, he decided pulling might be tough, but it wasn't as messy as pushing. While Debargio groaned and pulled the hand truck up one stair after another, Espinosa pushed and heaved against the container with both ham-hock hands. A gray trail of body fluids squirted from a tear in the plastic, painting a macabre squiggle on the stair wall as they went.

Zack watched in disgust, holding his breath and waiting for his comm link to please reconnect. The scene was a comedy from hell, with two bumbling oafs in the lead and two corpses playing supporting roles. It would've been a lot funnier if Zack hadn't been the captive audience. His gut churned in active protest. He could no longer tell if it was sniper instinct or just plain nausea.

Between their cursing, huffing and puffing, Debargio and Espinosa finally got the disintegrating body up the stairs. Zack could only hope they didn't drop Lord back down into the basement. Even the best plastic wrap would only hold for so long.

He strained to hear above the steady hum of the furnace motor. The loud noise of the side door slamming was the only recognizable sign that Lord had left the building. It was past time to change locations, and one thing was certain. Zack wanted out.

Just as he stepped from the cover of the closet, the furnace clicked off. A fragment of Murphy's frantic voice blasted into his ear. "...coming back!"

THIRTY

"And this little piggy had roast beef, but this little piggy had none."

Mei watched Junior Agent Rory Dennison rocking the very unsmiling Baby Song on his lap while he tugged at her bare toes. She didn't seem to be afraid of him, but neither did she seem to know how to respond to the simple childhood game. He continued despite her stoic expression, her lips pursed like she had a lot to think about.

"And this little piggy went to market." His dark brows raised in comic surprise when he latched onto her middle toe. "Oh no! But this little piggy stayed home."

Baby Song's dark eyes fell to her foot only to return quickly to Rory's face.

"What did the tiniest little piggy say?" he asked, his forehead pressed to hers as if he expected an answer.

Mei allowed a small smile. Zack needed to see the serious look on Baby Song's pretty face. The little girl just did not get the concept of social interaction yet, which stood to reason. A child raised in a playpen her first two years of life had a huge hurdle to overcome. The only indication she'd ever given that she might be breaking through the mindset in her love-deprived little brain was with Zack. Whatever bond they had, it had been forged in that single moment back in the foster home.

Rory brought the rocking chair to a sudden halt. He wiggled Song's baby toe. She studied him sternly, not cracking the slightest hint of a smile.

"This teeny, tiny baby toe said, 'Wee, wee, wee, all the way home'." He sat back still wiggling his eyebrows, again as if he expected a response.

Song settled against him with a big yawn.

Rory grinned, wrapping her bare foot into the blanket and rocking again. "Yep. Just like I planned. Bored her into another nap."

"Do you have any kids?" Mei had to ask. He seemed so natural with children.

"What? In a job like this?" He arched a devilish brow at her, not exactly offering a direct answer. Mei let it go. He called to Connor, who was busy in the kitchen. "How's lunch coming?"

"Grilled chicken sandwiches are almost ready," Connor replied. "Warming the baby bottle. You want to feed the Princess again?"

"Heck yeah," Rory answered.

The fact that she was once more under guard and unable to search for her daughter, did not escape Mei. She'd been fighting her anxiety since Zack returned to work earlier, but these two bodyguards helped ease the situation. Both were as easy on the eye as they were on her ragged emotions. Rory was the proverbial tall, dark, and handsome type who'd instantly taken to Song. Easy-going Connor maintained the computer support, and volunteered to fix all the meals. The only thing that would make her life complete was LiLi. And Zack.

BLAM!

Zack ducked, the hiss of a damned big shell warming his earlobe as it impacted with the two-by-four wall stud behind him. He'd intended to get out of the basement while Debargio and Espinosa moved Lord outside. That was not going to happen.

"We got us a prowler," Espinosa yelled from the top of the basement stairs.

"Move over, Vinnie!" Debargio growled. "You're in my way."

BLAM! Another volley peppered the sheetrock around Zack. Dust and plaster flew. Wood splintered, hitting the back of his head and neck enough to pepper him, but not enough to knock him out. He brushed it off. Dying in Lord's basement was not an option.

"I got him!" Vinnie yelled.

Zack charged, his Ruger spitting round after round as he dived to the floor, aiming his weapon up the staircase and into the hefty bodies blocking the door. He saw one round hit the center mass of Espinosa. The man didn't go down, even as the narrow chute of the stairway transformed into a shooting galley. Zack expelled his spent magazine and reloaded his spare in one smooth move, not willing to waste a second of the time he had left.

The damnedest thought flashed through his head. *I should have married Mei.*

Espinosa fell, or was shoved to the side by Debargio. Zack could not tell. All he knew was Espinosa was no longer shooting. Debargio filled the doorway, aiming a damned big

.45 Magnum down the stairs. Zack took careful aim, but Debargio dropped to his knees, the side of his face gone in a splash of red spray. Both men were down.

What the hell?

Zack rolled to his knees, his smoking hot weapon still pointed to the second floor where the nice clean kitchen had once been. He had to be sure. With his ears ringing, he climbed the steps, his Ruger extended in both hands, ready to finish the job once and for all. It became quickly apparent who'd saved the day.

The north facing windows were shattered. Both gangsters were missing parts of their skulls, some of their brains, and a lot of blood. He'd gotten a few body shots in, but it was David and Roy who'd sniped these thugs. Through the kitchen windows, no less.

Zack stepped over the sprawled remains, damned ready to get the hell out of the Lord estate. The ringing in his ears cleared as he made his way through the kitchen.

"You copy?" David's voice was as calm as ever in Zack's earpiece.

Before he could answer, Murphy shot back an angry volley. "Sonofabitch! Do I copy what?"

"Zack."

No wonder Murphy was spun up. David was so calm, while Murphy was pinging. The two did not mix well. Zack opened his mouth to advise his status, but once again his anxious second-in-command pre-empted him with an angry bellow. "Damn it to hell, David! You got Zack or not?"

"Yes, Murphy. Got him in my sights. Safe and sound."

Zack allowed a weary smile when Murphy snarled back to David. "I am too damned old for this bullshit!"

Ah. The brotherhood of men who've got your back. Nothing in the world like it.

He pushed open the side door and stumbled into the fresh December air. Cold had never felt so good. But like he often did after the battle was done, he grabbed his knees and threw up. After he wiped his mouth, he holstered his pistol as Murphy roared up to him, mad as hell.

"You okay?" Zack eyed the older man as he peeled his earpiece off.

"Me? Am I okay?" Murphy was steaming. "How about you tell me why you shut your comm link off and left me high and dry without a word outta you?"

Before Zack could answer, Murphy pushed him back a foot as adrenaline took charge. The older man was shaking. Zack got it. He was shaking, too.

"Next thing I know, all hell breaks loose. You don't answer me and all I hear is the whole damned world falling apart, only I don't have a clue where you are or what you're doing!" Murphy yelled, stabbing a finger in Zack's chest with every step he took. Before he was done, Zack was back at the side door, too weak to resist his friend's panic-motivated battering. "What kind of bullshit is that, Lennox? You want to tell me?"

Zack accepted the brunt of Murphy's wrath. He'd just crawled out of the mouth of hell. He didn't mind the butt-chewing he was getting. Murphy was scared. Hell, *he* was scared. Finnegan's wrath was nothing compared to what could have happened down in the cellar. Zack huffed the only answer he had. "Interference...from their furnace motor...I think. All I know is, I lost communication...when the furnace cycled on. Couldn't hear any of you."

Murphy stared, blowing out great plumes of vapor into the frigid air. He was still shaking with too much anger and not enough relief, his fists clenched, and Zack prepared for a literal beat down.

Go on, Murph. Hit me. Maybe then I'll feel better, too.

"I'd never not check in with you." Zack panted his own adrenaline away. "Damned glad you got through to me. You saved my life."

Murphy brushed Zack's hand off and stalked away, muttering, "Damn kids. You think you're all so sonofabitchin' smart."

"Don't worry. He'll cool off," Roy offered. "It just scared the hell out of us when we lost contact. Almost came in after you."

Zack nodded, still blowing the excess adrenaline away. "Me, too. Man, what a mess."

"We saw the tubs Debargio and Espinosa hauled out," Roy said, nodding to the open carriage-house garage doors. "Were those what I think they were?"

"Yeah. Lord and his wife. Guess Dom and Vinnie got stuck doing their own dirty work."

"Are you okay?" David peered into Zack's face.

"You need a minute?" Roy asked.

"My ears are still ringing," Zack admitted. *Hell, my whole body's ringing.*

"What happened?" Murphy was back, his eyes sharp and red-rimmed. "After you lost contact. What happened?"

Zack recounted the gory comedy of Dom and Vinnie. "They must've seen me. All I know is I heard your warning come through and the next thing, Debargio and Espinosa are firing at me. Bastards damned near hit me." Zack turned his head to show where the splinters had imbedded into the back of his head and neck. "I got a couple hits in, but man, those guys were big. They just would not go down."

"So how'd you get out of there?" Murphy had his arms crossed, still a little hot under the collar.

"I had some help." Zack nodded his chin toward David and Roy.

David gave one short, quick nod.

"Thanks, man." Zack clamped his shoulder. "Damned good shooting through the back window. And you." He turned to Roy. "I owe you guys."

Roy wiped his eyes. "Nah. Couldn't let you get yourself killed now that you finally got something worth living for, could I?"

Zack gulped at the very accurate assessment of his life. Roy was spot on. He had everything to live for and these two snipers to thank.

"You're a stupid kid, you know that, Lennox?" Murphy grabbed Zack by the back of his neck and hauled him in for one of those chest bump kind of man hugs. "Thought you was smarter than that."

Speechless, Zack could only slap Murphy's back and endure the fatherly praise.

"So who were these guys waiting for?" Roy asked.

"Don't know," Zack muttered. "Debargio mentioned they had a boss. You guys know who that might be?"

"No," Murphy replied. "With these two dead, seems to me we're running out of bosses."

"We may never know." David glanced at the house. "It's a crime scene now. Re-entering would be tampering with evidence. It's up to the police."

"How do we explain us being inside?" Zack asked. He hadn't worried when it was just breaking and entering. Murder gave it a whole new spin.

"We tell the truth," Roy said calmly. "As far as the police are concerned, we were following up on an Interpol operation. We noticed Dom and Vinnie's van and we suspected foul play. Heck, tell 'em about Gus and Dick, Lord too. Let Peters do some explaining for a change."

THIRTY-ONE

"Tell us what they said again," David asked.

"Debargio distinctly said their boss didn't want them to set Lord's place on fire. Vinnie argued, but Dom said the boss wanted time to get out of town," Zack answered.

The TEAM had reconvened back in their own Situation Room the next morning instead of reporting to Director Peters. The fire department had released the office portion of the arson crime scene, as long as everyone entered through the lobby and utilized the front stairway. The elevator and parking garage were off limits but the office was intact, more or less.

Kelsey called earlier to let Murphy know Alex was doing better. He'd had a good night's sleep and except for his hearing loss, he was feeling better. She'd laughed. He insisted he was going to install a hot tub in their backyard while he was off work and recuperating. Even sick, the man couldn't hold still.

David had invited all agents to the conference table, even junior agents Mark Houston and Harley Mortimer, who'd barely returned from Afghanistan and had their own debriefing to look forward to. Mother and Ember attended as well.

"Hell, who's left?" Roy muttered. He ticked the names off his fingers. "First Brown, then Carducci, Gus, Dick,

Senator Lord, his wife, Debargio, and Espinosa. That's eight murders, not counting the baby in the morgue. Am I missing anyone?"

Zack rubbed a hand over his head. "Todd," he muttered, surprised Roy could have forgotten.

"You're right." Roy added another finger. "Sorry. Damned near Alex too. That's nine murders and one attempted."

"Maybe Dom and Vinnie were sick of working for Lord," Murphy offered. "You guys know how gangsters operate. They've got no problem killing each other."

Zack spoke up. "No, they were following someone else's orders. Someone is still out there running the show. Besides, I was there. I saw those guys in Lord's basement. They weren't bright enough to hit a U. S. Senator without being told or paid to do it."

"It's like we're going around in a big old circle here, only we keep ending back at Lord," Murphy muttered.

"Like we're being led." Zack frowned.

"Damn, but you guys have been busy." Harley squinted at the overhead screen, ruffling a hand over his sandy-colored hair as he yawned. "And here I thought only us in the field did any real work."

"You don't mind if I take over for a minute, do you, David?" Mark snagged the laser pointer and focused on the overhead screen.

"No. Feel free. That's why you're here." David leaned back in his chair with a tired sigh. "I think the rest of us are too close to this operation. Murphy and Zack are right. Despite all we think we know, it feels like we're going around in circles."

"It sounds like it's been an ugly operation," Mark agreed. "I guess if we follow Murphy and Zack's gut, the real question is—"

"Who the hell's left?" Zack growled. "What are we not seeing?"

"It's impossible to quantify feelings." Mark scanned everyone at the table. "Let's look at the evidence differently. Where'd all this good information come from?"

"Most of it came from me and Ember." Mother spoke timidly as if she might incriminate herself. "The boss asked us to track some transactions. Ember came up with a boatload in the Caymans. They all originated in China."

Zack glanced at Ember, still wearing dark glasses and plenty of black.

"We're not worried about you and Ember. Who else provided information?" Mark asked.

"Alex," David offered thoughtfully. "He worked privately with Interpol Director Daniel Peters. Peters gave him the FBI dossiers on Debargio and Lord."

"Definitely not worried about Alex. So what about the FBI?" Mark asked.

"They're a pain in the ass to work with," Roy offered.

"They don't share intel," Zack said.

"They're arrogant," Murphy remarked.

"They don't do thorough reconnaissance," Harley said.

"They think one death is acceptable collateral damage," Mark answered his own question with a subdued voice.

"And they have the easiest firewalls around to hack." Mother smiled, but then her eyes widened at what had come out of her mouth. "I mean...umm, not that I would ever do such a thing. I might know someone who said they knew someone who mighta done something like that. Maybe. Once upon a time. A long time ago."

Mark cast a sideways smirk at Mother's unexpected disclosure. "I'm going to pretend I didn't hear that. Listen folks, I know we don't care to work with the FBI, and yes, they're a pain in the ass, but I'd like to think we're on the same side. What was in the dossiers?"

"Alex didn't want the information shared." David pursed his lips. "But it did prove the links between Huang, Lord, Carducci, and Debargio."

"But did it prove Lord was Huang?" Mark asked.

"No. It only proved someone in Mainland China made deposits to specific accounts in the Caymans."

"We need to see those dossiers," Zack said. "Then we need Mother and Ember to double-check everything in them. It sure looks like we've trusted our federal brethren a little too quickly."

"Like Carducci," Murphy commented drily. "Sure didn't see that coming."

"We heard about it over in Afghanistan. It's pretty bad when you've got to cross-check the government folks who hire you in the first place," Harley said. "Man, I'm suffering from jet lag something awful. I need coffee. Y'all go ahead with your arguing and I'll be right back. Clear me a spot on the table. I'm bringing the twenty-cup percolator." With that, he headed out.

"Don't forget the creamer," Roy called after him.

"Okay, so we talk to Alex, check out what's in those FBI files, and then we'll know for sure if Lord is the top dog in this fight, if he's really the Chinese mastermind known as Huang." Mark glanced at Mother and Ember. "You know that means you two will be doing all the double-checking, don't you?"

"Not a problem," Mother replied. "It's what we do, Mark honey."

Ember nodded, and Zack wanted to reach out and give her a hug. Her current choice of black hair dye only made her look scrawny and sad, like she was drowning and no one could save her. Survivor's guilt slapped him down. That stupid gangster had intended to kill him, not Todd. Looking at poor Ember, Zack almost wished he'd been the one to die that day. Did she wish the same? Did she blame him? He couldn't help but wonder, because he sure as hell blamed himself.

"Enough said about the FBI. What about Director Peters? What information did he provide?" Mark drew a red laser circle around the Interpol director's name on the screen.

David's brows furrowed. "Alex met privately with Director Peters several times. I wasn't privy to those meetings, but according to Alex, Interpol has no hard evidence Huang exists. He supposedly has a private home in China, but no one has a photo of the man. Peters was the one who provided Alex with copies of the Huang emails that originated right here in D.C."

Mark glanced at Ember. "Did you double-check what Peters provided Alex?"

Ember nodded. "I was the one who tracked the IP address to Lord. It was easy. In fact," she turned to Zack, "it was too easy."

"Why do you say that?" he asked gently. This was the first time she'd addressed him since Todd's murder. He couldn't see her eyes through the dark glasses, but in her own way she'd reached out to him.

"I don't know." She shrugged. "But it was like you said. I was being led. I didn't think of it until...." Her voice trailed away. Of course she hadn't noticed it. She'd been consumed with grief. The poor woman should be on some kind of antidepressant, but Zack knew why she wasn't. Same reason he wasn't.

"Would you mind taking another look at them?" he asked. "Maybe look past Lord. Maybe we were only seeing what Peters told us to see."

She pushed away from the table. "Sure. I can do that."

He turned to Mother. "How long would it take you to double-check the Interpol findings on Huang?"

"By double-check, do you mean *double-check?*" Mother's eyes were wide with surprise. "I mean, it's Interpol, Boss, I mean, Zack. I've never *double-checked* Interpol files before. I'm not real sure how long it will take to get into their, umm, mainframe." She cringed when she said the last word. The truth was out, like everyone didn't already know she dabbled in the black art of hacking.

"Yeah, but you're the *Mother around here*, right?" Mark repeated her often-stated self-declaration. "Who else could do it if not you or Ember?"

"I didn't say I couldn't do it. I just haven't done it before. It's probably as easy as pie." Mother's eyes twinkled as she and Ember headed out to their shared workstation. "Sure good to have you back home, Mark honey."

"Okay," Mark continued while everyone else smirked at her *motherly* endearment. "What else do we know about this Director Peters guy? He's beginning to look interesting."

"Right after we lost Agent Chandler, he told Alex to butt out of the Mainland China investigation," Zack muttered, thankful Ember was no longer in the room. "He said that was Interpol's jurisdiction, that he'd go after Huang himself."

"We heard about Agent Chandler in Afghanistan." Mark's voice softened. "That was a hard break. I'm sorry."

"Thanks," David replied. "It was hard on everyone, but I have to ask–how are you hearing about office business while you're overseas on a remote op?"

Mark nodded toward the outer office. "Someone keeps us informed, but you already know that."

David sighed. "I'm glad it's Mother and not someone else. I guess."

"We don't need a leak. We've got Mother," Zack said. "But now that I think about it, didn't Director Peters work with Alex on the emergency response plan to evacuate and take down the foster homes? Don't get me wrong. I'm glad we rescued those little girls, but didn't it all go down a little too smoothly? I mean, I wasn't there, but I heard the FBI and police swarmed in and grabbed everyone," he snapped his fingers, "just like that, and no one got hurt. It couldn't have gone smoother if Jun had invited the FBI over for coffee and said, '*Come on in, y'all*'."

"Except you were lying in some hole in the mud, huh?" Mark's eyes twinkled with mischief.

"Mother told you?" Zack grimaced. "Yeah. Not my finest moment."

"It did go extremely easy, now that you mention it." David's answer was guarded.

"We were pretty stoked when we saved all those little girls," Murphy said. "I mean it, Mark. You should've seen the foster homes. Looked more like warehouses."

"It was quite an emotional event for the whole city, wasn't it?" Mark asked.

"It hit us all pretty hard," David agreed.

"So hard that you and Zack both have new daughters." Mark smiled again.

"That's it. I'm talking to Mother," Zack exclaimed. "That woman can't shut her mouth to save her life."

"She can't help it. We're her family," Mark replied. "But think about this op from the perspective of whoever's running the show. Saving three hundred little girls distracted everyone, didn't it? So, naturally, everyone thought the child trafficking ring was broken up for good. It's what I would have thought."

Zack's mood had turned more serious with Mark's fresh analysis of the evidence.

"Then Peters declared he'd take care of the China connection, which made perfect sense. It's in his jurisdiction," Mark continued.

Roy spoke up. "Now you've got me wondering. Were we missing the big picture all along?"

Mark shut off the laser pointer. "If Peters is the powerbroker behind this operation, what better way to make the problem go away than to make it look like it did when it really didn't?"

"So everyone involved–the FBI, Metro PD, and us–we all go back to our jobs thinking we've done a great thing, saved all these girls, caught the bad guys, and—" Murphy said.

"And he opens up shop in a different city or country." David finished the thought. "He cleans up loose ends here and—"

"My God. How big is this ring?" Zack interrupted.

"Alex did mention Peters was the Assistant Director in the Beijing Interpol office before he came to D.C.," David replied. "He worked out of Hong Kong before that. In fact, he's only been D.C. Director for two years."

"He could have connections all over the world," Murphy said.

"Certainly in China," Zack said, the magnitude of what he was looking at worse than he imagined. Any business that could write off three hundred and eleven children as an acceptable business loss was beyond despicable.

"If what we suspect is true," Mark said somberly, "we've just proved motive and means."

"We need to see those FBI files. The sooner the better." Zack couldn't keep the excitement out of his voice. "And we need to double-check every word that came out of Peters' big mouth."

"Let's talk to Alex first," Mark said. "I've got the same gut feeling. Give Kelsey a call. Tell her we're on our way. Maybe Alex feels it too."

THIRTY-TWO

"How about we don't go visit your boss just yet?" a familiar man's voice interrupted.

Harley bumped the door open with the percolator in his hands and a madder-than-hell look on his face as Director Daniel Peters walked in behind him, a pearl-handled revolver stuck in Harley's back. Peters waved for Harley to join the group at the table. Four more black-uniformed guards poured in behind him, all with weapons drawn. The six TEAM agents were instantly surrounded and out-gunned.

Peters gave Zack a cold look as he took the empty chair between Zack and Murphy. "Why can't you for once in your screwed up, jarhead life follow orders like you're told to?"

Zack didn't answer. Peters didn't sign his paycheck.

"All you jokers had to do was hit Vinnie's hangout and report back to me. I told you to call if you ran into trouble, but could you do that? Hell, no." He turned to Murphy. "Who's the boss around here, anyway?"

"Not you, that's for sure." Murphy smirked, and Peters' hand shot out, striking Murphy full in the face. All the agents jumped to his aid, but Peters' men were already engaged, the barrels of their weapons in The TEAM's backs. Murphy settled into his chair, wiping the blood off his cheekbone with the back of his hand.

"Sit," Peters hissed. "I don't have time for fun and games."

The men sat, tension thick and heavy in the room.

"You morons should've contacted me like I told you."

"Why? So you could keep running the show?" Zack shot back at him, his arm tensed to block the quick hand of Peters' and the pistol-whipping that came with it.

"No. So I wouldn't have to kill you stupid damned cowboys!" Peters snapped. "You guys always think you can do as you please."

Zack grunted. Sure looked like Peters thought that, not him.

"Let me tell you how this is going to go down. Lay your weapons on the table. Come on. Let's see 'em."

David shook his head. "We're not carrying."

Peters looked surprised, glancing around the table. "That right? None of you carrying? Well, hell, that's a damned good office policy. Makes a hostile takeover a lot smoother."

Zack caught the latent hostility glowering across the table from Mark's eyes. He was planning his own hostile takeover, and Zack planned to be ready to go when it happened.

"Word on the streets is the police didn't apprehend all the Tigers yesterday like they were supposed to. Apparently, they can't do what they're told, either." Peters turned, his revolver digging into Zack's bicep. "Guess the Tigers are a little upset they killed that redheaded punk instead of you. They're going down to some fancy hotel in Alexandria to finish the job."

Zack bristled at the inference.

"And you." Peters aimed at David next. "You weren't supposed to show up at Lord's place yesterday. It was none of your business."

"Then why'd you tell Alex he was involved?" David asked, as calm as always.

"Because he was. How do you think he got to be Senator? And that greaseball, Carducci. How do you think he got so far up the ladder? It wasn't cuz they were smart. Hell, no. I owned them. I would've owned Brown too, but there's another punk for you. Brown wasn't smart enough to know when he had it good." Peters' eyes glittered as he scanned the men around the table. "And Stewart ate it up like a dog with a bone, but no more. That's why I'm here–clean up the loose ends. It's what I do."

"Why'd you kill Carducci?" Zack asked. "He just another loose end?"

Peters turned to him and the office stilled. He took a minute to answer, but the man wasn't even breathing hard. "I should've known better with good old Kev. He figured he could pull you guys off Debargio's scent with that stunt. Thought if he tossed one of them little girls at you, you couldn't resist. He was right. It almost worked, but he never shoulda used one of my girls to do it. Lord tried to save his ass with a Senate investigation on Stewart, but Kev just kept making one mess after another. Gotta hand it to Stewart, though. Never thought he'd tackle Richards and Debargio like he did. He's tougher than I thought."

"He's better than you," Harley growled.

Peters' raised brow and shrug matched his lack of concern. "Won't matter after today. He'll be just as dead."

"You planted information with the FBI," David stated.

Peters smirked. "It's amazing how a little comment here and a little comment there can change the direction of an entire operation."

"Like building a contingency plan to storm the foster homes," Zack said.

"Whoa." Peters leaned back with an appraising grunt. "As dumb as you are, you're still pretty sharp for a junior agent. What are you complaining about? You all got to feel like heroes. It almost worked."

"How many more foster homes are there?" David asked softly.

"Wrong question, Tao. You guys don't have a clue what you're up against. This is big business. I'm not even close to the top rung. I'm just the clean-up man."

"The east coast business was an acceptable loss then," Mark said quietly.

"More like insignificant. We don't do too bad here in the States, but the real money is overseas," Peters replied. "But I'm done talking. Time to do what I do best."

Mark gripped the table, and Zack matched his move.

"You're missing a button." Zack stared at Peters' suit jacket sleeve. This was the man who'd dumped Zhen Ting into the trash, the master manipulator behind Carducci, and the snake who'd employed Jun. He was the reason the tiny, unnamed toddler had been branded and drowned. Zack clenched his fist and planned, with or without Mark's participation. He might not have his Ruger, but Peters was going to die today. "Bet you're diabetic, too."

Peters shot him a look of incredulity before his gaze shifted to one of his men. "Do it."

That man pushed the conference room windows open wide before he pulled out a couple cans of spray paint. Within minutes, he'd tagged everything in the room with the bright orange and black stick letters and upside down religious graffiti, with a two-bit gang from Anacostia brightly taking credit for the murders of Alex Stewart and his team.

"Once the police arrive, they'll chalk the whole mess up to the Tigers. Case closed. Those clowns won't think a minute past the spray paint. It's too bad your boss isn't here." Peters aimed his gun at David again. At the same time, Zack felt the sharp dig of a gun barrel at the back of his head. He glanced around the table. Murphy, Mark, and Roy were all subdued in the same way. The only one not skewered with a weapon was Harley, who still held the percolator.

"When we're through here, Lennox, the Tigers are gonna visit your little girlfriend. Oughta be a touching scene, don't you think?" Peters winked like he was sharing a dirty secret. "You dog, you."

Zack's mind went to Rory Dennison, dutifully keeping watch over Mei and Song. Rory hailed from Nebraska. Farm country. Cornhuskers. The heartland of America. And a few generations of damned proud United States Marines.

And then there was Connor Maher, a Boston man raised by a determined widow who'd single-handedly raised seven boys, most of who'd followed in Connor's footsteps to join the Corps. The only brothers who hadn't were still in high school. Peters and his men were in for one hell of a firefight.

"Then we're going over to visit Tao's kids, I think there's about five of 'em, isn't that right? Any last words you want me to tell Nancy?" Peters taunted David, his pistol in continual motion until he ended at Mark. "Then I've got plans for a blonde chick who lives in Rose Creek. That wouldn't be a baby bump, would it, Houston? That's kinda like two for the price of one."

"You're not leaving here alive," Mark hissed, the promise of death in his eyes. Zack agreed with him, ready to spring into action at the first opportunity.

"You don't think so?" Peters waved his revolver again. "Maybe you oughta check with Tony Brown and Kevin Carducci. They said the same thing."

The four false Interpol agents grunted while Mark's knuckles turned white against the edge of the table. Zack studied his friend's deadly calm. He and Mark were both weightlifters. They could crush these guys. There was still hope.

"Woodley Park's next." Peters jabbed Murphy. "What'd ya do, Finnegan, rob the cradle with that one?"

If looks could kill, Peters would've been dead and buried with the insinuation, but there was little Murphy could do with the gun at the back of his head.

"Finally I'm going to chat with your poor, injured boss. Ya think I oughta include that little wife of his, that little Kelsey who gets all dreamy-eyed whenever they're together? That's another hard one to figure. What's a doll like her see in a bastard like Stewart?"

Tension pulsed from TEAM agent to agent. Despite the open windows, the room seemed full of darkness. Zack glared at Mark, but all he offered was a scant nod. Harley shifted his feet.

"Hell, instead of killing the women and kids, maybe we oughta put them to work. Always looking for new talent. I've got appetites for young women all over the world, even pregnant ones."

Mark's eyes darkened and Zack held his breath. *Keep making Houston mad, Peters, and he'll take you and your goons down singlehanded.*

As if on cue, Peters' agents dug their guns harder into the backs of their victims' skulls. Mark, Roy, Zack, David, and Murphy's heads were pushed so far forward that they were looking down at the table. Zack couldn't see his fellow agents anymore, but he knew them. He could sense them. All were primed to blow.

"Then there's you, Mortimer." Peters pushed his chair back, his legs stretched out in relaxation. "You're the only smart one here. No wife. No kids. Killing you won't matter, so I'm going to make you a deal. How about I let you be the sole survivor again?"

"How about I let you be the sole survivor again? Tie him up, boys."

By the sounds of it, one of Peters' men holstered his pistol. Zack tensed. He caught the slight shifting of weight across the table from Mark, the way a man anchors his feet before he launches into a brawl. Zack prepared to follow suit.

Peters pushed his chair back and stood. "Let's get it done. I've got a real job to get back to."

Zack sucked in a deep breath. Time to move. Time to do something. Anything!

Peters stood behind Zack. So did one of his guards. Peters must've been aiming at Harley, though. Zack already had a gun digging into his skull. Peters wouldn't be planning on wasting two bullets on a dumb junior agent, would he?

"On the count of three," Peters' slick voice ordered. "One."

Zack tensed, all his energy ready to propel him off his chair.

"Two."

Time had run out. Zack jumped to his feet and—

CRACK!

A gunshot shattered the air. The obnoxious Interpol Director lurched backward, a marionette blown off its feet. It was Alex at the door, his SIG locked in both hands as he advanced into the room.

Chaos erupted.

That one nanosecond of shocked surprise propelled Zack. His elbow caught the man behind him full in the face, knocking him off balance so Zack's fist could do the rest. The guy's gun flew. So did Zack's fist. He hit the man's nose. His cheek. His mouth. The guy never got a punch in. By the time Zack shoved his limp body aside, hamburger never looked so ugly.

Someone fired again. Had to be Alex. Another of Peters' men went down with Murphy on top of him. Mark had barely pushed off the floor at the other side of the table, his fists red and bruised. Somehow, David Tao still looked clean and professional. No doubt he'd relied on his martial art skills.

The percolator was shattered. Harley was covered in water and coffee grounds, but he had the cocky Mortimer swagger on. *Take that, PTSD!* Roy was just releasing one tough guy from a stranglehold. Either the man had passed out, or...Zack didn't think beyond that point. Didn't much care, either. Dead was just as good.

Pride ratcheted up Zack's spine. This was his team. His friends. His brothers. *No one messes with MY FAMILY!*

"Murph, that's enough," Alex shouted, but Murphy was suddenly just as deaf as Alex. He kept punching an unconscious assassin's bloody face again and again, his jaw clenched as tight as his fist.

"Murphy," Alex shouted, like he wasn't already loud enough.

Zack crouched beside Murphy, his hand restraining another blow to a face that no longer felt anything. Poor Murphy was spattered in blood and still mad as hell. "It's okay. You can stop now. We're done here. You done good."

Murphy made eye contact, for a moment ready to strike Zack. It took a second for him to shift mindsets. When he climbed to his feet, he kicked the bloodied, dead body of Director Peters and bellowed, "You sonofabitch. I ain't never too old I can't take care of my Moira!"

"I got it, man." Zack steered his senior agent away from Peters. "Look around. You're in good company."

Murphy was still ready to fight until he caught sight of Alex. "What the hell are you doing here?" he snapped. "Aren't you supposed to be home taking it easy?"

Alex pointed at one ear as he secured his pistol inside the holster under his arm. "Mother! Ember!" he shouted out the door.

Zack grinned. The man was deaf, still bossy as all get out, and a damned sight for sore eyes.

Mother and Ember entered the room, each with a revolver drawn. Zack grinned harder.

"No one messes with my guys," Mother said as she holstered her weapon, her chin stuck out in self-righteous bravado.

Ember calmly secured her pistol. She'd lost her dark glasses. The sadness in her eyes had been replaced by the look of the tough Navy Corpsman she'd once been. Zack was glad she was on his side. She was Amazonian again–tall, voluptuous, and deadly. He snagged one arm around her slender waist as he strolled out of the Sit Room behind his boss.

"I think it's time for you and me to do some serious target practice," he teased. Ember was the weapons expert. Target practice was the last thing she needed, but she took the bait.

"I already shoot better than you, Zack." The light was back in her green eyes. Still fragile. Still more glimmer than audacious, but Ember was on her way back from the grave. She was going to be okay.

Alex shouted to David, "Call the police. They were supposed to be here by now."

As if on cue, a swarm of officers poured up from the damaged stairwell, rifles drawn, and, like the cavalry in the old cowboy movies, late as usual.

Zack joined Alex and everyone else around Mother and Ember's workstation. For some reason, Alex was sitting behind a laptop, something Zack doubted he knew how to use. The man didn't do technology very well. It wasn't until Alex started talking that Zack put two and two together. Ember was typing the conversation so Alex could read what everyone had to say.

"Man, Boss, you never looked so pretty." Harley grunted as he flopped his lanky body into the chair beside Alex. "I was thinking I could take out maybe two of those guys with my trusty coffeepot, but I was worried it could get awful ugly."

Alex read the message Ember typed. He shot her a small smile before lowering his booming voice to a conversational level. "It did get ugly, just not like Peters planned."

"Boss, what are you doing here? You're supposed to be home resting." David pulled up the chair on the other side of Alex.

Ember typed David's words and Zack smiled. She looked happy to be helping Alex.

"And where were Mother and Ember during all this?" Roy asked. "Not that I minded you showing up like you did, but why didn't Peters grab you gals?"

Alex didn't have to wait for Ember to type, as fast as she was. His biggest problem was maintaining eye contact while reading the screen. "They were in the supply room. They saw him intercept Harley. And I'm here because I finally did what I should've done."

THIRTY-THREE

"What's that?" Zack asked. He'd taken a seat directly across from his boss.

"I talked with Shawn Washington."

"The gangbanger who shot Todd?" Zack asked, instantly angry. "Why?"

"Remember he wanted immunity in exchange for information? It turns out the big fish he was ready to turn on wasn't Carducci like I thought." Alex sighed deeply. "It was Peters."

"Yeah, none of us saw that coming," Zack said.

"How would a punk like Washington know Peters?" Roy asked.

Ember's fingertips flew over her keyboard, keeping her boss on track.

"He drove the car when Peters dumped Zhen Ting. Apparently, the little girl had seen Peters at one of the homes. The dumpster was supposed to have been picked up the same night. She should've been crushed in the back of a garbage truck and stuck on some garbage scow. It's a miracle the old man found her when he did."

"Marty. His name is Marty," Zack said quietly, thinking of his friend. Maybe it was time to adopt him, too.

"Too many other things didn't add up," Alex said, quieter still.

"Like the emails from Lenny Huang that mysteriously originated in D.C.?" Zack asked.

"Like a lot of things," Alex said. "The explosion yesterday made me damned mad. Hell, I've got a couple loose teeth, and those people at the hospital put me through a whole battery of tests on my heart before they'd let me leave. And not being able to hear is aggravating, but one good thing came out of it. For the first time in months, I ate dinner with my wife last night. That's rare around our place, and I got to bed at a reasonable hour. I woke up around two this morning, and I could see every single disconnect in the case. It's like I was looking at a road map."

"That's what we've been going over." Zack nodded toward the Situation Room where the FBI was now in control. "Seems everyone had a gut feeling about all the perfectly aligned evidence we'd been handed by our Interpol friend in there. We'd barely figured it out when Peters showed up with his goon squad."

"And to think I invited these guys into our operation." Alex sat back heavily in his chair.

"You were right to invite them," Roy said. "We couldn't have tackled a global operation by ourselves. We should've been able to trust ATF and Interpol."

"This game had a lot of heavy hitters," Murphy muttered, the wind finally out of his sails.

"Greed knows no boundaries," Mark offered. "Makes me want to go home and hug my wife."

"We are definitely off the case now," Alex said wearily. "I talked with Senator Matt Burlington from Wyoming. He's an honest man by the way, one you can trust. He's working closely with the FBI. They're point for civil rights violations like child trafficking, and unfortunately this one," Alex rubbed a hand over the back of his neck, "is the biggest they've ever seen."

"We came to the same conclusion," David said.

"Just a little too late," Zack whispered. The tremendous feeling of relief he'd experienced was tempered by those last comments from Peters about the stateside business being insignificant in comparison to the rest of the world. All those sad babies' faces in the foster homes still haunted him. Mark was right. Zack needed to hold his girls again, the sooner the better.

"Here, guys." Mother had made coffee in two of the smaller coffee makers in the office. She brought a tray of powdered creamer, sweetener, coffee mugs, and spoons to the table.

"Thanks." Harley reached for the nearest cup. "I need a gallon."

"Me, too." Roy helped himself.

Zack took his hot and black. Normally, he'd doctor it with plenty of cream and sugar, but black seemed to fit the mood. He sipped as he stared at the bluster of activity in the usually quiet TEAM office. The coroner had arrived with body bags and several assistants. Hell had come to the last place on earth he'd expected it to come.

Armchair quarterbacks and the all-knowing television pundits liked to say that a person who lived by the sword died by the sword, but Zack saw it differently. It was only because of the 'sword' carried into battle by honorable men that all those loud mouth pundits and know-it-alls had the freedom to shoot their faces off in the first place. David was right when he'd said, *'You and I are not like most of the people around us. We know what it means to fight for peace'.*

"The police want us to hang around for questioning, but right now, they're looking at us as victims first," Murphy said as he handed the two video surveillance tapes from the Situation Room to Alex. "You might want to look at this before you surrender it to the police, but these tapes should prove what went down here today."

"Bet you're glad I talked you into inner office surveillance now, aren't you?" Mother spiked a sassy eyebrow at her boss.

"I am," Alex said readily as he took the tapes. "Almost as glad as the day I hired you."

Zack couldn't help but smile. Mother had just been blindsided by her boss. She sputtered and got all teary-eyed.

"Those tapes will corroborate everything that happened here today?" Alex asked.

"It will document our evidence against Peters and his ring of associates," Mark said.

Alex handed Mother the tapes. "Make three copies. One for me, the police, and Senator Burlington."

She nodded, silently obedient.

Mei's sweet face came to Zack's mind. He wanted to run to her and Song, to make sure they were safe, but he didn't at the same time. Peters' death threats against each agent's wife and children revealed the extreme evil of the man. This had evolved into an intensely personal operation that rocked each of them to their core. They seemed paralyzed, still needing each other's company.

Predictably, it was Mother who ended the silence. As she cleared her throat to speak, Ember went dutifully back to typing. "You know, Boss, I wish we could fix the whole world and make everyone happy, and cure hunger and greed and all them things that make this old world sick, cuz it is a sick old place and it needs a powerful lot of help. I do wish that, but I'm looking at my family right now, and...and I don't care if I make a fool of myself."

Zack gulped. She might not be a trained sniper, but Mother's words were right on target. Her blue eyes overflowed, making it worse and better at the same time.

"You all wonder why I don't start my own business and make a million, but I'll tell you why. It's not the first time and it won't be the last time I say it, but...I love you guys. I do. That's all there is to it. I'm as happy as a pig in a bushel of peaches that you guys aren't the ones lying in there with holes in your heads. It could've been you if Alex hadn't shown up like he did. And you know what else? I love all your pretty little wives and your kids, too. I don't know what I'd have done if any of you were killed today. I'm not over losing Todd yet. None of us are."

By now she'd grabbed a box of tissues off her counter and mopped her face, crying openly. "And Boss." She dabbed her eyes and her nose. "I think I love you most of all, and I ain't ashamed to say it. You can tell Kelsey, too. I don't mind sharing you."

Alex grunted, and Zack had to turn away. There it was, the truth behind Mother's allegiance to her boss, out in the open for all to hear. Poor Alex.

Mother sputtered, too emotional to go on.

Thank God. Zack pushed away from the counter. Any more of this and he'd be bawling, too. He glanced at Harley who was wiping his face and not ashamed in the slightest, but that was different. Everyone knew Harley had a soft heart. David and Mark looked pretty subdued, but Zack was still hoping he had the tough guy mystique going for him.

"I think what Mother is trying to say, Alex," Ember lifted her quiet voice above Mother's sniffling while she began typing her own thoughts, her eyes never once straying to her flying fingertips, "is that we do good work here. Even if we couldn't save the world like we wanted, we did save three hundred and eleven little girls. Little Chai Yenn is safe and sound with David and his family. And little Baby Song?" She turned to Zack. "Wow."

He clenched his jaw. Ember was playing dirty.

"All we've got to do is look at him." She reached a hand to his knee and squeezed before she went back to typing. "He's happier than he's ever been. That's another sweet picture, watching our big old muscle-bound Zack sitting on the floor with his hands bandaged and playing with his sweet baby girl. You guys should've seen it."

Zack could not stop his eyes from filling. Ember was right. Song had opened his heart to the Technicolor world of real love. Mei had made him weak and strong in the same instant. There was no going back. He'd been converted, lock, stock and barrel, but he'd lost a good friend. Todd had also been there that day, watching him coax little Song to pick up the sock monkey.

Ember turned to Alex next, her voice tight with emotion. "And I saw you the day the police raided the first foster home."

Suddenly, Alex looked surprised and as vulnerable as Zack had just been. His eyes widened and just as quickly shadowed. A secret was about to be revealed.

"Wow, Alex. I saw you pick up that little girl when we went to help. She was scared and you snuggled her inside your jacket. You didn't know anyone was watching you, but I was."

He nodded one quick affirmation, his hand lifted to brush her words off like they were nothing.

"I saw the look on your face. I saw you kiss her forehead. You were thinking of Abby."

He did not speak, but Zack saw the cords in his neck tighten.

"Wow. There you were, holding that little orphan like she was the most precious thing in the whole world."

The hustle and bustle of the emergency responders faded. All Zack could see was the pain on his boss's face as the tender memory was relived. That was sacred ground. No one mentioned the daughter he'd lost to an automobile accident years ago. Not in the office. Ever.

"Cuz she was." Ember brought the point home. "It's a very good thing to rescue just one child, Alex. It's enough."

Her green eyes brimmed by the time she stopped typing and Zack wanted to hug her all over again. Here she was, devastated by her own loss, yet bolstering The TEAM like only a woman could.

Alex reached across the table for her hand, clearing his throat to speak. "You're right. Maybe we didn't save the world, but we've done a damned good job." He turned to the rest of his team. "Get out of here. Go home. This place can wait. Take two weeks. All of you."

Harley couldn't help himself. He cupped a hand to his ear and leaned across the table. "Huh? What'd you say, Boss? Huh?"

Alex almost repeated himself until he caught everyone's smiles. He snapped the laptop closed and stood up. "Get the hell outta here."

Unexpectedly, he turned to Zack. "Everyone but you."

THIRTY-FOUR

DAVID

"No, Daddy! No!"

Chai Yenn screamed all the way through the *Pirates of the Caribbean* ride at Disneyland. And then she screamed all the way through *Sleeping Beauty's* castle. Like a frantic, human growth on David's hip, she couldn't be quieted until at last they were outside of the dark, scary castle and back into the bright California sun.

The crowds of people milling through the castle gateway were no help as the frightened little girl clung to David in sheer terror, gulping back tears at the wonderful, horrible place. He stroked her hair as he soothed Chai in the circle of his arms. At last her screams reduced to sobbing hiccups. She peeked out from the safety of her hands and fingers. Nancy and his four boys sat with him.

"Maybe it would be better if I sat here with Chai for awhile." David studied his wife's impassive face across the table. "You and the boys go on some rides and have fun. We'll catch up in an hour or two."

Nancy Tao's eyes were unreadable behind her sunglasses. "I have a better idea. The boys and I will be right back." And with that, she was gone.

David and Nancy's four boys were Michael, age ten; Nathan, age eight; Ryan, age six; and the baby, Matthew, age two. And maybe it was the difference in gender, but ever since David and Nancy had brought five-year-old Chai Yenn into their home, the boys had turned into either her protectors or her slaves. No sibling rivalry had presented itself yet, but the continual jousting and competition among the boys to see who could make her smile first, or who could bring her a treat before another brother thought of it was an interesting phenomenon to watch. Even now, as Nancy walked away with Ryan and Matt's hands in hers, three of the boys were waving at their little sister, trying to get her attention. She finally waved back with both hands.

"Are you feeling better?" he asked her in soft Mandarin.

Chai nodded, looking around with wide, wondering eyes. He rarely spoke to her in anything but English, preferring that she acclimate as quickly as possible. But today was different. The whole Disneyland adventure had not proven to be one of his brighter ideas. So far, all he'd done was traumatize the very one he'd hoped to please.

After sitting for a few minutes, he scooped her up and walked with her still clinging like a baby orangutan to his side. Her nightmare was over, but apparently she could not transition to normal life yet. The oddest things frightened her. Extension cords. Matthew's trike. Even yogurt held a sad story he could not yet fathom. Who knew what this little one had seen and lived through? He truly wished he did. Maybe then he could erase them one by one.

They stopped to watch the carousel. It might make a better ride for a little girl who'd spent the first five years of her life in an orphanage. Maybe the magical horses or laughing tigers would help her enjoy the Wonderful World of Disney. The minute he stepped into line, she screamed. They didn't ride the carousel.

They watched the fantastical flying elephants soar overhead with their laughing child passengers. Chai's eyes were bright with curiosity. Maybe she'd enjoy a ride with Dumbo and his flying friends. Once again he was wrong. Her frantic screams upset the other children. They didn't ride the flying elephants.

He patiently rearranged his daughter on his hip and turned back the way he came. Since they'd taken her to their hearts, the little girl had put on weight. Nancy could no longer carry her, especially not all day long like Chai preferred. He'd either have to rent a stroller, or she'd have to learn to walk on her own. Still fearful, she hummed to herself in what he'd come to recognize as her attempt to self-comfort.

"We're back." Nancy tapped his shoulder.

Chai yelped when she found herself surrounded by Goofy and Donald Duck, Chip and Dale, and the beautiful Princess Mulan. Chai all but climbed up to David's shoulder as she whined, taking in the frightening scene around her. The big furry chipmunks were so funny-looking. It was Chip who broke the ice when he offered a feather-flower to the little girl.

Scared at first, she stretched her arm as far as it would go, not letting go of her Daddy while Chip put the flower in her hand. A cautious smile tugged the corners of her mouth. He blew her a kiss. She blew him a return kiss just like she'd learned to do from her brothers, only without a smile.

Chai climbed down into David's arms. By now, he and Nancy were seated on a rock ledge that ran the concourse to Never Neverland.

Beautiful Princess Mulan took her crown off and rested it carefully on Chai's head. Of course, Chai pulled it right off, but she let Mulan stroke her hair. All the while, Goofy and Donald danced and partied around her. Chip and Dale persisted with their antics.

Chai Yenn planted herself squarely between David's feet. Goofy and Donald joined her, then Chip and Dale. Soon Mickey Mouse arrived with his entourage. He sat at David's feet. The Tao family had become a Disney attraction.

David nudged Nancy's arm. Chai was playing pat-a-cake with Mulan. And smiling.

Nancy scooted in beside him as they watched their children cavort within the now cordoned-off area. Snow White and Cinderella arrived, along with more Disney security escorts. It was a totally unscripted party designed on the spur of the moment for a little girl who'd never seen such magical things as a fluffy duck in a sailor suit, chipmunks bigger than she was, or a mouse wearing red shorts.

"How did you arrange this?" David hugged his beaming wife, planting a kiss on the side of her very smart head.

"Easy." Nancy smiled. "The entire country knows about how you guys rescued all those orphans. I still had her adoption papers in my bag. Besides, Disney really is all about children."

He smiled past the knot in his throat. He couldn't bring them all home, but he was eternally grateful he'd saved this particular little girl. Now Chai Yenn would live the best happily ever after life he could give her.

Chai's brother, Ryan, pulled her to her feet while he played tag with Chip and Dale. "Come on, Chai. You can do it," he squealed.

Chip rolled on the ground, catching Chai as she ran by. He lifted her high in the air like a human airplane. She looked across the crowded space at David. The smile slipped.

He waved to her. *You're safe, Chai. Don't be afraid anymore. The world is yours for the taking.* The momentary frown was replaced by the breathtaking smile of a happy little girl playing with a giant furry chipmunk. He turned his head and wiped the tear.

Nancy whispered in his ear. "You old softy."

THIRTY-FIVE

EMBER

The capricious wind whistled around Ember Davis as she stood in solitary vigil at the headstone of Agent Todd Chandler.

Like the soldiers they represent, the endless rows of identical white headstones marched across acres of snow-drifted lawn in reverent Arlington Cemetery. The morning stillness gave way to the first of many twenty-one-gun salutes that would sound throughout the day while honor guards assigned heroes and heroines to their final posts. Solemn words would be spoken, the noble flag folded and presented. Another warrior safely home.

Yeah, right.

Ember didn't see it that way. A wild spirit whose perspective was eternally different from the world around her, all she saw was that she stood alone. She'd recognized a kindred spirit in Todd. He was the perfect complement to her perpetually searching soul, the steadiness to her unbounded enthusiasm, and the ground wire to her stream of effervescent energy. And now he was gone. Taken from her and buried here, among all the noble dead.

Even in death, he'd conformed to the strict military code of the cemetery. He'd lived by the code he was now interred by. Interment was another unsolved puzzle for this computer genius. When her time came, her remains would be cremated, the ashes tossed high into the jet stream to be scattered at its pleasure, not left within the cold bosom of a neglectful mother earth, forgotten and alone for eternity. No. Give her the sky and its endless sunshine. Give her night stars and solar flares. Give her–light.

Give me Todd back!

Tears coursed down her reddened cheeks. It wasn't long ago she'd shared the hope with Mother that maybe–just maybe–Todd was the one. He'd pestered her so much at first, almost like a younger brother who was always in her way. Finally, Ember had recognized his attention for what it was. He'd loved her at first sight, like no other before him. He just wasn't sure how to approach her, or if she even cared. Now he was gone, consigned to death while she was left behind, consigned to life.

She cared like hell.

So engrossed in grief, she didn't hear the quiet footfall until her boss stood beside her. Alex. Always Alex. She didn't understand how the man seemed to know when a member of his team was hurting. He just did.

Many times, she'd watched him shape attitudes with a few words that made them stronger, more focused, or mad as hell. She'd seen him bring comfort into mayhem just by showing up. She'd also seen him bring chaos the same way. With a glance or a word, he could build as easily as destroy. Alex was the strength and power behind The TEAM, the fiery core the rest of them moved around, like satellites in orbit around a temperamental sun.

Damn Alex.

She mopped her sleeve across her face, but if he'd noticed, he didn't say a word. Thankfully, he honored Todd in silence, alone with his thoughts while she stood alone with hers. Did he miss Todd half as much as she did?

Another twenty-one-gun salute sounded from far across the frozen ground. Still her boss waited with her. Of course, he hadn't come for Todd as much as he'd come for her. She didn't want to face anyone yet. Hiding was easier. Avoiding was better. Not having to talk was the only way she made it through the day. Talking meant opening up. Letting people in. Being normal again. Although she'd had plenty to say the day of the shooting in the Sit Room, she'd gone silent again. Living alone will do that to a person. Even her fat yellow tabby, Maple Syrup, figured it out. She wanted to be left alone.

"What do you want, Alex?" she asked without turning to face him. Eye contact with this guy was not in the cards. Not today. One hint of kindness and she'd fall apart.

He didn't answer. Alex stood ramrod straight, as always. Maybe he was still deaf; maybe he hadn't heard the nasty tone in her question.

She gulped. Maybe he did.

"Ember?"

Squeezing her eyes against Alex was like an ostrich sticking its head in the sand. He was still here.

"What?" she ground out, angry she sounded pitiful.

When he did not speak, she faltered. Peripheral vision was no help. There was no escape. She bit her lip and faced the man she refused to call Boss. He was Alex. No better. Certainly not smarter. Just damned Alex and he was here and she wanted to be alone!

Those dazzling blues looked straight into her soul, and she couldn't hide her pain. He saw her. He felt the same. And he could hear again.

"Todd was a good man," he said quietly.

Ember jerked her gaze away from that compelling blue light and sniffed the frigid air, hoping it would bring composure. It didn't. The man beside her was made of steel, and she was melted taffy in the summer sun, all sticky and turning to goo just because he'd shown up.

"Yes," she sputtered. "He was. Todd was...a very, very good man."

"He was in the middle of a mission when everything went wrong, you know."

"I didn't know he had a mission. He never said anything. I mean, not about any mission or anything. I mean...." Ember didn't know what she meant anymore. Grief swelled within her ocean of pain.

"It meant a lot to him, totally his idea. I'm not surprised you didn't know. Few agents did."

Ember straightened as she waited.

"I'd like you to finish it on his behalf, if you would."

"What? Me?"

"Only if you think you're up for it. I know it's a bad time."

"Are you serious? I'm not one of your snipers. It's been a long time since I held a gun."

"Not all our missions involve guns."

The damned man was as powerful when he was gentle as when he was mean. It set her off balance. She didn't know what to expect from him. Or herself.

"I know that, but...What? You came all the way out here to give me an assignment? What do you want?" The fury in her heart flew out of her mouth without thought or permission. She'd come here to cry and pray in peace, not work.

Damn Alex.

Instead of answering, he put his arm around her shoulders and tilted her body toward his. She was almost as tall as he was. Still dressed in mourning with her spiked hair as black as her eyes and her clothes as wild as ever, they must've looked quite the sight; him with his conservative trench coat embracing a totally free and angrily rebellious spirit in the middle of a freaking cemetery!

Ember groaned. She'd locked her heart away. He had no right to test the lock. She'd come here for solitude, not redemption. *Leave me alone. Not today, buddy. You can't break me today.*

"It's okay, sweetheart."

So not fair! Of all the things to say!

For a moment, they stood like two fence posts in the Arlington winterscape: straight, stiff, and separate. The bright white snow and granite blinded her. That's what the moisture was in her eyes. Without warning, it happened. That single gesture of gallant kindness and those gentle words filled the aching hole in her heart with something besides bottomless pain. She crumbled. The dam burst. Grief gulped out in a torrent that wouldn't stop.

Damn you, Alex. This is your fault. You're making me cry.

Ember leaned into him. He offered a cloth handkerchief. She shivered and wiped her raw, sore nose.

I look like a clown.

The winter wind spun flake and crystal around them in a sudden flurry that just as quickly departed, leaving them lightly frosted in its wake.

I miss him!

They stood together as the storm around and within abated.

"I'm sorry." She dabbed her eyes, the venom in her heart gone with the frozen breeze and a kind man's touch.

"Nothing to be sorry about." He squeezed her shoulder. "Sometimes tears are all we've got to give the friends we've lost."

"It's just that...it's just that...."

"You loved him." Alex's voice was more tender than she'd ever heard.

"Yeah." Ember gulped again. He read her like a book. She couldn't even cuss him anymore. "And he loved me. He was like, all starry-eyed when he was around me. You know?"

"Everyone knew."

"And now..."

"He's gone."

She leaned into his shoulder again, her resistance gone and her heart wide open. Alex held her tight while her pain poured out. "And I'm still here. And I hate it and I miss him and I'm still here!" she ground out, wishing she could shake some sense into the gods of karma and make them give Todd back. He wasn't the one who was supposed to die that day. It was Zack, only she didn't want Zack to die either. It just wasn't fair!

Alex held her steady until she calmed again.

Ember mopped her face and tried not to wipe her nose on her boss. "It comes in waves. One minute I'm normal, and the next, I'm so mad. And I'm sorry. I don't wish Zack was dead and I don't hate you."

"I know." He let her lean against him, his grip strong and firm. "What will you do now?"

She ignored his question with a question of her own. "What's the mission? What's so important Todd couldn't tell me?"

"I don't think it's that he couldn't. I think it's more he hadn't found the time to tell you yet. He was going to talk with you. That much I know."

"About what?" She brushed the tears off her face. *Spit it out, Alex. Then leave me alone.*

"There's a little girl at the city morgue." He reached into an inner pocket of his black trench coat. "Todd started a collection to—"

"To bury baby Jane Doe?" she finished for him. Jane Doe was the baby girl found in the Potomac around the same time Zack rescued Chai Yenn. She still rested in a stainless aluminum drawer–waiting for someone to care.

"He had this at his desk." Alex handed her a brown envelope full of bills of various denominations.

Ember accepted the lifeline. The envelope was part of the man she loved, and now, in a way, they would share and care about the forgotten child together. Warmth flooded the cold recess of her sad heart. It was so like Todd.

"I can do this." Her voice turned from sad to calm.

They trudged through the drifted snow together.

"He had green eyes just like mine."

Alex squeezed the smaller gloved hand in his. "He did. They were a shade lighter, though."

"They were." She pressed the brown envelope against her heart and sniffed her tears away. Alex was the best boss. Despite the incredibly pain-filled down side to her job, she wouldn't trade it for the world.

"If you need more money, let me know."

"Thanks." Ember felt stronger with every step.

"You do realize you can give her a name, don't you? You can put the name on her headstone."

"I didn't know that."

He nodded, his hand strong at her elbow as he accompanied her downhill to the parking lot.

"Her name is Chandler," she whispered.

If that little girl hadn't belonged to anyone before, she did now.

THIRTY-SIX

The frigid breeze full of glistening snowflakes blowing through the city of Paris fit the season. Christmas shoppers scurried along the narrow cobblestone street. Zack had been sent on the most important operation of his life. Even now, his heart beat contentedly while he observed his quarry from the warmth of a tiny, uncomfortable foreign rental car.

Mei had been less than pleased at his abrupt departure, arguing that LiLi was no closer to being located with him gone. He would have gladly told her the truth, but he could not risk breaking her heart or dashing her hopes again. So he opted for the Christmas gift of a lifetime. If she only knew.

Without fail, the man Zack followed left his home at precisely the same time every morning, and returned on the same tight schedule at dusk. He drove his own vehicle, a small black Peugeot sedan. Without a single day's variation, he parked in his assigned, numbered stall at the world-renowned Saint-Antoine University Hospital in Paris. Not once did the Caucasian gentleman step outside the hospital for lunch or other errands, neither did he detour from his established route to and from the hospital. By all appearances, he was a strict disciplinarian; his daily routine synchronized like finely-tuned clockwork.

His name? None other than the very prestigious and extremely devious Dr. Christopher Elias Jones II, the same man Mei had once given her heart to. He was the mastermind behind the abduction of the born out of wedlock daughter he'd once disowned. Born into a world where money solved all problems, he'd simply paid off a network of unscrupulous imposters and thieves to accomplish his goal. LiLi was never in danger. No. While poor Mei had been forced to suffer the most wretched nightmare a mother could endure, LiLi had been introduced to a life of luxury and French cuisine. By all appearances, Dr. Jones loved his daughter, but Zack freaking did not care. At the end of the mission, LiLi would be westbound to her mother where she belonged. Christopher Jones could go to hell.

From what he'd been able to observe in the three days he'd been in the country, the doctor employed two women at his very secluded villa east of the Paris metropolis. Zack pegged the sturdy, gray-haired woman to be the cook since she visited the markets daily, and, according to Mother's astute investigation, an occasional dress shop less frequently. The younger woman was rarely seen outside the villa walls. She did not venture far when she did leave, and the women never travelled together. At least one of them remained home at all times. If anyone else lived at the villa, they were never seen. But Zack suspected....

He sipped his steamy espresso while he waited. In five minutes, Dr. Jones was expected to rush home on the busy Parisian street. As usual, Zack would follow from a safe distance. After Dr. Jones drove out of town and entered the garage at his estate, the single door would close with a mechanical clank and seat tightly into place, offering no entry to rodent or man. That would conclude another day's surveillance. It would begin again in the morning, albeit in reverse, and again the next day until Zack's operation was complete.

There had not been a single change in the precise man's schedule for the last two weeks, according to Mother. Not one. Even the weather had no impact. But Alex had a hunch and Zack a gut feeling. Christmas was a time for children and pleasantry. Surely the doctor had a soft spot in his cold, hard heart. Surely he would falter. Zack blew softly over his cup to cool the drink. He double-checked his watch. It had finally happened. Dr. Jones was late.

Zack checked the GPS locator on his dash. The man might be late but he was close–damned close. The deviation was miniscule. Instead of passing Zack's parked car, he had parked behind it–of all places for parking to open up. Zack got out of his car and crossed to the opposite sidewalk for a clearer view. He could not help but smile. Dr. Jones had stopped at a toy store, a particularly expensive shop that proclaimed the most beautiful, the most rare, and the most desirable–dolls.

From his new position, Zack had an excellent view of the shop's cashier just beyond the plate glass window. The doctor wasted no time in making a selection. As expected, he paid in cash. There was no paper trail, which, along with his rather ordinary last name, had made him a bit difficult to locate. Zack snapped the camera shots that documented his findings and transmitted them across the Atlantic to Alexandria, Virginia. Mother's hard work had paid off.

Invisible in the hurry and scurry of holiday shoppers, Zack waited across the street until his quary was back on schedule. Weighing the change in the doctor's itinerary against the item he'd purchased, Zack decided.

Tomorrow was the day.

The iron gate needed a drop of oil in its creaky, rusted hinges, so Zack hopped over the stone wall instead. It was early morning. Dr. Jones was already en route back to Saint-Antoine's. The cook had driven off toward the day's bargains at the city markets. Within seconds Zack was inside the villa, alert and processing the daily minutiae that came with covert operations inside a residence not too different from Senator Lord's, minus a few bodies.

A machine hummed off to his right. Since he'd entered through the kitchen door at the rear of the home, he assumed the noise came from the automatic washing machine in the nearby utility room. A door quietly closed upstairs. Another muffled thud indicated a drawer had closed. The sound of water running upstairs meant a showerhead had been turned on. It was definitely not the sound of a bath being poured. Good. The younger woman was taking her morning shower.

It was now or never.

Three doors beckoned in the upstairs hallway. Zack paused at each until he was certain. As quiet as a whisper, he entered the darkened bedroom. It was not so dark he couldn't see the goal of his mission. With a single photograph in hand to explain his presence, he flicked his small flashlight on and spotlighted the picture.

"LiLi?"

"Yes?" a timid voice answered from the head of the bed.

"Would you like to go home to your mother?"

"Yes," she squeaked sadly.

"Then stand up. I'll wrap you in a blanket but we have to hurry."

She jumped to her feet on the bed, ready to go. "Who are you?" she asked, balancing her hands on his shoulders, trusting him to help her just as her mother had.

"Your Mommy sent me," he answered quickly. *My God, she looks just like Mei.* "I have to cover your head. It's cold outside."

She complied easily as he wrapped her snug and warm. Lifting her into his arms, he retraced his footsteps without a sound. The best thing about infiltrating an old French farmhouse was the solid wood flooring and steps, built by master craftsmen to endure forever. And they didn't squeak under a man's weight.

Within minutes, he was outside the villa walls, his precious bundle safe in his arms. Securing LiLi in the front seat of his rental, he made sure the seat belt was just right. The second he climbed inside, he cranked the heater to high. Zack unwrapped a chocolate energy bar and opened a bottle of water for his guest. LiLi Xing would be cared for like no other little girl on earth. Well, except maybe for Baby Song.

"Would you like something to eat?" he asked as he offered the treat.

Tearful blue eyes stared back at him. LiLi shook her head, her chin stuck out defiantly. "I want my Mommy," she demanded, and Zack was hooked. She was Mei all over again.

"Well, that's good because I'm taking you home to your Mommy today. We're going to fly on a big jet. Would you like to be her Christmas present?" He set the treat on the console between them and pulled his vehicle onto the road.

"No." LiLi crossed her hands over her chest, her head down and her lip quivering. "You said you were taking me home. I want Mommy. Now," she demanded, verging on tears.

"Should we call her?" he asked, one hand on the wheel and the other reaching for his cell phone.

All he got for an answer was a stream of tears down the saddest face. Zack would've pulled over right then and there if he knew for sure hugging LiLi wouldn't frighten her. He dialed the number at the hotel instead, certain the time difference meant nothing to the woman he loved.

Connor answered. "Hey Zack, what's up?"

"Is Mei still awake?"

"Ah, yeah. I think so. She was just feeding your little girl."

Ah, how Zack loved the sound of that–*his little girl.*

"Can you put her on the phone?"

"Hold on. Here she is."

Zack listened while the phone was handed off to Mei. His heart swelled at the sweet torture he would shortly put her through, but it was nothing compared to what she'd already endured.

"Zack?" She got right to the point. "When are you coming home?"

He smiled at the unspoken command behind her question. *We should be looking for LiLi. Why aren't we?*

"I am, but there's someone who needs to talk with you first." Without another word, he pulled to the side of the road and handed the phone to LiLi.

She placed it to her ear. "Mommy?"

He heard Mei's shriek through the phone.

"It's me, Mommy," LiLi bawled. "I wanna come home."

Zack groaned through his tears while mother and daughter cried, squealed, and spoke to each other for the first time in too many weeks. When LiLi hiccupped with sobs, he undid her seat belt and she scrambled onto his lap, her poor little body racked with the happiest cries.

"Mommy wants to talk to you," she said very seriously as she held the cell phone to his ear, her face drenched and her arm around his neck. "She says you're her best friend and you'll take good care of me. Here. Talk."

"Mei?" he asked, surprised he could find his voice. Half of him wanted to chuckle at LiLi's authoritarian demeanor, the other half wanted to cry for the joy Mei must be going through.

"Zack?" she choked, and that was the end of the conversation. She couldn't speak. Neither could he.

Finally he ground out, "I love you, Mei. Stop worrying. We're on our way."

"Hurry home," she whispered. "I love you so—"

LiLi pulled the phone away. "I wanna talk to my Mommy."

Zack would've laughed if he could've, but his heart was full. How he wished he were home, holding the matching bookend to this darling tyrant. He pitied Connor and Rory. Mei would be energized now and a bear to live with until LiLi was back in her arms.

Out of sheer satisfaction, he hummed an old-fashioned rendition of *'Twas the Night Before Christmas,* by Clement C. Moore. Mei was about to receive the only gift that truly

mattered, the purest reason for Christmas in the first place–
the unconditional love of a child. He pressed his new
daughter to his heart and wiped his eyes.

Merry Christmas to all and to all a good night!

EPILOGUE

Zack tucked sleeping LiLi into her bed while Mei pulled Song's pink tights off, changed her diaper, and snuggled the baby into her blankets. Rambunctious Song was a different child now. She could climb like a monkey, so her baby bed had been traded for a toddler-sized bed, and both were in LiLi's room. Not for long. Soon those beds would be in another home across the river in Pennsylvania. Moving would begin within the week. He couldn't wait.

Alex had insisted they stay at the hotel for as long as they needed. It made sense, but with his upcoming nuptials to Mei in less than a week, Zack was energized like never before. His girls and their mother deserved the best. He intended to deliver.

While their new home boasted marble countertops in the kitchen, crown-molding throughout, walk-in closets, and five bathrooms, it was the fenced-in backyard and the very real possibility of a big dog in their future that sealed the deal. David Tao had volunteered to help install a state of the art security system when he returned home from Disneyland. Harley promised he'd help train the dog, and there would be no more sleepless nights for any of his girls–ever. When Zack paused at the door to watch his daughters, Mei's hand snaked around his waist.

"I think we wore them out today," she whispered. "Song didn't make a peep when I laid her down."

"Neither did LiLi." He wrapped his arm around his wife-to-be, burying his nose in the soft fragrance of her hair. "What would you say if these little gals came with us on our honeymoon?"

This was not one of those moments when he had no clue what Mei was thinking. The way her eyes lit up was answer enough.

"It's just that LiLi isn't ready for time away from you, and—"

"And you aren't ready for time away from Song."

"And you aren't ready for time away from LiLi." Zack completed the circle.

He loved that Mei could read him like a book. The power of this woman had transformed him from a mindless playboy whose biggest problem away from the office was how many magnums of wine to pick up for the ladies and how many fifths of Jack for Jake. His life outside work had been one continual party, but he didn't miss it. Even his prize possession had fallen out of first place and would soon share their new heated garage. Who would have guessed he'd ever own something as mundane as a family van? He almost felt like David Tao. Almost.

Mei's hand on his chest drew his attention away from the girls. "I ordered pizza," she said. "Are you hungry?"

She took care of him, another thing he loved. Most of the other women he'd known wanted something, but all she'd ever wanted was her life and child back. And him.

"When will it be here?" he asked, his lips tasting the side of her very delectable and pretty face. With the girls tucked in bed, the possibilities were endless. Making love with Mei had become an insatiable appetite. Just the thought of a few stolen moments triggered his attention. It didn't happen often enough.

"Forty-five minutes." Mei turned to face him, her hands still on his chest and her happy heart in her eyes.

Hagatha had disappeared. Zack understood how the instinct to protect a child could transform the softest woman into the fiercest fighting machine. He felt the same way about all of his girls.

"That gives me enough time." Zack stooped low enough to lift Mei off her feet and into his arms. She came easily, her head soft against his chest and her arm around his neck. Ah, the gentle weight of a good woman enticed and pleased him to his core. The fire that glowed in her eyes glittered brightly. His woman was content. Nothing better in the world.

She trailed tender kisses up his neck and into the sensitive spot on his neck. Mei knew him too well. One tickle from the very tip of her index finger on his ear and he shivered. His damned ears seemed to be connected to his groin. How the hell did that work?

"Now?" she asked, her best innocent face on and seduction in her deep brown eyes.

He nodded. No words would be needed for the next forty-five minutes. He angled the love of his life through their bedroom door and toed it shut. Somehow, they'd find room and time for each other on their honeymoon without excluding their children. The day would come when they might take off for a weekend by themselves, but it was not this day.

Not yet.

THE END

A Hint of Things to Come...

Harley meant to go home. Really, he did, but for some reason his victory-red Jeep pulled into long-term parking at Reagan National Airport instead. It's not like anyone was waiting for him at home, anyway. Yeah, he could always head over to Alex and Kelsey's to wrestle with their dogs, Whisper and Smoke. Kelsey would feed him. He could hang out for a while, but for two weeks?

God, grant me the serenity to accept the things I cannot change...

Jet lag plagued him, but more than sleep, Harley wanted companionship. He wanted the feeling of someone special waiting for him, watching for him, maybe even wishing he was already there with them–wherever that was. And if she couldn't be waiting for him, at least he wanted to know she'd be back soon, that she'd left a note on the counter, and that she was happy to be part of his everyday life. He knew a pretty little redhead who did those kinds of things. They might not seem like much to most folks. Suddenly, they seemed like everything.

The courage to change the things I can...

So he bought a ticket to the Mid-western state of Wisconsin, and his long distance girlfriend, Judy O'Brien. He'd placed a quick call from the ticket counter just to be sure. Since she'd first introduced herself at Mark and Libby's wedding, she and Harley had maintained an on and off again relationship of sorts. She was a registered nurse with a full time career, and he was overseas a lot on assignments. All their time apart had made it tough to really get to know each other. So much for good intentions.

And the wisdom to know the difference would sure be nice, too.

Yes, she'd be off at midnight. Yes, she could get more time off if she needed it. A week or two? Yes, she'd see what she could do. When would his flight get in, and did he need a ride from the airport? She'd be there. Fly safe.

With that settled, he relaxed. The irony of flying home from one of the world's most dangerous countries to nearly die in the land of the free did not escape him. Daniel Peters was right. Post traumatic stress disorder had wreaked havoc in Harley's life. He was one of those guys, the loser kind, who'd been in too many clinics and rehab centers to count, the kind who protected himself at all cost. Some days he was a waste of skin. Other days he managed. It was a daily struggle. Most days he could deal. Not today.

Those other words Peters threw at him before the shooting bugged him. What did he mean? Sole survivor? Harley knew he'd been injured in an IED explosion in Iraq. That much was obvious, but the sole survivor bit? No way. That implied others died. He'd remember them, wouldn't he? He pushed the thought away as usual. Too many holes in his memory still haunted, holes he couldn't explain much less fill. Someday he'd have to break down and read the Army's incident report to find out what really happened, but not now. No need to go looking for trouble.

The mantra began again. *God, grant me the serenity to accept the things I cannot change...*

The airport was full of couples and families rushing by with all their noisy chatter and laughter. Husbands kissed pretty wives they'd missed on business trips. Happy little children skipped and danced around fathers come home from wherever they'd been. For the first time since he'd stuck himself in that Texas Rehab and thought he was cured of all his torments and addictions, Harley wasn't happy. The bliss of others pointed out the lack of it in his life. He wanted more than a twelve-step program.

The courage to change the things I can...

Something was missing, and it wasn't drugs, booze, or even the camaraderie of dogs. No. Ever since Mark had married Libby, and especially now that she was pregnant, Harley had grown more dissatisfied with himself. Life was slipping away. He hated to admit it because it sounded dumb, but it seemed like his biological clock was running out on him.

Heck, all my clocks are running out on me.

A shudder slinked across his shoulders, like a sick old friend who wouldn't die. Too many ghosts haunted him. They always would. He pushed them back and faced the truth.

I want Judy.

With luxurious copper-colored hair and soft emerald eyes, Judy was a strikingly beautiful woman, but she was also intelligent and practical, a take-charge kind of woman who supervised other nurses and care-providers at the clinic where she worked. It was no wonder she'd taken the first step in their relationship when she'd asked him to dance. He'd never have done it. Anyone could see she deserved better.

He wandered through the concourse, his mind a thousand miles away. She wasn't so much intimidating, although Harley was sometimes intimidated. She knew what she wanted, and she wasn't afraid to go after it. And it's not like he was afraid of her. Overwhelmed was more like it. Overwhelmed by her beauty, brains, and her love for him. Sometimes all that strength and confidence was more than he could handle.

How could a woman like her really love a messed-up man like him? And yet he'd told her everything, about all the drugs, every needle he'd ever stuck in his arm, everything he'd ever stuck up his nose, and every rehab in between. He'd told her how he'd trashed his parents' lives until they hated the sight of him, and about those other women too. She knew him inside out. All he had to offer her was the truth, so he did. She still loved him. Go figure.

And I miss her.

When he looked up from his wanderings, he was standing in front of a jewelry store, an eclectic little tourist trap with baubles and bangles galore. The clerk had red hair. He entered, in case that was a good omen for a lost man like him. The case of glittering gems and jewels beckoned.

Wow. So many choices. What the heck would Judy like?

An interesting item caught his eye, a ring with something called a chocolate diamond. The clerk was beside herself, telling him everything he didn't care about anyway. It did have an interesting fire to it, though.

Does Judy like chocolate? Most women do, don't they? Kelsey does. Libby, too. Heck, I should know something like that about my girlfriend, shouldn't I?

Still, it was a nice fourteen-carat, rose-gold band with a round cut, quarter-carat chocolate stone surrounded by a circle of smaller, brilliant white diamonds. The white made the chocolate look darker. He did something almost as impulsive as the time he'd committed himself to that Texas Rehab.

Heck. That turned out to be a good decision, didn't it?

He bought the ring.

And then he waited for the jet that would fly him to the Midwest to arrive and refuel. Then he waited for the passengers in first class seating to board. At last he was in the air. He dozed away some of his jet lag until the wintery checkered landscape below identified he was back in the dairy state. The weak winter sun cast a golden glow across the Styrofoam-like snow.

I have not been a good friend. I will admit my faults to the woman I...love?

The word warmed him from the inside out.

I love you, Judy, he told the breeze of the Jetway as he jogged around slower passengers in his way. *I love you so much it hurts.*

She stood waiting for him, the look on her face more worried than happy. No big smile lit her green eyes like it had on his previous visits.

He faltered. *I was gonna tell you something, only now....*

Harley gulped at the impromptu flight he'd taken. Heck, he didn't even have a bag of clothes to claim off the revolving carousel, he'd acted so foolishly fast. Maybe his impulsive flight was the result of the shootings in the office. Maybe it was because it could've been him as easily as Peters. Maybe because he could've lost everyone he loved that day. All he had in the world was his friends.

So many maybes....

Judy looked unhappy. Worried. He knew it then. He should've visited more often. Long distance relationships were hard enough for normal folks to maintain. Why'd he ever think he could handle one? Guilt for being dumb pierced his heart. This was the perpetual downside to being a man, the not knowing what was going on in his woman's mind.

Well, now that I'm here...

She didn't wait for him to cross the distance between them. With a rush, she ran the last dozen steps and threw herself into his arms. With a breath of peppermint, she planted her lips against his, her tears wet on his face.

His heart started beating again. He held her face to his and met her kisses with equal parts relief and passion.

"Harley. I took the month off." She came up for air.

"I only have two weeks off," he said between mouthfuls.

"I don't care. I don't want you to leave."

"I can't stay. I'm only here for—" He buried his face in the midst of her thick, red tresses and breathed her into his soul. This woman was everything to him. Life. Light. The best damned reason to live.

"Then...I can't do this any more." She pulled back, upsetting the calm. With a stomp of her booted foot, she let her temper fly. "Don't you get it? This long distance dating? This never seeing each other? It's too hard!"

He held her at arm's length to see her better. They were both breathing hard. Those green eyes were firing sparks and cinders. He thought he'd read her body language correctly, but somewhere between the first *"Harley"* and the last kiss, the conversation had taken a scary U-turn.

"I mean it." Tears tracked over her flushed cheeks. She bit her lip. It seemed she was making the biggest decision of her life. "I can't do it any more."

His heart sank. Was she waiting for him to say that elusive right thing lovers were supposed to say to each other at times like this? Heck, he was a man. He had no idea what she needed to hear. And was he seeing things? Was he wrong? Did he not see love shining behind those teary emerald greens?

What the hell's going on?

"I don't know what to say," he confessed, his heart reeling with confusion. He let his hands slip off her arms. If she didn't love him, it didn't matter what came out of his stupid mouth next. Peters was right. He was the biggest loser ever.

"No, Harley. No. I can't do this anymore. This!" She pushed him backward with all her strength, angry and– something else. *What?*

He could not for the life of him understand her. She'd gone from sad to angry so fast he couldn't keep up. Loving someone shouldn't be so complicated.

What should I do? Hug you? Get back on the plane and leave? Help me out here, Judy. Tell me what you want me to do.

"I can't keep seeing you just a couple days at a time." She pushed him back another step. "I can't keep crying myself to sleep at night."

She came at him again. He cringed, sure she might shove him again. *I get the point. I'll just go.*

She didn't. Instead, she grabbed the open zipper of his jacket and pulled him close, all her sweet peppermint breath in his face again. "So I'm going home with you."

He couldn't jump tracks fast enough, so he said it out loud. "W-w-what?"

By then, Judy had his tall, lanky body flattened against the beige-tiled terminal wall while she gripped his head with one hand and smothered him in kisses and hugs. The long, delicate fingers of her other hand peeled open the collar of the already too-loose and comfortable golf shirt beneath his jacket. His heart started beating again when her hand smoothed over his collarbone to grip the bare skin of his shoulder. Her hips kept pushing and he kept agreeing with her. *Yeah, that's the spot. Push. Keep on pushing.*

"Do you have room for me or not? Do you want me or not?" Her words tumbled out in a heated rush over his lips. "I love you. Do you hear me? And I miss you too much to keep living so far apart. Would you please take me home with you this time? Would you do that?"

They'd talked about this a couple times before, but leaving her job and family behind seemed such a big thing for a man to ask a woman to do. She had a way of making it sound like the perfect solution all of a sudden.

Hell, yeah.

He lifted her off her feet. She nipped his bottom lip, growling in that sexy, feline way she had. With suffocating warmth, he devoured her lips like he'd never kissed her before.

Oh, hell yeah.

Breathlessly, he backed her against the same beige-colored tile wall, his heart a pounding freight train coming down the Mortimer track. This was the bravest thing he'd ever done, no doubt about it. He was pretty sure there was nothing in all of his past life to compare with the words that were going to come out of his mouth next.

"Judy." Regardless of the passerbys watching, his hands roamed her body like they were the only two people in the world. Hands that had done so many stupid things in the past finally did something worthwhile when they cupped her ass and squeezed. If love was what she wanted, love was what she was going to get. Right here. Right now. Well, okay, so maybe not exactly right here, but he wasn't letting her go.

"Yes?" She planted burning kisses in his neck that echoed all the way to his groin, her feet still off the ground and those luscious breasts pushing warm and friendly into his chest. Thinking was getting more and more difficult.

"Sweetheart. Honey. Judy, darling, I have to know." He kissed her hard, pouring every ounce of promise into her lips that he could without catching a full breath.

"Yes?" she asked, just as breathlessly.

"Do you like chocolate?" Okay, that wasn't what he had meant to ask. It was important, yeah, but not what he meant. Why did his dumb old brain trick him like this?

"What?" She pulled back, trying to read him like the idiot he was. She had to know by now. He wasn't going to grow any more brainpower overnight.

But Harley did start over, his forehead pressed to hers, their noses touching. The ring could wait. Chocolate could wait. His heart needed to say its piece first. "I love you, Judy O'Brien, and yes. If you're willing, I'm taking you home with me. I've got two weeks. We'll load up a truck and get you moved. Is that what you really want?"

The fire in her eyes melted a welding link between them. Something sizzled deep inside. It might have been his soul to hers.

"I've loved you since our first dance," she murmured, her fingertips gentle on his cheek. "It's all I want, Harley. To be with you."

Why did he feel the need to say thank you? Harley didn't know why, but that's what he felt. His mantra settled in warm and right, alongside that other warm feeling in his heart: the courage to know the difference and the smarts to recognize love when he saw it. He finally got something right. And her name was–Judy.

Author's Note

I hope you enjoyed this short story about Harley and Judy. It is not a preview of the book as much as a glimpse into Junior Agent Harley Mortimer's personal life to get you in the mood for more.

Watch for it at Amazon, Kindle, Barnes and Noble, and Smashwords.

Thank you for reading Zack!

Be sure to check out the rest of the guys and gals of Irish Winters' series: *In the Company of Snipers*

Other Irish Winters' books:

King of Hearts, Deuces Wild Series, *#1*
Joker Joker, Deuces Wild Series, *#2*
Smoke, Hearts and Ashes Series, *#1*
Ash, Hearts and Ashes Series, *#2*

Coming soon!

Seth, In the Company of Snipers, #17
One-Eyed Jack, Deuces Wild Series, #3

YOU are the key to this book's success!

Please tell other readers why you liked Zack and Mei's story by leaving an honest review at the retail site where you purchased it.
Recommend it to your friends. Lend it.
Most of all, enjoy it!

The best way to keep up with my new releases, giveaways, and actionable intel is to sign up for my spam-free newsletter at IrishWinters.com.

About the Author

Irish Winters is an award winning, Amazon best-selling author who, when she isn't writing, dabbles in poetry, grandchildren, and rarely (as in extremely rarely) the kitchen. More prone to be outdoors than in, she grew up the quintessential tomboy on a dairy farm in rural Wisconsin, spent her teenage years in the Pacific Northwest, but calls the Wasatch Mountains of Northern Utah home. For now.

She believes in making every day count for something, and follows the wise admonition of her mother to, "Look out the window and see something!"

Connect with Irish!
On Facebook: https://www.facebook.com/author.irishwinters
On Twitter: https://twitter.com/irishwinters1
Or at www. IrishWinters.com

www.ingramcontent.com/pod-product-compliance
Lightning Source LLC
Chambersburg PA
CBHW061040190726
48286CB00006B/1543